DIANA PALMER

WILL OF STEEL
& RELUCTANT FATHER

Published by Silhouette Books
America's Publisher of Contemporary Romance

SILHOUETTE BOOKS

ISBN-13: 978-0-373-28598-3

WILL OF STEEL & RELUCTANT FATHER

Copyright © 2010 by Harlequin Books, S.A.

The publisher acknowledges the copyright holder of the
individual works as follows:

WILL OF STEEL
Copyright © 2010 by Diana Palmer

RELUCTANT FATHER
Copyright © 1988 by Diana Palmer

Recycling programs
for this product may
not exist in your area.

DIANA PALMER

has a gift for telling the most sensual tales with charm and humor. With more than 40 million copies of her books in print, Diana Palmer is one of North America's most beloved authors and considered one of the top ten romance authors in the United States.

Diana's hobbies include gardening, archaeology, anthropology, art, astronomy and music. She has been married to James Kyle for over thirty-five years. They have one son, Blayne, who is married to the former Christina Clayton, and a granddaughter, Selena Marie.

CONTENTS

Dear Reader,

Will of Steel started out to be a different sort of book altogether, a comedy about a young girl and a police chief who came together because of their respective uncles' wills. But that isn't how it turned out, as you will discover.

Authors know that characters tend to take on lives of their own once they are created. You can have a pattern for a book, but the hero and heroine can revise it to their own liking. No, I'm not certifiable: this is actually how the creative process works. So I plot the book, and the characters write it their own way.

Rourke was in *Tough to Tame* and *Dangerous,* and he popped up again in this book, with a bit more background. I didn't invite him, he just came along for the ride. He's one of those men I can't get rid of. Cash Grier was another. He'll get a book of his own down the line, I guess.

Thanks for your support and your kindness, and all the prayers and hugs. I am doing well, although I'm a little less mobile than I used to be. Chronic illness forces changes, not many of them welcome. I am grateful to have loyal fans and laptop computers and a thoughtful husband and understanding family. Those are blessings worth rubies in this world. The most beautiful ruby is my granddaughter, Selena, but I won't go on about that, although I could!

Much love to all of you, and thanks again for staying around and reading my books. You're the reason I can't stop writing them.

Love,

Diana Palmer

WILL OF STEEL

To the readers, all of you, many of whom are my friends on my Facebook page. You make this job wonderful and worthwhile. Thank you for your kindness and your support and your affection through all the long years. I am still your biggest fan.

Chapter 1

He never liked coming here. The stupid calf followed him around, everywhere he went. He couldn't get the animal to leave him alone. Once, he'd whacked the calf with a soft fir tree branch, but that had led to repercussions. Its owner had a lot to say about animal cruelty and quoted the law to him. He didn't need her to quote the law. He was, after all, the chief of police in the small Montana town where they both lived.

Technically, of course, this wasn't town. It was about two miles outside the Medicine Ridge city limits. A small ranch in Hollister, Montana, that included two clear, cold trout streams and half a mountain. Her uncle and his uncle had owned it jointly during their lifetimes. The two of them, best friends forever, had recently died, his uncle from a heart attack and hers, about a month later, in an airplane crash en route to a cattleman's convention. The property was set to go up on the auction block, and a California real estate developer was skulking in the wings, waiting to put in the winning bid. He was going to build a rich man's resort here, banking on those pure trout streams to bring in the business.

If Hollister Police Chief Theodore Graves had his way, the man would never set foot on the property. She felt that way, too. But the wily old men had placed a clause in both their wills pertaining to ownership of the land in question. The clause in her uncle's will had been a source of shock to Graves and the girl when the amused attorney read it out to them. It had provoked a war of words every time he walked in the door.

"I'm not marrying you," Jillian Sanders told him firmly the minute he stepped on the porch. "I don't care if I have to live in the barn with Sammy."

Sammy was the calf.

He looked down at her from his far superior height with faint arrogance. "No problem. I don't think the grammar school would give you a hall pass to marry me anyway."

Her pert nose wrinkled. "Well, you'd have to get permission from the old folks' home, and I'll bet you wouldn't get it, either!"

It was a standing joke. He was thirty-one to her almost twenty-one. They were completely mismatched. She was small and blonde and blue-eyed, he was tall and dark and black-eyed. He liked guns and working on his old truck when he wasn't performing his duties as chief of police in the small Montana community where they lived. She liked making up recipes for new sweets and he couldn't stand anything sweet except pound cake. She also hated guns and noise.

"If you don't marry me, Sammy will be featured on

the menu in the local café, and you'll have to live in the woods in a cave," he pointed out.

That didn't help her disposition. She glared at him. It wasn't her fault that she had no family left alive. Her parents had died not long after she was born of an influenza outbreak. Her uncle had taken her in and raised her, but he was not in good health and had heart problems. Jillian had taken care of him as long as he was alive, fussing over his diet and trying to concoct special dishes to make him comfortable. But he'd died not of ill health, but in a light airplane crash on his way to a cattle convention. He didn't keep many cattle anymore, but he'd loved seeing friends at the conferences, and he loved to attend them. She missed him. It was lonely on the ranch. Of course, if she had to marry Rambo, here, it would be less lonely.

She glared at him, as if everything bad in her life could be laid at his door. "I'd almost rather live in the cave. I hate guns!" she added vehemently, noting the one he wore, old-fashioned style, on his hip in a holster. "You could blow a hole through a concrete wall with that thing!"

"Probably," he agreed.

"Why can't you carry something small, like your officers do?"

"I like to make an impression," he returned, tongue-in-cheek.

It took her a minute to get the insinuation. She glared at him even more.

He sighed. "I haven't had lunch," he said, and managed to look as if he were starving.

"There's a good café right downtown."

"Which will be closing soon because they can't get a cook," he said with disgust. "Damnedest thing, we live in a town where every woman cooks, but nobody wants to do it for the public. I guess I'll starve. I burn water."

It was the truth. He lived on takeout from the local café and frozen dinners. He glowered at her. "I guess marrying you would save my life. At least you can cook."

She gave him a smug look. "Yes, I can. And the local café isn't closing. They hired a cook just this morning."

"They did?" he exclaimed. "Who did they get?"

She averted her eyes. "I didn't catch her name, but they say she's talented. So you won't starve, I guess."

"Yes, but that doesn't help our situation here," he pointed out. His sensual lips made a thin line. "I don't want to get married."

"Neither do I," she shot back. "I've hardly even dated anybody!"

His eyebrows went up. "You're twenty years old. Almost twenty-one."

"Yes, and my uncle was suspicious of every man who came near me," she returned. "He made it impossible for me to leave the house."

His black eyes twinkled. "As I recall, you did escape once."

She turned scarlet. Yes, she had, with an auditor who'd come to do the books for a local lawyer's office. The man, much older than her and more sophisticated, had charmed her. She'd trusted him, just as she'd trusted another man two years earlier. The auditor had taken her back to his motel room to get something he forgot. Or so he'd told her. Actually he'd locked the door and proceeded to try to remove her clothes. He was very nice about it, he was just insistent.

But he didn't know that Jillian had emotional scars already from a man trying to force her. She'd been so afraid. She'd really liked the man, trusted him. Uncle John hadn't. He always felt guilty about what she'd been through because of his hired man. She was underage, and he told her to stay away from the man.

But she'd had stars in her eyes because the man had flirted with her when she'd gone with Uncle John to see his attorney about a land deal. She'd thought he was different, nothing like Uncle John's hired man who had turned nasty.

He'd talked to her on the phone several times and persuaded her to go out with him. Infatuated, she sneaked out when Uncle John went to bed. But she landed herself in very hot water when the man got overly amorous. She'd managed to get her cell phone out and punched in 911. The result had been…unforgettable.

"They did get the door fixed, I believe…?" she said, letting her voice trail off.

He glared at her. "It was locked."

"There's such a thing as keys," she pointed out.

"While I was finding one, you'd have been…"

She flushed again. She moved uncomfortably. "Yes, well, I did thank you. At the time."

"And a traveling mathematician learned the dangers of trying to seduce teenagers in my town."

She couldn't really argue. She'd been sixteen at the time, and Theodore's quick reaction had saved her honor. The auditor hadn't known her real age. She knew he'd never have asked her out if he had any idea she was under legal age. He'd been the only man she had a real interest in, for her whole life. He'd quit the firm he worked for, so he never had to come back to Hollister.

She felt bad about it. The whole fiasco was her own fault.

The sad thing was that it wasn't her first scary episode with an older man. The first, at fifteen, had scarred her. She'd thought that she could trust a man again because she was crazy about the auditor. But the auditor became the icing on the cake of her withdrawal from the world of dating for good. She'd really liked him, trusted him, had been infatuated with him. He wasn't even a bad man, not like that other one...

"The judge did let him go with a severe reprimand about making sure of a girl's age and not trying to persuade her into an illegal act. But he could have gone to prison, and it would have been my fault," she recalled. She didn't mention the man who had gone to prison for assaulting her. Ted didn't know about that and she wasn't going to tell him.

"Don't look to me to have any sympathy for him," he said tersely. "Even if you'd been of legal age, he had no right to try to coerce you."

"Point taken."

"Your uncle should have let you get out more," he said reluctantly.

"I never understood why he kept me so close to home," she replied thoughtfully. She knew it wasn't all because of her bad experience.

His black eyes twinkled. "Oh, that's easy. He was saving you for me."

She gaped at him.

He chuckled. "He didn't actually say so, but you must have realized from his will that he'd planned a future for us for some time."

A lot of things were just becoming clear. She was speechless, for once.

He grinned. "He grew you in a hothouse just for me, little orchid," he teased.

"Obviously your uncle never did the same for me," she said scathingly.

He shrugged, and his eyes twinkled even more. "One of us has to know what to do when the time comes," he pointed out.

She flushed. "I think we could work it out without diagrams."

He leaned closer. "Want me to look it up and see if I can find some for you?"

"I'm not marrying you!" she yelled.

He shrugged. "Suit yourself. Maybe you can put up some curtains and lay a few rugs and the cave will be more comfortable." He glanced out the window. "Poor Sammy," he added sadly. "His future is less, shall we say, palatable."

"For the last time, Sammy is not a bull, he's a cow. She's a cow," she faltered.

"Sammy is a bull's name."

"She looked like a Sammy," she said stubbornly. "When she's grown, she'll give milk."

"Only when she's calving."

"Like you know," she shot back.

"I belong to the cattleman's association," he reminded her. "They tell us stuff like that."

"I belong to it, too, and no, they don't, you learn it from raising cattle!"

He tugged his wide-brimmed hat over his eyes. "It's useless, arguing with a blond fence post. I'm going back to work."

"Don't shoot anybody."

"I've never shot anybody."

"Ha!" she burst out. "What about that bank robber?"

"Oh. Him. Well, he shot at me first."

"Stupid of him."

He grinned. "That's just what he said, when I visited him in the hospital. He missed. I didn't. And he got sentenced for assault on a police officer as well as the bank heist."

She frowned. "He swore he'd make you pay for that. What if he gets out?"

"Ten to twenty, and he's got priors," he told her. "I'll be in a nursing home for real by the time he gets out."

She glowered up at him. "People are always getting out of jail on technicalities. All he needs is a good lawyer."

"Good luck to him getting one on what he earns making license plates."

"The state provides attorneys for people who can't pay."

He gasped. "Thank you for telling me! I didn't know!"

"Why don't you go to work?" she asked, irritated.

"I've been trying to, but you won't stop flirting with me."

She gasped, but for real. "I am *not* flirting with you!"

He grinned. His black eyes were warm and sensuous as they met hers. "Yes, you are." He moved a step closer. "We could do an experiment. To see if we were chemically suited to each other."

She looked at him, puzzled, for a few seconds, until it dawned on her what he was suggesting. She moved back two steps, deliberately, and her high cheekbones flushed again. "I don't want to do any experiments with you!"

He sighed. "Okay. But it's going to be a very lonely marriage if you keep thinking that way, Jake."

"Don't call me Jake! My name is Jillian."

He shrugged. "You're a Jake." He gave her a long look, taking in her ragged jeans and bulky gray sweatshirt and boots with curled-up toes from use. Her long blond hair was pinned up firmly into a topknot, and she wore no makeup. "Tomboy," he added accusingly.

She averted her eyes. There were reasons she didn't accentuate her feminine attributes, and she didn't want to discuss the past with him. It wasn't the sort of thing she felt comfortable talking about with anyone. It made Uncle John look bad, and he was dead. He'd cried about his lack of judgment in hiring Davy Harris. But it was too late by then.

Ted was getting some sort of vibrations from her. She was keeping something from him. He didn't know what, but he was almost certain of it.

His teasing manner went into eclipse. He became a policeman again. "Is there something you want to talk to me about, Jake?" he asked in the soft tone he used with children.

She wouldn't meet his eyes. "It wouldn't help."

"It might."

She grimaced. "I don't know you well enough to tell you some things."

"If you marry me, you will."

"We've had this discussion," she pointed out.

"Poor Sammy."

"Stop that!" she muttered. "I'll find her a home. I could always ask John Callister if he and his wife, Sassy, would let her live with them."

"On their ranch where they raise purebred cattle."

"Sammy has purebred bloodlines on both sides," she muttered. "Her mother was a purebred Hereford cow and her father was a purebred Angus bull."

"And Sammy is a 'black baldy,'" he agreed, giving it the hybrid name. "But that doesn't make her a purebred cow."

"Semantics!" she shot back.

He grinned. "There you go, throwing those one-dollar words at me again."

"Don't pretend to be dumb, if you please. I happen to know that you got a degree in physics during your stint with the army."

He raised both thick black eyebrows. "Should I be flattered?"

"Why?"

"That you take an interest in my background."

"Everybody knows. It isn't just me."

He shrugged.

"Why are you a small-town police chief, with that sort of education?" she asked suddenly.

"Because I don't have the temperament for scientific research," he said simply. "Besides, you don't get to play with guns in a laboratory."

"I hate guns."

"You said."

"I really mean it." She shivered dramatically. "You could shoot somebody by accident. Didn't one of your patrolmen drop his pistol in a grocery store and it went off?"

He looked grim. "Yes, he did. He was off duty and carrying his little .32 wheel gun in his pants pocket. He reached for change and it fell out and discharged."

He pursed his lips. "A mistake I can guarantee he will never make again."

"So his wife said. You are one mean man when you lose your temper, do you know that?"

"The pistol discharged into a display of cans, fortunately for him, and we only had to pay damages to the store. But it could have discharged into a child, or a grown-up, with tragic results. There are reasons why they make holsters for guns."

She looked at his pointedly. "That one sure is fancy," she noted, indicating the scrollwork on the soft tan leather. It also sported silver conchos and fringe.

"My cousin made it for me."

"Tanika?" she asked, because she knew his cousin, a full-blooded Cheyenne who lived down near Hardin.

"Yes." He smiled. "She thinks practical gear should have beauty."

"She's very gifted." She smiled. "She makes some gorgeous *parfleche* bags. I've seen them at the trading post in Hardin, near the Little Bighorn Battlefield." They were rawhide bags with beaded trim and fringe, incredibly beautiful and useful for transporting items in the old days for native people.

"Thank you," he said abruptly.

She lifted her eyebrows. "For what?"

"For not calling it the Custer Battlefield."

A lot of people did. He had nothing against Custer, but his ancestry was Cheyenne. He had relatives who had died in the Little Bighorn Battle and, later, at Wounded Knee. Custer was a sore spot with him. Some tourists didn't seem to realize that Native Americans considered that people other than Custer's troops were killed in the battle.

She smiled. "I think I had a Sioux ancestor."

"You look like it," he drawled, noting her fair coloring.

"My cousin Rabby is half and half, and he has blond hair and gray eyes," she reminded him.

"I guess so." He checked the big watch on his wrist. "I've got to be in court for a preliminary hearing. Better go."

"I'm baking a pound cake."

He hesitated. "Is that an invitation?"

"You did say you were starving."

"Yes, but you can't live on cake."

"So I'll fry a steak and some potatoes to go with it."

His lips pulled up into a smile. "Sounds nice. What time?"

"About six? Barring bank robberies and insurgent attacks, of course."

"I'm sure we won't have one today." He considered her invitation. "The Callisters brought me a flute back from Cancún when they went on their honeymoon. I could bring it and serenade you."

She flushed a little. The flute and its connection with courting in the Native American world was quite well-known. "That would be nice."

"It would?"

"I thought you were leaving." She didn't quite trust that smile.

"I guess I am. About six?"

"Yes."

"I'll see you then." He paused with his hand on the doorknob. "Should I wear my tuxedo?"

"It's just steak."

"No dancing afterward?" he asked, disappointed.

"Not unless you want to build a bonfire outside and

dance around it." She frowned. "I think I know one or two steps from the women's dances."

He glared at her. "Ballroom dancing isn't done around campfires."

"You can do ballroom dances?" she asked, impressed.

"Of course I can."

"Waltz, polka…?"

"Tango," he said stiffly.

Her eyes twinkled. "Tango? Really?"

"Really. One of my friends in the service learned it down in Argentina. He taught me."

"What an image that brings to mind—" she began, tongue-in-cheek.

"He didn't teach me by dancing with me!" he shot back. "He danced with a girl."

"Well, I should hope so," she agreed.

"I'm leaving."

"You already said."

"This time, I mean it." He walked out.

"Six!" she called after him.

He threw up a hand. He didn't look back.

Jillian closed the door and leaned back against it. She was a little apprehensive, but after all, she had to marry somebody. She knew Theodore Graves better than she knew any other men. And, despite their quarreling, they got along fairly well.

The alternative was to let some corporation build a holiday resort here in Hollister, and it would be a disaster for local ranching. Resorts brought in all sorts of amusement, plus hotels and gas stations and businesses. It would be a boon for the economy, but Hollister would lose its rural, small-town appeal. It wasn't something

Jillian would enjoy and she was certain that other people would feel the same. She loved the forests with their tall lodgepole pines, and the shallow, diamond-bright trout streams where she loved to fish when she had free time. Occasionally Theodore would bring over his spinning reel and join her. Then they'd work side by side, scaling and filleting fish and frying them, along with hush puppies, in a vat of hot oil. Her mouth watered, just thinking about it.

She wandered into the kitchen. She'd learned to cook from one of her uncle's rare girlfriends. It had delighted her. She might be a tomboy, but she had a natural affinity for flour and she could make bread from scratch. It amazed her how few people could. The feel of the dough, soft and smooth, was a gift to her fingertips when she kneaded and punched and worked it. The smell of fresh bread in the kitchen was a delight for the senses. She always had fresh homemade butter to go on it, which she purchased from an elderly widow just down the road. Theodore loved fresh bread. She was making a batch for tonight, to go with the pound cake.

She pulled out her bin of flour and got down some yeast from the shelf. It took a long time to make bread from scratch, but it was worth it.

She hadn't changed into anything fancy, although she did have on a new pair of blue jeans and a pink checked shirt that buttoned up. She also tucked a pink ribbon into her long blond hair, which she tidied into a bun on top of her head. She wasn't elegant, or beautiful, but she could at least look like a girl when she tried.

And he noticed the minute he walked in the door. He cocked his head and stared down at her with amusement.

"You're a girl," he said with mock surprise.

She glared up at him. "I'm a woman."

He pursed his lips. "Not yet."

She flushed. She tried for a comeback but she couldn't fumble one out of her flustered mind.

"Sorry," he said gently, and became serious when he noted her reaction to the teasing. "That wasn't fair. Especially since you went to all the trouble to make me fresh rolls." He lifted his head and sniffed appreciably.

"How did you know that?"

He tapped his nose. "I have a superlative sense of smell. Did I ever tell you about the time I tracked a wanted murderer by the way he smelled?" he added. "He was wearing some gosh-awful cheap cologne. I just followed the scent and walked up to him with my gun out. He'd spent a whole day covering his trail and stumbling over rocks to throw me off the track. He was so shocked when I walked into his camp that he just gave up without a fight."

"Did you tell him that his smell gave him away?" she asked, chuckling.

"No. I didn't want him to mention it to anybody when he went to jail. No need to give criminals a heads-up about something like that."

"Native Americans are great trackers," she commented.

He glowered down at her. "Anybody can be a good tracker. It comes from training, not ancestry."

"Well, aren't you touchy," she exclaimed.

He averted his eyes. He shrugged. "Banes has been at it again."

"You should assign him to school crossings. He hates that," she advised.

"No, he doesn't. His new girlfriend is a widow. She's

got a little boy, and Banes has suddenly become his hero. He'd love to work the school crossing."

"Still, you could find some unpleasant duty to assign him. Didn't he say once that he hates being on traffic detail at ball games?"

He brightened. "You know, he did say that."

"See? An opportunity presents itself." She frowned. "Why are we looking for ways to punish him this time?"

"He brought in a new book on the Little Bighorn Battle and showed me where it said Crazy Horse wasn't in the fighting."

She gave him a droll look. "Oh, sure."

He grimaced. "Every so often, some writer who never saw a real Native American gets a bunch of hearsay evidence together and writes a book about how he's the only one who knows the true story of some famous battle. This guy also said that Custer was nuts and had a hand in the post trader scandal where traders were cheating the Sioux and Cheyenne."

"Nobody who reads extensively about Custer would believe he had a hand in something so dishonest," she scoffed. "He went to court and testified against President Ulysses S. Grant's own brother in that corruption trial, as I recall. Why would he take such a risk if he was personally involved in it?"

"My thoughts exactly," he said, "and I told Banes so."

"What did Banes say to that?"

"He quoted the author's extensive background in military history."

She gave him a suspicious look. "Yes? What sort of background?"

"He's an expert in the Napoleonic Wars."

"Great! What does that have to do with the campaign on the Greasy Grass?" she asked, which referred to the Lakota name for the battle.

"Not a damned thing," he muttered. "You can be brilliant in your own field of study, but it's another thing to do your research from a standing start and come to all the wrong conclusions. Banes said the guy used period newspapers and magazines for part of his research."

"The Lakota and Cheyenne, as I recall, didn't write about current events," she mused.

He chuckled. "No, they didn't have newspaper reporters back then. So it was all from the cavalry's point of view, or that of politicians. History is the story of mankind written by the victors."

"Truly."

He smiled. "You're pretty good on local history."

"That's because I'm related to people who helped make it."

"Me, too." He cocked his head. "I ought to take you down to Hardin and walk the battlefield with you sometime," he said.

Her eyes lit up. "I'd love that."

"So would I."

"There's a trading post," she recalled.

"They have some beautiful things there."

"Made by local talent," she agreed. She sighed. "I get so tired of so-called Native American art made in China. Nothing against the Chinese. I mean, they have aboriginal peoples, too. But if you're going to sell things that are supposed to be made by tribes in this country, why import them?"

"Beats me. Ask somebody better informed."

"You're a police chief," she pointed out. "There isn't supposed to be anybody better informed."

He grinned. "Thanks."

She curtsied.

He frowned. "Don't you own a dress?"

"Sure. It's in my closet." She pursed her lips. "I wore it to graduation."

"Spare me!"

"I guess I could buy a new one."

"I guess you could. I mean, if we're courting, it will look funny if you don't wear a dress."

"Why?"

He blinked. "You going to get married in blue jeans?"

"For the last time, I am not going to marry you."

He took off his wide-brimmed hat and laid it on the hall table. "We can argue about that later. Right now, we need to eat some of that nice, warm, fresh bread before it gets cold and butter won't melt on it. Shouldn't we?" he added with a grin.

She laughed. "I guess we should."

Chapter 2

The bread was as delicious as he'd imagined it would be. He closed his eyes, savoring the taste.

"You could cook, if you'd just try," she said.

"Not really. I can't measure stuff properly."

"I could teach you."

"Why do I need to learn how, when you do it so well already?" he asked reasonably.

"You live alone," she began.

He raised an eyebrow. "Not for long."

"For the tenth time today…"

"The California guy was in town today," he said grimly. "He came by the office to see me."

"He did?" She felt apprehensive.

He nodded as he bit into another slice of buttered bread with perfect white teeth. "He's already approached contractors for bids to build his housing project." He bit the words off as he was biting the bread.

"Oh."

Jet-black eyes pierced hers. "I told him about the clause in the will."

"What did he say?"

"That he'd heard you wouldn't marry me."

She grimaced.

"He was strutting around town like a tom turkey," he added. He finished the bread and sipped coffee. His eyes closed as he savored it. "You make great coffee, Jake!" he exclaimed. "Most people wave the coffee over water. You could stand up a spoon in this."

"I like it strong, too," she agreed. She studied his hard, lean face. "I guess you live on it when you have cases that keep you out all night tracking. There have been two or three of those this month alone."

He nodded. "Our winter festival brings in people from all over the country. Some of them see the mining company's bankroll as a prime target."

"Not to mention the skeet-and-trap-shooting regional championships," she said. "I've heard that thieves actually follow the shooters around and get license plate numbers of cars whose owners have the expensive guns."

"They're targets, all right."

"Why would somebody pay five figures for a gun?" she wondered out loud.

He laughed. "You don't shoot in competition, so it's no use trying to explain it to you."

"You compete," she pointed out. "You don't have a gun that expensive and you're a triple-A shooter."

He shrugged. "It isn't that I wouldn't like to have one. But unless I take up bank robbing, I'm not likely to be able to afford one, either. The best I can do is borrow one for the big competitions."

Her eyes popped. "You know somebody who'll loan you a fifty-thousand-dollar shotgun?"

He laughed. "Well, actually, yes, I do. He's police chief of a small town down in Texas. He used to do shotgun competitions when he was younger, and he still has the hardware."

"And he loans you the gun."

"He isn't attached to it, like some owners are. Although, you'd never get him to loan his sniper kit," he chuckled.

"Excuse me?"

He leaned toward her. "He was a covert assassin in his shady past."

"Really?" She was excited by the news.

He frowned. "What do women find so fascinating about men who shoot people?"

She blinked. "It's not that."

"Then what is it?"

She hesitated, trying to put it into words. "Men who have been in battles have tested themselves in a way most people never have to," she began slowly. "They learn their own natures. They…I can't exactly express it…"

"They learn what they're made of, right where they live and breathe," he commented. "Under fire, you're always afraid. But you harness the fear and use it, attack when you'd rather run. You learn the meaning of courage. It isn't the absence of fear. It's fear management, at its best. You do your duty."

"Nicely said, Chief Graves," she said admiringly, and grinned.

"Well, I know a thing or two about being shot at," he reminded her. "I was in the first wave in the second incursion in the Middle East. Then I became a police officer and then a police chief."

"You met the other police chief at one of those conventions, I'll bet," she commented.

"Actually I met him at the FBI academy during a training session on hostage negotiation," he corrected. "He was teaching it."

"My goodness. He can negotiate?"

"He did most of his negotiations with a gun before he was a Texas Ranger," he laughed.

"He was a Ranger, too?"

"Yes. And a cyber-crime expert for a Texas D.A., and a merc, and half a dozen other interesting things. He can also dance. He won a tango contest in Argentina, and that's saying something. Tango and Argentina go together like coffee and cream."

She propped her chin in her hands. "A man who can do the tango. It boggles the mind. I've only ever seen a couple of men do it in movies." She smiled. "Al Pacino in *Scent of a Woman* was my favorite."

He grinned. "Not the 'governator' in *True Lies?*"

She glared at him. "I'm sure he was doing his best."

He shook his head. "I watched Rudolph Valentino do it in an old silent film," he sighed. "Real style."

"It's a beautiful dance."

He gave her a long look. "There's a new Latin dance club in Billings."

"What?" she exclaimed with pure surprise.

"No kidding. A guy from New York moved out here to retire. He'd been in ballroom competition most of his life and he got bored. So he organized a dance band and opened up a dance club. People come up from Wyoming and across from the Dakotas just to hear the band and do the dances." He toyed with his coffee cup. "Suppose you and I go up there and try it out? I can teach you the tango."

Her heart skipped. It was the first time, despite all the banter, that he'd ever suggested taking her on a date.

He scowled when she hesitated.

"I'd love to," she blurted out.

His face relaxed. He smiled again. "Okay. Saturday?"

She nodded. Her heart was racing. She felt breathless.

She was so young, he thought, looking at her. He hesitated.

"They don't have grammar school on Saturdays," she quipped, "so I won't need an excuse from the principal to skip class."

He burst out laughing. "Is that how I looked? Sorry."

"I'm almost twenty-one," she pointed out. "I know that seems young to you, but I've had a lot of responsibility. Uncle John could be a handful, and I was the only person taking care of him for most of my life."

"That's true. Responsibility matures people pretty quick."

"You'd know," she said softly, because he'd taken wonderful care of his grandmother and then the uncle who'd owned half this ranch.

He shrugged. "I don't think there's a choice about looking after people you love."

"Neither do I."

He gave her an appraising look. "You going to the club in blue jeans and a shirt?" he asked. "Because if you are, I plan to wear my uniform."

She raised both eyebrows.

"Or have you forgotten what happened the last time I wore my uniform to a social event?" he added.

She glowered at him.

"Is it my fault if people think of me as a target the minute they realize what I do for a living?" he asked.

"You didn't have to anoint him with punch."

"Sure I did. He was so hot under the collar about a speeding ticket my officer gave him that he needed instant cooling off."

She laughed. "Your patrolman is still telling that story."

"With some exaggerations he added to it," Theodore chuckled.

"It cured the guy of complaining to you."

"Yes, it did. But if I wear my uniform to a dance club where people drink, there's bound to be at least one guy who thinks I'm a target."

She sighed.

"And since you're with me, you'd be right in the thick of it." He pursed his lips. "You wouldn't like to be featured in a riot, would you?"

"Not in Billings, no," she agreed.

"Then you could wear a skirt, couldn't you?"

"I guess it wouldn't kill me," she said, but reluctantly.

He narrowed his eyes as he looked at her. There was some reason she didn't like dressing like a woman. He wished he could ask her about it, but she was obviously uncomfortable discussing personal issues with him. Maybe it was too soon. He did wonder if she still had scars from her encounter with the auditor.

He smiled gently. "Something demure," he added. "I won't expect you to look like a pole dancer, okay?"

She laughed. "Okay."

He loved the way she looked when she smiled. Her whole face took on a radiance that made her pretty. She didn't smile often. Well, neither did he. His job was a somber one, most of the time.

"I'll see you about six, then."

She nodded. She was wondering how she was going to afford something new to wear to a fancy nightclub, but she would never have admitted it to him.

She ran into Sassy Callister in town while she was trying to find something presentable on the bargain table at the single women's clothing store.

"You're looking for a dress?" Sassy exclaimed. She'd known Jillian all her life, and she'd never seen her in anything except jeans and shirts. She even wore a pantsuit to church when she went.

Jillian glared at her. "I do have legs."

"That wasn't what I meant." She chuckled. "I gather Ted's taking you out on a real date, huh?"

Jillian went scarlet. "I never said...!"

"Oh, we all know about the will," Sassy replied easily. "It's sensible, for the two of you to get married and keep the ranch in the family. Nobody wants to see some fancy resort being set up here," she added, "with outsiders meddling in our local politics and throwing money around to get things the way they think they should be."

Jillian's eyes twinkled. "Imagine you complaining about the rich, when you just married one of the richest men in Montana."

"You know what I mean," Sassy laughed. "And I'll remind you that I didn't know he was rich when I accepted his proposal."

"A multimillionaire pretending to be a ranch foreman." Jillian shook her head. "It came as a shock to a lot of us when we found out who he really was."

"I assure you that it was more of a shock to me," came the amused reply. "I tried to back out of it, but he wouldn't let me. He said that money was an accessory, not a character trait. You should meet his brother and sister-in-law," she added with a grin. "Her parents were missionaries and her aunt is a nun. Oh, and her godfather is one of the most notorious ex-mercenaries who ever used a gun."

"My goodness!"

"But they're all very down-to-earth. They don't strut, is what I mean."

Jillian giggled. "I get it."

Sassy gave her a wise look. "You want something nice for that date, but you're strained to the gills trying to manage on what your uncle left you."

Jillian started to deny it, but she gave up. Sassy was too sweet to lie to. "Yes," she confessed. "I was working for old Mrs. Rogers at the florist shop. Then she died and the shop closed." She sighed. "Not many jobs going in a town this small. You'd know all about that," she added, because Sassy had worked for a feed store and was assaulted by her boss. Fortunately she was rescued by her soon-to-be husband and the perpetrator had been sent to jail. But it was the only job Sassy could get. Hollister was very small.

Sassy nodded. "I wouldn't want to live anyplace else, though. Even if I had to commute back and forth to Billings to get a job." She laughed. "I considered that, but I didn't think my old truck would get me that far." Her eyes twinkled. "Chief Graves said that if he owned a piece of junk like I was driving, he'd be the first to agree to marry a man who could afford to replace it for me."

Jillian burst out laughing. "I can imagine what you said to that."

She laughed, too. "I just expressed the thought that he wouldn't marry John Callister for a truck." She cocked her head. "He really is a catch, you know. Theodore Graves is the stuff of legends around here. He's honest and kindhearted and a very mean man to make an enemy of. He'd take care of you."

"Well, he needs more taking care of than I do," came the droll reply. "At least I can cook."

"Didn't you apply for the cook's job at the restaurant?"

"I did. I got it, too, but you can't tell Theodore."

"I won't. But why can't I?"

Jillian sighed. "In case things don't work out, I want to have a means of supporting myself. He'll take it personally if he thinks I got a job before he even proposed."

"He's old-fashioned."

"Nothing wrong with that," Jillian replied with a smile.

"Of course not. It's just that some men have to be hit over the head so they'll accept that modern women can have outside interests without giving up family. Come over here."

She took Jillian's arm and pulled her to one side. "Everything in here is a three-hundred-percent markup," she said under her breath. "I love Jessie, but she's overpriced. You're coming home with me. We're the same size and I've got a closet full of stuff you can wear. You can borrow anything you like. Heck, you can have what you like. I'll never wear all of it anyway."

Jillian flushed red and stammered, "No, I couldn't…!"

"You could and you're going to. Now come on!"

Jillian was transported to the Callister ranch in a Jaguar. She was so fascinated with it that she didn't hear half of what her friend was saying.

"Look at all these gadgets!" she exclaimed. "And this is real wood on the dash!"

"Yes," Sassy laughed. "I acted the same as you, the first time I rode in it. My old battered truck seemed so pitiful afterward."

"I like my old car. But this is amazing," she replied, touching the silky wood.

"I know."

"It's so nice of you to do this," Jillian replied. "Theodore wanted me to wear a skirt. I don't even own one."

Sassy looked at her briefly. "You should tell him, Jilly."

She flushed and averted her eyes. "Nobody knows but you and your mother. And I know you won't say anything."

"Not unless you said I could," Sassy replied. "But it could cause you some problems later on. Especially after you're married."

Jillian clenched her teeth. "I'll cross that bridge if I come to it. I may not marry Theodore. We may be able to find a way to break the will."

"One, maybe. Two, never."

That was true. Both old men had left ironclad wills with clauses about the disposition of the property if Theodore and Jillian refused to get married.

"The old buzzards!" Jillian burst out. "Why did they have to complicate things like that? Theodore and I could have found a way to deal with the problem on our own!"

"I don't know. Neither of you is well-off, and that California developer has tons of money. I'll bet he's already trying to find a way to get to one of you about buying the ranch outright once you inherit."

"He'll never get it," she said stubbornly.

Sassy was going to comment that rich people with intent sometimes knew shady ways to make people do what they wanted them to. But the developer wasn't local and he didn't have any information he could use to blackmail either Theodore or Jillian, so he probably couldn't force them to sell to him. He'd just sit and wait and hope they couldn't afford to keep it. Fat chance, Sassy thought solemly. She and John would bail them out if they had to. No way was some out-of-state fat cat taking over Jillian's land. Not after all she'd gone through in her young life.

Maybe it was a good thing Theodore didn't know everything about his future potential wife. But Jillian was setting herself up for some real heartbreak if she didn't level with him. After all, he was in law enforcement. He could dig into court records and find things that most people didn't have access to. He hadn't been in town when Jillian faced her problems, he'd been away at the FBI Academy on a training mission. And since only Sassy and her mother, Mrs. Peale, had been involved, nobody else except the prosecuting attorney and the judge and the public defender had knowledge about the case. Not that any of them would disclose it.

She was probably worrying unnecessarily. She smiled at Jillian. "You are right. He'll never get the ranch," she agreed.

* * *

They pulled up at the house. It had been given a makeover and it looked glorious.

"You've done a lot of work on this place," Jillian commented. "I remember what it looked like before."

"So do I. John wanted to go totally green here, so we have solar power and wind generators. And the electricity in the barn runs on methane from the cattle refuse."

"It's just fantastic," Jillian commented. "Expensive, too, I'll bet."

"That's true, but the initial capital outlay was the highest. It will pay for itself over the years."

"And you'll have lower utility bills than the rest of us," Jillian sighed, thinking about her upcoming one. It had been a colder than usual winter. Heating oil was expensive.

"Stop worrying," Sassy told her. "Things work out."

"You think?"

They walked down the hall toward the master bedroom. "How's your mother?" Jillian asked.

"Doing great. She got glowing reports from her last checkup," Sassy said. The cancer had been contained and her mother hadn't had a recurrence, thanks to John's interference at a critical time. "She always asks about you."

"Your mother is the nicest person I know, next to you. How about Selene?"

The little girl was one Mrs. Peale had adopted. She was in grammar school, very intelligent and with definite goals. "She's reading books about the Air Force," Sassy laughed. "She wants to be a fighter pilot."

"Wow!"

"That's what we said, but she's very focused. She's good at math and science, too. We think she may end up being an engineer."

"She's smart."

"Very."

Sassy opened the closet and started pulling out dresses and skirts and blouses in every color under the sun.

Jillian just stared at them, stunned. "I've never seen so many clothes outside a department store," she stammered.

Sassy chuckled. "Neither did I before I married John. He spoils me rotten. Every birthday and holiday I get presents from him. Pick something out."

"You must have favorites that you don't want to loan," Jillian began.

"I do. That's why they're still in the closet," she said with a grin.

"Oh."

Sassy was eyeing her and then the clothes on the bed. "How about this?" She picked up a patterned blue skirt, very long and silky, with a pale blue silk blouse that had puffy sleeves and a rounded neckline. It looked demure, but it was a witchy ensemble. "Try that on. Let's see how it looks."

Jillian's hands fumbled. She'd never put on something so expensive. It fit her like a glove, and it felt good to move in, as so many clothes didn't. She remarked on that.

"Most clothes on the rack aren't constructed to fit exactly, and the less expensive they are, the worse the fit," Sassy said. "I know, because I bought clothes off the sales rack all my life before I married. I was shocked to find that expensive clothes actually fit. And when they do, they make you look better. You can see for yourself."

Jillian did. Glancing in the mirror, she was shocked to find that the skirt put less emphasis on her full hips and more on her narrow waist. The blouse, on the other hand, made her small breasts look just a little bigger.

"Now, with your hair actually down and curled, instead of screwed up into that bun," Sassy continued, pulling out hairpins as she went and reaching for a brush, "you'll look so different that Ted may not even recognize you. What a difference!"

It was. With her long blond hair curling around her shoulders, she looked really pretty.

"Is that me?" she asked, shocked.

Sassy grinned. "Sure is."

She turned to her friend, fighting tears. "It's so nice of you," she began.

Sassy hugged her. "Friends look out for each other."

They hadn't been close friends, because Sassy's home problems had made that impossible before her marriage. But they were growing closer now. It was nice to have someone she could talk to.

She drew away and wiped at her eyes. "Sorry. Didn't mean to do that."

"You're a nice person, Jilly," Sassy told her gently. "You'd do the same for me in a heartbeat, if our situations were reversed, and you know it."

"I certainly would."

"I've got some curlers. Let's put up your hair in them and then we can snap beans."

"You've got beans in the middle of winter?" Jillian exclaimed.

"From the organic food market," she laughed. "I have them shipped in. You can take some home and plant up. Ted might like beans and ham hocks."

"Even if he didn't, I sure would. I'll bet it's your own pork."

"It is. We like organic all the way. Put your jeans back on and we'll wash your hair and set it. It's thin enough that it can dry while we work."

And it did. They took the curlers out a couple of hours later. Jillian was surprised at the difference a few curls made in her appearance.

"Makeup next," Sassy told her, grinning. "This is fun!"

"Fun and educational," Jillian said, still reeling. "How did you learn all this?"

"From my mother-in-law. She goes to spas and beauty parlors all the time. She's still gorgeous, even though she's gaining in years. Sit down."

Sassy put her in front of a fluorescent-lit mirror and proceeded to experiment with different shades of lipstick and eye shadow. Jillian felt as spoiled as if she'd been to an exclusive department store, and she said so.

"I'm still learning," Sassy assured her. "But it's fun, isn't it?"

"The most fun I've had in a long time, and thank you. Theodore is going to be shocked when he shows up Saturday!" she predicted.

Shocked was an understatement. Jillian in a blue ensemble, with her long hair soft and curling around her shoulders, with demure makeup, was a revelation to a man who'd only ever seen her without makeup in ragged jeans and sweatshirts or, worse, baggy T-shirts. Dressed up, in clothes that fit her perfectly, she was actually pretty.

"You can close your mouth, Theodore," she teased, delighted at his response.

He did. He shook his head. "You look nice," he said. It was an understatement, compared to what he was thinking. Jillian was a knockout. He frowned as he thought how her new look might go down in town. There were a couple of younger men, nice-looking ones with wealthy backgrounds, who might also find the new Jillian a hot item. He might have competition for her that he couldn't handle.

Jillian, watching his expressions change, was suddenly insecure. He was scowling as if he didn't actually approve of how she looked.

"It isn't too revealing, is it?" she worried.

He cleared his throat. "Jake, you're covered from stem to stern, except for the hollow of your throat, and your arms," he said. "What do you think is revealing?"

"You looked...well, you looked..."

"I looked like a man who's considering the fight ahead."

"Excuse me?"

He moved a step closer and looked down at her with pure appreciation. "You really don't know what a knockout you are, all dressed up?"

Her breath caught in her throat. "Me?"

His big hands framed her face and brought it up to his dancing black eyes. "You." He rubbed his nose against hers. "You know, I really wonder if you taste as good as you look. This is as good a time as any to find out."

He bent his head as he spoke and, for the first time in their relationship, he kissed her, right on the mouth. Hard.

Whatever he expected her reaction to be, the reality of it came as a shock

Chapter 3

Jillian jerked back away from him as if he'd offended her, flushing to the roots of her hair. She stared at him with helpless misery, waiting for the explosion. The auditor had cursed a blue streak, called her names, swore that he'd tell every boy he knew that she was a hopeless little icicle.

But Theodore didn't do that. In fact, he smiled, very gently.

She bit her lower lip. She wanted to tell him. She couldn't. The pain was almost physical.

He took her flushed face in his big hands and bent and kissed her gently on the forehead, then on her eyelids, closing them.

"We all have our own secret pain, Jake," he whispered. "One day you'll want to tell me, and I'll listen." He lifted his head. "For the time being, we'll be best buddies, except that you're wearing a skirt," he added, tongue-in-cheek. "I have to confess that very few of my buddies have used a women's restroom."

It took her a minute, then she burst out laughing.

"That's better," he said, and grinned. He cocked his head and gave her a very male appraisal. "You really do look nice." He pursed his lips as he contemplated the ensemble and its probable cost.

"They're loaners," she blurted out.

His black eyes sparkled with unholy glee. "Loaners?"

She nodded. "Sassy Callister."

"I see."

She grinned. "She said that she had a whole closet of stuff she never wore. I didn't want to, but she sort of bulldozed me into it. She's a lot like her new husband."

"He wears petticoats?" he asked outrageously.

She glared at him. "Women don't wear petticoats or hoop skirts these days, Theodore."

"Sorry. Wrong era."

She grinned. "Talk about living in the dark ages!"

He shrugged. "I was raised by my grandmother and my uncle. They weren't forthcoming about women's intimate apparel."

"Well, I guess not!"

"Your uncle John was the same sort of throwback," he remarked.

"So we both come by it honestly, I suppose." She noted his immaculate dark suit and the spotless white shirt and blue patterned tie he was wearing with it. "You look nice, too."

"I bought the suit to wear to John Callister's wedding," he replied. "I don't often have the occasion to dress up."

"Me, neither," she sighed.

"I guess we could go a few places together," he commented. "I like to hunt and fish."

"I do not like guns," she said flatly.

"Well, in my profession, they're sort of a necessity, Jake," he commented.

"I suppose so. Sorry."

"No problem. You used to like fishing."

"It's been a while since I dipped a poor, helpless worm into the water."

He chuckled. "Everything in life has a purpose. A worm's is to help people catch delicious fish."

"The worm might not share your point of view."

"I'll ask, the next time I see one."

She laughed, and her whole face changed. She felt better than she had in ages. Theodore didn't think she was a lost cause. He wasn't even angry that she'd gone cold at his kiss. Maybe, she thought, just maybe, there was still hope for her.

His black eyes were kind. "I'm glad you aren't wearing high heels," he commented.

"Why?"

He glanced down at his big feet in soft black leather boots. "Well, these aren't as tough as the boots I wear on the job. I'd hate to have holes in them from spiked heels, when you step on my feet on the dance floor."

"I will not step on your feet," she said with mock indignation. She grinned. "I might trip over them and land in a flowerpot, of course."

"I heard about that," he replied, chuckling. "Poor old Harris Twain. I'll bet he'll never stick his legs out into the walkway of a restaurant again. He said you were pretty liberally covered with potting soil. You went in headfirst, I believe...?"

She sighed. "Most people have talents. Mine is lack

of coordination. I can trip over my own feet, much less someone else's."

He wondered about that clumsiness. She was very capable, in her own way, but she often fell. He frowned.

"Now, see, you're thinking that I'm a klutz, and you're absolutely right."

"I was wondering more about your balance," he said. "Do you have inner ear problems?"

She blinked. "What do my ears have to do with that?"

"A lot. If you have an inner ear disturbance, it can affect balance."

"And where did you get your medical training?" she queried.

"I spend some time in emergency rooms, with victims and perps alike. I learn a lot about medical problems that way."

"I forgot."

He shrugged. "It goes with the job."

"I don't have earaches," she said, and averted her eyes. "Shouldn't we get going?"

She was hiding something. A lot, maybe. He let it go. "I guess we should."

"A Latin dance club in Billings." She grinned. "How exotic!"

"The owner's even more exotic. You'll like him." He leaned closer. "He was a gun runner in his wild youth."

"Wow!"

"I thought you'd be impressed. So was I."

"You have an interesting collection of strange people in your life," she commented on the way to his truck.

"Goes with the—"

"Job. I guess." She grinned when she saw the truck. "Washed and waxed it, huh?" she teased.

"Well, you can't take a nice woman to a dance in a dirty truck," he stated.

"I wouldn't have minded."

He turned to her at the passenger side of the truck and looked down at her solemnly in the light from the security lamp on a pole nearby. His face was somber. "No, you wouldn't. You don't look at bank accounts to judge friendships. It's one of a lot of things I like about you. I dated a woman attorney once, who came here to try a case for a client in district court. When she saw the truck, the old one I had several years ago, she actually backed out of the date. She said she didn't want any important people in the community to see her riding around in a piece of junk."

She gasped. "No! How awful for you!"

His high cheekbones had a faint flush. Her indignation made him feel warm inside. "Something you'd never have said to me, as blunt as you are. It turned me off women for a while. Not that I even liked her. But it hurt my pride."

"As if a vehicle was any standard to base a character assessment on," she huffed.

He smiled tenderly. "Small-town police chiefs don't usually drive Jaguars. Although this guy I know in Texas does. But he made his money as a merc, not in law enforcement."

"I like you just the way you are," she told him quietly. "And it wouldn't matter to me if we had to walk to Billings to go dancing."

He ground his teeth together. She made him feel taller, more masculine, when she looked at him like that. He was struggling with more intense emotions than he'd felt in years. He wanted to grab her and eat her alive. But she needed careful handling. He couldn't be forward with her. Not until he could teach her to trust him. That would take time.

She felt uneasy when he scowled like that. "Sorry," she said. "I didn't mean to blurt that out and upset you…"

"You make me feel good, Jake," he interrupted. "I'm not upset. Well, not for the reasons you're thinking, anyway."

"What reasons upset you?"

He sighed. "To be blunt, I'd like to back you into the truck and kiss you half to death." He smiled wryly at her shocked expression. "Won't do it," he promised. "Just telling you what I really feel. Honesty is a sideline with most people. It's first on my list of necessities."

"Mine, too. It's okay. I like it when you're up-front."

"You're the same way," he pointed out.

"I guess so. Maybe I'm too blunt, sometimes."

He smiled. "I'd call it being forthright. I like it."

She beamed. "Thanks."

He checked his watch. "Got to go." He opened the door for her and waited until she jumped up into the cab and fastened her seat belt before he closed it.

"It impresses me that I didn't have to tell you to put that on," he said as he started the engine, nodding toward her seat belt. "I don't ride with people who refuse to wear them. I work wrecks. Some of them are horrific, and the worst fatalities are when people don't have on seat belts."

"I've heard that."

He pulled out onto the highway. "Here we go, Jake.

Our first date." He grinned. "Our uncles are probably laughing their ghostly heads off."

"I wouldn't doubt it." She sighed. "Still, it wasn't nice of either of them to rig the wills like that."

"I guess they didn't expect to die for years and years," he commented. "Maybe it was a joke. They expected the lawyer to tell us long before they died. Except he died first and his partner had no sense of humor."

"I don't know. Our uncles did like to manipulate people."

"Too much," he murmured. "They browbeat poor old Dan Harper into marrying Daisy Kane, and he was miserable. They thought she was a sweet, kind girl who'd never want anything more than to go on living in Hollister for the rest of her life."

"Then she discovered a fascination for microscopes, got a science degree and moved to New York City to work in a research lab. Dan wouldn't leave Hollister, so they got a divorce. Good thing they didn't have kids, I guess."

"I guess. Especially with Dan living in a whiskey bottle these days."

She glanced at him. "Maybe some women mature late."

He glanced back. "You going to develop a fascination with microscopes and move to New York?" he asked suspiciously.

She laughed out loud. "I hope not. I hate cities."

He grinned again. "Me, too. Just checking."

"Besides, how could I leave Sammy? I'm sure there isn't an apartment in a big city that would let you keep a calf in it."

He laughed. "Well, they would. But only in the fridge. Or the freezer."

"You bite your tongue!" she exclaimed. "Nobody's eating my cow!"

He frowned thoughtfully. "Good point. I'm not exactly sure I know how to field dress a cow. A steer, sure. But cows are, well, different."

She glared at him. "You are not field dressing Sammy, so forget it."

He sighed. "There go my dreams of a nice steak."

"You can get one at the restaurant in town anytime you like. Sammy is for petting, not eating."

"If you say so."

"I do!"

He loved to wind her up and watch the explosion. She was so full of life, so enthusiastic about everything new. He enjoyed being with her. There were all sorts of places he could take her. He was thinking ahead. Far ahead.

"You're smirking," she accused. "What are you thinking about?"

"I was just remembering how excited you get about new things," he confessed. "I was thinking of places we could go together."

"You were?" she asked, surprised. And flattered.

He smiled at her. "I've never dated anybody regularly," he said. "I mean, I've had dates. But this is different." He searched for a way to put into words what he was thinking.

"You mean, because we're sort of being forced into it by the wills."

He frowned. "No. That's not what I mean." He stopped at an intersection and glanced her way. "I haven't had regular dates with a woman I've known well for years and years," he said after a minute. "Somebody I like."

She beamed. "Oh."

He chuckled as he pulled out onto the long highway that led to Billings. "We've had our verbal cut-and-thrust encounters, but despite that sharp tongue, I enjoy being with you."

She laughed. "It's not that sharp."

"Not to me. I understand there's a former customer of the florist shop where you worked who could write a testimonial for you about your use of words in a free-for-all."

She flushed and fiddled with her purse. "He was obnoxious."

"Actually they said he was just trying to ask you out."

"It was the way he went about it," she said curtly. "I don't think I've ever had a man talk to me like that in my whole life."

"I don't think he'll ever use the same language to any other woman, if it's a consolation." He teased. "So much for his inflated ego."

"He thought he was irresistible," she muttered. "Bragging about his fast new car and his dad's bank balance, and how he could get any woman he wanted." Her lips set. "Well, he couldn't get this one."

"Teenage boys have insecurities," he said. "I can speak with confidence on that issue, because I used to be one myself." He glanced at her with twinkling black eyes. "They're puff adders."

She blinked. "Excuse me?"

"I've never seen one myself, but I had a buddy in the service who was from Georgia. He told me about them. They're these snakes with insecurities."

She burst out laughing. "Snakes with insecurities?"

He nodded. "They're terrified of people. So if humans come too close to them, they rise up on their tails and weave back and forth and blow out their throats and start hissing. You know, imitating a cobra. Most of the time, people take them at face value and run away."

"What if people stand their ground and don't run?"

He laughed. "They faint."

"They faint?"

He nodded. "Dead away, my buddy said. He took a friend home with him. They were walking through the fields when a puff adder rose up and did his act for the friend. The guy was about to run for it when my buddy walked right up to the snake and it fainted dead away. I hear his family is still telling the story with accompanying sound effects and hilarity."

"A fainting snake." She sighed. "What I've missed, by spending my whole life in Montana. I wouldn't have known any better, either, though. I've never seen a cobra."

"They have them in zoos," he pointed out.

"I've never been to a zoo."

"What?"

"Well, Billings is a long way from Hollister and I've never had a vehicle I felt comfortable about getting there in." She grimaced. "This is a very deserted road, most of the time. If I broke down, I'd worry about who might stop to help me."

He gave her a covert appraisal. She was such a private person. She kept things to herself. Remembering her uncle and his weak heart, he wasn't surprised that she'd learned to do that.

"You couldn't talk to your uncle about most things, could you, Jake?" he wondered out loud.

"Not really," she agreed. "I was afraid of upsetting him, especially after his first heart attack."

"So you learned to keep things to yourself."

"I pretty much had to. I've never had close girlfriends, either."

"Most of the girls your age are married and have kids, except the ones who went into the military or moved to cities."

She nodded. "I'm a throwback to another era, when women lived at home until they married. Gosh, the world has changed," she commented.

"It sure has," he agreed. "When I was a boy, television sets were big and bulky and in cabinets. Now they're so thin and light that people can hang them on walls. And my iPod does everything a television can do, right down to playing movies and giving me news and weather."

She frowned. "That wasn't what I meant, exactly."

He raised his eyebrows.

"I mean, that women seem to want careers and men in volume."

He cleared his throat.

"That didn't come out right." She laughed self-consciously. "It just seems to me that women are more like the way men used to be. They don't want commitment. They have careers and they live with men. I heard a newscaster say that marriage is too retro a concept for modern people."

"There have always been people who lived out of the mainstream, Jake," he said easily. "It's a choice."

"It wouldn't be mine," she said curtly. "I think people should get married and stay married and raise children together."

"Now that's a point of view I like."

She studied him curiously. "Do you want kids?"

He smiled. "Of course. Don't you?"

She averted her eyes. "Well, yes. Someday."

He sighed. "I keep forgetting how young you are. You haven't really had time to live yet."

"You mean, get fascinated with microscopes and move to New York City," she said with a grin.

He laughed. "Something like that, maybe."

"I could never see stuff in microscopes in high school," she recalled. "I was so excited when I finally found what I thought was an organism and the teacher said it was an air bubble. That's all I ever managed to find." She grimaced. "I came within two grade points of failing biology. As it was, I had the lowest passing grade in my whole class."

"But you can cook like an angel," he pointed out.

She frowned. "What does that have to do with microscopes?"

"I'm making an observation," he replied. "We all have skills. Yours is cooking. Somebody else's might be science. It would be a pretty boring world if we all were good at the same things."

"I see."

He smiled. "You can crochet, too. My grandmother loved her crafts, like you do. She could make quilts and knit sweaters and crochet afghans. A woman of many talents."

"They don't seem to count for much in the modern world," she replied.

"Have you ever really looked at the magazine rack, Jake?" he asked, surprised. "There are more magazines on handicrafts than there are on rock stars, and that's saying something."

"I hadn't noticed." She looked around. They were just coming into Billings. Ahead, she could see the awesome outline of the Rimrocks, where the airport was located, in the distance. "We're here?" she exclaimed.

"It's not so far from home," he said lazily.

"Not at the speed you go, no," she said impudently.

He laughed. "There wasn't any traffic and we aren't overly blessed with highway patrols at this hour of the night."

"You catch speeders, and you're local law enforcement," she pointed out.

"I don't catch them on the interstate unless they're driving on it through my town," he replied. "And it's not so much the speed that gets them caught, either. It's the way they're driving. You can be safe at high speeds and dangerous at low ones. Weaving in and out of traffic, riding people's bumpers, running stop signs, that sort of thing."

"I saw this television program where an experienced traffic officer said that what scared him most was to see a driver with both hands white-knuckled and close together on the steering wheel."

He nodded. "There are exceptions, but it usually means someone who's insecure and afraid of the vehicle."

"You aren't."

He shrugged. "I've been driving since I was twelve. Kids grow up early when they live on ranches. Have to learn how to operate machinery, like tractors and harvesters."

"Our ranch doesn't have a harvester."

"That's because our ranch can't afford one," he said, smiling. "But we can always borrow one from neighbors."

"Small towns are such nice places," she said dreamily. "I love it that people will loan you a piece of equipment that expensive just because they like you."

"I imagine there are people in cities who would do the same, Jake, but there's not much use for them there."

She laughed. "No, I guess not."

He turned the corner and pulled into a parking lot next to a long, low building. There was a neon sign that said Red's Tavern.

"It's a bar?" she asked.

"It's a dance club. They do serve alcohol, but not on the dance floor."

"Theodore, I don't think I've ever been in a bar in my life."

"Not to worry, they won't force you to drink anything alcoholic," he told her, tongue-in-cheek. "And if they tried, I'd have to call local law and have them arrested. You're underage."

"Local law?"

"I'm not sanctioned to arrest people outside my own jurisdiction," he reminded her. "But you could make a citizen's arrest. Anybody can if they see a crime being committed. It's just that we don't advise it. Could get you killed, depending on the circumstances."

"I see what you mean."

He got out and opened her door, lifting her gently down from the truck by the waist. He held her just in front of him for a minute, smiling into her soft eyes. "You're as light as a feather," he commented softly. "And you smell pretty."

A shocked little laugh left her throat. "I smell pretty?"

"Yes. I remember my grandmother by her scent. She wore a light, flowery cologne. I recognize it if I smell it anywhere. She always smelled so good."

Her hands rested lightly on his broad shoulders. He was very strong. She loved his strength, his size.

She smiled into his dark eyes. "You smell good, too. Spicy."

He nuzzled her nose with his. "Thanks."

She sighed and slid her arms around his neck. She tucked her face into his throat. "I feel so safe with you," she said softly. "Like nothing could ever hurt me."

"Now, Jake, that's not the sort of thing a man likes to hear."

She lifted her head, surprised. "Why?"

He pursed his lips. "We want to hear that we're dangerous and exciting, that we stir you up and make you nervous."

"You do?"

"It's a figure of speech."

She searched his eyes. "You don't want me to feel comfortable with you?" she faltered.

"You don't understand what I'm talking about, do you?" he wondered gently.

"No…not really. I'm sorry."

It was early days yet, he reminded himself. It was disappointing that she wasn't shaky when he touched her. But, then, she kept secrets. There must be a reason why she was so icy inside herself.

He set her down but he didn't let her go. "Some things have to be learned," he said.

"Learned."

He framed her face with his big, warm hands. "Passion, for instance."

She blinked.

It was like describing ice to a desert nomad. He smiled wistfully. "You haven't ever been kissed in such a way that you'd die to have it happen again?"

She shook her head. Her eyes were wide and innocent, unknowing. She flushed a little and shifted restlessly.

"But you have been kissed in such a way that you'd rather undergo torture than have it happen again," he said suddenly.

She caught her breath. He couldn't know! He couldn't!

His black eyes narrowed on her face. "Something happened to you, Jake. Something bad. It made you lock yourself away from the world. And it wasn't your experience with the traveling auditor."

"You can't know...!"

"Of course not," he interrupted impatiently. "You know I don't pry. But I've been in law enforcement a long time, and I've learned to read people pretty good. You're afraid of me when I get too close to you."

She bit down hard on her lower lip. She drew blood.

"Stop that," he said in a tender tone, touching her lower lip where her teeth had savaged it. "I'm not going to try to browbeat you into telling me something you don't want to. But I wish you trusted me enough to talk to me about it. You know I'm not judgmental."

"It doesn't have anything to do with that."

He cocked his head. "Can't you tell me?"

She hesitated noticeably. She wanted to. She really wanted to. But...

He bent and kissed her eyelids shut. "Don't. We have all the time in the world. When you're ready to talk, I'll listen."

She drew in a long, labored breath and laid her forehead against his suit coat. "You're the nicest man I've ever known."

He smiled over her head. "Well, that's a start, I guess."

She smiled, too. "It's a start."

Chapter 4

It was the liveliest place Jillian had ever been to. The dance band was on a platform at the end of a long, wide hall with a polished wooden floor. Around the floor were booths, not tables, and there was a bar in the next room with three bartenders, two of whom were female.

The music was incredible. It was Latin with a capital *L*, pulsing and narcotic. On the dance floor, people were moving to the rhythm. Some had on jeans and boots, others were wearing ensembles that would have done justice to a club in New York City. Still others, apparently too intimidated by the talent being displayed on the dance floor, were standing on the perimeter of the room, clapping and smiling.

"Wow," Jillian said, watching a particularly talented couple, a silver-haired lean and muscular man with a willowy blonde woman somewhat younger than he was.

They whirled and pivoted, laughing, with such easy grace and elegance that she couldn't take her eyes off them.

"That's Red Jernigan," he told her, indicating the silver-haired man, whose thick, long hair was in a ponytail down his back.

"He isn't redheaded," she pointed out.

He gave her an amused look. "It doesn't refer to his coloring," he told her. "They called him that because in any battle, he was the one most likely to come out bloody."

She gasped. "Oh."

"I have some odd friends." He shrugged, then smiled. "You'll get used to them."

He was saying something profound about their future. She was confused, but she returned his smile anyway.

The dance ended and Theodore tugged her along with him to the dance floor, where the silver-haired man and the blonde woman were catching their breath.

"Hey, Red," he greeted the other man, who grinned and gripped his hand. "Good to see you."

"About time you came up for a visit." Red's dark eyes slid to the small blonde woman beside the police chief. His eyebrows arched.

"This is Jillian," Theodore said gently. "And this is Red Jernigan."

"I'm Melody," the pretty blonde woman said, introducing herself. "Nice to meet you."

Red slid his arm around the woman and pulled her close. "Nice to see Ted going around with somebody," he observed. "It's painful to see a man come alone to a dance club and refuse to dance with anyone except the owner's wife."

"Well, I don't like most modern women." Theodore

excused himself. He smiled down at a grinning Jillian. "I like Jake, here."

"Jake?" Red asked, blinking.

"He's always called me that," Jillian sighed. "I've known him a long time."

"She has," Theodore drawled, smiling. "She likes cattle."

"I don't," Melody laughed. "Smelly things."

"Oh, but they're not smelly if they're kept clean," Jillian protested at once. "Sammy is always neat."

"Her calf," Theodore explained.

"Is he a bull?" Red asked.

"She's a heifer," Jillian inserted. "A little black baldy."

Red and Melody were giving her odd looks.

"As an acquaintance of mine in Jacobsville, Texas, would say," Red told them, "if Johnny Cash could sing about a girl named Sue, a person can have a girl animal with a boy's name." He leaned closer. "He has a female border collie named Bob."

They burst out laughing.

"Well, don't stand over here with us old folks," Red told them. "Get out there with the younger generation and show them how to tango."

"You aren't old, Bud," Theodore told his friend with twinkling eyes. "You're just a hair slower than you used to be, but with the same skills."

"Which I hope I'm never called to use again," Red replied solemnly. "I'm still on reserve status."

"I know."

"Red was a bird colonel in spec ops," Theodore explained to Jillian later when they were sitting at a table sampling the club's exquisitely cooked seasoned steak and fancy baked sweet potatoes, which it was as famous as for its dance band.

"And he still is?" she asked.

He nodded. "He can do more with recruits than any man I ever knew, and without browbeating them. He just encourages. Of course, there are times when he has to get a little more creative, with the wilder sort."

"Creative?"

He grinned. "There was this giant of a kid from Milwaukee who was assigned to his unit in the field. Kid played video games and thought he knew more about strategy and tactics than Red did. So Red turns him loose on the enemy, but with covert backup."

"What happened?" she asked, all eyes.

"The kid walked right into an enemy squad and froze in his tracks. It's one thing to do that on a computer screen. Quite another to confront armed men in real life. They were aiming their weapons at him when Red led a squad in to recover him. Took about two minutes for them to eliminate the threat and get Commando Carl back to his own lines." He shook his head. "In the excitement, the kid had, shall we say, needed access to a restroom and didn't have one. So they hung a nickname on him that stuck."

"Tell me!"

He chuckled. "Let's just say that it suited him. He took it in his stride, sucked up his pride, learned to follow orders and became a real credit to the unit. He later became mayor of a small town somewhere up north, where he's still known, to a favored few, as 'Stinky.'"

She laughed out loud.

"Actually, he was in good company. I read in a book on World War II that one of our better known generals did the same thing when his convoy ran into a German attack. Poor guy. I'll bet Stinky cringed every time he saw that other general's book on a rack."

"I don't doubt it."

She sipped her iced tea and smiled. "This is really good food," she said. "I've never had a steak that was so tender, not even from beef my uncle raised."

"This is Kobe beef," he pointed out. "Red gets it from Japan. God knows how," he added.

"I read about those. Don't they actually massage the beef cattle?"

"Pamper them," he agreed. "You should try that sweet potato," he advised. "It's really a unique combination of spices they use."

She frowned, picking at it with her fork. "I've only ever had a couple of sweet potatoes, and they were mostly tasteless."

"Just try it."

She put the fork into it, lifted it dubiously to her lips and suddenly caught her breath when the taste hit her tongue like dynamite. "Wow!" she exclaimed. "What do they call this?"

"Red calls it 'the ultimate jalapeño-brown-sugar-sweet-potato delight.'"

"It's heavenly!"

He chuckled. "It is, isn't it? The jalapeño gives it a kick like a mule, but it's not so hot that even tenderfeet wouldn't eat it."

"I would never have thought of such a combination. And I thought I was a good cook."

"You are a good cook, Jake," he said. "The best I ever knew."

She blushed. "Thanks, Theodore."

He cocked his head. "I guess it would kill you to shorten that."

"Shorten what?"

"My name. Most people call me Ted."

She hesitated with the fork in midair. She searched his black eyes for a long time. "Ted," she said softly.

His jaw tautened. He hadn't expected it to have that effect on him. She had a soft, sweet, sexy voice when she let herself relax with him. She made his name sound different; special. New.

"I like the way you say it," he said, when she gave him a worried look. "It's—" he searched for a word that wouldn't intimidate her "—it's stimulating."

"Stimulating." She didn't understand.

He put down his fork with a long sigh. "Something happened to you," he said quietly. "You don't know me well enough to talk to me about it. Or maybe you're afraid that I might go after the man who did it."

She was astounded. She couldn't even manage words. She just stared at him, shocked.

"I'm in law enforcement," he reminded her. "After a few years, you read body language in a different way than most people do. Abused children have a look, a way of dressing and acting, one that's obvious to a cop."

She went white. She bit her lower lip and her fingers toyed with her fork as she stared at it, fighting tears.

His big hand curled around hers, gently. "I wish you could tell me. I think it would help you."

She looked up into quiet, patient eyes. "You wouldn't...think badly of me?"

"For God's sake," he groaned. "Are you nuts?"

She blinked.

He grimaced. "Sorry. I didn't mean to put it that way. Nothing I found out about you would change the way I feel. If that's why you're reluctant."

"You're sure?"

He glared at her.

She lowered her eyes and curled her small hand into his big one, a trusting gesture that touched him in a new and different way.

"When I was fifteen, Uncle John had this young man he got to do odd jobs around here. He was a drifter, very intelligent. He seemed like a nice, trustworthy person to have around the house. Then one day Uncle John felt bad and went to bed, left me with the hired man in the kitchen."

Her jaw clenched. "At first, he was real helpful. Wanted to put out the trash for me and sweep the floor. I thought it was so nice of him. Then all of a sudden, he asked what was my bra size and if I wore nylon panties."

Theodore's eyes began to flash.

She swallowed. "I was so shocked I didn't know what to do or say. I thought it was some sick joke. Until he tried to take my clothes off, mumbling all the time that I needed somebody to teach me about men and he was the perfect person, because he'd had so many virgins."

"Good God!"

"Uncle John was asleep. There was nobody to help me. But the Peales lived right down the road, and I knew a back way through the woods to their house. I hit him in a bad place and ran out the door as fast as my legs could carry me. I was almost naked by then." She closed her eyes, shivering with the memory of the terror she'd felt, running and hearing him curse behind her as he crashed through the undergrowth in pursuit,

"I didn't think what danger I might be placing Sassy Peale and her mother and stepsister in, I just knew they'd help me and I was terrified. I banged on the door and Sassy came to it. When she saw how I looked, she ran for the shotgun they kept in the hall closet. By the time the hired man got on the porch, Sassy had the shotgun loaded and aimed at his stomach. She told him if he moved she'd blow him up."

She sipped tea while she calmed a little from the remembered fear. Her hand was shaking, but just a little. Her free hand was still clasped gently in Theodore's.

"He tried to blame it on me, to say I'd flirted and tried to seduce him, but Sassy knew better. She held him at bay until her mother called the police. They took him away." She drew in a breath. "There was a trial. It was horrible, but at least it was in closed session, in the judge's chambers. The hired man plea-bargained. You see, he had priors, many of them. He drew a long jail sentence, but it did at least spare me a public trial." She sipped tea again. "His sister lived over in Wyoming. She came to see me, after the trial." Her eyes closed. "She said I was a slut who had no business putting a sweet, nice guy like him behind bars for years." She managed a smile. "Sassy was in the kitchen when the woman came to the door. She marched into the living room and gave that woman hell. She told her about her innocent brother's priors and how many young girls had suffered because of his inability to control his own desires. She was eloquent. The woman shut up and went away. I never heard from her again." She looked over at him. "Sassy's been my friend ever since. Not a close one, I'm sorry to say. I was so embarrassed at having her know about it that it inhibited me with her and everyone else. Everyone would believe the man's sister, and that I'd asked for it."

His fingers curled closer into hers. "No young woman asks for such abuse," he said softly. "But abusers use that argument to defend themselves. It's a lie, like all their other lies."

"Sometimes," she said, to be fair, "women do lie, and men, innocent men, go to jail for things they didn't do."

"Yes," he agreed. "But more often than not, such lies are found out, and the women themselves are punished for it."

"I guess so."

"I wasn't here when that happened."

"No. You were doing that workshop at the FBI Academy. And I begged the judge not to tell you or anybody else. She was very kind to me."

He looked over her head, his eyes flashing cold and black as he thought what he might have done to the man if he'd been in town. He wasn't interested in Jillian as a woman back then, because she was still almost a child, but he'd always been fond of her. He would have wiped the floor with the man.

His expression made her feel warm inside. "You'd have knocked him up and down main street," she ventured.

He laughed, surprised, and met her eyes. "Worse than that, probably." He frowned. "First the hired man, then the accountant."

"The accountant was my fault," she confessed. "I never told him how old I was, and I was infatuated with him. He was drinking when he tried to persuade me." She shook her head. "I can't believe I even did that."

He stared at her. "You were a kid, Jake. Kids aren't known for deep thought."

She smiled. "Thanks for not being judgmental."

He shrugged. "I'm such a nice man that I'm never judgmental."

Her eyebrows arched.

He grinned. "And I really can do the tango. Suppose I teach you?"

She studied his lean, handsome face. "It's a very, well, sensual sort of dance, they say."

"Very." He pursed his lips. "But I'm not an aggressive man. Not in any way that should frighten you."

She colored a little. "Really?"

"Really."

She drew in a long breath. "I guess every woman should dance the tango at least once."

"My thoughts exactly."

He wiped his mouth on the linen napkin, took a last sip of the excellent but cooling coffee and got to his feet.

"You have to watch your back on the dance floor, though," he told her as he led her toward it.

"Why is that?"

"When the other women see what a great dancer I am, they'll probably mob you and take me away from you," he teased.

She laughed. "Okay." She leaned toward him. "Are you packing?"

"Are you kidding?" he asked, indicating the automatic nestled at his waist on his belt. "I'm a cop. I'm always packing. And you keep your little hands off my gun," he added sternly. "I don't let women play with it, even if they ask nicely."

"Theodore, I'm scared of guns," she reminded him. "And you know it. That's why *you* come over and sit on the front porch and shoot bottles on stumps, just to irritate me."

"I'll try to reform," he promised.

"Lies."

He put his hand over his heart. "I only lie when I'm salving someone's feelings," he pointed out. "There are times when telling the truth is cruel."

"Oh, yeah? Name one."

He nodded covertly toward a woman against the wall. "Well, if I told that nice lady that her dress looks like she had it painted on at a carnival, she'd probably feel bad."

She bit her lip trying not to laugh. "She probably thinks it looks sexy."

"Oh, no. Sexy is a dress that covers almost everything, but leaves one little tantalizing place bare," he said. "That's why Japanese kimonos have that dip on the back of the neck, that just reveals the nape, when the rest of the woman is covered from head to toe. The Japanese think the nape of the neck is sexy."

"My goodness!" She stared up at him, impressed. "You've been so many places. I've only ever been out of Montana once, when I drove to Wyoming with Uncle John to a cattle convention. I've never been out of the country at all. You learn a lot about other people when you travel, don't you?"

He nodded. He smiled. "Other countries have different customs. But people are mostly the same everywhere. I've enjoyed the travel most of all, even when I had to do it on business."

"Like the time you flew to London with that detective from Scotland Yard. Imagine a British case that involved a small town like Hollister!" she exclaimed.

"The perpetrator was a murderer who came over here fishing to provide himself with an alibi while his wife committed the crime and blamed it on her absent husband. In the end, they both drew life sentences."

"Who did they kill?" she asked.

"Her cousin who was set to inherit the family estate and about ten million pounds," he said, shaking his head. "The things sensible people will do for money never ceases to amaze me. I mean, it isn't like you can take it with you when you die. And how many houses can you live in? How many cars can you drive?" He frowned. "I think of money the way the Crow and Cheyenne people do. The way most Native Americans do. The man in the tribe who is the most honored is always the poorest, because he gives away everything he has to people who need it more. They're not capitalists. They don't understand societies that equate prestige with money."

"And they share absolutely everything," she agreed. "They don't understand private property."

He laughed. "Neither do I. The woods and the rivers and the mountains are ageless. You can't own them."

"See? That's the Cheyenne in you talking."

He touched her blond hair. "Probably it is. We going to dance, or talk?"

"You're leading, aren't you?"

He tugged her onto the dance floor. "Apparently." He drew her gently to him and then hesitated. After what she'd told him, he didn't want to do anything that would make her uncomfortable. He said so.

"I don't…well, I don't feel uncomfortable, like that, with you," she faltered, looking up into his black eyes. She managed a shaky little smile. "I like being close to you." She flushed, afraid she'd been too bold. Or that he'd think she was being forward. Her expression was troubled.

He just smiled. "You can say anything to me," he said gently. "I won't think you're being shallow or vampish. Okay?"

She relaxed. "Okay. Is this going to be hard to learn?"

"Very."

She drew in a long breath. "Then I guess we should get started."

His eyes smiled down at her. "I guess we should."

He walked her around the dance floor, to her amusement, teaching her how the basic steps were done. It wasn't like those exotic tangos she'd seen in movies at first. It was like kindergarten was to education.

She followed his steps, hesitantly at first, then a little more confidently, until she was moving with some elegance.

"Now, this is where we get into the more exotic parts," he said. "It involves little kicks that go between the legs." He leaned to her ear. "I think we should have kids one day, so it's very important that you don't get overenthusiastic with the kicks. And you should also be very careful where you place them."

It took her a minute to understand what he meant, and then she burst out laughing instead of being embarrassed.

He grinned. "Just playing it safe," he told her. "Ready? This is how you do it."

It was fascinating, the complexity of the movements and the fluid flow of the steps as he paced the dance to the music.

"It doesn't look like this in most movies," she said as she followed his steps.

"That's because it's a stylized version of the tango," he told her. "Most people have no idea how it's supposed to be done. But there are a few movies that go into it in depth. One was made in black and white by a British woman. It's my favorite. Very comprehensive. Even about the danger of the kicks." He chuckled.

"It's Argentinian, isn't it? The dance, I mean."

"You'd have to ask my buddy about that, I'm not sure. I know there are plenty of dance clubs down there that specialize in tango. The thing is, you're supposed to do these dances with strangers. It's as much a social expression as it is a dance."

"Really?"

He nodded. He smiled. "Maybe we should get a bucket and put all our spare change into it. Then, when we're Red's age, we might have enough to buy tickets to Buenos Aires and go dancing."

She giggled. "Oh, I'm sure we'd have the ticket price in twenty or thirty years."

He sighed as he led. "Or forty." He shook his head. "I've always wanted to travel. I did a good bit of it in the service, but there are plenty of places I'd love to see. Like those ruins in Peru and the pyramids, and the Sonoran desert."

She frowned. "The Sonoran desert isn't exotic."

He smiled. "Sure it is. Do you know, those Saguaro cacti can live for hundreds of years? And that if a limb falls on you, it can kill you because of the weight? You don't think about them being that heavy, but they have a woody spine and limbs to support the weight of the water they store."

"Gosh. How do you know all that?"

He grinned. "The *Science Channel,* the *Discovery Channel,* the *National Geographic Channel...*"

She laughed. "I like to watch those, too."

"I don't think I've missed a single nature special," he told her. He gave her a droll look. "Now that should tell you all you need to know about my social life." He grinned.

She laughed, too. "Well, my social life isn't much better. This is the first time I've been on a real date."

His black eyebrows arched.

She flushed. She shrugged. She averted her eyes.

He tilted her face up to his and smiled with a tenderness that made her knees weak. "I heartily approve," he said, "of the fact that you've been saving yourself for me, just like your uncle did," he added outrageously.

She almost bent over double laughing. "No fair."

"Just making the point." He slid his arm around her and pulled her against him. She caught her breath.

He hesitated, his dark eyes searching hers to see if he'd upset her.

"My…goodness," she said breathlessly.

He raised his eyebrows.

She averted her eyes and her cheeks took on a glow. She didn't know how to tell him that the sensations she was feeling were unsettling. She could feel the muscles of his chest pressed against her breasts, and it was stimulating, exciting. It was a whole new experience to be held close to a man's body, to feel its warm strength, to smell the elusive, spicy cologne he was wearing.

"You've danced with men before."

"Yes, of course," she confessed. She looked up at him with fascination. "But it didn't, well, it didn't…feel like this."

That made him arrogant. His chin lifted and he looked down at her with possession kindling in his eyes.

"Sorry," she said quickly, embarrassed. "I just blurt things out."

He bent his head, so that his mouth was right beside

her ear as he eased her into the dance. "It's okay," he said softly.

She bit her lip and laughed nervously.

"Well, it's okay to feel like that with me," he corrected. "But you should know that it's very wrong for you to feel that way with any other man. So you should never dance with anybody but me for the rest of your life."

She burst out laughing again.

He chuckled. "You're a quick study, Jake," he noted as she followed his steps easily. "I think we may become famous locally for this dance once you get used to it."

"You think?" she teased.

He turned her back over his arm, pulled her up, and spun her around with skill. She laughed breathlessly. It was really fun.

"I haven't danced in years," he sighed. "I love to do it, but I'm not much of a party person."

"I'm not, either. I'm much more at home in a kitchen than I am in a club." She grimaced. "That's not very modern, either, for a woman. I always feel that I should be working my way up a corporate ladder somewhere or immersing myself in higher education."

"Would you like to be a corporate leader?"

She made a face. "Not really. Jobs like that are demanding, and you have to want them more than anything. I'm just not ambitious, I guess. Although," she mused, "I think I might like to take a college course."

"What sort?" he asked.

"Anthropology."

He stopped dancing and looked down at her, fascinated. "Why?"

"I like reading about ancient humans, and how archaeologists can learn so much from skeletal material.

I go crazy over those *National Geographic* specials on Egypt."

He laughed. "So do I."

"I'd love to see the pyramids. All of them, even those in Mexico and Asia."

"There are pyramids here in the States," he reminded her. "Those huge earthen mounds that primitive people built were the equivalent of pyramids."

She stopped dancing. "Why do you think they built them?"

"I don't know. It's just a guess. But most of the earthen mounds are near rivers. I've always thought maybe they were where the village went to get out of the water when it flooded."

"It's as good a theory as any other," she agreed. "But what about in Egypt? I don't think they had a problem with flooding," she added, tongue in cheek.

"Now, see, there's another theory about that. Thousands of years ago, Egypt was green and almost tropical, with abundant sources of water. So who knows?"

"It was green?" she exclaimed.

He nodded. "There were forests."

"Where did you learn that?"

"I read, too. I think it was in Herodotus. They called him the father of history. He wrote about Egypt. He admitted that the information might not all be factual, but he wrote down exactly what the Egyptian priests told him about their country."

"I'd like to read what he said."

"You can borrow one of my books," he offered. "I have several copies of his *Histories*."

"Why?"

He grimaced. "Because I keep losing them."

She frowned. "How in the world do you lose a book?"

"You'll have to come home with me sometime and see why."

Her eyes sparkled. "Is that an invitation? You know, 'come up and see my books'?"

He chuckled. "No, it's not a pickup line. I really mean it."

"I'd like to."

"You would?" His arm contracted. "When? How about next Saturday? I'll show you my collection of maps, too."

"Maps?" she exclaimed.

He nodded. "I like topo maps, and relief maps, best of all. It helps me to understand where places are located."

She smiled secretively. "We could compare maps."

"What?"

She sighed. "I guess we do have a lot in common. I think I've got half the maps Rand McNally ever published!"

Chapter 5

"Well, what do you know?" He laughed. "We're both closet map fanatics."

"And we love ancient history."

"And we love shooting targets from the front porch."

She glowered up at him.

He sighed. "I'll try to reform."

"You might miss and shoot Sammy," she replied.

"I'm a dead shot."

"Anybody can miss once," she pointed out.

"I guess so."

They'd stopped on the dance floor while the band got ready to start the next number. When they did, he whirled her around and they started all over again. Jillian thought she'd never enjoyed anything in her life so much.

* * *

Ted walked her to the front door, smiling. "It was a nice first date."

"Yes, it was," she agreed, smiling back. "I've never had so much fun!"

He laughed. She made him feel warm inside. She was such an honest person. She wasn't coy or flirtatious. She just said what she felt. It wasn't a trait he was familiar with.

"What are you thinking?" she asked curiously.

"That I'm not used to people who tell the truth."

She blinked. "Why not?"

"Almost all the people I arrest are innocent," he ticked off. "They were set up by a friend, or it was a case of mistaken identity even when there were eyewitnesses. Oh, and, the police have it in for them and arrest them just to be mean. That's my personal favorite," he added facetiously.

She chuckled. "I guess they wish they were innocent."

"I guess."

She frowned. "There's been some talk about that man you arrested for the bank robbery getting paroled because of a technicality. Is it true?"

His face set in hard lines. "It might be. His attorney said that the judge made an error in his instructions to the jury that prejudiced the case. I've seen men get off in similar situations."

"Ted, he swore he'd kill you if he ever got out," she said worriedly.

He pursed his lips and his dark eyes twinkled. "Frightened for me?"

"Of course I am."

He sighed and pulled her close. "Now, that's exactly

the sort of thing that makes a man feel good about himself, when some sweet little woman worries about him."

"I'm not little, I'm not sweet and I don't usually worry," she pointed out.

"It's okay if you worry about me," he teased. "As long as you don't do it excessively."

She toyed with the top button of his unbuttoned jacket. "There are lots of safer professions than being a police chief."

He frowned. "You're kidding, right?"

She grimaced. "Ted, Joe Brown's wife was one of my uncle's friends. She was married to that deputy sheriff who was shot to death a few years ago. She said that she spent their whole married lives sitting by the phone at night, almost shaking with worry every time he had to go out on a case, hoping and praying that he'd come home alive."

His hands on her slender waist had tightened unconsciously. "Anyone who marries someone in law enforcement has to live with that possibility," he said slowly.

She bit her lower lip. She was seeing herself sitting by the phone at night, pacing the floor. She was prone to worry anyway. She was very fond of Ted. She didn't want him to die. But right now, she wasn't in love. She had time to think about what she wanted to do with her life. She was sure she should give this a lot of thought before she dived headfirst into a relationship with him that might lead very quickly to marriage. She'd heard people talk about how it was when people became very physical with each other, that it was so addictive that they couldn't bear to be apart at all. Once that happened, she wouldn't have a chance to see things rationally.

Ted could almost see the thoughts in her mind. Slowly he released her and stepped back.

She felt the distance, and it was more than physical. He was drawing away in every sense.

She looked up at him. She drew in a long breath. "I'm not sure I'm ready, Ted."

"Ready for what?"

That stiffness in him was disturbing, but she had to be honest. "I'm not sure I'm ready to think about marriage."

His black eyes narrowed. "Jillian, if we don't get married, there's a California developer who's going to make this place into hot real estate with tourist impact, and Sammy could end up on a platter."

She felt those words like a body blow. Her eyes, tormented, met his. "But it's not fair, to rush into something without having time to think about it!" she exclaimed. "The wills didn't say we have to get married tomorrow! There's no real time limit!"

There was, but he wasn't going to push her. She had cold feet. She didn't know him that well, despite the years they'd been acquainted, and she wasn't ready for the physical side of marriage. She had hang-ups, and good reasons to have them.

"Okay," he said after a minute. "Suppose we just get to know each other and let the rest ride for a while?"

"You mean, go on dates and stuff?"

He pursed his lips. "Yes. Dates and stuff."

She noticed how handsome he was. In a crowd, he always stood out. He was a vivid sort of person, not like she was at all. But they did enjoy the same sorts of things and they got along, most of the time.

"I would like to see your place," she said.

"I'll come and get you Saturday morning," he said quietly.

He waited for her answer with bridled impatience. She could see that. He wasn't sure of her at all. She hated being so hesitant, but it was a rushed business. She would have to make a decision in the near future or watch Uncle John's ranch become a resort. It didn't bear thinking about. On the other hand, if she said yes to Ted, it would mean a relationship that she was certain she wasn't ready for.

"Stop gnawing your lip off and say yes," Ted told her. "We'll work out the details as we go along."

She sighed. "Okay, Ted," she said after a minute.

He hadn't realized that he'd been holding his breath. He smiled slowly. She was going to take the chance. It was a start.

"Okay." He frowned. "You don't have any low-cut blouses and jeans that look like you've been poured into them, do you?"

"Ted!"

"Well, I was just wondering," he said. "Because if you do, you can't wear them over at my place. We have a dress code."

"A dress code." She nodded. "So your cowboys have to wear dresses." She nodded again.

He burst out laughing. He bent and kissed her, hard, but impersonally, and walked down the steps. "I'll see you Saturday."

"You call that a kiss?" she yelled after him, and shocked herself with the impertinent remark that had jumped out of her so impulsively.

But he didn't react to it the way she expected. He just threw up his hand and kept walking.

* * *

They worked side by side in his kitchen making lunch. He was preparing an omelet while she made cinnamon toast and fried bacon.

"Breakfast for lunch," she scoffed.

"Hey, I very often have breakfast for supper, if I've been out on a case," he said indignantly. "There's no rule that says you have to have breakfast in the morning."

"I suppose not."

"See, you don't know how to break rules."

She gasped. "You're a police chief! You shouldn't be encouraging anybody to break rules."

"It's okay as long as it's only related to food," he replied.

She laughed, shaking her head.

"You going to turn that bacon anytime soon?" he asked, nodding toward it, "or do you really like it raw on one side and black on the other?"

"If you don't like it that way, you could fry it yourself."

"I do omelets," he pointed out. "I don't even eat bacon."

"What?"

"Pig meat," he muttered.

"I like bacon!"

"Good. Then you can eat it. I've got a nice country ham all carved up and cooked in the fridge. I'll have that with mine."

"Ham is pig meat, too!"

"I think of it as steak with a curly tail," he replied.

She burst out laughing. He was so different off the job. She'd seen him walking down the sidewalk in town, somber and dignified, almost unapproachable. Here, at home, he was a changed person.

"What are you brooding about?" he wondered.

"Was I? I was just thinking how different you are at home than at work."

"I should hope so," he sighed, as he took the omelet up onto a platter. "I mean, think of the damage to my image if I cooked omelets for the prisoners."

"Chief Barnes used to," she said. "I remember Uncle John talking about what a sweet man he was. He'd take the prisoners himself to funerals when they had family members die, and in those days, when the jail was down the hall from the police department, he'd cook for them, too."

"He was a kind man," Ted agreed solemnly.

"To think that it was one of the prisoners who killed him," she added quietly as she turned the bacon. "Of all the ironies."

"The man was drunk at the time," Ted said. "And, if you recall, he killed himself just a few weeks later while he was waiting for trial. He left a note saying he didn't want to put the chief's family through any more pain."

"Everybody thought that was so odd," she said. "But people forget that murderers are just like everybody else. They aren't born planning to kill people."

"That's true. Sometimes it's alcohol or drugs that make them do it. Other times it's an impulse they can't control. Although," he added, "there are people born without a conscience. They don't mind killing. I've seen them in the military. Not too many, thank goodness, but they come along occasionally."

"Your friend who was a sniper, was he like that?"

"Not at all," he said. "He was trained to think of it as just a skill. It was only later, when it started to kill his soul, that he realized what was happening to him. That was when he got out."

"How in the world did he get into law enforcement, with such a background?" she wondered.

He chuckled. "Uncle Sam often doesn't know when his left hand is doing something different than his right one," he commented. "Government agencies have closed files."

"Oh. I get it. But those files aren't closed to everyone, are they?"

"They're only accessible to people with top-secret military clearance." He glanced at her amusedly. "Never knew a civilian, outside the executive branch, who even had one."

"That makes sense."

He pulled out her chair for her.

"Thank you," she said, with surprise in her tone.

"I'm impressing you with my good manners," he pointed out as he sat down across from her and put a napkin in his lap.

"I'm very impressed." She tasted the omelet, closed her eyes and sighed. "And not only with your manners. Ted, this is delicious!"

He grinned. "Thanks."

"What did you put in it?" she asked, trying to decide what combination of spices he'd used to produce such a taste.

"Trade secret."

"You can tell me," she coaxed. "After all, we're almost engaged."

"The 'almost' is why I'm not telling," he retorted. "If things don't work out, you'll be using my secret spices in your own omelets for some other man."

"I could promise."

"You could, but I'm not telling."

She sighed. "Well, it's delicious, anyway."

He chuckled. "The bacon's not bad, either," he conceded, having forgone the country ham that would need warming. He was hungry.

"Thanks." She lifted a piece of toast and gave it a cold look. "Shame we can't say the same for the toast. Sorry. I was busy trying not to burn the bacon, so I burned the toast instead."

"I don't eat toast."

"I do, but I don't think I will this time." She pushed the toast aside.

After they ate, he walked her around the property. He only had a few beef steers in the pasture. He'd bought quite a few Angus cattle with his own uncle, and they were at the ranch that Jillian had shared with her uncle John. She was pensive as she strolled beside him, absently stripping a dead branch of leaves, thinking about the fate of Uncle John's prize beef if she didn't marry Ted sometime soon.

"Deep thoughts?" he asked, hands in the pockets of his jeans under his shepherd's coat.

She frowned. She was wearing her buckskin jacket. One of the pieces of fringe caught on a limb and she had to stop to disentangle it. "I was thinking about that resort," she confessed.

"Here. Let me." He stopped and removed the branch from the fringe. "Do you know why these jackets always had fringe?"

She looked up at him, aware of his height and strength so close to her. He smelled of tobacco and coffee and fir trees. "Not really."

He smiled. "When the old-timers needed something to tie up a sack with, they just pulled off a piece of fringe and used that. Also, the fringe collects water and drips it away from the body."

"My goodness!"

"My grandmother was full of stories like that. Her grandfather was a fur trapper. He lived in the Canadian wilderness. He was French. He married a Blackfoot woman."

She smiled, surprised. "But you always talk about your Cheyenne heritage."

"That's because my other grandmother was Cheyenne. I have interesting bloodlines."

Her eyes sketched his high-cheekboned face, his black eyes and hair and olive complexion. "They combined to make a very handsome man."

"Me?" he asked, surprised.

She grinned. "And not a conceited bone in your body, either, Ted."

He smiled down at her. "Not much to be conceited about."

"Modest, too."

He shrugged. He touched her cheek with his fingertips. "You have beautiful skin."

Her eyebrows arched. "Thank you."

"You get that from your mother," he said gently. "I remember her very well. I was only a boy when she died, but she was well-known locally. She was the best cook in two counties. She was always the first to sit with anyone sick, or to take food when there was a funeral."

"I only know about her through my uncle," she replied. "My uncle loved her. She was his only sister, much older than he was. She and my father had me unexpectedly, late in life."

Which, he thought, had been something of a tragedy.

"And then they both died of the flu, when I was barely

crawling," she sighed. "I never knew either of them." She looked up. "You did at least know your parents, didn't you?"

He nodded. "My mother died of a stroke in her early thirties," he said. "My father was overseas, working for an oil corporation as a roughneck, when there was a bombing at the installation and he died. My grandmother took me in, and my uncle moved in to help support us."

"Neither of us had much of a childhood," she said. "Not that our relatives didn't do all they could for us," she added quickly. "They loved us. Lots of orphaned kids have it a lot worse."

"Yes, they do," he agreed solemnly. "That's why we have organizations that provide for orphaned kids."

"If I ever get rich," she commented, "I'm going to donate to those."

He grinned. "I already do. To a couple, at least."

She leaned back against a tree and closed her eyes, drinking in the sights and sounds and smells of the woods. "I love winter. I know it isn't a popular season," she added. "It's cold and there's a lot of snow. But I enjoy it. I can smell the smoke from fireplaces and woodstoves. If I close my eyes, it reminds me of campfires. Uncle John used to take me camping with him when I was little, to hunt deer."

"Which you never shot."

She opened her eyes and made a face. "I'm not shooting Bambi."

"Bull."

"People shouldn't shoot animals."

"That attitude back in colonial times would have seen you starve to death," he pointed out. "It's not like those old-timers could go to a grocery store and buy meat and vegetables. They had to hunt and garden or die."

She frowned. "I didn't think about that."

"In fact," he added, "people who refused to work were turned out of the forts into the wilderness. Some stole food from the Indians and were killed for it. Others starved or froze to death. It was a hard life."

"Why did they do it?" she wondered aloud. "Why leave their families and their homes and get on rickety old ships and go to a country they'd never even seen?"

"A lot of them did it to escape debtor's prison," he said. "They had debts they couldn't pay. A few years over here working as an indentured servant and they could be free and have money to buy their own land. Or the people they worked for might give them an acre or two, if they were generous."

"What about when the weather took their crops and they had nothing to eat?"

"There are strings of graves over the eastern seaboard of pilgrims who starved," he replied. "A sad end to a hopeful beginning. This is a hostile land when it's stripped of supermarkets and shopping centers."

A silence fell between them, during which he stared at the small rapids in the stream nearby. "That freezes over in winter," he said. "It looks pretty."

"I'd like to see it then."

He turned. "I'll bring you over here."

She smiled. "Okay."

His black eyes looked long and deep into hers across the distance, until she felt as if something snapped inside her. She caught her breath and forced her eyes away.

Ted didn't say anything. He just smiled. And started walking again.

* * *

She loved it that he didn't pressure her into a more physical relationship. It gave her a breathing space that she desperately needed.

He took her to a play in Billings the following weekend, a modern parody of an old play about two murderous old women and their assorted crazy relatives.

She laughed until her sides ached. Later, as they were driving home, she realized that it had been a long time since she'd been so amused by anything.

"I'm so glad I never had relatives like that," she ventured.

He laughed. "Me, too. The murderous cousin with the spooky face was a real pain, wasn't he?"

"His associate was even crazier."

She sat back against the seat, her eyes closed, still smiling. "It was a great play. Thanks for asking me."

"I was at a loose end," he commented. "We have busy weekends and slow weekends. This was a very slow one, nothing my officers couldn't handle on their own."

That was a reminder, and not a very pleasant one, of what he did for a living. She frowned in the darkness of the cab, broken only by the blue light of the instrument panel. "Ted, haven't you ever thought about doing something else for a living?"

"Like what?" he asked. "Teaching chemistry to high school students?"

He made a joke of it, but she didn't laugh. "You're not likely to be killed doing that."

"I guess you don't keep up with current events," he remarked solemnly, and proceeded to remind her of several terrible school shootings.

She grimaced. "Yes, but those are rare incidents. You

make enemies in your work. What if somebody you locked up gets out and tries to kill you?"

"It goes with the job," he said laconically. "So far, I've been lucky."

Lucky. But it might not last forever. Could she see herself sitting by the phone every night of her life, waiting for that horrible call?

"You're dwelling on anticipation of the worst," he said, glancing her way. "How in the world do you think people get by who have loved ones with chronic illness or life-threatening conditions?"

She looked at him in the darkness. "I've never thought about it."

"My grandmother had cancer," he reminded her. "Had it for years. If I'd spent that time sitting in a chair, brooding on it, what sort of life would it have been for her?"

She frowned. "Lonely."

"Exactly. I knew it could happen, anytime. But I lived from day to day, just like she did. After a while, I got used to the idea, like she did, and we went on with our lives. It was always there, in the background, but it was something we just—" he searched for the word "—lived with. That's how husbands and wives of people in law enforcement and the military deal with it."

It was a new concept for her, living with a terrifying reality and getting used to it.

"You're very young," he said heavily. "It would be harder for you."

It probably would. She didn't answer him. It was something new to think about.

He walked her up the steps to her front door. He looked good in a suit, she thought, smiling.

"What are you thinking?" he teased.

"That you look very elegant in a suit."

He shrugged. "It's a nice suit."

"It's a nice man wearing it."

"Thanks. I like your dress."

She grinned. "It's old, but I like the color. It's called Rose Dust."

He fingered the lacy collar. He wouldn't have told her, because it would hurt her feelings, but it looked like the sort of dress a high school girl would wear. It wasn't sophisticated, or even old enough for her now. But he just smiled.

"Nice color," he agreed.

She cocked her head, feeling reckless. "Going to kiss me?" she asked.

"I was thinking about it."

"And what did you decide?"

He stuck his hands in his pockets and just smiled down at her. "That would be rushing things a little too much," he said gently. "You want to date and get to know each other. I think that's a good idea. Plenty of time for the other, later."

"Well, my goodness!"

"Shocked by my patience, are you?" he asked with a grin. "Me, too."

"Very."

His eyes were old and wise. "When things get physical, there's a difference in the way two people are, together. There's no time to step back and look at how things really are."

She nodded. "You mean, like Sassy and her husband, John Callister, when they first got married. They couldn't stand to be apart, even for an hour or two. They still pretty much go everywhere together. And they're always standing close, or touching."

"That's what I mean."

She frowned. "I haven't ever felt like that," she said.

He smiled. "I noticed."

She flushed. "I'm sorry, I just blurt things out…"

"I don't mind that you're honest," he said. "It helps. A lot."

She bit her lower lip. "I'd give anything if Uncle John hadn't hired that man to come work for him."

"I'm sure your uncle felt the same way. I'm surprised that he never told me about it," he added curtly.

"I imagine he thought you'd hold him responsible for it. He blamed himself," she added softly. "He never stopped apologizing." She sighed. "It didn't help very much."

"Of course it didn't." He stepped closer and tilted her chin up. "You'll deal with it. If you don't think you can, there are some good psychologists. Our department works with two, who live in Billings."

She made a face. "I don't think I could talk about something like that to a total stranger."

He stared at her for a long time. "How about me?" he asked suddenly. "Could you talk about it to me?"

Chapter 6

Jillian stared up at him with conflicting emotions. But after a minute she nodded. "I think I could," she replied finally.

He beamed. His black eyes were twinkling. "That's a major step forward."

"Think so?"

"I know so."

She moved a step closer. "I enjoyed tonight. Thank you."

He gave her a teasing look and moved a step away. "I did, too, and I'll thank you to keep your distance. I don't want to be an object of lust to a single woman who lives alone."

She gasped theatrically. "You do so!"

"I do?"

"Absolutely!" she agreed. She grinned. "But not right now. Right?"

He laughed. "Not right now." He bent and brushed a lazy kiss against her forehead. "Get some sleep. I'll call you Monday."

"You do that. Not early," she added, without telling him why. She had a secret, and she wasn't sharing it.

"Not early," he agreed. "Good night."

"Good night, Ted."

He bounded down the steps, jumped in his truck and sat there deliberately until she got the message. She went inside, locked the door and turned off the porch light. Only then did he drive away. It made her feel safe, that attitude of his. Probably it was instinctive, since he was in law enforcement, but she liked it. She liked it very much.

Snow came the next morning. Jillian loved it. She drove slowly, so that she didn't slip off the road. But there wasn't much traffic, and she lived close to town. It was easier than she expected to get in on the country roads.

When she left again, at noon, it was a different story. The snow had come fast and furiously, and she could barely crawl along the white highway. The road crews had been busy, spreading sand and gravel, but there were icy spots just the same.

She hesitated to go all the way back to the ranch when she couldn't see the road ahead for the blinding snow, so she pulled into the town's only restaurant and cut off the engine.

"Well," she said to herself, "I guess if worse comes to worst, they might let me sleep in a booth in the restaurant." She laughed at the imagery.

She grabbed her purse and got out, grateful for her high-heeled cowboy boots that made it easier to get a foothold in the thick, wet snow. This was the kind that made good snowmen. She thought she might make one when she finally got home. A calf, perhaps, to look like Sammy. She laughed. Ted would howl at that, if she did it.

She opened the door of the restaurant and walked right into a nightmare. Davy Harris, the man who had almost raped her, was standing by the counter, paying his bill. He was still thin and nervous-looking, with straggly brown hair and pale eyes. He looked at her with mingled distaste and hatred.

"Well, well, I hoped I might run into you again," he said in a voice dripping with venom. "I don't guess you expected to see me, did you, Jillian? Not the man you put in prison for trying to kiss you!"

The owner of the restaurant knew Jillian, and liked her, but he was suddenly giving her a very odd look. There was another customer behind him, one who'd known Jillian's uncle. He gave her an odd look, too.

"There was more to it than that," Jillian said unsteadily.

"Yes, I wanted to marry you, I can't imagine why, you little prude," he said with contempt. "Put a man in prison for trying to teach you about life."

She flushed. She had a good comeback for that, but it was too embarrassing to talk about it in public, especially around men she didn't really know. She felt sick all over.

He came up to her, right up to her, and looked down at her flushed face. "I'm going to be in town for a while, Jillian," he said. "And don't get any ideas about having your boyfriend try to boot me out, or I'll tell him a few things he doesn't know about you."

With that shocking statement, he smiled at the owner, praised the food again and walked out the door.

Jillian sat drinking coffee with cold, trembling hands. She felt the owner's eyes on her, and it wasn't in a way she liked. He seemed to be sizing her up with the new information his customer had given him about her.

People who didn't know you tended to accept even unsavory details with openhandedness, she thought miserably. After all, how well did you really know somebody who worked for you a few days a week? Jillian lived outside town and kept to herself. She wasn't a social person.

There would be gossip, she was afraid, started by the man who'd just gotten out of prison. And how had he gotten out? she wondered. He'd been sentenced to ten years.

When she finished her coffee, she paid for it and left a tip, and paused to speak to the owner. She didn't really know what to say. Her enemy had made an accusation about her, but how did she refute it?

"What he said," she stammered, "there's a lot more to it than it sounds like. I was...fifteen."

The owner wasn't a stupid man. He'd known Jillian since she was a child. "Listen," he said gently, "I don't pay any mind to gossip. I know Jack Haynes, the assistant circuit D.A. He'd never prosecute a man unless he was sure he could get a conviction."

She felt a little relieved. "Thanks, Mr. Chaney."

He smiled. "Don't worry about it. You might talk to Jack, though."

"Yes, I might." She hesitated. "You won't, well, fire me?"

"Don't be ridiculous. And you be careful out there in

the snow. If it gets worse, stay home. I can get old Mrs. Barry to sub for you in the morning, okay?"

"Okay," she said. "Thanks."

"We don't want to lose you in an accident," he replied.

She smiled back.

Jack Haynes had his office in the county courthouse, in Hollister. She walked in, hesitantly, and asked the clerk if he was there and could she see him.

"Sure," he said. "He's just going over case files." He grimaced. "Not a fun thing to do. Court's next week."

"I can imagine."

He announced her and she walked in. Jack Haynes smiled, shook hands with her and offered her a chair.

"Davy Harris is out of prison," she blurted out. "I walked right into him at the restaurant this morning."

He scowled. "Who's out?"

She repeated the man's name.

He pushed the intercom button. "Did we receive notification that they'd released Davy Harris in that attempted rape case?"

"Just a minute, sir, I'll check."

The prosecutor cursed under his breath. "I had no idea! You saw him?"

She nodded. "He told everybody in earshot that I had him put in prison for trying to kiss me." She flushed.

"What a whitewash job!"

"Tell me about it."

The intercom blared. "Sir, they sent a notification, but it wasn't on the server. I'm sorry. I don't know how it got lost."

"Electronic mail," Haynes scoffed. "In my day, we went to the post office to get mail!"

"And even there it gets lost sometimes, sir," his clerk said soothingly. "Sorry."

"So am I. How did Harris get out?"

"On a technicality, pertaining to the judge's instructions to the jury being prejudicial to his case," came the reply. "He's only out until the retrial."

"Yes, well, that could take a year or two," Haynes said coldly.

"Yes," his clerk said quietly.

"Thanks, Chet," he replied, and closed the circuit.

He turned his attention back to Jillian. "That's the second piece of unsettling news I've had from the court system this week," he said curtly. "They've released Smitty Jones, the bank robber, who threatened our police chief, also on a technicality. He's out pending retrial, too." His face hardened. "It shouldn't come as a surprise that they have the same lawyer, some hotshot from Denver."

Jillian clenched her teeth. "He said he'd kill Ted."

Haynes smiled reassuringly. "Better men than him have tried to kill Ted," he pointed out. "He's got good instincts and he's a veteran law enforcement officer. He can take care of himself, believe me."

"I know that, but anybody can be ambushed. Look at Chief Barnes. He was a cautious, capable law enforcement officer, too."

He grimaced. "I knew him. He was such a good man. Shame, what happened."

"Yes."

He gave her a long look. "Jillian, we can't do anything about Harris while he's out on bond," he told her. "But you can take precautions, and you should. Don't go anywhere alone."

"I live alone," she pointed out, worriedly.

He drew in a sharp breath. He'd seen cases like this before, where stalkers had vowed revenge and killed or raped their accusers when they were released from prison. He hated the thought of having something bad happen to this poor woman, who'd seen more than her share of the dark side of men.

"I'll tell Ted," she said after a minute.

His eyebrows arched.

She averted her eyes. "We're sort of in a situation, about the ranch. Our uncles left a clause that if we don't get married, the ranch has to be sold at public auction. Ted thinks we should get married very soon. But I've been hesitant," she said, and bit off the reason.

He knew, without being told by her. "You need to be in therapy," he said bluntly.

She grimaced. "I know. But I can't, I just can't talk about things like that to a stranger."

He had a daughter about her age. He thought how it would be for her in a similar circumstance. It made him sad.

"They're used to all sorts of terrible stories," he began.

"I can't talk about personal things to a stranger," she repeated.

He sighed. "It could ruin your whole life, lock you up in ways you don't even realize yet," he said gently. "I've seen cases where women were never able to marry because of it."

She nodded.

"Don't you want a husband and a family?"

"Very much," she said. She ground her teeth together. "But it seems just hopeless right now." She looked up. "That California developer is licking his lips over my ranch already. But I don't know if I can be a good wife.

Ted thinks so, but it's a terrible gamble. I know I have hang-ups."

"They'll get worse," he said bluntly. "I speak from experience. I've tried many cases like yours over the years. I've seen the victims. I know the prognosis. It isn't pretty."

Her eyes were haunted and sad. "I don't understand why he did it," she began.

"It's a compulsion," he explained. "They know it's wrong, but they can't stop. It isn't a matter of will." He leaned forward. "It's like addiction. You know, when men try to give up alcohol, but there's something inside them that pushes them to start drinking again. It doesn't excuse it," he said immediately. "But I'm told that even when they try to live a normal life, it's very difficult. It's one day at a time."

He shook his head. "I see the results of addiction all the time. Alcohol, sex, cards, you name it. People destroy not only their own lives, but the lives of their families because they have a compulsion they can't control."

"It's a shame there isn't a drug you can give people to keep them from getting addicted," she said absently.

He burst out laughing. "Listen to you. A drug. Drugs are our biggest headache."

She flushed. "Sorry. Wasn't thinking."

He gave her a compassionate smile. "Talk to Ted," he said. "He'll look out for you until our unwanted visitor leaves. In fact, there's a vagrancy law on the books that could give him a reason to make the man leave. Tell him I said so."

She smiled. "I will. Thanks so much, Mr. Haynes."

She stood up. He did, too, and shook her hand.

"If you need help, and you can't find Ted, you can

call me," he said unexpectedly. He pulled out a business card and handed it to her. "My Jessica is just your age," he added quietly. "Nothing like that ever happened to her. But if it had, I'd have a hard time remembering that my job is to uphold the law."

"Jessica is very nice."

"Why, thank you," he chuckled. "I think so, too."

They didn't discuss why he'd raised Jessica alone. Her mother had run off with a visiting public-relations man from Nevada and divorced Mr. Haynes. He'd been left with an infant daughter that his wife had no room for in her new and exciting life of travel and adventure. But he'd done very well raising her. Jessica was in medical school, studying to be a doctor. He was very proud of her.

"Don't forget," he told Jillian on the way out. "If you need me, you call."

She was very touched. "Thanks, Mr. Haynes."

He shrugged. "When I'm not working, which isn't often even after hours, my social life is playing World of Warcraft online." He smiled. "I don't get out much. You won't bother me if you call."

"I'll remember."

She went out and closed the door, smiling at the young clerk on her way outside.

She ran headlong into Ted, who had bounded up the steps, wearing an expression that would have stopped a charging bull.

"What did he say to you?" he demanded hotly. His black eyes were sparking with temper.

"What...Mr. Haynes?" she stammered, nodding toward the office she'd just left.

"Not him. That..." He used some language that lifted

both her eyebrows. "Sorry," he said abruptly. "I heard what happened."

She let out a breath. "He announced in the diner that he got put in prison because he wanted to marry me and I didn't want him to kiss me," she said coldly. "He's out on bond because of a technicality, Mr. Haynes said."

"I know. I phoned the prison board."

She tried to smile. "Mr. Haynes says you can arrest him for vagrancy if he stays in town long enough."

He didn't smile back. "He got a job," he said angrily.

She had to lean against the wall for support. "What?"

"He got a damned job in town!" he snapped. "Old Harrington at the feed store hired him on as a day laborer, delivering supplies to ranchers."

She felt sick to her stomach. It meant that Davy Harris had no plans to leave soon. He was going to stay. He was going to live in her town, be around all the time, gossip about her to anybody who would listen. She felt hunted.

Ted saw that and grimaced. He drew her into his arms and held her gently, without passion. "I'll find a way to get him out of here," he said into her hair.

"You can't break the law," she said miserably. She closed her eyes and felt the strong beat of his heart under her ear. "It gets worse. Smitty Jones, that man you arrested for bank robbery, got out, too, didn't he?"

He hesitated. "Yes."

"I guess it's our day for bad news, Ted," she groaned.

He hugged her, hard, and then let her go. "I don't like the idea of your living alone out at the ranch," he said curtly. "It makes you a better target if he came here with plans for revenge. Which he might have."

She bit her lower lip. "I don't want to get married yet."

He let out an exasperated sigh. "I don't have funds that I could use to get you police protection," he said angrily. "And even if I did, the man hasn't made any threats. He's just here."

"I know," she said. "And he's got a job, you said."

He nodded. "I could have a word with the owner of the feed store, but that would be crossing the line, big time. I can't tell a merchant who to hire, as much as I'd like to," he added.

"I know that. He'd just find another job, anyway, if he's determined to stay here." She closed her eyes on a grimace. "He'll talk to everybody he meets, he'll say I had him put away for some frivolous reason." She opened her eyes. "Ted, he makes it all sound like I was just a prude that he shocked with a marriage proposal. He can tell a lie and make it believeable."

"Some people will believe anything they hear," he agreed. His black eyes were turbulent. "I don't like it."

"I don't, either." She felt sick all over. She'd thought things were bad before. Now, they were worse. "I could leave town."

"That would make it worse," he said flatly. "If you run, it will give him credibility."

"I guess so." She looked up at him worriedly. "Don't you let him convince you that I had him put away for trying to kiss me. It was a lot more than that."

He only smiled. "I'm not easy to sway. Besides, I've known you most of your life."

That was true. She didn't add that Ted hadn't known her really well until just recent times.

"There are other people he won't convince, including the prosecutor."

"Mr. Haynes said I could call him if I got in trouble and you weren't available," she said.

He smiled. "He'd come, too. He's a good guy."

"I can't understand why a woman would run away from her husband and a little baby," she said. "He's such a nice person."

"Some women don't want nice, they want dangerous or reckless or vagabond."

"Not me," she said. "I want to stay in Hollister my whole life."

"And have kids?"

She looked up at Ted worriedly. "I want kids a lot," she told him. "It's just…"

"It's just what you have to do to make them," he replied.

She blushed.

"Sorry," he said gently. "I didn't mean for it to come out like that."

"I'm a prude. I really am."

"You're not."

She was beginning to wonder. She didn't like recalling what had happened with the man in her past, but his accusations had disturbed her. Was she really so clueless that she'd sent him to prison for something that wasn't his fault? Had she overreacted? She had been at fault with the auditor; she'd gone with him to the motel and at first she'd let him kiss her. Then things got out of hand and she panicked, largely because of what Davy Harris had done to her.

Ted was looking at his watch. "Damn! I've got a meeting with a defense attorney in my office to take a deposition in a theft case. I'll have to go." He bent and kissed her cheek. "You stay clear of that coyote, and if he gives you any trouble, any at all, you tell me. I'll throw his butt in jail."

She smiled. "I will. Thanks, Ted."

"What are friends for?" he asked, and smiled back.

She watched him walk away with misgivings. She wanted to tell him that she wasn't confident about her actions in the past, tell him that maybe the man she'd accused wasn't as guilty as she thought. She wished she had somebody to talk to about it.

She sighed and got in her truck and drove to the ranch. It was going to be the biggest problem of her life, and she didn't know how she was going to solve it.

Things went from bad to worse very quickly. She went in to work the next morning and Davy Harris was sitting in a booth the minute the doors opened. She had to come out to arrange pies and cakes in the display case for the lunch crowd. She didn't work lunch, but she did much of the baking after she'd finished making breakfast for the customers.

Every time she came out to arrange the confections, the man was watching her. He sat as close to the counter as he could get, sipping coffee and giving her malicious looks. He made her very nervous.

"Sir, can I get you anything else?" the waitress, aware of Jillian's discomfort, asked the man in a polite but firm tone.

He lifted his eyebrows. "I'm finishing my coffee."

"Breakfast is no longer being served, sir. We're getting ready for the lunch crowd."

"I know. I'll be back for lunch," he assured her. "I'm almost done."

"Yes, sir." She produced the check and put it next to

his plate, and went back to her other customer, the only other one left in the room.

"You always did cook sweets so well, Jilly," Harris told her with a long visual appraisal. "I loved the lemon cake you used to make for your uncle."

"Thanks," she muttered under her breath.

"You live all alone in that big ranch house, now, don't you?" he asked in a pleasant tone that was only surface. His eyes were full of hate. "Don't you get scared at night?"

"I have a shotgun," she blurted out.

He looked shocked. "Really!"

"Really," she replied with a cold glare. "It would be so unwise for anybody to try to break in at night."

He laughed coldly. "Why, Jilly, was that a threat?" he asked, raising his voice when the waitress came back to that side of the restaurant. "Were you threatening to shoot me?"

"I was saying that if anybody broke into my house, I would use my shotgun," she faltered.

"Are you accusing me of trying to break in on you?" he asked loudly.

She flushed. "I didn't say that."

"Are you sure? I mean, accusing people of crimes they haven't committed, isn't that a felony?" he persisted.

The waitress marched back to his table. "Are you finished, sir?" she asked with a bite in her voice, because she was fond of Jillian. "We have to clear the tables now."

He sighed. "I guess I'm finished." He looked at the bill, pulled out his wallet, left the amount plus a ten-cent tip. He gave the waitress an amused smile. "Now, don't you spend that whole tip all in one place," he said with dripping sarcasm.

"I'll buy feed for my polo ponies with it," she quipped back.

He glared at her. He didn't like people one-upping him, and it showed. "I'll see you again, soon, Jilly," he purred, with a last glance.

He left. Jillian felt her muscles unlocking. But tears stung her eyes.

"Oh, Jill," the waitress, Sandra, groaned. She put her arms around Jillian and hugged her tight. "He'll go away," she said. "He'll have to, eventually. You mustn't cry!"

Jillian bawled. She hadn't known the waitress well at all, until now.

"There, there," Sandra said softly. "I know how it is. I was living with this guy, Carl, and he knocked me around every time he got drunk. Once, he hit me with a glass and it shattered and cut my face real bad. I loved him so much," she groaned. "But that woke me up, when that happened. I moved out. He made threats and even tried to set fire to my house. But when he finally realized I meant it, he gave up and found another girlfriend. Last I heard, she was making weekly trips to the emergency room up in Billings."

Jillian pulled back, wiping her eyes. "It wasn't like that," she whispered. "I was fifteen, and he tried to…"

"Fifteen?"

Jillian bit her lower lip. "My uncle hired him as a handy man."

"Good Lord! You should have had him arrested!"

"I did," Jillian said miserably. "But he got out, and now he's going to make my life hell."

"You poor kid! You tell Chief Graves," she said firmly. "He'll take care of it."

Jillian's eyes were misty. "You can't have somebody

thrown out of town without good reason," she said. "He hasn't threatened me or done anything except show up here to eat all the time. And it's the only restaurant in town, Sandra," she added.

"Yes, but he was making some pretty thick accusations," she reminded the other girl.

"Words. Just words."

"They can hurt as bad as fists," Sandra said curtly. "I ought to know. My father never hesitated to tell me how ugly and stupid I was."

Jillian gasped. Nobody in her family had ever said such things to her.

"I guess you had nice people to live with, huh?" Sandra asked with a worldly smile. "That wasn't the case with me. My father hated me, because I wasn't his. My mother had an affair. People do it all the time these days. She came back, but he could never get over the fact that she had me by somebody else. She died and he made me pay for it."

"I'm so sorry."

"You're a nice kid," Sandra told her quietly. "That guy makes any trouble for you in here, he'll have to deal with me."

Jillian chuckled. "I've seen you handle unruly customers. You're good at it."

"I ought to be. I was in the army until two years ago," she added. "I worked as military police. Not much I don't know about hand-to-hand combat."

Jillian beamed. "My heroine!"

Sandra just laughed. "Anyway, you get those cakes arranged and go home. I'll deal with the visiting problem while you're away."

"Thanks. For everything."

"Always wished I had a kid sister," Sandra scoffed.

She grinned. "So now I do. You tell people I'm your sister and we'll have some laughs."

That would have been funny, because Sandra's skin was a very dark copper, compared to Jillian's very pale skin. Sandra was, after all, full-blooded Lakota.

"Chief Graves is Cheyenne," she said aloud.

"Nothing wrong with the Cheyenne, now that we're not bashing each other's brains out like we did a century ago," came the amused reply. Sandra winked. "Better get cracking. The boss is giving us dark looks."

Jillian grinned. "Can't have that!" she laughed.

Jillian did feel better, and now she had an ally at work. But she was still worried. That man had obviously come to Hollister to pay her back for his jail sentence, and now she was doubting her own story that had cost him his freedom.

Chapter 7

Jillian had never considered that she might become a victim of a stalker. And she wondered if it could even be called stalking. Davy Harris came into the restaurant every morning to eat. But it was the only diner in town. So was that stalking?

Ted thought so, but the law wasn't on the victim's side in this case. A man couldn't be arrested for stalking by eating in the only restaurant in town.

But he made Jillian uptight. She fumbled a cake onto the floor two mornings later, one that had taken a lot of trouble to bake, with cream filling. Harris laughed coldly.

"Why, Jilly, do I make you nervous?" he chided. "I'm only having breakfast here. I haven't tried to touch you or anything."

She cleaned the floor, flushed and unsettled. Sandra had called in sick that morning, so they had a substitute waitress, one who just did her job and didn't waste time on getting to know the other employees. She had no one to back her up, now.

"I only wanted to marry you," Harris said in a soft, quiet tone. "You were real young, but I thought you were mature enough to handle it. And you liked me. Remember when the little white kittens were born and they were going to have to be put down because you couldn't keep them all? I went around to almost every house in town until I found places for them to live."

She bit her lip. That was true. He'd been kind.

"And when your uncle John had that virus and was so sick that he couldn't keep the medicine down? I drove both of you to the hospital."

"Yes," she said reluctantly.

He laughed. "And you repaid my kindness by having me put in prison with murderers."

Her face was stricken as she stared at him.

He got to his feet, still smiling, but his eyes were like a cobra's. "Did you think I'd just go away and you'd never have to see me again?"

She got up, a little wobbly. "I didn't realize…"

"What, that I really would go to prison because you exaggerated what happened?" he interrupted. "What kind of woman does that to a man?"

She felt really sick. She knew her face was white.

"I just wanted to marry you and take care of you, and your uncle," he said. "I wouldn't have hurt you. Did I ever hurt you, Jilly?"

She was growing less confident by the second. Had she misjudged him? Was he in prison because she'd blown things out of proportion?

He put a five-dollar bill down beside his plate. "Why don't you think about that?" he continued. "Think about what you did to me. You don't know what it's like in prison, Jilly. You don't know what men can do to other men, especially if they aren't strong and powerful." His face was taut with distaste. "You stupid little prude," he said harshly. "You landed me in hell!"

"I'm…I'm sorry," she stammered.

"Are you really?" he asked sarcastically. "Well, not sorry enough, not yet." He leaned toward her. "But you're going to be," he said in a voice that didn't carry. "You're going to wish you never heard my name when I'm through with you."

He stood back up again, smiling like a used car salesman. "It was a really good breakfast, Jilly," he said out loud. "You're still a great little cook. Have a nice day, now."

He walked out, while the owner of the restaurant and the cashier gave him a thoughtful look. Jillian could imagine how it would sound. Here was the poor, falsely accused man trying to be nice to the woman who'd put him away. Jillian wasn't going to come out smelling like roses, no matter what she said or did. And now she had her own doubts about the past. She didn't know what she was going to do.

Ted came by the next day. She heard his car at the front door of the ranch house and she went to the steps with a feeling of unease. She didn't think Ted would take the side of the other man, but Davy could be very convincing.

Ted came up the steps, looking somber. He paused when he saw her expression.

"What's happened?" he asked.

She blinked. "What do you mean?"

"You look like death warmed over."

"Do I? It must be the flour," she lied, and forced a laugh. "I've been making a cherry pie."

Once, he would have made a joke, because it was his favorite. But he was quiet and preoccupied as he followed her into the kitchen.

"Any coffee going?" he asked as he sailed his hat onto the counter.

"I can make some."

"Please."

She started a pot, aware of his keen and penetrating gaze, following her as she worked.

"What's going on with you and Harris?" he asked suddenly.

The question startled her so much that she dropped a pan she'd been putting under the counter. Her hands were shaking.

She turned back to him. "No…nothing," she stammered, but her cheeks had flushed.

His face hardened. "Nothing."

"He comes in the restaurant to have breakfast every day," she said.

"And you'd know this, how?"

She put the pan down gently on the counter and drew in a breath. "Because I've got a job there, cooking for the breakfast crowd."

He looked angry. "Since when?"

She hesitated. She hadn't realized how difficult it was going to be, telling him about her job, and explaining why she'd decided to keep it secret from him. It would look bad, as if she didn't trust him.

The guilt made him angrier.

She poured coffee into a mug and put it in front of him on the table. Her hands were unsteady. "I realize it must seem like I'm keeping secrets," she began.

"It sounds a lot like that."

"I was going to tell you," she protested.

"When?"

She hesitated.

"You said you didn't want to get married yet. Is that why?" he persisted. "You got a job so you could take care of your bills here, so that you could refuse to honor the terms of our uncles' wills?"

It was sounding worse than it was. He was mad. He couldn't even hide it.

He hadn't touched his coffee. He got to his feet. "You back away every time I come close to you. When I take you out, you dress like a teenager going to a dance in the gym. You get a job and don't tell me. You're being overheard flirting with the man who supposedly assaulted you years ago." His eyes narrowed as she searched for ways to explain her behavior. "What other secrets are you keeping from me, Jillian?"

She didn't know what to say that wouldn't make things worse. Her face was a study in misery.

"I'm not flirting with him," she said.

"That isn't what one of the diners said," he returned.

She bit her lower lip. "I've been wondering," she began.

"Wondering what?"

She lifted one shoulder. "Maybe I made a mistake," she blurted out. "Maybe I did exaggerate what happened, because I was so naive." She swallowed hard. "Like with the auditor, when I went out with him and didn't tell him my age, and he got in trouble."

Ted's expression wasn't easily explained. He just stared at her with black eyes that didn't give any quarter at all.

"Davy Harris was kind to Uncle John," she had to admit. "And he was always doing things for him, and for me." She lowered her eyes to the floor, so miserable that she almost choked on her own words. "He said the other men did things to him in prison."

He still hadn't spoken.

She looked up, wincing at his expression. "He wasn't a mean sort of person. He never hurt me…"

He picked up his hat, slammed it over his eyes, and walked out the door.

She ran after him. "Ted!"

He kept walking. He went down the steps, got into his truck and drove off without a single word.

Jillian stared after him with a feeling of disaster.

Sandra gaped at her the next morning at work. "You told Ted Graves that you made a mistake?" she asked. "What in the world is the matter with you? You were so young, Jillian! What sort of man tries to get it on with a kid barely in high school?"

"He was just twenty-one," she protested.

"He should have known better. No jury in the world would have turned him loose for making advances to you."

"Yes, but he, well, while he was in prison, some of the men…" She hesitated, searching for the words to explain.

"I know what you mean," Sandra replied shortly. "But you're missing the whole point. A grown man tried to make you go to bed with him when you were young then. Isn't that what happened?"

Jillian drew in a long breath. "Yes. I guess so."

"Then why are you trying to take the blame for it? Did you lead him on? Did you wear suggestive clothing, flirt with him, try to get him to come into your room when your uncle wasn't around?"

"Good heavens, no!" Jillian protested.

Sandra's black eyes narrowed. "Then why is it your fault?"

"He went to prison on my testimony."

"Sounds to me like he deserved to," Sandra replied curtly.

"But he was a kind man," she said. "He was always doing things for other people. One week when Uncle John was real sick, he even did the grocery shopping for us."

"A few years back in a murder trial, a witness testified that the accused murderer helped her take her groceries into the house. Another told the jury that he tuned up her old car when it wouldn't start. What does that have to do with a man's guilt or innocence?"

Jillian blinked. "Excuse me?"

"Don't you think that a man can do kind things and still kill someone, given the motive?" she asked.

"I never thought of it like that."

"Even kind people can kill, Jillian," Sandra said bluntly. "I knew this guy on the reservation, Harry. He'd give you the shirt off his back. He drove old Mr. Hotchkiss to the doctor every month to get his checkup. But he killed another man in an argument and got sent to prison for it. Do you think they should have acquitted him because he did a couple of kind things for other people?"

"Well, no," she had to admit.

"We all have good and evil in us," the older woman replied. "Just because we're capable of good doesn't mean we can't do something evil."

"I guess I understand."

"You think about that. And stop trying to assume responsibility for something that wasn't your fault. You were just out of grade school when it happened. You weren't old enough or mature enough to permit any man liberties like that, at the time. You weren't old enough to know better, Jillian, but he was."

She felt a little better.

"Besides that, did you like it?"

"Are you kidding?" Jillian exclaimed. "No, I hated it!"

"Then that should tell you who's at fault, shouldn't it?"

Jillian began to relax. "You have a way with words."

"I should have been a writer," Sandra agreed. She grinned, showing perfect white teeth. "Now you stop spouting nonsense and start working on that bacon. We'll have customers ranting because breakfast isn't ready!"

Jillian laughed. "I guess we will. Thanks."

Sandra grinned. "You're welcome."

Jillian didn't go out front when the doors opened, not even to put out the cakes and pies. Sandra did that for her.

"Curious," she said when she came back into the kitchen.

"What is?"

"Your old friend Davy wasn't out there."

"Maybe he decided to leave," Jillian said hopefully.

"It would take somebody more gullible than me to believe that," the older woman replied.

"Yes, but I can hope."

"Know what the Arabs say?" Sandra asked. "They

say, trust in Allah, but tie up your camel. Sound advice," she added, shaking a long finger at the other woman.

Jillian did hope for the best, anyway, and not only about Davy Harris leaving town. She hoped that Ted might come by to talk, or just smooth things over with her. But he didn't come to the restaurant, or to the ranch. And the next morning, Davy Harris was right back in the same booth, waiting for his breakfast.

"Did you miss me?" he teased Jillian, having surprised her as she was putting a pound cake in the display case.

"I didn't notice you were gone," she lied, flushing.

"We both know better than that, don't we?" He leaned back in the booth, his pale eyes so smug that it made her curious. "I've been talking to people about you."

She felt uneasy. "What people?"

"Just people."

She didn't know what to say. She got to her feet and went back into the kitchen. Her stomach was cutting somersaults all the way.

That afternoon, as she went out to get into her old vehicle to go home, she walked right into Davy.

She gasped and jumped back. He laughed.

"Do I make you nervous?" he chided. "I can't imagine why. You know, I never tried to hurt you. I never did. Did I?"

"N-no," she blurted out, embarrassed, because a few people standing outside the bank were listening, and watching them.

"I told your uncle I wanted to marry you," he said, without lowering his voice. He even smiled. "He said that he hoped I would, because he liked me and he knew

I'd take care of you. But that was before you told those
lies about me, wasn't it, Jilly? That was before you got
me put in jail for trying to kiss you."

She was embarrassed because they were talking
about something private in a very public location, and
several people were listening.

"It wasn't...wasn't like that," she stammered, flushing.

"Yes, it was, you just don't like admitting that you
made a mistake," he said, his voice a little louder now.
"Isn't that the truth?"

She was fumbling for words. She couldn't get her
mind to work at all.

"You lied about me," he continued, raising his voice.
"You lied."

She should have disputed that. She should have said
that it was no lie, that he'd tried to assault her in her
own home. But she was too embarrassed. She turned
and almost ran to her truck. Once inside, she locked the
door with cold, trembling fingers.

Davy stood on the sidewalk, smiling. Just smiling.
A man and woman came up to him and he turned and
started talking to them as Jillian drove away. She wondered what they were saying. She hoped it wasn't about
her.

But in the next few days, she noticed a change in
attitude, especially in customers who came to the restaurants. Her pretty cakes had been quickly bought before,
but now they stayed in the case. Jill took most of them
back home. When she went to the bank, the teller was
polite, but not chatty and friendly as she usually was.

Even at the local convenience store where she bought

gas, the clerk was reserved, all business, when she paid at the counter.

The next morning, at work, she began to understand why she was being treated to a cold shoulder from people she'd known most of her life.

"Everybody thinks you did a job on me, Jilly," Davy said under his breath when she was putting a cake on the counter—only one cake today, instead of the variety she usually produced, since they weren't selling.

She glared at him over the cake. "It wouldn't do to tell them the truth."

"What is the truth?" He leaned back in the booth, his eyes cold and accusing. "You had me sent to jail."

She stood up, tired of being harassed, tired of his unspoken accusations, tired of the way local people were treating her because of him.

"I was a freshman in high school and you tried to force me to have sex with you," she said shortly, aware of a shocked look from a male customer. "How hard is that to understand? It's called statutory rape, I believe...?"

Davy flushed. He got to his feet and towered over her. "I never raped you!"

"You had my clothes off and the only reason you stopped was because I slugged you and ran. If Sassy Peale hadn't had a shotgun, you never would have stopped! You ran after me all the way to her house!"

He clenched his fists by his side. "I went to jail," he snapped. "You're going to pay for that. I'll make sure you pay for that!"

She took the cake, aimed it and threw it right in his face.

"I could have you arrested for assault!" he sputtered.

"Go ahead," she said, glaring at him. "I'll call the police for you, if you like!"

He took a quick step toward her, but the male customer stood up all at once and moved toward him. He backed away.

"You'll be sorry," he told Jillian. He glared at the other customer, and walked out, wiping away cake with a handkerchief.

Jillian was shaking, but she hadn't backed down. She took a shaky breath, fighting tears, and started picking up cake.

"You think he'll go away," the customer, a tall blond man with a patch over one eye, said quietly, in an accented tone, like a British accent, but with a hard accent on the consonants. She recalled hearing accents like that in one of the *Lethal Weapon* movies. "He won't."

She stopped picking up cake and got to her feet, staring at him.

He was tall and well built. His blond hair was in a ponytail. His face was lean, with faint scars, and he had one light brown eye visible. He looked like the sort of man who smiled a lot, but he wasn't smiling now. He had a dangerous look.

"You should talk to a lawyer," he said quietly.

She bit her lip. "And say what? He eats here every day, but this is the only restaurant in town."

"It's still harassment."

She sighed. "Yes. It is. But I can't make him leave."

"Talk to Ted Graves. He'll make him leave."

"Ted isn't speaking to me."

He lifted an eyebrow expressively.

"I ticked him off, too, by saying I might have made a mistake and overreacted to what Davy did to me," she said miserably. "Davy made it sound as if I did. And then he reminded me about all the kind things he did for my uncle and me…"

"Adolph Hitler had a dog. He petted it and took it for walks and threw sticks for it to chase," he said blandly.

She grimaced. She went back down and picked up more cake.

"If you were so young and it took a shotgun to deter him," the man continued, "it wasn't an innocent act."

"I'm just beginning to get that through my thick skull," she sighed.

"This sort of man doesn't quit," he continued, sticking his hands deep in the pockets of his jeans. His eye was narrow and thoughtful. "He's here for more than breakfast, if you get my drift. He wants revenge."

"I guess so."

"I hope you keep a gun."

She laughed. "I hate guns."

"So do I," he mused. "I much prefer knives."

He indicated a huge Bowie knife on one hip, in a fringed leather sheath.

She stared at it. "I don't guess you'd have to do much more than show that to somebody to make them back off."

"That's usually the case."

She finished cleaning up the cake. "They aren't selling well lately, but I thought this one might. Davy seems to have been spending all his spare time telling people what an evil woman I am. There's a distinct chill in the air wherever I go now."

"That's because he's telling his side of the story to anybody who'll listen," he replied. "And that's harassment, as well."

"I can see Ted arresting him for talking to someone," she said sarcastically.

"It depends on what he's saying. I heard what he said in here. If you need a witness, I'm available."

She frowned. "He didn't say much."

"He said enough," he replied.

She shrugged. "I like to handle my own problems."

"Ordinarily I'd say that's admirable. Not in this case. You're up against a man who's done hard time and came out with a grudge. He wants blood. If you're not very careful, he'll get it. He's doing a number on your character already. People tend to believe what they want to believe, and it isn't always the truth. Especially when a likeable young man who's apparently been railroaded by a nasty young girl tells the right kind of story."

She blinked. "I'd be the nasty young girl in this story?"

He nodded.

She put the remnants of her cake into the trash can behind the counter. She shrugged. "I never thought of myself as a bad person."

"It's his thoughts that you have to worry about. If he's mad enough, and I think he is if he came here expressly to torment you, he won't stop with gossip."

That thought had occurred to her, too. She looked up at the customer with wide, worried eyes. "Maybe I should get a job over in Billings."

"And run for it?" he asked. "Fat chance. He'd follow you."

She gasped. "No…!"

His face hardened. "I've seen this happen before, in a similar case," he said tersely. "In fact, I was acting as an unpaid bodyguard as a favor to a friend. The perp not only got out of jail, he went after the girl who testified against him and beat her up."

She glared. "I hope you hurt him."

"Several of us," he replied, "wanted to, but her boyfriend got to him first. He's back in jail. But if she'd been alone, there might not have been anybody to testify."

She felt sick to her stomach. "You're saying something, aren't you?"

"I'm saying that such men are unpredictable," he replied. "It's better to watch your back than to assume that everything will work itself out. In my experience, situations like this don't get better."

She put down the rag she'd been cleaning with, and looked up with worried eyes. "I wish Ted wasn't mad at me," she said quietly.

"Go make up with him," he advised. "And do it soon." He didn't add that he'd seen the expression on her assailant's face and he was certain the man would soon resort to violence to pay her back.

"I suppose I should," she said. She managed a smile. "Thanks, Mr....?"

"Just call me Rourke," he said, and grinned. "Most people do."

"Are you visiting somebody local?"

His eyebrows arched. "Don't I look like a local?"

She shook her head, softening the noncomment with a smile.

He laughed. "Actually," he said, "I came by to see the police chief. And not on a case. Ted and I were in the military together. I brought a message from an old friend who works as a police chief down in Texas."

She cocked her head. "That wouldn't be the one who taught him to tango?"

He blinked his single eye. "He taught Ted to dance?"

She nodded. "He's pretty good, too."

Rourke chuckled. "Wonders never cease."

"That's what I say."

He smiled down at her. "Talk to Ted," he advised. "You're going to need somebody who can back you up, if that man gets violent."

"I'll do that," she said after a minute. "And thanks."

"You're welcome, but for what?"

"For making me see the light," she replied flatly. "I've been blaming myself for sending Davy to prison."

"You mark my words," he replied. "Very soon, Davy is going to prove to you that it was where he belonged."

She didn't reply. She just hoped it wasn't a prophecy. But she was going to see Ted, the minute she got off work.

Chapter 8

Before Jillian could finish her chores and get out of the restaurant, Sassy Peale Callister came into the restaurant and dragged her to one side.

"I can't believe what I just heard," she said shortly. "Did you actually say that you might have been wrong to have Davy Harris put in jail?"

Jillian flushed to the roots of her hair. "How did you hear about that?" she stammered.

"Hollister is a very small town. You tell one person and everybody else knows," the other woman replied. "Come on, is it true?"

Jillian felt even more uncomfortable. "He was reminding me how much he helped me and Uncle John around the ranch. He was always kind to us. Once, when we were sick, he went to the store and pharmacy for us, and then nursed us until we were well again."

Sassy wasn't buying it. Her face was stony. "That

means he's capable of doing good deeds. It doesn't mean he can't do bad things."

"I know," Jillian said miserably. "It's just...well, he's been in here every day. He makes it sound like I overreacted..."

"You listen to me, he's no heartsick would-be suitor," Sassy said firmly. "He's a card-carrying coyote with delusions of grandeur! I wasn't sure that he wasn't going to try to take the shotgun away from me, even if I'd pulled the trigger. He was furious! Don't you remember what he said?"

Jillian glanced around her. The restaurant was empty, but the owner was nearby, at least within earshot.

"He said that he'd get both of us," Sassy replied. "John thinks he meant it and that he's here for revenge. He hired me a bodyguard, if you can believe that." She indicated the tall man with a long blond ponytail and a patch over one eye.

"That's Rourke," Jilly exclaimed.

Sassy blinked. "Excuse me?"

"That's Rourke. He was in here this morning, when I threw a cake at Davy." She ignored Sassy's gasp and kept going. "He said that I was nuts trying to make excuses for the man, and that I should make up with Ted. He thinks Davy is dangerous."

"So do I," Sassy said quietly. "You should come and stay with us until this is over, one way or the other."

Jillian was tempted. But she thought of little Sammy and a means of revenge that might occur to a mind as twisted as Davy's. He might even burn the house down. She didn't dare leave it unattended.

"Thanks," she said gently, "but I can't do that. Anyway, I've got my uncle's shotgun."

"Which you've never touched," Sassy muttered. "I doubt it's been cleaned since he died."

Jillian stared at the floor. "Ted would clean it for me if I asked him to."

"Why don't you ask him to?" came the short reply. "And then tell him why you need it cleaned. I dare you."

"I don't think Davy would hurt me, really," she said slowly.

"He assaulted you."

"Maybe he just got, well, overstimulated, and…"

"He assaulted you," Sassy replied firmly.

Jillian sighed. "I hate unpleasantness."

"Who doesn't? But this isn't just a man who let a kiss go too far. This is a man who deliberately came to Hollister, got a job and devils you every day at your place of work," Sassy said quietly. "It's harassment. It's stalking. Maybe you can't prove it, but you should certainly talk to Ted about it."

"He'll think I'm overreacting."

"He's a policeman," Sassy reminded her. "He won't."

Jillian was weakening. She was beginning to feel even more afraid of Davy. If Sassy's husband thought there was a threat, and went so far as to hire his wife a bodyguard, he must be taking it seriously.

"John tried to have him arrested, but Ted reminded him that you can't put somebody behind bars for something he said years ago. He has to have concrete evidence."

That made things somehow even worse. Jillian's worried eyes met her friend's. "Davy does scare me."

Sassy moved closer. "I'm going to have Rourke keep an eye on you, too, when I'm safely home with

John. We've got enough cowboys at the ranch who have federal backgrounds to keep me safe," she added with a chuckle. "One of them used to work for the godfather of John's sister-in-law. He was a mercenary with mob connections. He's got millions and he still comes to see her." She leaned forward, so that Rourke couldn't hear. "There was gossip once that Rourke was his son. Nobody knows and Rourke never talks about him."

"Wow," Jillian exclaimed. "That would be K.C. Kantor, wouldn't it?"

Sassy was impressed. "How did you know?"

"I wouldn't have, but your husband was talking about him at the restaurant one morning when you were on that shopping trip to Los Angeles and he had to eat in town."

"Eavesdropping, were you?" Sassy teased.

Jillian smiled. "Sorry. Sometimes a waitress can't help it."

"I don't mind." She drew in a breath. "I have to go. But if you need anything, you call. I'll lend Rourke to you."

"My ears work, even if I'm missing one eye," the tall blond man drawled.

Both women turned, surprised.

"And K.C. Kantor is not my father." He bit off every word. "That's malicious gossip, aimed at my dad, who was a military man in South Africa and made enemies because of his job."

"Sorry," Sassy said at once, and looked uneasy. Rourke rarely did anything except smile pleasantly and crack jokes, but his pale brown eye was glittering and he looked dangerous.

He saw the consternation his words had produced, and fell back into his easygoing persona with no visible effort. He grinned. "I eavesdrop shamelessly, too," he added. "I never know when some pretty young woman might be making nice remarks about me. Wouldn't want to miss it."

They both relaxed.

"Sorry," Sassy said again. "I wasn't saying it to be unkind."

He shrugged. "I know that. Kantor took me in when I was orphaned, because he and my dad were friends. It's a common misconception." He frowned. "You're right about Jillian. Living alone is dangerous when you've got an enemy with unknown intentions. Mrs. Callister is safe at night, unless she's going out without her husband. I could come over and sleep on your sofa, if you like."

"Yes, he could," Sassy seconded at once.

That made Jillian visibly uncomfortable. She averted her eyes. "That's very kind of you, thanks, but I'll manage."

Rourke lifted an eyebrow. "Is it my shaving lotion? I mean, it does sometimes put women off," he said blandly.

Sassy laughed. "No. It's convention."

"Excuse me?"

"She won't stay alone at night with a man in the house," Sassy said. "And before you say anything—" she stopped him when he opened his mouth to reply "—I would have felt exactly the same way when I was single. Women in small towns, brought up with certain attitudes, don't entertain single men at night."

He looked perplexed.

"You've never lived in a small town," Jillian ventured.

"I was born in Africa," he said, surprisingly. "I've lived in small villages all my life. But I don't know much about small American towns. I suppose there are similarities. Well, except for the bride price that still exists in some places."

"Bride price?" Jillian stared at him, waiting.

"A man who wants to marry a woman has to give her father a certain number of cattle."

She gaped at him.

"It's a centuries-old tradition," he explained. He pursed his lips and smiled at Jillian. "I'll bet your father would have asked a thousand head for you."

She glared at him. "My father would never have offered to sell me to you!" she exclaimed.

"Different places, different customs," he said easily. "I've lived in places, in ways, that you might never imagine."

"John said you were a gunrunner," Sassy mused.

He glared at her. "I was not," he said indignantly. Then he grinned. "I was an arms dealer."

"Semantics!" she shot back.

He shrugged again. "A man has to make a living when he's between jobs. At the time, there wasn't much action going on in my part of Africa for mercenaries."

"And now you work as a bodyguard?" Jillian asked.

He hesitated. "At times, when I'm on vacation. I actually work as an independent contractor these days. Legit," he added when they looked at him with open suspicion. "I don't do mercenary work anymore."

"So that case in Oklahoma where you helped free a kidnapping victim was legit, too?" Sassy asked.

"I was helping out a friend," he replied, chuckling. "He works for the same federal agency I work for these days."

"But you're an African citizen, aren't you?" Jillian asked. "I mean, if you were born there…?"

"I have American citizenship now," he said, and looked uncomfortable.

"When he went to work for Mr. Kantor, he had to have it," Sassy murmured. "I imagine he pulled some strings at the state department?"

Rourke just looked at her, without speaking.

She held out her hands, palms up. "Okay, I'm sorry, I won't pry. I'm just grateful you're around to look out for me." She glanced at Jillian. "But you still have a problem. What if Harris decides he wants to get even one dark night, and you can't get to that shotgun in time? The one that hasn't been cleaned since your uncle died?"

"I said I'd get Ted to clean it for me," the other woman protested.

"You and Ted aren't speaking."

"I'll come over and clean it for you," Rourke said quietly. "And teach you to shoot it."

Jillian looked hunted. "I hate guns," she burst out. "I hated it when Ted would come over and shoot targets from the front porch. I'll never get used to the sound of them. It's like dynamite going off in my ears!"

Rourke looked at her with shocked disdain. "Didn't anybody ever tell you about earplugs?"

"Earplugs?"

"Yes. You always wear them on the gun range," he explained, "unless you want to go deaf at an early age. Ear protectors are fine on the range, but earplugs can be inserted quickly if you're on a job and expecting trouble."

"How do you hear?"

"They let in sound. They just deaden certain fre-

quencies of sound," he explained. He glanced at Sassy.
"You won't need me tonight. I heard your husband say
he's lined up a new werewolf movie to watch with you
on pay-per-view."

She laughed. "Yes. It's the second in a vampire
trilogy, actually. I love it!"

He didn't react. He glanced toward Jillian. "So I'll be
free about six. I can come over and clean the shotgun
and do a security sweep. If you need locks and silent
sentries, I can install them."

She bit her lip, hard. She couldn't afford such things.
She could barely pay the bills on what she made as a
cook.

The owner of the restaurant, who had been blatantly
eavesdropping, joined them. "You can have an advance
on your salary anytime you need it," he told Jillian
gently. "I'd bar Harris from coming on the premises,
if I could, but he's the sort who'd file a lawsuit. I can't
afford that," he added heavily.

"Thanks, Mr. Chaney," Jillian said quietly. "I thought
you might fire me, because of all that's going on right
now."

"Fat chance," he said amusedly. "You're the best cook
I've ever had."

"He shouldn't be allowed to harass her while she's
doing her job," Sassy said curtly.

"I agree," the restaurant owner said gently. "But this
is a business and I can't bar people I dislike without
proof they're causing problems. I've never heard him
threaten Jillian or even be disrespectful to her."

"That's because he whispers things to me that he
doesn't want anybody to overhear," she said miserably.
"He made me believe that I had him locked up for no
reason at all."

"I live in Hollister," he said quietly. "Even if it's not in blaring headlines, most of us know what's going on here. I remember the case. My sister, if you recall, was the assistant prosecutor in the case. She helped Jack Haynes with the precedents."

"I do remember," Jillian said. She folded her arms over her slight breasts. "It's so scary. I never thought he'd get out."

"People get out all the time on technicalities," Rourke said. "A case in point is the bank robber your police chief put away. And a friend of mine in the FBI in Texas has a similar problem. A man he sent away for life just got out and is after him. My friend can't do much more than you're doing. The stalker doesn't do anything he could even be charged with."

"Life is hard," Sassy said.

"Then you die," Rourke quipped, and grinned. "Did you watch that British cop show, too? You're pretty young."

"Everything's on disc now, even those old shows. It's one of John's favorites," Sassy chuckled.

"Mine, too," Chaney added, laughing. "They were an odd mix, the female British cop and the American one, in a team."

"Pity it ended before we knew how things worked out between them," Rourke sighed. "I would have loved a big, romantic finale."

Both women and the restaurant owner stared at him.

"I'm a romantic," he said defensively.

The women stared pointedly at the pistol in the shoulder holster under his loose jacket.

"I can shoot people and still be romantic," he said

belligerently. "Out there somewhere is a woman who can't wait to marry me and have my children!"

They stared more.

He moved uncomfortably. "Well, my profession isn't conducive to child-raising, I guess, but I could still get married to some nice lady who wanted to cook and darn my socks and take my clothes to the dry cleaner when I was home between jobs."

"That's not romantic, that's delusional," Sassy told him.

"And you're living in the wrong century," Jillian added.

He glared. "I'm not shacking up with some corporate raider in a pin-striped business suit."

"It's not called shacking up, it's called cohabiting," Sassy said drolly. "And I really can't see you with a corporate raider. I should think a Dallas Cowboy linebacker would be... Don't hit me, I'll tell John!" she said in mock fear when he glowered and took a step forward.

"A woman in a pin-striped suit," he qualified.

Sassy nodded. "A female mob hit-person."

He threw up his hands. "I can't talk to you."

"You could if you'd stop mixing metaphors and looking for women who lived in the dark ages." She frowned. "You don't get out much, do you?"

He looked out the window of the restaurant. "In this burg, it wouldn't matter if I did. I think there are two unmarried ladies who live in this town, and they're both in their sixties!"

"We could ask if anybody has pretty cousins or nieces who live out of town," Jillian offered.

He gave her a pursed-lip scrutiny. "You're not bad. You have your own ranch and you can cook."

"I don't want to get married," Jillian said curtly.

"That's true," Sassy said sadly. "I think Harris has put her off men for life. She won't even marry Ted, and that means she'll lose the ranch to a developer."

"Good grief," Rourke exclaimed. "Why?"

"It's in my uncle's will and his uncle's will that we have to marry each other or the ranch gets sold at public auction," Jillian said miserably. "There's a California developer licking his lips in the background, just waiting to turn my ranch into a resort."

Rourke was outraged. "Not that beautiful hunk of land!"

She nodded. "It will look like the West Coast when he gets through. He'll cut down all the trees, pave the land, and build expensive condominiums. I hear he even has plans for a strip mall in the middle. Oh, and an amusement park."

Rourke was unusually thoughtful. "Nice piece of land, that," he remarked.

"Very nice."

"But that doesn't solve your problem," Sassy replied.

"I can be over about six, if that's okay?" he told Jillian, with a questioning glance at Sassy.

"That will be fine with us," Sassy assured him. She glared at Jillian, who was hesitating. "If Ted won't talk to you, somebody has to clean the shotgun."

"I suppose so."

"Enthusiasm like that has launched colonies," Rourke drawled.

Jillian laughed self-consciously. "Sorry. I don't mean to sound reluctant. I just don't know what Ted will think. He's already mad because I said I might have overreacted to Davy Harris when I had him arrested."

"It wasn't overreaction," the restaurant owner, Mr. Chaney, inserted indignantly. "The man deserved what he got. I'm just sorry I can't keep him out of here. If he ever insults you or makes a threat, you tell me. I'll bar him even if I do get sued."

"Thanks, boss. Really," Jillian said.

"Least I could do." He glanced at the front door. "Excuse me. Customers." He left with a smile.

"He always greets people when they come in," Jillian explained with a smile, "and then he comes around to the tables and checks to make sure the service and the food are okay with them. He's a great boss."

"It's a good restaurant," Rourke agreed. "Good food." He grinned at Jillian.

"So. Six?" he added.

Jillian smiled. "Six. I'll even feed you."

"I'll bring the raw materials, shall I?" he asked with a twinkle in his eyes. "Steaks and salad?"

"Lovely!" Jillian exclaimed. "I haven't had a steak in a long time!"

"You've got all that beef over there and you don't eat steak?" he exclaimed. "What about that prime young calf, the little steer…?"

"Sammy?" Jillian gasped. "She's not eating beef!"

"She?" he asked.

"She's a cow. Or she will be one day."

"A cow named Sammy." He laughed. "Sounds like Cy Parks, down in Jacobsville, Texas. He's got a girl dog named Bob."

Everyone laughed.

"See?" Jillian said indignantly. "I'm not the only person who comes up with odd names for animals."

Sassy hugged her. "No, you aren't. I'm going home. You let Rourke clean that shotgun."

"Okay. Thanks," she added.

"My pleasure," Rourke said.

Sassy grinned. "And don't let him talk you into marrying him," she added firmly. "Ted will never speak to us again."

"No danger of that," Jillian sighed. "Sorry," she added to Rourke.

"Don't be so hasty, now," Rourke said. "I have many good qualities. I'll elaborate on them tonight. See you at six."

He left with Sassy. Jillian stared after them, grateful but uneasy. What was Ted going to think?

Rourke showed up promptly at six with a bag of groceries.

He put his purchases out on the table. Expensive steaks, lettuce, all the ingredients for salad plus a variety of dressings, and a cherry pie and a pint of vanilla ice cream.

"I know you cook pies and cakes very well," he explained, "but I thought you might like a taste of someone else's cooking. Mrs. Callister's new cook produced that. It's famous where she comes from, up in Billings, Montana."

"I'll love it. Cherry pie is one of my favorites."

"Mine, too."

He started the steaks and then used her gourmet knives to do a fantastic chopping of vegetables for the salad.

Jillian watched his mastery of knives with pure fascination. "It must have taken you a long time to learn to do that so effortlessly."

"It did. I practiced on many people."

She stared at him, uncertain how to react.

He saw that and burst out laughing. "I was joking," he explained. "Not that I've never used knives on people, when the occasion called for it."

"I suppose violence is a way of life to someone in your position."

He nodded. "I learned to handle an AK-47 when I was ten years old."

She gasped.

"Where I grew up, in Africa, there were always regional wars," he told her. "The musclemen tried to move in and take over what belonged to the local tribes. I didn't have family at that time, was living in an orphanage, so I went to fight with them." He laughed. "It was an introduction to mean living that I've never been able to get past. Violence is familiar."

"I suppose it would have to be."

"I learned tactics and strategy from a succession of local warlords," he told her. "Some of them were handed down from the time of Shaka Zulu himself."

"Who was that?"

"Shaka Zulu? The most famous of the Zulu warriors, a strategist of the finest kind. He revolutionized weaponry and fighting styles among his people and became a great warlord. He defeated the British, with their advanced weapons."

"Good grief! I never heard of him."

"There was a miniseries on television about his exploits," he said while he chopped celery and cucumbers into strips. "I have it. I watch it a lot."

"I saw *Out of Africa*."

He smiled. "That's a beaut."

"It is. I loved the scenery." She laughed. "Imagine, playing Mozart for the local apes."

"Inventive." He stopped chopping, and his eye became dreamy. "I think Africa is the most beautiful place on earth. It's sad that the animals are losing habitat so quickly. Many of the larger ones will go extinct in my lifetime."

"There are lots of people trying to save them. They raise the little ones and then turn them back out onto the land."

"Where poachers are waiting to kill them," he said laconically. "You can still find ivory, and elephant feet used for footstools, and rhinoceros horn in clandestine shops all over the world. They do catch some of the perps, but not all of them. It's tragic to see a way of life going dead. Like the little Bushmen," he added quietly. "Their culture was totally destroyed, denigrated, ridiculed as worthless by European invaders. The end result is that they became displaced people, living in cities, in slums. Many are alcoholics."

"I could tell you the same is true here, where Native Americans received similar treatment," she told him.

He smiled. "It seems that the old cultures are so primitive that they're considered without value. Our greatest modern civilizations are less than two thousand years old, yet those of primitive peoples can measure in the hundreds of thousands. Did you know that the mighty civilizations of Middle America were based on agriculture? Ours are based on industry."

"Agriculture. Farming."

He nodded. "Cities grew up around irrigated lands where crops were planted and grew even in conditions of great drought. The Hohokam in Arizona had canals. The Mayan civilization had astronomy." He glanced at her. "The medical practitioners among the Incas knew how to do trepanning on skulls to relieve pressure in the brain. They used obsidian scalpels. It isn't well-known, but they're still in use today in scalpels for surgery."

"How did you learn all that?" she wondered.

"Traveling. It's one of the perks of my job. I get to see things and mix with people who are out in the vanguard of research and exploration. I once acted as bodyguard to one of the foremost archaeologists on earth in Egypt."

"Gosh!"

"Have you ever traveled?" he asked.

She thought about that. "Well, I did go to Oklahoma City, once," she said. "It was a long drive."

He was holding the knife in midair. "To Oklahoma City."

She flushed. "It's the only place outside Montana that I've ever been," she explained.

He was shocked. "Never to another country?"

"Oh, no," she replied. "There was never enough money for..." She stopped and glanced out the window. A pickup truck pulled up in the yard, very fast. The engine stopped, the door opened and was slammed with some fury.

Rourke's hand went involuntarily to the pistol under his arm.

"Oh, dear," Jillian said, biting her lip.

"Harris?" he asked curtly.

She sighed. "Worse. It's Ted."

Chapter 9

There were quick, heavy footsteps coming up onto the porch. Jillian didn't have to ask if Ted was mad. When he wasn't, his tread was hardly audible at all, even in boots. Now, he was walking with a purpose, and she could hear it.

He knocked on the door. She opened it and stepped back.

His black eyes glittered at her. "I hear you have company," he said shortly.

Rourke came out of the kitchen. His jacket was off, so the .45 automatic he carried was plainly visible in its holster. "She does, indeed," he replied. He moved forward with easy grace and extended a hand. "Rourke," he introduced himself. "I'm on loan from the Callisters."

Ted shook the hand. "Theodore Graves. Chief of police," he added.

Rourke grinned. "I knew that. I came to town to try to see you the other day, but you were out on a case. Cash Grier said to tell you hello."

Ted seemed surprised. "You know him?"

"We used to work together under, shall we say, unusual conditions, in Africa," came the reply.

Ted relaxed a little. "Rourke. I think he mentioned you."

He shrugged. "I get around. I really came over to clean her shotgun for her, but I'm cooking, too." He gave Ted an appraisal that didn't miss much, including the other man's jealousy. "I'm impressing her with my culinary skills, in hopes that she might want to marry me after supper."

Ted gaped at him. "What?"

"He's just kidding," Jillian said, flushing.

"I am?" Rourke asked, and raised both eyebrows.

Ted glared at the other man. "She's engaged to me."

"I am not!" Jillian told him emphatically.

Rourke backed up a step and held up a hand. "I think I'll go back into the kitchen. I don't like to get mixed up in family squabbles," he added with a grin.

"We are not a family, and we're not squabbling!" Jillian raged.

"We're going to be a family, and yes, we are," Ted said angrily.

Rourke discreetly moved into the kitchen.

"I could have cleaned the shotgun, if you'd just asked me," he said angrily.

"You stormed out of here in a snit and never said a word," she returned. "How was I supposed to ask you, mail a letter?"

"Email is quicker," came a droll voice from the kitchen.

"You can shut up, this is a private argument," Ted called back.

"Sorry," Rourke murmured. "Don't be too long now, cold steak is unappetizing."

"You're feeding him steak?" Ted exclaimed. "What did he do, carve up Sammy?"

"I don't eat ugly calves!" Rourke quipped.

"Sammy is not ugly, she's beautiful!" Jillian retorted.

"If you say so," Rourke said under his breath.

"There's nothing wrong with black baldies," she persisted.

"Unless you've never seen a Brahma calf," Rourke sighed. "Gorgeous little creatures."

"Brahmas are the ugliest cattle on earth," Ted muttered.

"They are not!" Rourke retorted. "I own some of them!"

Ted stopped. "You run cattle around here?" he asked.

Rourke came back into the room, holding a fork. "In Africa. My home is in Kenya."

Ted's eyes narrowed. "So that's how Cash met you."

"Yes. I was, shall we say, gainfully employed in helping oust a local warlord who was slaughtering children in his rush to power."

"Good for you," Ted replied.

"Now you're teaming up?" Jillian said, fuming.

"Only as far as cattle are concerned," Rourke assured her with a flash of white teeth. "I'm still a contender in the matrimonial sweepstakes," he added. "I can cook and clean and make apple strudel." He gave Ted a musing appraisal, as if to say, top that.

Ted was outdone. It was well-known that he couldn't boil water. He glared at the blond man. "I can knock pennies off bottles with my pistol," he said, searching for a skill to compare.

"I can do it with an Uzi," Rourke replied.

"Not in my town, you won't—that's an illegal weapon."

"Okay, but that's a sad way to cop out of a competition." He blinked. "I made a pun!"

"I'm not a cop, I'm a police chief."

"Semantics," Rourke said haughtily, borrowing Jillian's favorite word, and walked back to the kitchen.

Ted looked down at Jillian, who was struggling not to laugh. He was more worried than he wanted to admit about her assailant, who kept adding fuel to the fire in town with gossip about Jillian's past. He knew better, but some people wouldn't. He'd been irritable because he couldn't find a way to make the little weasel leave town. Jillian was pale and nervous. He hadn't helped by avoiding her. It was self-defense. She meant more to him than he'd realized. He didn't want her hurt, even if she couldn't deal with marrying him.

He rested his hand on the butt of the automatic holstered on his belt. "I heard about what happened in the restaurant. You should listen to Sassy. It's possible that Harris may try to get revenge on you here, where you're alone."

"She's not alone," Rourke chimed in. "I'm here."

"Not usually, and he'll know that," Ted said irritably. He didn't like the other man assuming what he thought of as his own responsibility.

"Mrs. Callister already asked her to come stay at the ranch, but she won't," came the reply.

Ted didn't like the idea of Jillian being closer to Rourke, either. But he had to admit that it was the safest thing for her, if she wouldn't marry him.

"We could get married," he told her, lowering his voice.

"Can you cook?" Rourke asked. "Besides, I have all my own teeth."

Ted ignored him. He was worried, and it showed. He searched her eyes. "Harris bought a big Bowie at the hardward store yesterday."

"It's not illegal to own a knife," Rourke said.

"Technically it's not, although a Bowie certainly falls under the heading of an illegal weapon if he wears it in town. It has a blade longer than three-and-a-quarter inches. It's the implication of the purchase that concerns me," he added.

Rourke quickly became more somber. "He's making a statement of his intentions," he said.

"That's what I thought," Ted agreed. "And he knows there's not a damned thing I can do about it, unless he carries the weapon blatantly. He's not likely to do that."

Rourke didn't mention that he'd been wearing his own Bowie knife in town. "You could turn your back and I could have a talk with him," Rourke suggested, not completely facetiously.

"He'd have me arrest you, and he'd call his lawyer," was the reply.

"I suppose so."

"Maybe I could visit somebody out of state," Jillian said on a sigh.

"He'd just follow you, and pose a threat to anybody

you stayed with," Ted said. "Besides that, you don't know anybody out of state."

"I was only joking," Jillian replied. "I'm not running," she added firmly.

The men looked at her with smiling admiration.

"Foolhardy," Rourke commented.

"Sensible," Ted replied. "Nobody's getting past me in my own town to do her harm."

"I'm not needed at the ranch at night," Rourke said. "I could stay over here."

Ted and Jillian both glared at him.

He threw up his hands. "You people have some incredible hang-ups for twenty-first century human beings!"

"We live in a small town," Jillian pointed out. "I don't want to be talked about. Any more than I already am, I mean," she said miserably. "I guess Harris has convinced half the people here that I'm a heartless flirt who had him arrested because he wanted to marry me."

"Good luck to anybody brain-damaged enough to believe a story like that," Rourke said. "Especially anybody who knows you at all."

"Thanks, Rourke," Jillian replied.

Ted shook his head. "There are people who will believe anything. I'd give real money if I could find a law on the books that I could use to make him leave town."

"Vagrancy would have been a good one until he got that job."

"I agree," Ted said.

"It's not right," Jillian blurted out. "I mean, that somebody can come here, harass me, make my life miserable and just get away with it."

Ted's expression was eloquent. His high cheekbones flushed with impotent bad temper.

"I'm not blaming you," Jillian said at once. "I'm not, Ted. I know there's nothing you can do about it."

"Oh, for the wild old days in Africa," Rourke sighed. "Where we made up the laws as we went along."

"Law is the foundation of any civilization," Ted said firmly.

"True. But law, like anything else, can be abused." Rourke pursed his lips. "Are you staying for supper? I actually brought three steaks."

Jillian frowned. "Three?"

He chuckled. "Let's say I anticipated that we might have company," he said with a wry glance at Ted.

Ted seemed to relax. He gave Jillian an appraising look. "After supper, we might sit on the front porch and do a little target shooting."

She glared at him.

"We could practice with her shotgun," Rourke agreed, adding fuel to the fire.

"I only have two shells," Jillian said curtly.

Rourke reached into a bag he'd placed on a nearby shelf. "I anticipated that, too." He handed the shells to Ted with a grin.

"Double ought buckshot," Ted mused. "We use that in our riot shotguns."

"I know."

"What does that mean?" Jillian wanted to know.

"It's a heavy load, used by law enforcement officers to ensure that criminals who fire on them pay dearly for the privilege," Ted said enigmatically.

"Tears big holes in things, love," Rourke translated.

Ted didn't like the endearment, and his black eyes glittered.

Rourke laughed. "I'll just go turn those steaks."

"Might be safer," Ted agreed.

Rourke left and Ted took Jillian's hand and led her into the living room. He closed the door.

"I don't like him being over here with you alone," he said flatly.

She gave him a hunted look. "Well, I wasn't exactly overflowing with people trying to protect me from Davy!"

He averted his eyes. "Sorry."

"Why did you get so angry?"

"You were making excuses for him," he said, his voice curt. "Letting him convince you that it was all a mistake. I got access to the court records, Jillian."

She realized what he was saying, and flushed to her hairline.

"Hey," he said softly. "It's not your fault."

"He said I wore suggestive things…"

"You never wore suggestive things in your life, and you were fifteen," he muttered. "How would you feel, at your age now, if a fifteen-year-old boy actually flirted with you?"

"I'd tell his mama," she returned.

"Exactly." He waited for that to register.

Her eyes narrowed. "You mean, I didn't have the judgment to involve myself with a man, even one just six years older than me."

"You didn't. And you never wore suggestive things."

"I wasn't allowed, even if I'd wanted to. My uncle was very conservative."

"Harris was a predator. He still is. But in his own mind, he didn't do anything wrong. That's why he's giving you the business. He really feels that he had every right to pursue you. He can't understand why he was arrested for it."

"But that's crazy!"

"No crazier than you second-guessing your own re-actions, when you actually had to run to a neighbor's house to save yourself from assault," he pointed out.

She gnawed her lower lip. "I was scared to death." She looked up at him. "Men are so strong," she said. "Even thin men like Davy. I almost didn't get away. And when I did, he went nuts. He was yelling threats all the way to the Peales' house. I really think he would have killed me if Sassy hadn't pulled that shotgun. He might have killed her, too, and it would have been my fault, for running over there for help. But it was the only house close enough."

"I'm sure Sassy never blamed you for that. She's a good person."

"So are you," she commented quietly. "I'm sorry I've been such a trial to you."

His face softened. His black eyes searched hers. "I should have been more understanding." He grimaced. "You don't get how it is, Jake, to go out with a woman you want and be apprehensive about even touching her."

She had a blank look on her face.

"You don't know what I'm talking about, do you?" he asked in a frustrated tone. He moved closer. "Maybe it's time you did."

He curled her into his body with a long, powerful arm and bent his head. He kissed her with soft persuasion at first, then, when she relaxed, his mouth became invasive. He teased her lips apart and nibbled them. He felt her stiffen at first, but after a few seconds, she became more flexible. She stopped resisting and stood very still.

She hadn't known that she could feel such things. Up until now, Ted had been almost teasing when he kissed her. But this time, he wasn't holding anything back. His arm, at her back, arched her up against him. His big hand smoothed up from her waist and brushed lightly at the edges of her small, firm breast.

She really should protest, she told herself. She shouldn't let him do that. But as the kisses grew longer and hungrier, her body began to feel swollen and hot. She ached for more than she was getting, but she didn't understand what she wanted.

Ted felt those vague longings in her and knew how to satisfy them. His mouth ground down onto hers as his fingers began to smooth over the soft mound of flesh, barely touching, kindling hungers that Jillian had never known before.

She gasped when his fingers rubbed over the nipple and it became hard and incredibly sensitive. She tried to draw back, but not with any real enthusiasm.

"Scared?" he whispered against her mouth. "No need. We have a chaperone."

"The door…it's closed."

"Yes, thank goodness," he groaned, "because if it wasn't, I wouldn't dare do this."

"This" involved the sudden rise of her shirt and the bra up under her chin and the shocking, delicious, invasion of Ted's warm mouth over her breast.

She shuddered. It was the most intense pleasure she'd ever felt. Her short nails dug into his broad shoulders as she closed her eyes and arched backward to give him even better access to the soft, warm flesh that ached for his tender caress.

She felt his hand cupping her, lifting her, as his mouth

opened over the nipple and he took it between his lips and tongue.

Her soft gasp was followed by a harsh, shivering little moan that cost him his control. Not only had it been a long, dry spell, but this woman was the most important person in his life and he wanted her with an obsessive hunger. He hadn't been able to sleep for thinking about how sweet it would be to make love to her. And now she was, despite her hang-ups, not only welcoming his touch, but enjoying it.

"You said you didn't want to marry me," he whispered roughly as his mouth became more demanding.

Her nails dug into his back. "I said a lot of things," she agreed. Her eyes closed as she savored the spicy smell of his cologne, the tenderness of his mouth on forbidden flesh. "I might have even...believed them, at the time."

He lifted his head and looked down at her. His expression tautened at the sight of her pretty, firm breasts, and his body clenched. "I took it personally. Like you thought there was something wrong with me."

"Ted, no!" she exclaimed.

He pulled back the hand that was tracing around her nipple.

She bit her lip. "I wasn't saying no to that," she said with hopeless shyness, averting her eyes. "I meant, I don't think there's anything wrong with you...!"

She gasped as he responded to the blatant invitation in her voice and teased the hard rise of flesh with his thumb and forefinger.

"You don't?" he whispered, and smiled at her in a way that he never had before.

"Of course not! I was just scared," she managed, because what he was doing was creating sensations in some very private places. "Scared of marriage, I mean."

"Marriage is supposed to be a feast of pleasure for two people who care about each other," he pointed out, watching with delight her fascination with what he was doing to her willing body. He drew in a long breath and bent his head. "I'm beginning to believe it."

He opened his mouth over her soft breast and drew it inside, suckling it with his lips and his tongue in a slow, easy caress that caused her whole body to clench and shiver. As his ardor increased, he felt with wonder the searching fingers on the buttons of his shirt. They hesitated.

"Men like to be touched, too," he whispered into her ear.

"Oh."

She finished opening the button, a little clumsily, and spread her hands over the thick, curling mass of hair that covered his chest. "Wow," she whispered when sensations rippled through her body and seemed to be echoed coming from his. "You like that?" she asked hesitantly.

"I love it," he gritted.

She smiled with the joy of discovery as she looked up at him, at his mussed hair, his sensuous mouth, his sparkling black eyes. It was new, this shared pleasure. And she'd been so certain that she'd never be able to feel it with him, with anyone.

He bent to her mouth and crushed his lips down over it as his body eased onto hers. She felt the press of his bare chest against her breasts and arched up to increase the contact. Her arms went around him tightly, holding on as the current of passion swept her along.

He eased one long, powerful leg between both of hers

and moved against her in a rhythm that drew shudders and soft moans from her throat. She buried her teeth in his shoulder as the sensations began to rise and become obsessive. He must have felt something comparable, because he suddenly pushed down against her with a harsh groan as his control began to slip.

The soft knock on the door came again and again, until it was finally a hammering.

Ted lifted his head, his shocked eyes on Jillian's pretty pink breasts with visible passion marks, her face flushed and rigid with desire, her eyes turbulent as they met his.

"What?" Ted said aloud.

"Steak's ready! Don't let it get cold!" Rourke called, and there were audible footsteps going back down the hall.

With the passion slowly receding, Jillian was disturbed at letting Ted see her like this. Flushed, she fumbled her blouse and bra back on, wincing as the sensitive nipple was brushed by the fabric.

"Sorry," he whispered huskily. "I lost my head."

She managed a shaky smile. "It's okay. I lost mine, too." She looked at him with absolute wonder. "I didn't know it could feel like that," she stammered. "I mean, I never felt like that with anybody. Not that I ever let any man do that…!"

He put a long finger over her lips and smiled at her in a way he never had before. "It's okay, Jake."

She was still trying to catch her breath, and not doing a good job of it.

"I think you could say that we're compatible, in that way," he mused, enjoying her reaction to him more than he could find a way to express.

She laughed softly. "Yes, I think you could."

He smiled. "So, suppose we get married. And you can live with me, here on the ranch, and you'll never have to worry about Harris again."

She hesitated, but not for very long. She nodded, slowly. "Okay."

His high cheekbones went a ruddy color. It flattered him that she'd agree after a torrid passionate interlude, when he hadn't been able to persuade her with words.

"Don't get conceited," she said firmly, figuring out his thoughts.

His eyes twinkled. "Not possible."

She laughed. It was as if the world had changed completely in those few minutes. All her hang-ups had gone into eclipse the minute Ted turned the heat up.

"I wondered," he confessed, "if you'd be able to respond to a man after what happened to you."

"I did, too." She moved close to him and put her hands on his chest. "It was one reason I was afraid to let things go, well, very far. I didn't want to lead you on in any way and then pull away and run. I almost did that once."

"Yes," he said.

"If we get married, you'll give me a little time, won't you?" she asked worriedly. "I mean, I think I can do what you want me to. But it's just getting used to the idea."

Ted, who knew more than she did about women's reactions when passion got really hot, only smiled. "No problem."

She grinned. "Okay, then. Do we get married in the justice of the peace's office…?"

"In a church," he interrupted. "And you have to have a white gown and carry a bouquet. I'll even wear my good suit." He smiled. "I'm only getting married once, you know. We have to do it right."

She loved that attitude. It was what she'd wanted, but she was sensitive about being pushy. "Okay," she said.

"You'll be beautiful in a wedding gown," he murmured, bending to kiss her tenderly. "Not that you aren't beautiful in blue jeans. You are."

"I'm not," she faltered.

"You are to me," he corrected. His black eyes searched hers and he thought about the future, about living with her, about loving her... He bent and kissed her hungrily, delighting when she returned the embrace fervently.

"The steak's going to be room temperature in about thirty seconds!" Rourke shouted down the hall.

Ted pulled back, laughing self-consciously. "I guess we could eat steak, since he's been nice enough to cook it," he told her. His eyes glittered. "We can tell him we're engaged before we even start eating."

"Rourke's not interested in me that way," she said easily, smiling. "He's a nice man, but he's just protective of women. It isn't even personal."

Ted had his doubts about that. Jillian underestimated her appeal to men.

"Come on," she said, and slid her little hand into his big one.

That knocked the argument right out of him. It was the first physical move she'd made toward him. Well, not the first, but a big one, just the same. He slid his fingers between hers sensually, and smiled at her.

She smiled back. Her heart was hammering, her senses were alive and tumultuous. It was the beginning of a whole new life. She could hardly wait to marry Ted.

* * *

Rourke gave them a knowing smile when he noticed the telltale signs of what they'd been doing. He served up supper.

"This is really good," Ted exclaimed when he took the first bite of his steak.

"I'm a gourmet chef," Rourke replied, surprisingly. "In between dangerous jobs, I used to work in one of the better restaurants in Jo'burg," he said, giving Johannesburg it affectionate abbreviation.

"Wonders will never cease," Jillian said with a grin. "From steaks to combat."

"Oh, it was always combat first," Rourke said easily, "since I was born in Africa."

"Africa was always a rough venue, from what Cash told me," Ted said.

Rourke nodded. "We have plenty of factions, all trying to gain control of the disputed African states, although each is a sovereign nation in the Organization of African Unity, which contains fifty-four nations. The wars are always bloody. And there are millions upon millions of displaced persons, trying to survive with their children. A mercenary doesn't even have to look for work, it's all around him." His face hardened. "What's hardest is what they do to the kids."

"They must die very young there," Jillian commented sadly.

"No. They put automatic weapons in their hands when they're grammar school age, teach them to fire rocket launchers and set explosive charges. They have no sense of what childhood should actually be."

"Good heavens!" she exclaimed.

"You've never traveled, Jake," Ted said gently. "The world is a lot bigger than Hollister."

"I guess it is. But I never had the money, even if I'd had the inclination," she said.

"That's why I joined the army." Ted chuckled. "I knew it was the only way I'd get to travel."

"I wanted to see the world, too." Rourke nodded. "But most of what I've seen of it wouldn't be appropriate for any travel magazine."

"You have a ranch?" Ted asked.

He smiled. "Yes, I do. Luckily it's not in any of the contested areas, so I don't have to worry about politicians seizing power and taking over private land."

"And you run Brahmas," Ted said, shaking his head. "Ugly cattle."

"They're bred to endure the heat and sometimes drought conditions that we have in Africa," Rourke explained. "Our cattle have to be hearty. And some of your American ranchers use them as breeding stock for that very reason."

"I know. I've seen a lot of them down in Texas."

"They don't mind heat and drought, something you can't say for several other breed of cattle," Rourke added.

"I guess," Jillian said.

Rourke finished his steak and took a sip of the strong coffee he'd brewed. "Harris has been frustrated because Jillian got one of the waitresses to start putting cakes out for her in the display case."

"They haven't been selling," Jillian said sadly. "They used to be very popular, and now hardly anybody wants slices of them. I guess Davy has convinced people that they shouldn't eat my cooking because I'm such a bad person."

"Oh, that's not true," Ted said at once. "Don't you know about the contest?"

She frowned. "What contest?"

"You don't read the local paper, do you?" Rourke chided her.

She shook her head. "We already know what's going on, we only read a paper to know who got caught. But I have him," she pointed at Ted, "to tell me that, so why do I need to spend money for a newspaper?"

They both laughed.

"The mayor challenged everyone in Hollister to give up sweets for two weeks. It's a competition between businesses and people who work for them. At the end of the two weeks, everybody gets weighed, and the business with the employees who lost the most weight gets a cash prize, put up by the businesses themselves. The employees get to decide how the money's spent, too, so they can use it for workplace improvements or cash bonuses."

Jillian perked up. "Then it isn't about me!"

"Of course not," Ted chuckled. "I've heard at least two men who eat in that restaurant complain because they couldn't eat those delicious cakes until the contest ended."

"I feel so much better," she said.

"I'm glad," Rourke told her. "But that still doesn't solve your problem. Harris bought a Bowie knife and he doesn't hunt." He let the implication sink in. "He's facing at least ten to fifteen on the charges if he goes back to trial and is convicted again. He's been heard saying that he'll never go back to that hellhole voluntarily. So basically he's got nothing to lose." He glanced at Ted. "You know that already."

Ted nodded. "Yes, I do," he replied. He smiled at Jillian. "Which is why we're getting married Saturday."

She gasped. "Saturday? But there's not enough time...!"

"There is. We'll manage. Meanwhile," Ted said, "you're going to take Sassy's invitation seriously and stay out at her ranch until the ceremony. Right?"

She wanted to argue, but both males had set faces and determined expressions. So she sighed and said, "Right."

Chapter 10

Not only did John and Sassy Callister welcome Jillian as a houseguest, Sassy threw herself into wedding preparations and refused to listen to Jillian's protests.

"I've never gotten to plan a wedding, not even my own," Sassy laughed. "John hired a professional to do it for us because so many important people came to the ceremony. So now I'm taking over preparations for yours."

"But I can't afford this store," the younger woman tried to complain. "They don't even put price tags on this stuff!"

Sassy gave her a smile. "John and I agreed that our wedding present to you is going to be the gown and accessories," she said. "So you can hand it down through your family. You might have a daughter who'd love to wear it at her own wedding."

Jillian hadn't thought about that. She became dreamy.

A child. A little girl that she could take on walks, cuddle and rock, read stories to. That was a part of marriage she'd never dwelled on before. Now, it was a delightful thought.

"So stop arguing," Sassy said gently, "and start making choices."

Jillian hugged her. "Thanks. For the gown and for letting me stay with you until the wedding."

"This is what friends are for. You'd do it for me in a heartbeat if our situations were reversed."

"Yes, but I could have gotten you killed that night by running to you for help," Jillian said. "It torments me."

"I was perfectly capable of handling Davy Harris. And now I've got John, who can handle anything."

"You're very lucky. He's a good man."

"Yes, he is," Sassy agreed with a smile.

"I've never seen anything as beautiful as these dresses," Jillian began.

"I hear you're getting married Saturday, Jilly," came a cold, taunting voice from behind her.

Both women turned. Davy Harris was watching them, a nasty look on his face.

"Yes, I'm getting married," Jillian told him.

"There was a time when I thought you'd marry me," he said. "I had it all planned, right down to what sort of dress you'd wear and where we'd live. I'd lined up a full-time job with a local rancher. Everything was set." His lips twisted. "Then you had to go and get outraged when I tried to show you how I felt."

"I'll show you how I feel," Sassy said pertly. "Where's my shotgun?"

"Terroristic threats and acts, Mrs. Callister," he shot

back. "Suppose I call the news media and tell them that you're threatening me?"

Jillian was horrified.

Sassy just smiled. "Well, wouldn't it be a shame if that same news media suddenly got access to the trial transcripts?" she asked pleasantly.

His face hardened. "You think you're so smart. Women are idiots. My father always said so. My mother was utterly worthless. She couldn't even cook without burning something!"

Jillian stared at him. "That doesn't make a woman worthless."

"She was always nervous," he went on, as if she hadn't spoken. "She called the police once, but my father made sure she never did it again. They put him in prison. I never understood why. She had him locked up. He was right to make her pay for it."

Sassy and Jillian exchanged disturbed looks.

Harris gave Jillian a chilling smile. "He died in prison. But I won't. I'm never going back." He shrugged. "You enjoy thinking about that wedding, Jilly. Because all you're going to get to do is think about it. Have a nice day, now."

He walked out.

The shopping trip was ruined for Jillian. Sassy insisted that they get the gown and the things that went with it, but Jillian was certain that Davy had meant what he said. He was going to try to kill her. Maybe he'd even kill himself, afterward. In his own mind, he was justified. There was no way to reason with such a person, a man who thought that his own mother deserved to die because she'd had his father arrested for apparently greatly abusing her.

"You know, there are scary people in the world,"

Jillian told Sassy in a subdued tone. "I'll bet if Uncle John had ever really talked to Davy, he'd never have let him in the front door in the first place. He's mentally disturbed, and it isn't apparent until he starts talking about himself."

"I noticed that," Sassy replied. She drew in a long breath. "I'm glad we have Rourke."

Jillian frowned. "Where is he?"

"Watching us. If Harris had made a threatening move, he'd already be in jail, probably after a trip to the emergency room. I've never seen Rourke mad, but John says it's something you don't want to experience."

"I got that impression." She laughed. "He cooked steaks for Ted and me."

"I heard about that," the other woman said in an amused tone. "Ted was jealous, was he?"

"Very. But after he realized that Rourke was just being friendly and protective, his attitude changed. Apparently he knows a police chief in Texas that Ted met at a workshop back east."

"Rourke does get around." She glanced at Jillian. "He acts like a perpetual clown, but if you see him when he thinks he's alone, it's all an act. He's a very somber, sad person. I think he's had some rough knocks."

"He doesn't talk about them much. Just about his ranch."

"He doesn't talk about K.C. Kantor, either," Sassy replied. "But there's some sound gossip about the fact that Rourke's mother was once very close to the man."

"From what everybody says about that Kantor man, he isn't the sort to have kids."

"That's what I thought. But a man can get into a situation where he doesn't think with his mind," Sassy chuckled. "And when people get careless, they have kids."

"I'd be proud of Rourke, if I was his father."

"You're the wrong age and gender," Sassy said, tongue in cheek.

"Oh, you know what I mean. He's a good person."

"He is," Sassy said as she pulled up in front of the ranch house. "I'm glad John hired him. At least we don't have to worry about being assassinated on the way to town!"

"Amen," Jillian sighed.

John Callister was an easygoing, friendly man. He didn't seem at all like a millionaire, or at least, Jillian's vision of one. He treated her as he would a little sister, and was happy to have her around.

Jillian also liked Sassy's mother, who was in poor health, and her adopted sister, Selene, who was a whiz at math and science in grammar school. John took care of them, just as he took care of Sassy.

But the easygoing personality went into eclipse when he heard that Davy Harris had followed them into the dress shop in Billings.

"The man is dangerous," he said as they ate an early supper with Rourke.

"He is," Rourke agreed. "He shouldn't be walking around loose in the first place. What the hell is wrong with the criminal justice system in this country?"

John gave him a droll look. "It's better than the old vigilante system of the distant past," he pointed out. "And it usually works."

"Not with Harris," Rourke replied, his jaw set as he munched on a chef's salad. "He can put on a good act for a while, but he can't keep it up. He starts talking, and you see the lunacy underneath the appearance of sanity."

"Disturbed people often don't know they're disturbed," Sassy said.

"That's usually the case, I'm sad to say," Rourke added. "People like Harris always think they're being persecuted."

"I knew a guy once who was sure the government sent invisible spies to watch him," John mused. "He could see them, but nobody else could. He worked for us one summer on the ranch back home. Gil and I put up with him because he was the best horse wrangler we'd ever had. But that was a mistake."

"How so?" Rourke asked.

"Well, he had this dog. It was vicious and he refused to get rid of it. One day it came right up on the porch and threatened Gil's little girls. Gil punched him and fired him. Then he started cutting fences and killing cattle. At the last, he tried to kill us. He ended up in prison, too."

"Good heavens!" Jillian said. "No wonder you hired a bodyguard for Sassy."

"Exactly," John replied tersely. He didn't mention that Sassy had been the victim of a predator herself, in the feed store where she was working when they met. That man was serving time now.

His eyes lingered on Sassy with warm affection. "Nobody's hurting my best girl. Or her best friend," he declared with a grin at Jillian.

"Not while I'm on the job," Rourke added, chuckling. "You could marry me, you know," he told Jillian. "I really do have most of my own teeth left, and I can cook. Your fiancé can't boil water, I hear."

"That's true," Jillian said, smiling. "But I've known

him most of my life, and we think the same way about most things. We'll have a good marriage." She was sure of that. Ted would be gentle, and patient, and he'd rid her of the distaste Davy had left in her about physical relationships. She'd never been more certain of anything.

"Well, it's a great shame," Rourke said with a theatrical sigh. "I'll have to go back home to my ugly cattle and live in squalor because nobody wants to take care of me."

"You'll find some lovely girl who will be happy living on a small farm in Africa," Jillian assured him.

John almost choked on his coffee.

Rourke gave him a cold glare.

"What is wrong with you?" Sassy asked her husband.

He wiped his mouth, still stifling laughter. "Private joke," he said, sharing a look with Rourke, who sighed and shrugged.

"But it had better be somebody who can dress bullet wounds," John added with a twinkle in his eyes as he glanced at the other man.

"I only get shot occasionally," Rourke assured him. "And I usually duck in time."

"That's true," John agreed, forking another piece of steak into his mouth. "He only has one head wound, and it doesn't seem to have affected his thinking processes." He didn't mention the lost eye, because Rourke was sensitive about it.

"That was a scalp wound," Rourke replied, touching a faint scar above his temple. He glared at the other man from a pale brown eye. "And not from a bullet. It was from a knife."

"Poor thing," Jillian murmured.

John choked on his steak.

"Will you stop?" Rourke muttered.

"Sorry." John coughed. He sipped coffee.

Jillian wished she knew what they were talking about. But it was really none of her business, and she had other worries.

The wedding gown was exquisite. She couldn't stop looking at it. She hung it on the door in the guest bedroom and sighed over it at every opportunity.

Ted came by to visit frequently and they took long walks in the woods, to talk and to indulge in a favorite of dating couples, the hot physical interludes that grew in intensity by the day.

He held her hand and walked with her down a long path through the snow, his fingers warm and strong in hers.

"I can't stand it if I go a whole day without seeing you," he said out of the blue.

She stopped walking and looked up at him with pure wonder. "Really?"

He pulled her into his arms. "Really." He bent and kissed her slowly, feeling her respond, feeling her warm lips open and move tenderly. She reached her arms up around his neck as if it was the most natural thing in the world. He smiled against her lips. It was a delightful surprise, her easy response to him.

"Maybe I can get used to Sammy following me around, and you can get used to me shooting targets off the front porch," he teased.

She grinned. "Maybe you can teach me to shoot, too."

He looked shocked. "I can?"

"We should share some interests," she said wisely.

"You always go to that shooting range and practice. I could go with you sometimes."

He was surprised and couldn't hide it.

She toyed with a shirt button. "I don't like being away from you, either, Ted," she confessed and flushed a little. "It's so sweet…"

He pulled her close. One lean hand swept down her back, riveting her to his powerful body. "Sweeter than honey," he managed before he kissed her.

His hand pushed her hips against the sudden hardness of his own, eliciting a tiny sound from her throat. But it wasn't protest. If anything, she moved closer.

He groaned out loud and ground her hips into his.

"I can't wait until Saturday," he said in a husky tone, easing his hands under Jillian's blouse, under the bra to caress her soft breasts. "I'm dying!"

"So am I," she whispered shakily. "Oh, Ted!" she gasped when he pulled the garments out of his way and covered her breast with his mouth. It was so sweet. Too sweet for words!

He didn't realize what he was doing until they were lying on the cold ground, in the snow, while he kissed her until she was breathless.

She was shaking when he lifted his head, but not from cold or fear. Her eyes held the same frustrated desire that his held.

"I want to, so much!" she whispered.

"So do I," he replied.

For one long instant, they clung together on the hard ground, with snow making damp splotches all down Jillian's back and legs, while they both fought for control.

Ted clenched his hands beside her head and closed

his eyes as he rested his forehead against hers. He was rigid, helplessly aroused and unable to hide it.

She smoothed back his black hair and pressed soft, undemanding little kisses all over his taut face, finally against the closed eyelids and short thick black lashes.

"It's all right," she whispered. "It's all right."

He was amazed at the effect those words, and the caresses, had on him. They eased the torment. They calmed him, in the sweetest way he'd ever imagined. He smiled against her soft throat.

"Learning how to tame the beast, aren't you?" he whispered in a teasing tone.

She looked up at him with soft, loving eyes. "How to calm him down, anyway," she said with a little laugh. "I think marriage is going to be an adventure."

"So do I."

He stood and tugged her up, too, helping to rearrange her disheveled clothing. He grinned at her. "We both love maps and the tango. We'll go dancing every week."

Her eyes brightened. "I'd like that."

He enveloped her against him and stood holding her, quietly, in the silence of the snow-covered woods. "Heaven," he whispered, "must be very like this."

She smiled, hugging him. "I could die of happiness."

His heart jumped. "So could I, sweetheart."

The endearment made her own heart jump. She'd never been so happy in her life.

"Saturday can't come soon enough for me," he murmured.

"Or for me. Ted, Sassy bought me the most beautiful wedding gown. I know you aren't supposed to see it before the ceremony, but I just have to show it to you."

He drew back, smiling. "I'd like that."

They walked hand in hand back to the ranch house, easy and content with each other in a way they'd never been before. They looked as if they'd always been together, and always would be.

Sassy, busy in the kitchen with the cook, grinned at them. "Staying for lunch, Ted? We're having chili and Mexican corn bread."

"I'd love to, if you have enough to share."

"Plenty."

"Then, thanks, I will. Jillian wants me to see the wedding gown."

"Bad luck," Sassy teased.

"We make our own luck, don't we, honey?" he asked Jillian in a husky, loving tone.

She blushed at the second endearment in very few minutes and squeezed his hand. "Yes, we do."

She opened her bedroom door and gasped, turning pale. There, on the floor, were the remains of her wedding gown, her beautiful dress. It had been slashed to pieces.

"Stop right there," Ted said curtly, his arm preventing Jillian from entering the room. "This is now a crime scene. I'll get the sheriff's department's investigator out here right now, and the state crime-lab techs. I know who did this. I only want enough proof to have him arrested!"

Jillian wrapped her arms around her chest and shivered. Davy had come right into the house and nobody knew. Not even Rourke. It was chilling. Sassy, arriving late, took in the scene with a quick glance and hugged Jillian.

"It will be all right," she promised. But her own eyes were troubled. It was scary that he'd come into the house without being seen.

* * *

Rourke, when he realized what had happened, was livid. "That polecat!" he snarled. "Right under my bloody nose, and me like a raw recruit with no clue he was on the place! That won't happen again! I'm calling in markers. I'll have this place like a fortress before Saturday!"

Nobody argued with him. The situation had become a tragedy in the making. They'd all underestimated Davy Harris's wilderness skills, which were apparently quite formidable.

"He was a hunter," Jillian recalled. "He showed me how to track deer when he first started working with Uncle John, before he got to be a problem. He could walk so nobody heard a step. I'd forgotten that."

"I can ghost-walk myself," Rourke assured her.

"He used to set bear traps," Jillian blurted out, and reddened when everybody looked at her. "He said it was to catch a wolf that had been preying on the calves, but Uncle John said there was a dog caught in it…" She felt sick. "I'd forgotten that."

The men looked at each other. A bear trap could be used for many things, including catching unsuspecting people.

Jillian stared at Ted with horror. "Ted, he wouldn't use that on Sammy, would he?" she asked fearfully. Davy knew how much she loved her calf.

"No," he assured her with a comforting arm around her shoulders as he lied. "He wouldn't."

Rourke left the room for a few minutes. He came back, grim-faced. "We're going to have a lot of company very soon. All we need is proof that he was here, and he won't be a problem again."

* * *

Which would have been wonderful. Except that there wasn't a footprint in the dirt, a fingerprint, or any trace evidence whatsoever that Davy Harris had been near the Callister home. The technicians with all their tools couldn't find one speck of proof.

"So much for Locard's Exchange Principle," Ted said grimly, and then had to explain what it meant to Jillian. "A French criminalist named Edmond Locard noted that when a crime is committed, the perpetrator both carries away and leaves behind trace evidence."

"But Davy didn't," she said sadly.

"He's either very good or very lucky," Ted muttered. He slid a protective arm around Jillian. "And it won't save him. He's the only person in town who had a motive for doing this. It's just a matter of proving it."

She laughed hollowly. "Maybe you could check his new Bowie knife to see if it's got pieces of white lace sticking to it," she said, trying to make the best of a bad situation.

But he didn't laugh. He was thoughtful. "That might not be such a bad idea," he murmured. "All I'd need is probable cause, if I can convince a judge to issue a search warrant on the basis of it." He pursed his lips and narrowed his eyes, nodding to himself. "And that's just what I'm going to do. Stick close to the house today, okay?"

"Okay."

He kissed her and left.

But Ted came back a few hours later and stuck to her like glue. She noticed that he was suddenly visible near her, everywhere she went around the house and the barn. It was just after he'd received a phone call, to which nobody was privy.

"What's going on?" Jillian asked him bluntly.

He smiled, his usual easygoing self, as he walked beside her with his hands deep in the pockets of his khaki slacks. "What would be going on?"

"You're usually at work during the day, Ted," she murmured dryly.

He grinned at her. "Maybe I can't stay away from you, even on a workday," he teased.

She stopped and turned to him, frowning. "That's not an answer and you know…!"

She gasped as he suddenly whirled, pushing her to the ground as he drew his pistol and fired into a clump of snow-covered undergrowth near the house. Even as he fired, she felt a sting in her arm and then heard a sound like a high-pitched crack of thunder.

That sound was followed by the equally loud rapid fire of a .45 automatic above her. She heard the bullets as they connected with tree trunks in the distance.

"You okay?" he asked urgently.

"I think so."

He stopped firing, and eased up to his feet, standing very still with his head cocked, listening. Far in the distance was the sound of a vehicle door closing, then an engine starting. He whipped out his cell phone and made a call. He gave a quick explanation, a quicker description of the direction of travel of the vehicle and assurances that the intended victim was all right. He put up the cell phone and knelt beside a shaken Jillian.

There was blood on her arm. The sleeve of her gray sweatshirt was ripped. She looked at it with growing sensation. It stung.

"What in the world?" she stammered.

"You've been hit, sweetheart," he said curtly. "That's a gunshot wound. I didn't want to tell you, but one of my investigators learned that Harris bought a high-powered rifle with a telescopic sight this morning, after I had his rented room tossed for evidence."

"He's a convicted felon, nobody could have sold him a gun at all…!" she burst out.

"There are places in any town, even small ones, where people can buy weapons under the table." His face was hard as stone. "I don't know who sold it to him, but you'd better believe that I'm going to find out. And God help whoever did, when I catch up to him!"

She was still trying to wrap her mind around the fact that she'd been shot. Rourke, who'd been at the other end of the property, came screeching up in a ranch Jeep and jumped out, wincing when he saw the blood on Jillian's arm.

"I spotted him, I was tracking him, when I heard the gunshot. God, I'm sorry!" he exclaimed. "I should have been quicker. Do you think you hit him?" he asked Ted.

"I'm not sure. Maybe." He helped Jillian up. "I'll get you to a doctor." He glanced at Rourke. "I called the sheriff to bring his dogs and his best investigator out here," he added. "They may need some help. I told the sheriff you'd been on the case, working for the Callisters."

Rourke's pale brown eye narrowed. He looked far different from the man Jillian had come to know as her easygoing friend. "I let him get onto the property, and I'm sorry. But I can damned sure track him."

"None of us could have expected what happened here," Ted said reassuringly, and put a kindly hand on the other man's shoulder. "She'll be okay. Sheriff's department investigator is on his way out here. I gave the sheriff's investigator your cell phone number," Ted added.

Rourke nodded. He winced at Jillian's face. "I'm sorry," he said curtly.

She smiled, holding her arm. "It's okay, Rourke."

"I didn't realize he was on the place, either, until I heard the gunshots," Ted said.

"Not the first time you've been shot at, I gather?" she asked with black humor.

"Not at all. You usually feel the bullet before you hear the sound," he added solemnly.

"And that's a fact," Rourke added with faint humor.

"Let's go," Ted said gently.

She let him put her into the patrol car. She was feeling sick, and she was in some pain. "It didn't hurt at first," she said. "I didn't even realize I was shot. Oh, Ted, I'm sorry, you have to wait…!" She opened the door and threw up, then she cried with embarrassment.

He handed her a clean white handkerchief, put her back in the car, and broke speed limits getting her to the emergency room.

"It's never like that on television," she said drowsily, when she'd been treated and was in a semi-private room for the night. They'd given her something for pain, as well. It was making her sleepy.

"What isn't, sweetheart?"

She smiled at the endearment as he leaned over her, gently touching her face. "People getting shot. They don't throw up."

"That's not real life, either," he reminded her.

She was worried, but not only for herself.

"What is it?" he asked gently.

"Sammy," she murmured. "I know, it's stupid to be worried about a calf, but if he can't get to me, he might try to hurt something I love." She searched his eyes. "You watch out, too."

His dark eyes twinkled. "Because you love me?" he drawled.

She only nodded, her face solemn. "More than anyone in the world."

There was a flush on his high cheekbones. He cupped her head in his big hands and kissed her with blatant possession. "That goes double for me," he whispered against her lips.

She searched his eyes with fascination. "It does?"

"Why in the world do you think I'd want to marry you if I didn't love you?" he asked reasonably. "No parcel of land is worth that sort of sacrifice."

"You never said," she stammered.

"Neither did you," he pointed out, chuckling.

She laid her hand against his shoulder. "I didn't want to say it first."

He kissed her nose. "But you did."

She sighed and smiled. "Yes. I did."

For one long moment, they were silent together, savoring the newness of an emotion neither had realized was so intense.

Finally he lifted his head. "I don't want to leave you, but we've got a lot of work to do and not a lot of time to do it."

She nodded. "You be careful."

"I will."

"Ted, could you check on Sammy?" she asked worriedly.

"Yes. I'll make sure she's okay."

She smiled. "Thanks."

"No problem."

Sassy came and took her back to the Callister ranch as soon as the doctor released her.

"I still think they should have kept you overnight," Sassy muttered.

"They tried to, but I refused," Jillian said drowsily. "I don't like being in hospitals. Have you heard anything more?"

"About Harris?" Sassy shook her head. "I know they've got dogs in the woods, hunting him. But if he's a good woodsman, he'll know how to cover his trail."

"He talked about that once," Jillian recalled. "He said there were ways to cover up a scent trail so a dog couldn't track people. Funny, I never wondered why he'd know such a thing."

"I'm sorry he does," Sassy replied. "If he didn't have those skills, he'd be a lot easier to find."

"I guess so."

"I've got a surprise for you," Sassy said when they walked into the house. She smiled mysteriously as she led Jillian down the hall to the guest bedroom she'd been occupying.

"What is it?" Jillian asked.

Sassy opened the door. There, hanging on the closet door, was a duplicate of the beautiful wedding gown that Sassy had chosen, right down to the embroidery.

"They only had two of that model. The other was in a store in Los Angeles. I had them overnight it," Sassy chuckled. "Nothing is going to stop this wedding!"

Jillian burst into tears. She hugged Sassy, as close as her wounded arm would permit. "Thank you!"

"It's little enough to do. I'm sorry the other one was ruined. We're just lucky that there was a second one in your size."

Jillian fingered the exquisite lace. "It is the most beautiful gown I'd ever seen. I'll never be able to thank you enough, Sassy."

The other woman was solemn. "We don't talk about it, but I'm sure you know that I had a similar experience, with my former boss at the feed store where I worked just before I married John. I was older than you were, and it wasn't quite as traumatic as yours, but I know how it feels to be assaulted." She sighed. "Funny thing, I had no idea when you came running up to the door with Harris a step behind you that I'd ever face the same situation in my own life."

"I'm sorry."

"Yes, so am I. There are bad men in the world. But there are good ones, too," Sassy reminded her. "I'm married to one of them, and you're about to marry another one."

"If Davy doesn't find some horrible new way to stop it," Jillian said with real concern in her voice.

"He won't," Sassy said firmly. "There are too many people in uniforms running around here for him to take that sort of a chance."

She bit her lower lip. "Ted was going to see about Sammy. I don't know if Harris might try to hurt her, to get back at me."

"He won't have the chance," Sassy said. "John and two of our hands took a cattle trailer over to your house a few minutes before I left to pick you up at the hospital. They're bringing her over here, and she'll stay in our barn. We have a man full-time who does nothing but look after our prize bulls who live in it."

"You've done so much for me," Jillian said, fighting tears.

"You'd do it for me," was the other woman's warm reply. "Now stop worrying. You have two days to get well enough to walk down the aisle."

"Maybe we should postpone it," she began.

"Not a chance," Sassy replied. "We'll have you back on your feet by then if we have to fly in specialists!" And she meant it.

Chapter 11

Jillian carried a small bouquet of white and pale pink roses as she walked down the aisle of the small country church toward Ted, who was waiting at the altar. Her arm was sore and throbbing a little, and she was still worried about whether or not Davy Harris might try to shoot one of them through the window. But none of her concerns showed in her radiant expression as she took her place beside Ted.

The minister read the marriage ceremony. Jillian repeated the words. Ted repeated them. He slid a plain gold band onto her finger. She slid one onto his. They looked at each other with wonder and finally shared a kiss so tender that she knew she'd remember it all her life.

They held hands walking back down the aisle, laughing, as they were showered with rose petals by two little girls who were the daughters of one of Ted's police officers.

"Okay, now, stand right here while we get the photos," Sassy said, stage-managing them in the reception hall where food and punch were spread out on pristine white linen tablecloths with crystal and china to contain the feast. She'd hired a professional photographer to record the event, over Jillian's protests, as part of the Callisters' wedding gift to them.

Jillian felt regal in her beautiful gown. The night before, she'd gone out to the barn with Ted to make sure little Sammy was settled in a stall. It was silly to be worried about an animal, but she'd been a big part of Jillian's life since she was first born, to a cow that was killed by a freak lightning strike the next day. Jillian had taken the tiny calf to the house and kept her on old blankets on the back porch and fed her around the clock to keep her alive.

That closeness had amused Ted, especially since the calf followed Jillian everywhere she went and even, on occasion, tried to go in the house with her. He supposed he was lucky that they didn't make calf diapers, he'd teased, or Jillian would give the animal a bedroom.

"Did anybody check to see if I left my jacket down that trail where I took Sammy for her walks?" Jillian asked suddenly. "The buckskin one, with the embroidery. It hasn't rained, but if it does, it will be soaked. I forgot all about it when I came to stay with Sassy."

"I'll look for it later," Ted told her, nuzzling her nose with his. "When we go home."

"Home." She sighed and closed her eyes. "I forgot. We'll live together now."

"Yes, we will." He touched her face. "Maybe not as

closely as I'd like for a few more days," he teased deeply and chuckled when she flushed. "That arm is going to take some healing."

"I never realized that a flesh wound could cause so much trouble," she told him.

"At least it was just a flesh wound," he said grimly. "Damned if I can figure out why we can't find that polecat," he muttered, borrowing Rourke's favorite term. "We've had men scouring the countryside for him."

"Maybe he got scared and left town," she said hopefully.

"We found his truck deserted, about halfway between the Callisters' ranch and ours," he said. "Dogs lost his trail when it went off the road." He frowned. "One of our trackers said that his footprints changed from one side of the truck to the other, as if he was carrying something."

"Maybe a suitcase?" she wondered.

He shook his head. "We checked the bus station and we had the sheriff's department send cars all over the back roads. He just vanished into thin air."

"I'm not sorry," she said heavily. "But I'd like to know that he wasn't coming back."

"So would I." He bent and kissed her. "We'll manage," he added. "Whatever happens, we'll manage."

She smiled up at him warmly. "Yes. We will."

They settled down into married life. Ted had honestly hoped to wait a day or so until her arm was a little less sore.

But that night while they were watching a movie on television, he kissed her and she kissed him back. Then they got into a more comfortable position on the sofa. Very soon, pieces of clothing came off and were discarded on the floor. And then, skin against skin, they learned each other in ways they never had before.

Just for a minute, it was uncomfortable. He felt her stiffen and his mouth brushed tenderly over her closed eyelids. "Easy," he whispered. "Try to relax. Move with me. Move with me, sweetheart…yes!"

And then it was all heat and urgency and explosions of sensation like nothing she'd ever felt in her life. She dug her nails into his hips and moaned harshly as the hard, fierce thrust of his body lifted her to elevations of pleasure that built on each other until she was afraid that she might die trying to survive them.

"Yes," he groaned, and he bruised her thighs with his fingers as he strained to get even closer to her when the pleasure burst and shuddered into ecstacy.

She cried out. Her whole body felt on fire. She moved with him, her own hips arching up in one last surge of strength before the world dissolved into sweet madness.

She was throbbing all over, like her sore arm that she hadn't even noticed until now. She shivered under the weight of Ted's body.

"I was going to wait," he managed in a husky whisper.

"What in the world for?" she laughed. "It's just a sore arm." Her eyes met his with shy delight.

He lifted an eyebrow rakishly. "Is anything else sore?" he asked

She grinned. "No."

He pursed his lips. "Well, in that case," he whispered, and began to move.

She clutched at him and gasped with pure delight. He only laughed.

Much later, they curled up together in bed, exhausted and happy. They slept until late the next morning, missing church and a telephone call from the sheriff, Larry Kane.

"Better call me as soon as you get this," Larry said grimly on the message. "It's urgent."

Ted exchanged a concerned glance with Jillian as he picked up his cell phone and returned the call.

"Graves," he said into the phone. "What's up?"

There was a pause while he listened. He scowled. "What?" he exclaimed.

"What is it?" Jillian was mouthing at him.

He held up a hand and sighed heavily. "How long ago?"

He nodded. "Well, it's a pity, in a way. But it's ironic, you have to admit. Yes. Yes. I'll tell her. Thanks, Larry."

He snapped the phone shut. "They found Davy Harris this morning."

"Where is he?" she asked, gnawing her lip.

"They've taken him to the state crime lab."

She blinked. "I thought they only took dead people... Oh, dear. He's dead?"

He nodded. "They found him with his leg caught in a bear trap. He'd apparently been trying to set it on the ranch, down that trail where you always walk with Sammy, through the trees where it's hard to see the ground."

"Good Lord!" she exclaimed, and the possibilities created nightmares in her mind.

"He'd locked the trap into place with a log chain, around a tree, and padlocked it in place. Sheriff thinks he lost the key somewhere. He couldn't get the chain loose or free himself from the trap. He bled to death."

She felt sick all over. She pressed into Ted's arms and held on tight. "What a horrible way to go."

"Yes, well, just remember that it was how he planned for Sammy to go," he said, without mentioning that Harris may well have planned to catch Jillian in it.

"His sister will sue us all for wrongful death and say we killed him," Jillian said miserably, remembering the woman's fury when her brother was first arrested.

"His sister died two years ago," he replied. "Of a drug overdose. A truly troubled family."

"When did you find that out?" she wondered.

"Yesterday," he said. "I didn't want to spend our wedding day talking about Harris, but I did wonder if he might run to his sister for protection. So I had an investigator try to find her."

"A sad end," she said.

"Yes. But fortunately, not yours," he replied. He held her close, glad that it was over, finally.

She sighed. "Not mine," she agreed.

Rourke left three days later to go back to Africa. He'd meant to leave sooner, but Sassy and John wanted to show him around Montana first, despite the thick snow that was falling in abundance now.

"I've taken movies of the snow to show back home," he mentioned as he said his farewells to Jillian and Ted while a ranch hand waited in the truck to drive him to the airport in Billings. "We don't get a lot of snow in Kenya," he added, tongue in cheek.

"Thanks for helping keep me alive," Jillian told him.

"My pleasure," he replied, and smiled.

Ted shook hands with him. "If you want to learn how to fish for trout, come back in the spring when the snows melt and we'll spend the day on the river."

"I might take you up on that," Rourke said.

They watched him drive away.

Jillian slid her arm around Ted's waist. "You coming home for lunch?" she asked as they walked to his patrol car.

"Thought I might." He gave her a wicked grin. "You going to fix food or are we going to spend my lunch hour in the usual way?"

She pursed her lips. "Oh, I could make sandwiches."

"You could pack them in a plastic bag," he added, "and I could take them back to work with me."

She flushed and laughed. "Of course. We wouldn't want to waste your lunch hour by eating."

He bent and kissed her with barely restrained hunger. "Absolutely not! See you about noon."

She kissed him back. "I'll be here."

He drove off, throwing up a hand as he went down the driveway. She watched him go and thought how far she'd come from the scared teenager that Davy Harris had intimidated so many years before. She had a good marriage and her life was happier than ever before. She still had her morning job at the local restaurant. She liked the little bit of independence it gave her, and they could use the extra money. Ted wasn't likely to get rich working as a police chief.

On the other hand, their lack of material wealth only

brought them closer together and made their shared lives better.

She sighed as she turned back toward the house, her eyes full of dreams. Snow was just beginning to fall again, like a burst of glorious white feathers around her head. Winter was beautiful. Like her life.

* * * * *

RELUCTANT FATHER

For Margaret, with love.

Chapter 1

Blake Donavan didn't know which was the bigger shock—the dark-haired, unsmiling little girl at his front door or the news that the child was his daughter by his ex-wife.

Blake's pale green eyes darkened dangerously. It had been a hell of a day altogether, and now this. The lawyer who'd just imparted the information stepped closer to the child.

Blake raked his fingers through his unruly black hair and glared down at the child through thick black lashes. His daughter? The scowl grew and his expression hardened, emphasizing the harsh scar down one lean, tanned cheek. He looked even taller and more formidable than he really was.

"I don't like him," the little girl murmured, glaring at Blake as she spoke for the first time. She thrust her lower lip out and moved closer to the lawyer, clinging to his trouser leg. She had green eyes. That fact registered almost immediately—that and her high cheekbones. Blake had high cheekbones, too.

"Now, now." The tall, bespectacled man cleared his throat. "We mustn't be naughty, Sarah."

"My wife," Blake said coldly, "left me five years ago to take up residence with an oilman from Louisiana. I haven't seen or heard from her since."

"If I might come in, Mr. Donavan…?"

He ignored the attorney's plea. "We only cohabited for a month—just long enough for her to find out that I was up to my neck in legal battles. She cut her losses and got out quick with her new lover." He smiled crookedly. "She didn't expect me to win. But I did."

The lawyer glanced around at the elegant, columned front porch, the well-kept gardens, the Mercedes in the driveway. He'd heard about the Donavan fortune and the fight Blake Donavan had when his uncle died and left him fending off numerous greedy cousins.

"The problem, you see," the attorney continued, glancing worriedly at the clinging child, "is that your ex-wife died earlier this month in an airplane crash. Understandably her second husband, from whom she was estranged, didn't want to assume responsibility for the child. Sarah has no one else," he added on a weary sigh. "Your wife's parents were middle-aged when she was born, and she had no brothers or sisters. The entire family is dead. And Sarah is your child."

Blake stared down at the little girl half-angrily. He hadn't even kept a photograph of Nina to remind him of the fool he'd been. And now here was her child, and they expected him to want her.

"I don't have room in my life for a child," he said

curtly, furious at the curve fate had thrown him. "She can be put in a home somewhere, I suppose…."

And that was when it happened. The child began to cry. There wasn't a sound from her. She went from belligerence to heartrending sorrow in seconds, with great tears rolling from her green eyes down her flushed round cheeks. The effect was all the more poignant because of her silence and the stoic look on her face, as if she hated giving way to tears in front of the enemy.

Blake felt a stirring inside that surprised him. His mother had died soon after he was born. She hadn't been a particularly moral woman, according to his uncle, and all he knew about her was what little he'd been told. His uncle had taken him in and had adopted him. He, like Sarah, had been an extra person in the world, unwanted by just about everyone. He had no idea who his father was. If it hadn't been for his very wealthy uncle, he wouldn't even have a name. That lack of love and security in his young life had turned him hard. It would turn Sarah hard, too, if she had nobody to protect her.

He looked down at the little girl with a headful of angry questions, hating those tears. But the child had grit. She glared at him and abruptly wiped the tears away with a chubby little hand.

Blake lifted his chin pugnaciously. Already the kid was getting to him. But he wasn't going to be taken in by some scam. He trusted no one. "How do I know she's mine?" he demanded to the lawyer.

"She has your blood type," the man replied. "Your ex-wife's second husband has a totally different blood group. As you know, a blood test can only tell who the father wasn't. It wasn't her second husband."

Blake was about to remark that it could have been any one of a dozen other men, but then he remembered that Nina had married him for what she thought was his soon-to-be-realized wealth. He reasoned that Nina was too shrewd to have risked losing him by indulging in a fling. And after she knew what a struggle it was going to be to get that wealth, she hadn't wanted her newest catch to know she was already pregnant.

"Why didn't she tell me?" Blake asked coldly.

"She allowed her second husband to think the child was his," he said quietly. "It wasn't until she died and Sarah's birth certificate was found that he discovered she was yours. Nina had apparently decided that Sarah had a right to her own father's name. By then her second marriage was already on the rocks, from what I was told." He touched the child's dark hair absently. "You have the resources to double-check all this, of course."

"Of course." He stared down his broken nose at the little girl's face. "What's her name again? Sarah?"

"That's right. Sarah Jane."

Blake turned. "Bring her inside. Mrs. Jackson can feed her and I'll engage a nurse for her."

Just that quickly, he made the decision to keep the child. But, then, he'd been making quick decisions for a long time. When his uncle had attempted to link him with Meredith Calhoun, Blake had quickly decided to marry Nina. And as a last effort to force Blake into marrying Meredith, his uncle had left Meredith twenty percent of the stock in the real-estate conglomerate Blake was to inherit.

That had backfired. Blake had laughed at Meredith, in front of the whole family gathered for the reading of the will. And he'd told them all, his arm protectively around a smiling Nina, that he'd rather lose his inheritance and a leg than marry a skinny, plain, repulsive woman like

Meredith. He was marrying Nina and Meredith could take her stock and burn it, for all he cared.

His heart lay like lead in his chest as he remembered the harsh words he'd used that day to cut Meredith down. She hadn't even flinched, but he'd watched something die in her soft gray eyes. With a kind of ravished dignity, she'd walked out of the room with every eye on her straight back. That had been bad enough. But later she'd come to offer him the stock and he'd been irritated by the faint hunger in her soft eyes. Because she disturbed him, he'd kissed her roughly, bruising her mouth, and he'd said some things that sent her running from him. He regretted that most of all. He planned to marry Nina, but despite his feeling for her, Meredith had been a tiny thorn in his side for years. He hadn't really meant to hurt her. He'd only wanted to make her go away. Well, he had. And he hadn't seen her since. She'd become internationally famous with her women's novels, one of which had been adapted for television. He saw her books everywhere these days. Like Meredith, they haunted him.

It hadn't been until after Nina had left him that he'd found out the reason for Meredith's haste in getting away. She'd been in love with him, his uncle's attorney had told him ruefully as he handed Blake the documents to sign that would give him full control of the Donavan empire. His uncle had known it and had hoped to make Blake see what a good catch she was.

Blake remembered vividly the day he'd discovered his hunger for Meredith. It had shocked them both. His uncle had come into the stable just in time to break up what might have been a disastrous confrontation between them. Blake had lost control and frightened Meredith, although she'd been so sweetly responsive at first that he hadn't seen her fear until the sound of a car driving up had brought him to his senses. Even a blind man couldn't have missed the faint swell of Meredith's mouth, the color in her cheeks and the way she was trembling. That was probably when the old man got the idea about the stock.

What irony, Blake thought, that what he'd wanted most in life was just a little love. He'd never had his mother's. He'd never known his father. And his uncle, though fond of him, was a manipulative man interested in the survival of his empire through Blake. Blake had actually married Nina because she'd flattered him and played up to him and sworn that she loved him. Now, looking back, he could see that she'd loved his money, not him. Once there was any possibility of the fortune being lost, she'd walked out on him. But Meredith had genuinely loved Blake, and he'd been cruel to her. That had haunted him all these years—that he'd hurt the one human being on earth who'd ever wanted to love him.

Meredith's father had worked for Blake's uncle, but the two men were good friends, as well. Uncle Dan had been at Meredith's christening as her godfather, and when she'd grown into her teens and expressed an interest in writing local history for the school newspaper, Uncle Dan had opened his library to her and spent hours telling her stories he'd heard from his grandfather about the old days. Meredith would sit and listen, her big eyes wide, her mouth faintly smiling. And Blake would brood, because his uncle had never given him that kind of time and affection. Blake was useful, but his uncle loved Meredith. He felt as if she'd usurped the only place in the world he had, and he'd resented her bitterly. And it was more than just that. He'd already learned that he couldn't trust people. He knew that Meredith and her parents were dirt poor, and he often wondered if she might not have some mercenary reason for hanging around the Donavan house. Too late, he discovered that she hung around because of him. Knowing the truth put salt in an old wound.

Plain Meredith, with her stringy dark hair and her pale gray eyes and her heart-shaped face. His uncle had loved her. Blake had almost despised her, especially after what had happened in the stable when he lost control with her. But under the resentment was an obsessive desire for Meredith that angered him, until it reached flash point the day his uncle's will was read. He'd given his word to Nina that he'd marry her and he couldn't honorably go back on it, but he'd wanted Meredith. God, how he'd wanted her, for years!

She'd loved him, he thought wearily as he led the lawyer and child into the study. Nobody else ever had felt that way about him. His uncle had enjoyed their battles; they'd been friends. His death had been a terrible, unexpected blow, made worse by the fact that he'd always felt that his uncle might have cared for him if Meredith hadn't always been underfoot. Not that it was love that had caused his uncle to adopt him. That had been business.

Maybe his mother would have loved him if she'd lived, although his uncle had described her as a pretty, self-centered woman who simply liked men too much.

So it had come as a shock to find out what shy young Meredith had felt for him. It didn't help to remember how he'd cut her to pieces in public and private. Over the years since she'd left for Texas in the middle of the night on a bus, without a goodbye to anyone, he'd agonized over what he'd done to her. Twice, he'd almost gone to see her when her name started cropping up on book covers. But the past was best left in the past, he'd decided finally. And he had nothing to give her, anyway. Nina had destroyed that part of him that was capable of trust. He had no more to give—to anyone.

He dragged his thoughts away from the past and looked at the child, who was staring plaintively and a little apprehensively at the door, because the lawyer had just smiled and was now making his way out, patent relief written all over his thin features. Sarah sat very still on the edge of a blue wing chair, biting her lower lip, her eyes wide and frightened, although she tried to hide her fear from the cold, mean-looking man they said was her father.

Blake sat down across from her in his own big red leather armchair, aware that he looked more like a desperado in his jeans and worn chambray shirt than a man of means. He'd been out in the pasture helping brand cattle, just for the hell of it. At least when he was working with his hands on the small ranch where he ran purebred Hereford cattle, he could let his mind go. It beat the hell out of the trying board meeting he'd had to endure at his company headquarters in Oklahoma City that morning.

"So you're Sarah," he said. Children made him uncomfortable, and he didn't know how he was going to cope with this one. But she had his eyes and he couldn't let her go to strangers. Not if there was one chance in a million that she really was his daughter.

Sarah lifted her eyes to his, then glanced away, shifting restlessly. The lawyer had said she was almost four, but she seemed amazingly mature. She behaved as if she'd never known the company of other children. It was possible that she hadn't. He couldn't picture Nina entertaining children. It was totally out of character, but he hadn't realized that when he'd lost his head and married her. Funny how easy it was to imagine Meredith

Calhoun with a lapful of little girls, laughing and playing with them, picking daisies in the meadow....

He had to stop thinking about Meredith, he told himself firmly. He didn't want her, even if there was a chance in hell that she'd ever come back to Jack's Corner, Oklahoma. And he knew without a doubt that she certainly didn't want him.

"I don't like you," Sarah said after a minute. She shifted in the chair and glanced around her. "I don't want to live here." She glared at Blake.

He glared back. "Well, I'm not crazy about the idea, either, but it looks like we're stuck with each other."

Her lower lip jutted, and for an instant she looked just like him. "I'll bet you don't even have a cat."

"God forbid," he grumbled. "I hate cats."

She sighed and looked at her scuffed shoes with something like resignation and a patience far beyond her years. She appeared tired and worn. "My mommy isn't coming back." She pulled at her dress. "She didn't like me. You don't like me, either," she said, lifting her chin. "I don't care. You're not really my daddy."

"I must be." He sighed heavily. "God knows, you look enough like me."

"You're ugly."

His eyebrows shot up. "You're no petunia yourself, sprout," he returned.

"The ugly duckling turns into a swan," she told him with a faraway look in her eyes.

She twirled her hands in her dress. He noticed then, for the first time, that it was old. The lace was stained and the dress was rumpled. He frowned.

"Where have you been staying?" he asked her.

"Mommy left me with Daddy Brad, but he had to go out a lot, so Mrs. Smathers took care of me." She looked up, and the expression in her green eyes was old for a little girl's. "Mrs. Smathers says that children are horrible," she said dramatically, "and that they belong in cages. I cried when Mommy left, and she locked me up and said she'd leave me there if I didn't hush." Her lower lip trembled, but she didn't cry. "I got out, too, and ran away." She shrugged. "But nobody came to find me, so I went home. Mrs. Smathers was real mad, but Daddy Brad didn't care. He said I wasn't his real child and it didn't matter if I ran away."

Blake could imagine that "Daddy Brad" was upset to find that the child he'd accepted as his own was somebody else's, but taking it out on the child seemed pretty callous.

He leaned back in his chair, wondering what in hell he was going to do with his short houseguest. He didn't know anything about kids. He wasn't sure he even liked them. And this one already looked like a handful. She was outspoken and belligerent and not much to look at. He could see trouble ahead.

Mrs. Jackson came into the room to see if Blake wanted anything, and stopped dead. She was fifty-five, a spinster, graying and thin and faintly intimidating to people who didn't know her. She was used to a bachelor household, and the sight of a child sitting across from her boss was vaguely unnerving.

"Who's that?" she asked, without dressing up the question.

Sarah looked at her and sighed, as if saying, oh, no, here's another sour one. Blake almost laughed out loud at the expression on the child's face.

"This is Amie Jackson, Sarah," Blake said, introducing them. "Mrs. Jackson, Sarah Jane is my daughter."

Mrs. Jackson didn't faint, but she did go a shade

redder. "Yes, sir, that's hard to miss," she said, comparing the small, composed child's face with its older male counterpart. "Her mother isn't here?" she added, staring around as if she expected Nina to materialize.

"Nina is dead," Blake said without any particular feeling. Nina had knocked the finer feelings out of him years ago. His own foolish blindness to her real nature had helped her in the task.

"Oh, I'm sorry." Mrs. Jackson rubbed her apron between her thin hands for something to do. "Would she like some milk and cookies?" she asked hesitantly.

"That might be nice. Sarah?" Blake asked more curtly than he'd meant.

Sarah shifted and stared at the carpet. "I'd get crumbs on the floor." She shook her head. "Mrs. Smathers says kids should eat off the kitchen floor 'cause they're messy."

Mrs. Jackson looked uncomfortable, and Blake sighed heavily. "You can get crumbs on the floor. Nobody's going to yell at you."

Sarah glanced up hesitantly.

"I don't mind cleaning up crumbs," Mrs. Jackson said testily. "Do you want cookies?"

"Yes, please."

The older woman nodded curtly and went to get some.

"Nobody smiles here," Sarah murmured. "It's just like home."

Blake felt a twinge of regret for the child, who seemed to have been stuck away in the housekeeper's corner with no thought for her well-being. And not just since her stepfather had found out that she was Blake's child, apparently.

His eyes narrowed and he asked the question that was consuming him. "Didn't your mother stay with you?"

"Mommy was busy," Sarah said. "She said I had to stay with Mrs. Smathers and do what she said."

"Wasn't she home from time to time?"

"She and my daddy—" she faltered and grimaced "—my *other* daddy yelled at each other mostly. Then she went away and he went away, too."

This was getting them nowhere. He stood and began to pace, his hands in his pockets, his face stormy and hard.

Sarah watched him covertly. "You sure are big," she murmured.

He stopped, glancing down at her curiously. "You sure are little," he returned.

"I'll grow," Sarah promised. "Do you have a horse?"

"Several."

She brightened. "I can ride a horse!"

"Not on my ranch, you can't."

Her green eyes flashed fire. "I can so if I want to. I can ride any horse!"

He knelt in front of her very slowly, and his green eyes met hers levelly and without blinking. "No," he said firmly. "You'll do what you're told, and you won't talk back. This is my place, and I make the rules. Got it?"

She hesitated, but only for a minute. "Okay," she said sulkily.

He touched the tip of her pert nose. "And no sulking. I don't know how this is going to work out," he added curtly. "Hell, I don't know anything about kids!"

"Hell is where you go when you're bad," Sarah replied matter-of-factly. "My mommy's friend used to talk about it all the time, and about damns and sons of—"

"Sarah!" Blake burst out, shocked that a child her age should be so familiar with bad words.

"Do you have any cows?" she added, easily diverted.

"A few," he muttered. "Which one of your mummy's friends used language like that around you?"

"Just Trudy," she said, wide-eyed.

Blake whistled through his teeth and turned just as Mrs. Jackson came in with a tray of milk and cookies for Sarah and coffee for Blake.

"I like coffee," Sarah said. "My mommy let me drink it when she had hers in bed and she wasn't awake good."

"I'll bet," Blake said, "but you aren't drinking it here. Coffee isn't good for kids."

"I can have coffee if I want to," Sarah returned belligerently.

Blake looked at Mrs. Jackson, who was more or less frozen in place, staring at the little girl as she grabbed four cookies and proceeded to stuff them into her mouth as if she hadn't eaten in days.

"You quit, or even try to quit," Blake told the housekeeper, who'd looked after his uncle before him, "and so help me God, I'll track you all the way to Alaska and drag you back here by one foot."

"Me, quit? Just when things are getting interesting?" Mrs. Jackson lifted her chin. "God forbid."

"Sarah, when was the last time you ate?" Blake inquired, watching her grab another handful of cookies.

"I had supper," she said, "and then we came here."

"You haven't had breakfast?" he burst out. "Or lunch?"

She shook her head. "These cookies are good!"

"If you haven't eaten for almost a day, I imagine

so." He sighed. "You'd better make us an early dinner tonight," Blake told Mrs. Jackson. "She'll eat herself sick on cookies if we're not careful."

"Yes, sir. I'll go and make up the guest room for her," she said. "But what about clothes? Does she have a suitcase?"

"No, that lawyer didn't bring anything. Let her sleep in her slip tonight. Tomorrow," he added, "you can take her into town to do some shopping."

"Me?" Mrs. Jackson looked horrified.

"Somebody has to be sacrificed," he told her pithily. "And I'm the boss."

Mrs. Jackson's lips formed a thin line. "I don't know beans about little girls' clothes!"

"Well, take her to Mrs. Donaldson's shop," he muttered. "That's where King Roper and Elissa take their little girl to be outfitted. I heard King groan about the prices, but that won't bother us any more than it bothers them."

"Yes, sir." She turned to leave.

"By the way, where's the weekly paper?" he asked, because it always came on Thursday morning. "I wanted to see if our legal ad got in."

Mrs. Jackson shifted uncomfortably and grimaced. "Well, I didn't want to upset you..."

His eyebrows arched. "How could the weekly paper possibly upset me? Get it!"

"All right. If you're sure that's what you want." She reached into the drawer of one of the end tables and pulled it out. "There you go, boss. And I'll leave before the explosion, if you don't mind."

She exited, and Sarah took two more cookies while Blake stared down at the paper's front page at a face that had haunted him.

"Author Meredith Calhoun to autograph at Baker's Book Nook," read the headline, and underneath it was a recent picture of Meredith.

His eyes searched over it in shock. The plain, skinny woman he'd hurt bore no resemblance to this peacock. Her brown hair was pulled back from her face into an elegant chignon. Her gray eyes were serene in a high-cheekboned face that could have graced the cover of a magazine, and her makeup enhanced the raw material that had always been there. She was wearing a pale suit coat with a pastel blouse, and she looked lovely. More than lovely. She looked soft and warm and totally untouched at the age of twenty-five, which she had to be now.

Blake put the paper down after scanning what he already knew about her skyrocketing career and her latest book, *Choices*, about a man and a woman trying to manage careers, marriage and parenthood all at once. He'd read it, as he secretly read all Meredith's books, looking for traces of the past. Maybe even for a cessation of hostilities. But her feelings for him were buried and there was never a single trait he could recognize in her people that reminded him of himself. It was as if she sensed that he might look at them and had hidden anything that would give her inner feelings away.

Sarah Jane was standing beside him without his knowing it. She looked at the picture in the paper. "That's a pretty lady," Sarah said. She leaned forward and picked out a word in the column below the photograph. "*B…o…o…k* Book," she said proudly.

"So it is." He pointed to the name. "How about that?"

"*M…e…r*…Merry Christmas," she said.

He smiled faintly. "Meredith," he corrected. "That's her name. She's a writer."

"I had a book about the three bears," Sarah told him. "Did she write that?"

"No. She writes books for big girls. Finish your cookies and you can watch television."

"I like to watch *Mr. Rogers* and *Sesame Street*," she said.

He frowned. "What?"

"They come on television."

"Oh. Well, help yourself."

He moved out of the room, ignoring the coffee. Which was sad, because Sarah Jane discovered it in the big silver pot and proceeded to help herself to the now cool liquid while he was on the telephone in the hall. Her cry caused him to drop the receiver in mid-sentence.

She was drenched in coffee and screaming her head off. She wasn't the only wet thing, either. The carpet and part of the sofa were saturated and the tray was an inch deep with black liquid.

"I told you to stay out of the coffee, didn't I?" Blake said as he knelt to see if she had been burned. Which, thank God, she hadn't; she was more frightened than hurt.

"I wanted some," she murmured tearfully. "I ruined my pretty dress."

"That isn't all that's going to get ruined, either," he said ominously, and abruptly tugged her over his knee and gave her bottom a slap. "When I say no, I mean no. Do you understand me, Sarah Jane Donavan?" he asked firmly.

She was too surprised to cry anymore. She stared at him warily. "Is that my name now?"

"It's always been your name," he replied. "You're a Donavan. This is your home."

"I like coffee," she said hesitantly.

"And I said you weren't to drink it," he reminded her.

She took a deep breath. "Okay." She picked up the coffeepot, only to have it taken from her and put on the table. "I can clean it up," she said. "Mommy always made me clean up my mess."

"This is more than you can cope with, sprout. And God only knows what we're going to put on you while those things are washed."

Mrs. Jackson came in and put both hands to her mouth. "Saints alive!"

"Towels, quick," Blake said.

She went to get them, muttering all the way.

Minutes later the mess was gone, Sarah Jane was bundled up in a makeshift towel dress and her clothes were being washed and dried. Blake went into his study and locked the door, shamelessly leaving Mrs. Jackson to cope with Sarah while he had a few minutes' peace. He had a feeling that it was going to be more and more difficult to find any quiet place in his life from now on.

He wasn't sure he was going to like being a father. It was a whole new kind of responsibility, and his daughter seemed to have inherited his strength of will and stubbornness. She was going to be a handful. Mrs. Jackson knew no more about kids than he did, and that wasn't going to help, either. But he didn't feel right about sending Sarah off to a boarding school. He knew what it was like to be alone and unwanted and not too physically appealing. He felt a kind of kinship with this child, and he was reluctant to push her out of his life. On the other hand, how in hell was he going to live with her?

But over and above that problem was the newest one. Meredith Calhoun was coming to Jack's Corner for a whole month, according to that newspaper. In that length of time he was sure to see her, and he had mixed feelings about opening up the old wounds. He wondered if she felt the same way, or if, in her fame and wealth, she'd left the memories of him in the past. He wanted to see her all the same. Even if she still hated him.

Chapter 2

Blake and Mrs. Jackson usually ate their evening meal with a minimum of conversation. But that was another old custom that was going to change.

Sarah Jane was a walking encyclopedia of questions. One answer led to another why and another, until Blake was ready to get under the table. And just the mention of bedtime brought on a tantrum. Mrs. Jackson tried to cajole the child into obeying, but Sarah Jane only got louder. Blake settled the matter by picking her up and carrying her to her new room.

Mrs. Jackson helped her undress and get into bed and Blake paused at her bedside reluctantly to say goodnight.

"You don't like me," Sarah accused.

He almost bristled at her mutinous expression, but she was a proud child, and he didn't want to break her spirit. She'd need it as she grew older.

"I don't know you," he replied reasonably. "Any more than you know me. People don't become friends on the spur of the moment. It takes time, sprout."

She considered that as she lay there, swallowed whole by the size of the bed under her and the thick white coverlet over her. She watched him curiously. "You don't hate little children, do you?" she asked finally.

"I don't hate kids," he said. "I'm just not used to them. I've been by myself for a long time."

"Did you love my mommy?"

That question was harder to answer. His broad shoulders rose and fell. "I thought she was beautiful. I wanted to marry her."

"She didn't like me," Sarah confided. "Can I really stay here? And I don't have to go back to Daddy Brad?"

"No, you don't have to go back. We'll have to do some adjusting, Sarah, but we'll get used to each other."

"I'm scared with the light off," she confessed.

"We'll leave a night-light on."

"What if a monster comes?" she asked.

"I'll kill it, of course," he reassured her with a smile.

She shifted under the covers. "Aren't you scared of monsters?"

"Nope."

She smiled for the first time. "Okay." She stared at him for a minute. "You have a scar on your face," she said, pointing to his right cheek.

His fingers touched it absently. "So I do." He'd long ago given up being sensitive about it, but he didn't like going into the way he'd gotten it. "Good night, sprout."

He didn't offer to read her a story or tell her one. In fact, he didn't know any he could tell a child. And he didn't tuck her in or kiss her. That would have been awkward. But Sarah didn't ask for those things or seem to need them. Perhaps she hadn't had much affection. She acted very much like a child who'd been turned loose and not bothered with overmuch.

He went back downstairs and into his study, to finish the day's business that had been put on hold while he'd coped with Sarah's arrival. Tomorrow Mrs. Jackson would have to handle things. He couldn't steal time from a board meeting for one small child.

Jack's Corner was a medium-sized Oklahoma city, and Blake's office was in a new mall complex that was both modern and spacious. The next day, he and his board were just finalizing the financing for an upcoming project, when his secretary came in, flustered and apprehensive.

"Mr. Donavan, it's your housekeeper on the phone. Could you speak with her, please?"

"I told you not to interrupt me unless it was urgent, Daisy," he told the young blond woman curtly.

She hesitated nervously. "Please, sir?"

He got up and excused himself, striding angrily out into the waiting room to pick up the phone with a hard glare at Daisy.

"Okay, Amie, what's wrong?" he asked shortly.

"I quit."

"Oh, my God, not yet," he shot back. "Not until she starts dating, at least!"

"I can't wait that long, and I want my check today," Mrs. Jackson snorted.

"Why?"

She held out the receiver. "Do you hear that?"

He did. Sarah Jane was screaming her head off.

"Where are you?" he asked with cold patience.

"Meg Donaldson's dress shop downtown," she replied. "This has been going on for five minutes. I wouldn't let her buy the dress she wanted and I can't make her stop."

"Smack her on the bottom," Blake said.

"Hit her in public?" She sounded as if he'd asked her to tie the child to a moving vehicle by her hair. "I won't!"

He said something under his breath. "All right, I'm on my way."

He hung up. "Tell the board to go ahead without me," he told Daisy shortly, grabbing his hat off the hat rack. "I have to go administrate a small problem."

"When will you be back, sir?" Daisy asked.

"God knows."

He closed the door behind him with a jerk, mentally consigning fatherhood and sissy housekeepers to the netherworld.

It took him ten minutes to get to the small children's boutique in town, and as luck would have it, there was one empty space in front that he could slide the Mercedes into. Next to his car was a sporty red Porsche with the top down. He paused for a moment to admire it and wonder about the owner.

"Oh, thank God." Mrs. Jackson almost fell on him when he walked into the shop. "Make her stop."

Sarah was lying on the floor, her face red and tear stained, her hair damp with sweat, her old dress rumpled from her exertions. She looked up at Blake and the tantrum died abruptly. "She won't buy me the frilly one," she moaned, pouting with a demure femininity.

My God, Blake thought absently, they learn how to do it almost before they can walk.

"Why won't you buy her the frilly one?" he asked an

astonished Mrs. Jackson, the words slipping out before he could stop them, while Meg Donaldson smothered a smile behind her cupped hands at the counter.

Mrs. Jackson looked taken aback. She cleared her throat. "Well, it's expensive."

"I'm rich," he pointed out.

"Yes, but it's not suitable for playing in the backyard. She needs some jeans and tops and underthings."

"I need a dress to wear to parties," Sarah sobbed. "I never got to go to a party, but you can have one for me, and I can make friends."

He reached down and lifted her to her feet, then knelt in front of her. "I don't like tantrums," he said. "Next time Mrs. Jackson will spank you. In public," he added, glaring at the stoic housekeeper.

She turned beet red, and Mrs. Donaldson bent down beside the counter as if she were going to look for something and burst out laughing.

While Mrs. Jackson was searching for words, the shop door opened and two women came in. Elissa Roper was immediately recognizable. She was married to King Roper, a friend of Blake's.

"Blake!" Elissa smiled. "We haven't seen you lately. What are you and Mrs. Jackson doing in here? And who's this?"

"This is my daughter, Sarah Jane," Blake said, introducing the child. "We've just been having a tantrum."

"Speak for yourself," Mrs. Jackson sniffed. "I don't have tantrums. I just resign from jobs that have gotten too big for me."

"You're resigning, Mrs. Jackson? That would be one for the books, wouldn't it?" a soft, amused voice asked, and Blake's heart jumped.

He got slowly to his feet, oblivious to Sarah's curious stare, to come face to face with a memory.

Meredith Calhoun looked back at him with gray eyes that gave away nothing except faint humor. She was wearing a blue dress with a white jacket, and she looked expensive and sophisticated and lovely. Her figure had filled out over the years, and she was tall and exquisite, with full, high breasts and a narrow waist flaring to hips that were in exact proportion for her body. She had long legs encased in silk hose, and elegant feet in white sandals. And the sight of her made Blake ache in the most inconvenient way.

"Merry!" Mrs. Jackson enthused, and hugged her. "It's been so long!"

And it had been since Mrs. Jackson had made cake and cookies for her while she visited Blake's uncle, who was also her godfather.

She and the housekeeper had grown close. "Long enough, I guess, Amie," Meredith said as they stepped apart. "You haven't aged a day."

"You have," Mrs. Jackson said with a smile. "You're grown up."

"And famous," Elissa put in. "Bess—you remember my sister-in-law—and Meredith were in the same class at school and are still great friends. She's staying with Bess and Bobby."

"They've just bought the house next door to me," Blake replied, for something to say. He couldn't find the words to express what he felt when he looked at Meredith. So many years, so much pain. But whatever she'd felt for him was gone. That fact registered immediately.

"Has Nina come back with your daughter?" Elissa asked, trying not to appear poleaxed, which she was.

"Nina died earlier this year. Sarah Jane is living with

me now." He dragged his eyes away from Meredith to turn his attention to his child. "You look terrible. Go to the rest room and wash your face."

"You come, too," Sarah said mutinously.

"No."

"I won't go!"

"I'll take her," Mrs. Jackson said in her best martyred tone.

"No! You won't let me buy the frilly dress!" Sarah turned her attention to the two curious onlookers. "She's in the paper," she said, her eyes on Meredith. "She writes books. My daddy said so."

Meredith managed not to look at Blake. The unexpected sight of him after so much time was enough to knock her speechless. Thank God she'd learned to mask her emotions and hadn't given herself away. The last thing she wanted to do was let Blake Donavan see that she had any vulnerability left.

Sarah walked over to Meredith, staring up at her with rapt fascination. "Can you tell stories?"

"Oh, I guess I can," she said, smiling at the child who was so much like Blake. "You've got red eyes, Sarah. You shouldn't cry."

"I want the frilly dress and a party and other little children to play with. It's very lonely, and they don't like me." She indicated Blake and Mrs. Jackson.

"One day, and she's advertising to the world that we're Jekyll and Hyde." Mrs. Jackson threw up her hands.

"Which one are you?" Blake returned, glaring at her.

"Jckyll, of course. I'm prettier than you are," Mrs. Jackson shot back.

"Just like old times," Elissa said with a sigh, "isn't it, Merry?"

Meredith wasn't listening. Sarah Jane had reached up and taken her hand.

"You can come with me," the little girl told Meredith. "I like her," she said to her father belligerently. "She smiles. I'll let her wash my face."

"Do you mind?" Blake asked Meredith, speaking to her for the first time since she'd entered the shop.

"I don't mind." She didn't look at him fully, then turned and let Sarah lead her into the small bathroom in the back of the shop.

"She's changed," Mrs. Jackson said to Mrs. Donaldson. "I hardly knew her."

"It's been a long time, you know. And she's a famous woman now, not the child who left us."

Blake walked away uncomfortably, staring at the dresses. Elissa moved closer to him while the other two women talked. She'd been a little afraid of Blake when she'd first met him years ago, but she'd gotten to know him better. He and King were friends and visited regularly.

"How long has Sarah been with you?" she asked him.

"Since yesterday afternoon," he replied dryly. "It seems like years. I guess I'll get used to her, but it's hard going right now. She's a handful."

"She's just frightened and alone," Elissa replied. "She'll improve when she has time to settle down and adjust."

"I may be bankrupt by then," he mused. "I had to walk out of a board meeting. And all because Sarah Jane wanted a frilly dress."

"Why don't you buy it for her and she can come to my Danielle's birthday party next week? It will be nice for her to meet children her own age."

"She'll sit on the cake and wreck the house," he groaned.

"No, she won't. She's just a little girl."

"She wrecked my living room in just under ten minutes," he assured her.

"It takes mine five minutes to do that." Elissa grinned. "It's normal."

He stared toward the bathroom. Meredith and Sarah Jane were just coming out. "There are people in the world who have more than one," he murmured. "Do you suppose they're sane?"

Elissa laughed. "Yes. You'll understand it all one day."

"Look what Merry gave me!" Sarah enthused, showing Blake a snowy white handkerchief. "And it's all mine! It has lace!"

Blake shook his head as she turned abruptly and grabbed the dress she'd been screaming about. "It's mine. I want it. Oh, please." She changed tactics, staring up pie eyed at her daddy. "It will go so nicely with my new handkerchief."

Blake laughed and then caught himself. He looked at Mrs. Jackson. "What do you think?"

"I think that if you buy Sarah Jane that dress I'm going to put it on you," the older woman replied in a hunted tone.

"You really shouldn't give in because children have tantrums, Blake," Mrs. Donaldson volunteered. "I know. I raised four."

He stared at Mrs. Jackson. "You started this. Why would you tell her she couldn't have the damned thing in the first place?"

"I told you, it was too expensive for her to play in."

"She'll need a dress to come to Danielle's party," Elissa broke in.

"Now see what you've done," Blake growled at Mrs. Jackson.

"I won't take her shopping ever again. You can just let somebody else run your company and do it yourself," Mrs. Jackson grumbled.

"I don't know what to think of a woman who can't manage to buy a dress for one small child."

"That isn't just one small child, that's one small Donavan, and nobody could say she isn't your daughter!" Mrs. Jackson said.

Blake felt an unexpected surge of pleasure at the words. He looked down at the child who looked so much like him and had to agree that she did have some of his better qualities. Stubborn determination. Not to mention good taste.

"You can have the dress, Sarah," he told her, and was rewarded by a smile so delightful he'd have sold his Mercedes to buy the damned thing for her no matter what it cost.

"Oh, thank you!" Sarah gushed.

"You'll be sorry," Mrs. Jackson said.

"You can shut up," he told her. "It's your fault."

"You said to take her shopping, you didn't say what to buy," she reminded him huffily. "And I'm going home."

"Then go on. And don't burn lunch," he called after her.

"I couldn't burn a bologna sandwich if I tried, and that's all you'll get from me today!"

"I'll fire you!"

"Thank God!"

Blake glared at Mrs. Donaldson and Elissa, who

were trying not to smile. This byplay between Blake and Mrs. Jackson was old hat to them, and they found it amusing. Meredith's expression was less revealing. She was looking at Sarah and Blake wished he could see her eyes.

But she turned away. "We'd better get on," she told Elissa. "Bess will be waiting for us to pick her up at the beauty parlor."

"Okay," Elissa grinned. "Just let me get those socks for Danielle and I'll be ready."

She did, which left Meredith stranded with Blake and his daughter.

"Isn't it pretty?" Sarah sighed, pirouetting with the dress held in front of her. "I look like a fairy princess."

"Not quite," Blake said. "You'll need shoes, and some clothes to play in, too."

"Okay." She ran to the other racks and started looking through them.

"Is it normal for them to be so clothes conscious at this age?" Blake asked, turning his attention to Meredith.

"I don't know," she said uncomfortably. His unblinking green-eyed gaze was making her remember too much pain. "I haven't been around children very much. I must go…."

He touched her arm, and was astonished to find that she jerked away from his touch and stared fully at him with eyes that burned with resentment and pain and anger.

"So, you haven't forgotten," he said under his breath.

"Did you really think I ever would?" she asked on a shaky laugh. "You were the reason I never came back here. I almost didn't come this time, either, but I was tired of hiding."

He didn't know what to say. Her reaction was un-expected. He'd imagined that she might have some bitterness, but not this much. He searched what he could see of her face, looking for something he knew he wasn't going to find anymore.

"You've changed," he said quietly.

Her eyes looked up into his, and there was a flash of cold anger there. "Oh, yes, I've changed. I've grown up. That should reassure you. I won't be chasing after you like a lovesick puppy this time."

The reference stung, and she'd meant it to. He'd accused her of chasing him and more, after the reading of the will.

But being reminded of the past only made him bitter, and he hit back. "Thank God," he said with a mocking smile. "Could I have that in writing?"

"Go to hell," she said under her breath.

That, coming from shy little Meredith, floored him. He didn't even have a comeback.

Sarah came running up with an armload of things. "Look, aren't they pretty! Can I have them all?" she asked the scowling man beside Meredith.

"Sure," he said absently.

Meredith turned away from him, smiling. It was the first time in memory that she'd ever fought back—or for that matter, said anything to him that wasn't respectful and worshipful. What a delightful surprise to find he no longer intimidated her.

"Ready to go?" Meredith asked Elissa.

"Sure am. See you, Blake!"

"But you can't go." Sarah ran to Meredith and caught her skirt. "You're my friend."

The child couldn't know how that hurt—to have Blake's child, the child she might have borne him, cling to her. She knelt in front of Sarah, disengaging the small hand. "I have to go now. But I'll see you again, Sarah. Okay?"

Sarah looked lost. "You're nice. Nobody else smiles at me."

"Mrs. Jackson will smile at you tonight, I promise," Blake told the child. "Or she'll never smile again," he added under his breath.

"You don't smile," Sarah accused him.

"My face would break," he assured her. "Now get your things and we'll go home."

She sighed. "Okay." She looked up at Meredith. "Will you come to see me?"

Meredith went white. Go into that house again, where Blake had humiliated and hurt her? God forbid!

"You can come to see Danielle, Sarah," Elissa interrupted, and Meredith knew then that Elissa had heard the whole story from King. She was running interference, bless her.

"Who's Dan—Danielle?" Sarah asked.

"My daughter. She's four."

"I'm almost four," Sarah said. "Can she say nursery rhymes? I know all of them. 'Humpty Dumpty sat on the wall, Humpty Dumpty—'"

"I'll give your Daddy a call and he can bring you down to Bess's house, where Meredith is staying. Bess is my sister-in-law, and Danielle and I go to see her sometimes."

"I'd like to have a friend," Sarah agreed. "Could we do that?" she asked her father.

Blake was watching Meredith shift uncomfortably. "Sure we can," he said, just to irritate her.

Meredith turned away, her heart going like an overwound watch, her eyes restless and frightened. The very last thing she wanted was to have to cope with Blake.

"Bye, Merry!" Sarah called.

"Goodbye, Sarah Jane," she murmured, and forced a smile, but she wouldn't look at Blake.

He said the appropriate things as Elissa followed Meredith out the door, but the fact that Meredith wouldn't look at him cut like a knife.

He watched Meredith climb in under the wheel of the red Porsche. It didn't seem like the kind of car she'd drive, but she wasn't the girl she'd been. His eyes narrowed. He wondered if she was still as innocent as before, or if some man had taught her all the sweet ways to make love. His face hardened at the thought. No one had touched her until he had. But he'd been rough and he'd frightened her. He hadn't really meant to. The feel and taste of her had knocked him off balance, and at the time he hadn't been experienced himself. Nina had been his first woman, but his first real intimacy, even if it had been relatively chaste, had been with Meredith. Even after all the years in between, he could feel her mouth, taste its sweetness. He could see the soft alabaster of her breasts when he'd unbuttoned the top of her dress. He groaned silently. That was when he'd lost his senses—seeing her like that. He wondered if she knew how green he'd been in those days, and decided that she was too inexperienced herself to realize it. He'd wanted Meredith to the point of madness, and things had just gotten out of hand. But to a shy young virgin, his ardor must have seemed frightening.

He turned back to his daughter with memories of the past darkening his eyes. It seemed so long ago that the rain had found him in the stable and Meredith had come in looking for his uncle....

Chapter 3

It had been late spring that day five years ago, and Blake had been helping one of the men doctor a sick horse in the stable. Meredith had come along just in time to see the second man leave. Blake was still there. She'd come to ask where his uncle was, but it was a rainy day, and she and Blake had been caught in the barn while it stormed outside.

Blake had hungrily watched Meredith as she stood on her tiptoes to look toward the house. She was wearing a white sundress that buttoned up the front, and as she stretched, every line of her body had been emphasized and her dress had ridden up, displaying most of her long legs.

The sight of those slim, elegant legs and the sensuous curve of her body had caught him in the stomach like a body blow, and he'd stood there staring. It shouldn't have affected him. He had Nina, who was blond and beautiful and who loved him. Meredith was plain and shy and not at all the kind of woman who could attract him. But as he'd looked at her, his body had quickened and the shock of it had moved him helplessly toward where she stood in the wide doorway, just out of the path of the rain.

Meredith had heard him, or perhaps sensed him, because she turned, her eyes faintly covetous before she lowered them. "It's really coming down, isn't it?" she asked hesitantly. "I was just about to go home, but I needed to ask your Uncle Dan some more questions."

"You're always around these days," he'd remarked, half-angry because his body was playing cruel tricks on him.

She'd blushed. "He's helping me with some articles for the school paper, and I'm going to do a book with the same information," she'd begun.

"Book!" He scoffed at that. "You're barely twenty. What makes you think you've learned enough to write books? You haven't even started to live."

Her head came up and there had been a flash of anger in her pale gray eyes, which was instantly disguised. "You make me sound like a toddler."

"You look like one occasionally," he remarked with faint humor, noting the braid of her hair, which she'd tied with a ribbon. "And I'm almost twelve years older than you are." He pushed away from the barn door, noticing the faint hunger in her face as he went toward her.

The hunger was what touched him. It hadn't occurred to him that women besides Nina might find him physically attractive. He had that damned scar down one cheek, thanks to Meredith, and it made him look like a renegade. His arrogance didn't soften the impression.

He looked down his nose at Meredith when he was less than a foot from her, watching the expressions play across her face. It was a pretty good bet that she was innocent, and if she'd been kissed, probably it hadn't been often or seriously. That, at least, made him feel confident. She didn't have anyone to compare him with.

His eyes went to her soft bow of a mouth, and with an impulse he didn't even understand at the time, he tilted her chin up with a lean hand and bent to brush his lips over hers.

"Blake…!" she gasped.

He hadn't known if it was fear or shock…hadn't cared. The first contact with her mouth had caused a frightening surge of desire in his lean body. "Don't back away now," he bit off against her soft lips. "Come here."

He'd pulled her against him and his mouth had grown rough and hungry. Even now, five years later, he could feel the soft yielding of her body in his arms, smell the scent of her as she strained upward and gave him her mouth with such warm eagerness. He could hear the rain beating on the stable roof, and the soft sounds of a cow settling down in the darkness beyond where they stood silhouetted against the driving rain.

Blake had been amazed by the tentative response he got from her lips. That shy nibbling drove him over the edge. He eased her back against the wall of the barn, out of sight, with his mouth still covering hers. Then he let his body slide down against her so that his hips were pressing feverishly against hers, his chest crushing her soft young breasts.

He felt her quickened breathing, heard the soft "no!" as he felt for and found one firm breast and touched it through her clothing. The feel of her made him wild. He remembered the white-hot flames that had consumed him with the intimate touch. He'd wanted her with a shuddering passion and his mouth had grown more and more demanding. She gave in to him all at once, her body relaxing, shivering, her mouth shyly responding. His tongue pushed gently inside her lips and she stiffened, but she didn't try to pull away.

Confident now, his fingers worked at buttons and he lifted his head just fractionally to look down at what they uncovered. Her breasts were bare under the dress and he groaned as he bent to brush his mouth against them. He felt her gasp and her hands gripped his arms hard. The silky taste of her body stripped him of control entirely, the feel of her skin against his face made him wild. His hands grew roughly intimate in passion and his mouth closed hungrily over one firm breast.

What might have happened then was anyone's guess. He hardly heard Meredith's frantic voice. It wasn't until he caught the sound of a car driving up that his sanity returned.

He lifted his head, breathing fiercely, in time to see Meredith's eyes full of fear. He realized belatedly what he'd done. He took a sharp breath and levered himself back up, away from her, his body in torment with unsatisfied desire, his eyes smoldering as they met hers.

She blushed furiously as she fumbled buttons into buttonholes, making herself decent again. And only then did he realize how intimate the embrace had gotten. He didn't know what had possessed him. He'd frightened her and himself, because it was the first time he'd ever lost control like that. But, then, he hadn't been experienced, he realized now. Not until he and Nina were married. His first taste of sensual pleasure had been with Meredith that day in the stable.

He didn't speak—he was too shocked. The sudden arrival of his uncle had been a godsend at the time, but later it dawned on him that his uncle had guessed what had happened between Blake and Meredith and had altered his will to capitalize on it. His favorite godchild and his nephew—he would have considered them a perfect match. But Blake hadn't thought of it at the time. He'd been so drunk on Meredith's soft mouth that he'd almost gone after her when she mumbled some excuse and ran out into the rain as he and his uncle watched her.

Then, within days, his uncle was dead of a heart attack. Blake had been crushed. The sense of loneliness he felt when it happened was almost too great for words. Meredith had been around, with her parents, but he'd hardly noticed with Nina clinging to him, pretending sympathy. And then, suddenly they were reading the will. Blake was engaged to Nina, but still trying to cope with the turbulent emotions Meredith had aroused in him. The will was read, and he learned that Uncle Dan had left twenty percent of the stock in his real estate companies to Meredith. The only way Blake could have it would be by marrying her.

He had forty-nine percent of the stock, but his cousins had thirty-one shares between them. And although one of the cousins down in Texas would have sided with him in a proxy fight if Meredith sided against him, he could lose everything. Nina had laughed. He still remembered the look on her face as she scrutinized Meredith in a manner too contemptuous for words.

Blake had done much worse. The realization that his uncle had tried to control his life even from the grave and the embarrassment of having his haughty cousins snicker at him was just too much.

"Marry her?" he'd said slowly after the will had been read, rising out of his chair to confront Meredith in the dead silence that followed. "My God, marry that plain, dull, shadow of a woman? I'd rather lose the real estate companies, the money and my left leg than marry her!" He'd moved closer to Meredith, watching her cringe and go pale at the humiliation of having him say those things so loudly in front of the family. "No dice, Meredith," he said with venom. "Take the stock and go to hell with it. I don't want you!"

He'd expected her to burst into tears and run out of the room, but she hadn't. Deathly pale, shaking so hard she could barely stand, she lowered her eyes, turned away and walked out with dignity far beyond her twenty years. It had shamed him later to remember her stiff pride and his own loss of control that had prompted the outburst. The cousin from Texas had glared at him with black eyes and walked out without another word, leaving him alone with Nina and the other cousins, who subsequently filed suit to take control of the real estate companies from him.

But Nina had smiled and clung to him and promised heaven, because she was sure he'd get the stock back somehow. She'd advised him to talk to the lawyer.

He had. But the only way to get the stock back, apparently, was to marry Meredith or break the will. Both were equally impossible.

He was still smoldering when he found Meredith coming out the back door. She'd been in the kitchen saying goodbye to Mrs. Jackson.

She was pale and unusually quiet, and she looked as if she didn't want to stop. But he'd gotten in front of her in the deserted, shaded backyard and refused to let her pass.

"I don't want the shares," she said, without looking at him. "I never did. I knew nothing about what your uncle had planned, and I wouldn't have gone through with it if I had."

"Wouldn't you?" he demanded coldly. "Maybe you saw a chance to marry a rich man. Your family is poor."

"There are worse things than being poor," she replied quietly. "And people who marry for money earn it, as you'll find out one day."

"I will?" He caught her arms roughly. "What do you mean?"

"I mean that Nina wants what you have, not what you are," she replied with a sad smile.

"Nina loves me," he said.

"No."

"What does it matter to you, anyway?" he growled. "I haven't been able to turn around without running into you for the past two months. You're always here, getting in the way! What's the matter, did you decide that one kiss wasn't enough, and you're hot for more?"

In fact, it had been the other way around. He'd wanted her so desperately that his mind had gone into hiding, behind the anger he used to disguise the hunger that was driving him mad.

He pulled her into his arms, angry at life and circumstances, ignoring her faint struggles. "God forbid that you should go away with nothing," he added. And he kissed her with all his fury and frustration in his lips. He accused her of chasing him, of wanting his uncle's money. And then he turned around and walked off, leaving her in tears.

His eyes closed as he came back to the present, hating the memory, hating his cruelty. He'd been a different man then, a colder, less feeling man. It had irritated him that Meredith disturbed him physically, that he could be aroused by the sound of her voice, by the sight of her.

Because of what he thought he felt for Nina, he'd pushed his growing attraction to Meredith out of his mind. Nina loved him and Meredith just wanted what he had—or so he'd been sure at the time. Now he knew better, and it was too late.

Those few minutes he'd made love to Meredith in the stable that long-ago afternoon had been the sweetest and saddest of his entire life. He'd been cruel after the will was read because he'd felt betrayed by his uncle and by her. But he'd also been sad, because he wanted Meredith far more than Nina. He'd given his word to Nina that he was going to marry her, and honor made him stick to it. So he'd forced Meredith to run away to remove the temptation from his path. He'd known deep inside that he couldn't have resisted Meredith much longer. And he had no right to her.

It struck him as odd that he'd lost control with Meredith. He'd never lost it with Nina, although he'd had a lukewarm kind of feeling for her that had grown out of her adoration and teasing. But what he'd felt with Meredith had been fire and storm. The last time he'd seen her, he'd raged at her that she'd tempted him by following him around like a lovesick puppy, and that had been the last straw. She'd run then, all right, and she hadn't stopped. Not for five years. A week after she left, an attorney brought him the stock, legally signed over to him without a single request for money. Nina had been delighted, and she'd led him right to the altar. He'd been so cut up by his own conscience about what he'd done to Meredith that he hadn't protested, even though his yen for Nina had all but left him.

He went through the motions of making love to Nina, but it wasn't at all satisfying to him. And she always smiled at him so lovingly when they were in bed together.

Smiling. Until the day the court battle started, initiated by his cousins, and he was backed into a corner that Nina didn't think he'd get out of. So she left him and divorced him, and he'd had years to regret his own foolishness.

Meredith's attitude toward him in the shop hadn't really come as a surprise. He knew how badly he'd hurt her that day, frightened her. Probably she'd never had a lover or wanted one, because if appearances were anything to go by, he'd left some bad scars. He felt even guiltier about that. But it didn't seem as if he were going to get close enough to tell her the truth about what had happened—even if his pride would allow it.

And anyway, she'd made her feelings about the house clear. She wouldn't voluntarily set foot in it. He sighed heavily. Incredible, he thought, how a man could become his own worst enemy. Looking back, he knew his uncle had been right. If he'd married Meredith, she'd have loved him, and in time he might have been able to love her back. As things stood, that was something he'd never know.

Down the road at Bobby and Bess's house, Meredith Calhoun was halfheartedly watching a movie on Bess's VCR as she tried to come to grips with the unexpected confrontation with Blake.

She felt shaky inside. The sight of Blake, with his jet black hair, green eyes and arrogant, mocking smile, had twisted her heart. Over the years she'd tried to force herself to go out on dates, see other men. But it hadn't worked. She couldn't bear for any man to do more than kiss her, and even the kisses were bitter and unpleasant after Blake's. One part of her was afraid of Blake because of what he'd done to her, but another part remembered the first kiss in the stable, the sweet, slow hunger that had flared between them like summer lightning. And because of that kiss, no other man had ever been able to stir her.

Blake's daughter had come as the biggest surprise. Meredith hadn't known about the child. It seemed, from what Elissa said, that nobody had. Sarah Jane was a quirk of fate, and she wondered if Blake still loved Nina. If he did, Sarah Jane would be a comfort to him. But when he'd said that Nina was dead, it had been without a scrap of emotion in his face or his eyes. He didn't seem to care one way or another. That was strange, because he'd been so adamant about marrying Nina, so certain that she loved him.

Meredith got up, oblivious to the television, and began to wander restlessly around Bess's big living room. She stopped in front of the picture window. Beyond it, on a rise a few hundred yards away, was Blake's house. She sighed, remembering the happy times she'd had there before the will had been read. Blake had always seemed to resent her, but that day in the stable had been full of soft magic. Because of it, she'd actually expected something more from him than anger. She'd dreamed afterward that he'd left Nina and discovered that he loved Meredith and couldn't live without her. Dreams.

She laughed with a new cynicism. That would be the day, when Blake Donavan would feel anything but dislike for her. He hadn't been openly antagonistic today, but he'd verged on it just before she left the store. Sarah liked her and it was going to be difficult to keep the child at bay without hurting her. Meredith had a feeling that Sarah Jane's young life hadn't been a happy one. She didn't act like a contented child, and apparently she'd only been with Blake and Mrs. Jackson for a day or so. Meredith had wondered why, but hadn't dared ask Blake.

Sarah reminded her of herself at that age, a poor little kid from the wrong side of the tracks, with no brothers or sisters and parents who worked themselves into early graves trying to make a living with the sweat of their brows. Bess had been her only friend, and Bess had it even worse than she did at home. The two of them had become close as children and remained close as adults. So when Bess had invited Meredith, with Bobby's blessing, to come and stay for a few weeks, she'd welcomed the rest from work and routine.

She hadn't consciously considered that Blake was going to be a very big part of her visit. She'd actually thought she could come to Jack's Corner without having to see him at all. Which was silly. King and Elissa and Bess and Bobby all knew him, and Blake and King were best friends. She wondered if maybe she'd rationalized things because of Blake, because she'd wanted to see him again, to see if her fears had been real or just manifestations of unrequited love and sorrow. She wanted to see if looking at him could still make her knees go weak and her heart run away.

Well, now she knew. It could. And if she had any sense of self-preservation, she was going to have to keep some distance from him. She couldn't risk letting Blake get close to her heart a second time. Once had been enough—more than enough. She'd just avoid him, she told herself, and everything would be all right.

But avoiding him turned out to be a forlorn hope, because Sarah Jane liked Meredith and contrived to get her father to call Elissa about that visit she'd mentioned.

Blake listened to the request with mixed feelings. Sarah Jane was beginning to settle down a little, although she was still belligerent and not an overly joyful addition to the household. Mrs. Jackson was coping well enough, but she'd vanish the minute Blake came home from work, leaving him to try and talk to his sullen young daughter. He knew that the situation needed a woman's touch, but Mrs. Jackson wasn't the woman. Meredith already liked Sarah, and Sarah was drawn to her. If he could get Meredith to befriend the child, it would make his life easier. But in another way, he was uncertain about trying to force himself and Sarah on Meredith. After having seen how frightened she still was of him, how bitter she was about the past, he might open old wounds and rub salt in them. He didn't want to hurt Meredith, but Sarah Jane was driving him nuts, and he needed help.

"You have to call 'lissa," Sarah Jane said firmly, her mutinous mouth pouting up at him. "She promised I could play with her little girl. I want to see Mer'dith, too. She likes me." She glared at him, her eyes so like his only in her youthful face. "You don't like me."

"I explained that to you," he said with exaggerated patience as he perched on the corner of his desk. "We don't know each other."

"You don't ever come home," she said, sighing. "And Mrs. Jackson doesn't like me, either."

"She's not used to children, Sarah, any more than I am." A corner of his mouth twisted. "Look, sprout, I'll try to spend more time with you. But you've got to understand that I'm a busy man. A lot of people depend on me."

"Can't you call 'lissa?" she persisted. "Please?" she added. "Please?"

He found himself picking up the telephone. Sarah had a knack for getting under his skin. He was beginning to get used to the sound of her voice, the running footsteps in the morning, the sound of cartoons and children's programs coming from the living room. Maybe in time he and Sarah would get along better. They were still in the squaring off and glaring stages right now, and she was every bit as stubborn as he was.

He talked to Elissa, who was delighted to comply with Sarah's request. She promised to set things up for the following morning because it was Saturday and Blake could bring Sarah down to Bess's house. But first she wanted to check with Bess and make sure it was all right.

Blake and Sarah both waited for the phone to ring. Blake wondered how Meredith was going to feel about it, but apparently she didn't mind, because Elissa had called back within five minutes and said that Bess would be expecting the child about ten o'clock. Not only that, Sarah was invited to spend the day.

"I can spend the day?" Sarah asked, brightening.

"We'll see." Blake was noncommittal. "Why don't you find something to play with?"

Sarah shrugged. "I don't have any toys. I had a teddy bear, but he got lost and Daddy Brad wouldn't let me look for him before they brought me here."

His eyes narrowed. "Don't call him that again," he said gruffly. "He isn't your father. I am."

Sarah's eyes widened at his tone, and he felt uncomfortable for having said anything at all.

"Can I call you 'Daddy'?" Sarah asked after a long minute.

Blake's breath caught in his throat. He shifted. "I don't care," he said impassively. In fact, he did care. He cared like hell.

"Okay," she said, and went off to the kitchen to see if Mrs. Jackson had any more cookies.

Blake frowned, thinking about what she'd said about

toys. Surely a child of almost four still played with them. He'd have to ask Elissa. She'd know about toys and little girls.

The next morning, Sarah dressed herself in her new frilly dress and her shoes and went downstairs. Blake had to bite his lip to keep from howling. She had the dress on backward and unbuttoned. She had on frilly socks, but one was yellow and one was pink. Her hair was unruly, and the picture she made was of chaos, not femininity.

"Come here, sprout, and let's get the dress on properly," he said.

She glared at him. "It's all right."

"No, it's not." He stood. "Don't argue with me, kid. I'm twice your size."

"I don't have to mind you," she said.

"Yes, you do. Or else."

"Or else what?" she challenged.

He stared down at her. "Or else you'll stay home today."

She grimaced and stared down at the carpet. "Okay."

He helped her turn the dress around and cursed under his breath while he did up buttons that were hard for his big, lean hands to work. He finally got them fixed, then took her upstairs, where he searched until he found matching socks and then brushed her straight hair until it looked soft and shiny.

She turned before he finished, looking small and oddly vulnerable on the vanity stool, and her green eyes met his. "I never had any little children to play with. My mommy said I made her nervous."

He didn't say anything, but he could imagine Nina being uncomfortable around children.

"Can I stay here?" Sarah asked unexpectedly, and

there was a flash of real fear in her eyes. "You won't make me go away, will you?"

He had to bite down hard to keep back a harsh curse. "No, I won't make you go away," he said after a minute. "You're my daughter."

"You didn't want me when I was a baby," she accused mutinously.

"I didn't know about you," he said, sitting down and talking to her very seriously, as if she were already an adult. "I didn't know I had a little girl. Now I do. You're a Donavan, and this is your place in the world. Here, with me."

"And I can live here forever?"

"Until you grow up, anyway," he promised. His green eyes narrowed. "You aren't going to start crying or anything, are you?" he asked, because her eyes were glistening.

That snapped her out of it. She glared at him. "I never cry. I'm brave."

"I guess you've had to be, haven't you?" he murmured absently. He stood. "Well, if we're going, let's go. And you be on your best behavior. I'm going to tell Bess to swat you if you don't mind her."

"Mer'dith won't let her hit me," she said smugly. "She's my friend. Do you have any friends?"

"One or two," he said, holding her hand as they went down the long staircase.

"Do they come to play with you?" she asked seriously. "And could they play with me, too?"

He chuckled deep in his throat, trying to imagine King Roper sitting cross-legged on the living room carpet, dressing a doll.

"I don't think so," he replied. "They're grown-ups."

"Oh. Grown-ups are too big to play, I guess. I don't want to grow up. I wish I had a doll."

"What kind of doll?" he asked.

"A pretty one with long golden hair and pretty dresses. I could talk to her. And a teddy bear," she said sadly. "I want a teddy bear just like Mr. Friend. I miss Mr. Friend. He used to sleep with me. I'm ascared of the dark," she added.

"Yes, I know," he murmured, having had to help Mrs. Jackson get her to bed every night and chase out the monsters before she closed her eyes.

"Lots of monsters live in my room," she informed him. "You have to kill them every night, don't you?"

"So far, I'm ahead by one monster," he reassured her.

"You're awful big," she said, eyeing him with an unblinking scrutiny. "I bet you weigh one million pounds."

"Not quite."

"I'm ten feet tall," she said, going on tiptoe.

He led her out the door, calling goodbye to Mrs. Jackson. It seemed natural to hold her hand and smile at her chatter. There was magic in a child, even a hard case like this one. He wondered if security would soften her, and doubted it. She had spirit and inner strength. Those qualities pleased him. She'd need them if she lived with him.

Bess and Bobby's house was a split-level brick with exquisite landscaping and a small thicket of trees that separated their property from Blake's. In the driveway were Elissa's gray Lincoln, Meredith's red Porsche convertible and the blue Mercedes that Bess drove. Blake parked behind them on the long driveway and helped Sarah out.

She was at the front door before he reached it, excited as the door opened and a little blond girl about her age shyly greeted her.

"This is Danielle, Sarah. She's looked forward to meeting you," Elissa said with a smile. "Hi, Blake. Come on in."

He took off his gray Stetson and stood in the hall while Sarah went into the living room with Danielle, who'd brought a box of toys with her.

Sarah's eyes lit up like a Christmas tree, and she exclaimed over every single one of Danielle's things, as if she'd never seen toys before. She sat down on the carpet and handled each one gingerly, turning it over and examining it and telling Danielle how beautiful the dolls were.

"She doesn't have any toys," Blake told Elissa with a worried frown. "She seems so mature sometimes. I didn't realize…"

"Parenthood takes time," Elissa assured him. "Don't expect to learn everything at once."

"I don't think I've learned anything yet," he confessed. He frowned as he watched his daughter. "I expected her to push Danielle around and try to take her toys away. She isn't the easiest child to get along with."

"She's a frightened child," Elissa replied. "Underneath there are some sweet qualities. You see, she's playing very nicely, and she isn't causing trouble."

"Yet," Blake murmured, waiting for the explosion to come.

His head turned as Meredith came down the hall. She hesitated momentarily, then joined them.

"Bess is getting coffee," she said quietly. She was wearing a pale green sundress that slashed squarely over her high breasts, and her hair was loose, waving around her shoulders. She looked younger this way, and Blake almost sighed with memories.

"Will you stay and have a cup with us?" Elissa asked him.

"I guess so," he agreed. His eyes hadn't left Meredith.

She averted her gaze and started into the living room, too vulnerable to risk letting him see how easily he could get to her with that level, unblinking stare.

"Mer'dith!" Sarah jumped up, all eyes and laughing smile, and ran with her arms open to be picked up and hugged warmly. "Oh, Mer'dith, Daddy brought me to see Dani and he's going to get me another Mr. Friend and he says I can have a doll! Oh, he's just the nicest daddy…!"

Blake looked as if someone had poured ice into his shirt. He stared at the child blankly. She'd just called him 'Daddy' for the first time, and something stirred in the region of his heart, making him feel warm and needed. It was a new feeling, as if he weren't totally alone anymore.

"That's nice, darling," Meredith was telling the child. She let her down and knelt beside her, smiling as she pushed back Sarah's unruly hair. "You look very pretty this morning. I like your new dress."

"It's very pretty," Danielle agreed. She was dressed in slacks and a shirt for playing, but she didn't make fun of Sarah's dress. She was a quiet child and sweet natured.

"I put it on backward, but Daddy fixed it for me." She smiled at Meredith. "Can you stay and play with us? We can play with dolls."

"I wish I could," Meredith said, nervous because Blake was watching her so closely. She was frantic for a way out of the house, away from him. "But I have to go into town to the library and do some research."

"I thought this was supposed to be a holiday," Bess said as she came in with a tray of coffee and cake. "You're here to rest, not to work."

Meredith smiled at her lovely blond friend. "I know. But I'm not comfortable if I don't have something to do. I won't be long."

"I could drive you," Blake volunteered.

She blanched and started to refuse, but Elissa and Bess jumped in and teased and cajoled until they made it impossible for her to turn down his offer.

She wanted to scream. Alone with Blake in his car? What would they say to each other? What could they say to each other that wouldn't involve them in another terrible argument? The past was very much in Meredith's thoughts, and she wasn't about to risk a repeat of it. But she'd allowed herself to be manipulated by him, and it looked as though she wasn't going to be able to get out of going to town with him. Now, she thought, what are you going to do?

Chapter 4

Blake could sense the nervousness in Meredith as she sat stiffly in the seat beside him while he started the car. In the old days, he might have made some cutting remark about it, but the days were gone when he'd deliberately try to hurt her.

"Fasten your seat belt," he said, noticing that she hadn't.

"Oh." She did it absently. "I usually remember in my own car," she said with faint defensiveness.

"Don't you ever ride with other people?"

"Not if I can help it," she murmured, glancing at his hard profile as he backed the car out of the driveway and pulled onto the highway.

"Are your friends bad drivers," he asked, "or is it that you just don't like being out of control?"

"Who drives you, if we're going to throw stones?" she asked with a pleasantly cool smile.

His mouth twitched. "Nobody."

She toyed with her white leather purse, twisting the thin strap around her fingers while she stared out the window at the green crops and grazing cattle on the way to Jack's Corner. The flat horizon seemed to stretch forever, just as it did back in Texas.

"Sarah engineered this get-together," he remarked. "She damned near drove me crazy until I phoned Elissa to arrange it." His green eyes touched her stiff profile and went back to the road. "She likes you."

"I like her, too," she said quietly. "She's a sweet child."

"'Sweet' isn't exactly the word I'd choose."

"Can't you see what's under the belligerence?" she asked solemnly, and turned in the seat slightly so that she could look at him without having to move her head. "She's frightened."

"Elissa said that, too. What is she frightened of? Me?" he asked.

"I don't know what," she said. "I don't know anything about the situation, and I'm not prying." She stared at the clasp on her purse and unsnapped it. "She doesn't look like a happy child. And the way she enthused over Danielle's things, I'd almost bet she's hardly had a toy in her life."

"I'm a bachelor," he muttered angrily. "I don't know about children and toys and dresses. My God, until a few days ago I didn't even know I was a father."

Meredith wanted to ask why Nina had kept Sarah's existence a secret, but she didn't feel comfortable talking about such personal things with him. She had to remember that he was the enemy, in a very real sense. She couldn't afford to show any interest in his life.

He was already figuring that out by himself. She either

didn't care about how he'd found out, or she wasn't going
to risk asking him. He wished he smoked. She made him
nervous and he didn't have anything to do with his hands
except grip the steering wheel as he drove.

"Mrs. Jackson is one of your biggest fans," he said,
moving the conversation away from Sarah.

"Is she? I'm glad."

"I guess you make a fair living from what you do, if
that Porsche is any indication."

She lifted her eyes to his face, letting them run over
his craggy features. The broken nose was prominent, as
was that angry scar down his cheek. She felt a surge of
warmth remembering how he'd come by that scar. Her
eyes fell.

"I make a good living," she replied. "I'm rather well-
to-do, in fact. So if you think I came home looking for a
rich husband, you're well off the mark. You're perfectly
safe, Blake," she added coldly. "I'm the last woman on
earth you'll have to ward off these days."

He had to clamp down hard on his teeth to keep from
saying what came naturally. The past was dead, but she
had every reason for digging it up and throwing it at him.
He had to remember that. If she'd done to him what he'd
done to her, he'd have wanted a much worse revenge than
a few pithy remarks.

"I don't flatter myself that you'd come looking for me
without a loaded gun, Meredith," he returned. He glanced
at her, noting the surprise on her face.

She looked out the window again, puzzled and
confused.

He pulled the Mercedes into the parking lot behind
the library and shut off the engine.

"Don't do that. Not yet," he said when she started to
open the door. "Let's talk for a minute."

"What do we have to say to each other?" she asked distantly. "We're different people now. Let the past take care of itself. I don't want to remember—" she stopped short when she realized what she'd blurted out.

"I know." He leaned back against his door, his pale green eyes under thick black lashes searching her face. "I guess you think I was rough with you in the stable deliberately. And I said some cruel things, didn't I?"

She flushed and averted her eyes, focusing on his chest. "Yes," she said, taut with embarrassment and vivid memories.

"It wasn't planned," he replied. "And what I said wasn't what I felt." He sighed heavily. "I wanted you, Meredith. Wanted you with a passion that drove me right over the edge. But I'm sorry I hurt you."

"Nothing happened," she said icily. In her nervousness her hands gripped her purse like talons.

"Only because my uncle came driving up at the right moment," he said bitterly. He studied her set features. "You'll never know how it's haunted me all these long years. I was deliberately rough with you the day the will was read because guilt was eating me up. I'd promised to marry Nina, my cousins were talking lawsuits…and on top of all that, I'd just discovered that I wanted you to the point of madness."

"I don't want to talk about it," she said under her breath. Her eyes closed in pain. "I can't…talk about it."

His eyes narrowed. "I thought Nina loved me," he said gently. "She said she did, and all her actions seemed to prove it. I thought you only wanted the inheritance, that I was a stepping stone for you, a way to escape the poverty you'd lived in all your young life." He ran his fingers lightly over the steering wheel. "It wasn't until after…that day, that the lawyer told me why my uncle had wanted me to marry you." His eyes slid to catch hers and hold them. "I didn't know you were in love with me."

Her face lost every vestige of color. She sat and stared at him, her pride in rags, her deepest secret naked to his scrutiny.

"It wouldn't have made the slightest bit of difference," she choked out. "Nothing would have changed. Except that you'd have used the information to humiliate me even more. You and Nina would have laughed yourselves sick over that irony."

The cynicism in her tone made him feel even guiltier. She'd grown a shell, just like the one he'd lived inside most of his life. It kept people from getting too close, from wounding too deeply. Nina hadn't managed to penetrate it, but Meredith very nearly had. He'd pushed her out of his life at exactly the right moment, because it wouldn't have taken much to give her a stranglehold on his heart. He'd known that five years ago, and did everything he could to prevent it.

Now he was seeing the consequences of his reticence. His life had altered, and so had Meredith's. Her fame must have been poor recompense for the home and children she'd always wanted, for a husband to love and take care of and be loved by.

He couldn't answer her accusation without giving himself away, so he ignored it and let her think what she liked.

"You never used to be sarcastic," he said quietly. "You were quiet and shy—"

"And dull and plain," she added for him with a cold smile. "I still am all those things. But I write books that sell like hotcakes and I've got my own small following of loyal readers. I'm famous and I'm rich. So now it doesn't matter if I'm not a blond bombshell. I've learned to live with what I am."

"Have you?" He searched her eyes for a long moment. "You've learned to hide yourself away from the world so that you won't get hurt. You draw back from emotion, from involvement. Even today you were thinking of ways to keep Sarah from having any time with you. That's the whole point of this trip to the library. Your damned research could have been anytime, but you preferred not to be around while Sarah and I were at Bess's house."

"All right, maybe I did!" she said, goaded into telling the truth. "Sarah is a sweet child, and I could love her, but I don't want to have to look at you, much less be dragged up to that house when you're there. Mars wouldn't be far enough away from you to suit me!"

He was grateful that he'd learned to keep a poker face. She couldn't have known how those words hurt him. She had every reason to want to avoid him, to hate him. But he didn't want to avoid her, and hatred was the last emotion he felt for her now.

"So Sarah's going to have to pay because you don't want to be around me," he replied.

She glared at him. "Oh, no, you don't," she said. "You aren't laying any guilt trips on me. Sarah has you and Mrs. Jackson—"

"Sarah doesn't like me and Mrs. Jackson," he interrupted. "She likes you. She's done nothing but talk about you."

She turned away. "I can't," she said huskily.

"She could have been our child," he said unexpectedly. "Yours and mine. And that's what's eating you alive, isn't it?"

She couldn't believe he'd said that. She looked back

at him with tears welling in her gray eyes, blinding her. "Damn you!"

"I saw it in your face this morning when you looked at her," he went on relentlessly, driven to make her admit it. "It isn't fear of me that's stopping you—it's fear of admitting that Sarah reminds you too painfully of what you wanted and couldn't have."

She cried out as if he'd slapped her. She pushed the door open and ran toward the library, almost stumbling in her haste to get away from him. She made it to the lobby and stood there shaking, grateful that the librarian was away from the desk as she tried to get her composure back. She fumbled a handkerchief out of her purse and wiped her eyes. Blake was right. She was avoiding Sarah Jane because of the pain the child caused her. But knowing the truth didn't help. It only made things worse that he should be perceptive enough to sense what she was thinking.

She put the handkerchief away and went back to the reading room to pore over volumes on southwestern history. She didn't know how she was going to get back home. Blake would have gone and she'd just have to call Elissa or Bess.

An hour later, calmer and less flustered, she put the notebook she'd been scribbling in back in her purse, returned the reference books to the shelf and walked outside to find a public telephone.

Blake was there, leaning comfortably against the wall, waiting.

"Are you ready to go?" he asked pleasantly as if nothing at all had happened.

She stared at him. "I thought you'd gone."

His broad shoulders rose and fell. "It's Saturday," he said. "I don't usually work on Saturday unless I have to."

His eyes narrowed as he searched her face. "Are you all right?" he added quietly.

She nodded, her eyes avoiding him.

"I won't do that again, Meredith," he said deeply. "I didn't mean to upset you. Let's go."

She sat rigidly beside him on the ride home, afraid that he might start on her again despite what he'd said. But he didn't. He turned on the radio and kept it playing until he pulled into Bess's driveway again.

"You don't have to worry," he said before she got out of the car, and there was a resigned expression on his face. "I won't try to force you into a relationship with Sarah. She's my responsibility, not yours."

And that was that. Meredith went back into the house, and after he'd explained to Elissa and Bess that they could call him when Sarah was ready to come home, he drove off.

He didn't know what he was going to do as he drove away. He hadn't expected Meredith to react like that to his words. What he'd said had only been a shot in the dark, but he'd scored a hit. Sarah disturbed her. The child reminded her of Blake's cruelty, and Meredith was going to keep Sarah at a distance no matter what it took.

That was going to be sad for both of them. Meredith had grown cold and self-contained. She could use a child's magic to bring her back into the sunlight. Sarah likewise would profit from Meredith's tenderness. But it wasn't going to happen and he had to face it. He'd hoped that he might reach Meredith again through Sarah, but she wanted no part of him. She hated him.

He went back to the house and locked himself in his study with his paperwork, forcing his mind not to dwell on Meredith's anger. He had no one to blame but himself. And only time would tell if she could ever forgive him.

* * *

Later that afternoon, Meredith sat with Bess and Elissa and watched the little girls play.

"Isn't she the image of Blake?" Elissa smiled as she watched Sarah. "I guess it's hard for him, trying to raise a child on his own."

"He needs to marry again," Bess agreed.

"Well, he's rich enough to attract a wife," Meredith replied with cool disinterest.

"Another Nina would be the end of him," Elissa said. "And think of Sarah. She needs to be loved, not pushed aside. She looks as if she's never really been loved."

"She won't be with Blake," Meredith said. "He isn't a loving man."

Elissa looked at her curiously. "Considering his life so far, is that surprising? He's never been loved, has he? Even his uncle manipulated him, used him for the good of the real estate corporation. Blake has been an outsider looking in. He hasn't known how to love. Maybe Sarah will teach him. She's not the little terror she makes out to be. There's an odd softness about her, especially when she talks to Blake. And have you noticed how unselfish she is?" she added. "She hasn't fought with Dani or tried to take her toys away or break them. She's not what she seems."

"I noticed that, too," Meredith said reluctantly. She looked at the child who was so much like Blake and so little like her beautiful blond mother. Her heart ached at the sight of the little girl who could have been her own. If only Blake could have loved her. She smiled sadly. Oh, if only.

Sarah seemed to feel that scrutiny, because she got up and went to Meredith, her curious eyes searching the woman's. "Can you write a book about a little girl and she can have a daddy and mommy to love her?" she asked. "And it could have a pony in it, and lots of dolls like Dani has."

Meredith touched the small, dark head gently. "I might do that," she said, smiling involuntarily.

Sarah smiled back. "I like you, Merry."

She went back to play with Danielle, leaving a hopelessly touched Meredith staring hungrily at her. Tears stung her eyes.

"Merry, could you watch the girls for a bit while Elissa and I run down to the ice cream shop and get some cones for them?" Bess asked with a quickly concealed conspiratorial wink at Elissa.

"Of course," Meredith agreed.

"We won't be a minute," Bess promised. "Do you want a cone?"

"Yes, please. Chocolate." Meredith grinned.

"I want chocolate, too," Sarah pleaded. "A big one."

"I want vanilla," Danielle said.

"Forty-eight flavors, and we live with purists." Bess sighed, shaking her head. "Okay, chocolate and vanilla it is. Won't be a minute!"

Of course it was more than a minute. They were gone for almost an hour, and when they got back, Meredith was sitting in the middle of the carpet with Sarah and Danielle, helping them dress one of Danielle's dolls. Sarah was sitting as close as she could get to Meredith, and her young face was for once without its customary sulky look. She was laughing, and almost pretty.

The ice cream was passed out and another hour went by before Elissa said reluctantly that she and Danielle would have to go.

"I hate to, but King's bringing one of his business associates home for supper, and I have to get Danielle's bath and have her in bed by the time they get home," Elissa said. "But we'll have to do this again."

"Do you have to go?" Sarah asked Danielle sadly. "I wish you could come live with me, and we could be sisters."

"Me, too," Danielle said.

"I like your toys. I guess your mommy and daddy like you a lot."

"Your daddy likes you, too, Sarah," Meredith said gently, taking the child's hand in hers. "He just didn't know that you wanted toys. He'll buy you some of your own."

"Will he, truly?" Sarah asked her, all eyes.

"Truly," she replied, hoping she was right. The Blake she'd known in the past wouldn't have cared overmuch about a child's needs. Of course, the man she'd glimpsed today might. She could hardly reconcile what she knew about him with what she was learning about him.

"That's right," Bess agreed, smiling down at Sarah. "Your dad's a pretty nice guy. We all like him, don't we, Meredith?"

Meredith glared at her. "Oh, we surely do," she said through her teeth. "He's a prince."

Which was what Sarah Jane told her daddy that very night over the supper table. He'd picked her up at Bess's house, but Meredith's car was gone. She was avoiding him, he supposed wearily, and he listened halfheartedly to Sarah all the way home. Now she was telling him about the wonderful time she'd had playing dolls with Meredith, and he turned his attention from business problems to stare at her blankly as what she was saying began to register.

"She did *what*?" he asked.

"She played dolls with me," she said, "and she says

you're a prince. Does that mean you used to be a frog, Daddy?" Sarah added. "Because the princess kisses the frog and he turns into a prince. Did my mommy kiss you?"

"Occasionally, and no, I wasn't a frog. Meredith played dolls with you?" he asked, feeling a tiny glow deep inside himself.

"She really did." Sarah sighed. "I like Mer'dith. I wish she was my mommy. Can't she come to live with us?"

He couldn't explain that very easily. "No," he said simply. "You'd better get ready for bed."

"But, Daddy…" she moaned.

"Go on. No arguments."

"All right," she grumbled. But she went.

He looked after her, smiling faintly. She was a handful, but she was slowly growing on him.

He stayed home on Sunday and took Sarah Jane out to see the horses grazing in the pasture. One of the men, a grizzled old wrangler named Manolo, was working a gelding in the corral, breaking him slowly and gently to the saddle. Blake had complained that Manolo took too long to break horses, especially when he was doing it for the remuda in spring before roundup. The cowhands had to have a string of horses when they started working cattle. But Manolo used his own methods, despite the boss's arguments. No way, he informed Blake, was he going to mistreat a horse just to break it to saddle, and if Blake didn't like that, he could fire him.

Blake hadn't said another word about it. The horses Manolo broke were always gentle and easily managed.

But this horse was giving the old man a lot of trouble. It pranced and reared, and Blake was watching it instead of Sarah Jane when the lacy handkerchief Meredith had given her blew into the corral.

Like a shot, she climbed through the fence to go after it, just as the horse broke away from Manalo and came snorting and bucking in her direction.

Blake saw her and blinked, not believing what his eyes were telling him. All at once he was over the fence, just as Manalo yelled.

Sarah was holding her handkerchief, staring dumbly at the approaching horse.

Blake grabbed her and sent her through the fence, following her with an economy of motion. He thanked God for his own strength as it prevented what would have been a total disaster.

Sarah Jane clung to his neck tightly, crying with great sobs.

He hugged her to him, his eyes closed, a shudder running through his lean, fit body. Another few seconds and it would have been all over. Sarah would have become a tragic memory. It didn't bear thinking about. Worse than that, it brought back an older memory, of another incident with a bronc. He touched his lean cheek where the scar cut across his tan. How many years ago had it been that he'd saved Meredith just as he'd saved Sarah? A long time ago—long before the sight of her began to make him ache.

The fear he'd experienced, added to the unwanted memories, made him furious. He let go of Sarah and held her in front of him, his green eyes glittering with rage.

"Don't you know better than to go into the corral with a wild animal?" he snapped. "Where's your mind, Sarah?"

She stared at him as if he'd slapped her. Her lower lip trembled. "I had to get my…my hankie, Daddy." She held it up. "See? My pretty hankie that Mer'dith gave me…."

He shook her. "The next time you go near any enclosure with horses or cattle in it, you stay out! Do you understand me?" he asked in a tone that made her small body jerk with a sob. "You could have been killed!"

"I'm so—sorry," she faltered.

"You should be!" he jerked out. "Now get in the house."

She started crying, frightened by the way he looked. "You hate me," she whimpered. "I know you do. You yelled at me. You're mean and ugly…and…I don't like you!"

"I don't like you, either, at the moment," he bit off, glaring down at her, his legs still shaking from the exertion and fear. "Now get going."

"You mean old daddy!" she cried. She turned and ran wildly for the house as Blake stared after her in a blind rage.

"Is she all right, boss?" Manolo asked from the fence. "My God, that was quick! I didn't even see her!"

"Neither did I," Blake confessed. "Not until it was damned near too late." He let out a rough sigh. "I didn't mean to be so hard on her, but she's got to learn that horses and cattle are dangerous. I wanted to make sure she remembered this."

"She'll remember," Manolo said ruefully, and turned away before the boss could see the look on his face. Poor little kid. She needed hugging, not yelling.

Blake went in the house a few minutes later and looked for Sarah, but she was nowhere in sight. Mrs. Jackson had heard her come in, but she hadn't seen her because she was working in the front of the house.

He checked Sarah's bedroom, but she wasn't there,

either. Then he remembered what she'd said about being locked in the closet when she was bad....

He jerked open the closet door and there she sat, her face red and tear stained, sobbing and looking as if she hadn't a friend in the world.

"Go away," she sniffed.

He got down awkwardly on one knee. "You'll suffocate in here."

"I hate you."

"I don't want anything to happen to you," he said. "The horse could have hurt you very badly."

She touched the dusty lace handkerchief to her red eyes. "You yelled at me."

He grimaced. "You scared me," he muttered, averting his gaze. "I never thought I'd get to you in time."

She sniffed and got up on her knees under the hanging dresses and blouses and slacks. "You didn't want me to get hurt?"

"Of course I didn't want you to get hurt," he snapped, green eyes flashing.

"You're yelling at me again," she said, pouting.

He sighed angrily. "Well, I've been doing it for a lot of years, and I won't change. You'll just have to get used to my temper." He stared at her half-angrily. "I thought I was getting the hang of it, and you had to go crawl in with a bucking bronco and set me back."

"Everybody used to yell at me," she told him solemnly. "But they didn't do it just if I got hurt. They didn't like me."

"I like you. That's why I yelled," he muttered.

She smiled through her tears. "Really and truly?"

He grimaced. "Really and truly." He got up. "Come out of there."

"Are you going to spank me?" she asked.

"No."

"I won't do it again."

"You'd better not." He took her hand and led her downstairs. When Mrs. Jackson found out what had happened, she took a fresh coconut cake out of the pantry, sliced it up and poured Sarah a soft drink. She even smiled. Sarah dried her eyes and smiled back.

On Monday Blake took two hours off at lunch and went to a toy store. He bought an armful of dolls and assorted girlish toys and took them to the house without fully understanding his motives. Maybe it was relief that Sarah was all right or guilt because he'd hurt her.

But she sat down in the living room with her new friends—which included a huge stuffed teddy bear—and the way she handled her toys was enough to bring a tear to the eye. She hugged the teddy bear, then she hugged Blake, who was half delighted and half embarrassed by her exuberance.

"You're just the nicest daddy in the whole world," Sarah Jane said, and she was crying again. She wiped her eyes with her hands. "I have a new Mr. Friend now, and he can help you fight monsters."

"I'll keep that in mind. Behave yourself." He went out the door quickly, more moved than he wanted to admit by his daughter's reception to the impromptu toy surprise.

On the way back to work, he remembered what Sarah had said about Meredith playing dolls with her. Meredith had been trying to keep Sarah at arms' length, so he wondered at her actions. Had he been wrong about Meredith's motives? Had he misjudged what he thought was her reason for avoiding Sarah?

He remembered all too well the feel of Meredith's soft, innocent mouth under his that day in the stable, the wonder in her eyes when he'd lifted his head just briefly to look down at her. And then he'd lost control and frightened her, turning the wonder to panic.

That she'd loved him didn't bear thinking about. At least he and Sarah were closer than ever. But she needed more than a father. Sarah needed a mother. Someone to read her stories, to play with her. Someone like Meredith. It made him feel warm to think of Meredith doing those things with his daughter. In time she might even get over the past and start looking ahead. She might fall in love with him all over again.

His body reacted feverishly to that thought, and as quickly his mind rejected it. He didn't want her to love him. He felt guilt for the way he'd treated her and he still wanted her, but *love* wasn't a word in his vocabulary anymore. It hurt too much.

Letting her get close would be risky. Meredith had every reason in the world to want to get even with him. He scowled. Would Meredith want revenge if he could bring himself to tell her the truth about why he'd been so rough with her?

Not that *he* needed her, he assured himself. It was only that Sarah liked her and needed her. But Meredith wouldn't come to the house. She wasn't going to let him, or Sarah, get close to her, and that was the big hurdle. How, he wondered, could he overcome it?

He worried the thought for two days and still hadn't figured out a solution, when he had to fly to Dallas on business for the day. But fate was on his side.

While he was gone, Mrs. Jackson's only living sister had a heart attack and a neighbor called asking Amie to come to Wichita, Kansas, and help look after her. That left Mrs. Jackson with nobody to look after Sarah. She couldn't take the child with her while she tried to care for a heart patient. She called Elissa, but she and her husband and child were out of town. Bess wouldn't be able to cope with the angry little girl. That left only one person in Jack's Corner who might be willing to try.

Without hesitation, Mrs. Jackson picked up the phone and called Meredith Calhoun.

Chapter 5

Sarah Jane was almost dancing with pleasure when Meredith came in the door. She ran to her, arms outstretched, and Meredith instinctively picked her up and hugged her warmly. Maternal instincts she hadn't indulged since Blake had sent her running came to the fore, making her soft.

"Now don't you give Meredith any trouble, young lady," Mrs. Jackson cautioned Sarah Jane. "Meredith, this is my sister's phone number, but I'll call as soon as I know something and tell Mr. Blake what's going on. I hope he won't mind."

"You know very well he won't," Meredith said. "I'm sorry about your sister, but I'm sure she'll be all right."

"Well, we can hope, anyway," Mrs. Jackson said, forcing a smile. "There's my cab. I'll be back as soon as I can."

"Bye, Mrs. Jackson," Sarah called.

She turned at the door and smiled at the little girl. "Goodbye, Sarah. I'll miss you. Thanks again, Merry."

"No problem," Meredith said as the housekeeper left.

"We can play dolls now, Merry," Sarah said enthusiastically, repeating the nickname she'd heard for Meredith as she struggled to be put down. She then led Meredith by the hand into the living room. "Look what my daddy bought me!"

Meredith was pleasantly surprised by the array of dolls. There must have been two dozen of them, surrounding a huge, whimsical tan teddy bear who was wearing one of Blake's Stetsons on his shaggy head.

"He's supposed to be my daddy," Meredith said, pointing to the bear, "since my daddy's away. But actually he's Mr. Friend. My old Mr. Friend got lost, so Daddy bought me a new one."

Meredith sat down on the sofa, smiling as Sarah introduced every one of her new toys to her older friend.

"I dropped the pretty hankie you gave me inside the fence," Sarah explained excitedly, "and a big horse almost ran over me, but my daddy saved me. He yelled at me and I cried and hid in the closet, and he came to find me. He said I mustn't *ever* do it again because he liked me." She laughed. "And then he went to the store and brought me ever so many toys."

Meredith was feeling cold chills at the innocent story. She could imagine how Blake had felt, the fear that had gripped him. She remembered so well the day he'd had to rescue her from a wild horse. She wondered if it had brought back memories for him, too.

Sarah looked up at Meredith. "My daddy has an *awful* temper, Merry."

Meredith knew that already. She remembered his temper very well. A lot of things could spark it, but embarrassment, fear, or any kind of threat were sure to ignite it. She could imagine how frightened Sarah had been of him, but apparently toys could buy forgiveness. She chided herself for that thought. Blake could be unexpectedly kind. It was just that he seemed so cold and self-contained. She wondered if Nina had ever really touched him during their brief marriage, and decided that it was unlikely.

Meredith got down on the floor with Sarah, grateful, as they sprawled on the carpet, that she'd worn jeans and a yellow blouse instead of a dress. She and Sarah dressed dolls and talked for a long time before Meredith got the small girl ready for bed, tucked her in and helped her say her prayers.

"Why do I have to say prayers?" Sarah asked.

"To thank God for all the nice things He does for us." Meredith smiled.

"Daddy talks to God all the time," Sarah said. "Especially when I turn things over or get hurt—"

Meredith fought to keep her expression steady. "That's not what I meant, darling. Now you settle down and we'll talk."

"Okay, Merry." She moved her dark head on the pillow. "Merry, do you like me?"

Meredith looked down at the child she might have had. She smiled sadly, touching Sarah's dark hair gently. "Yes, I like you very much, Sarah Jane Donavan," she replied, smiling.

"I like you, too."

Meredith bent and kissed the clean, shiny face. "Would you like me to read you a story? Have you any books?"

The small face fell. "No. Daddy forgot."

"That's all right, then. I can think of one or two." She sat down on Sarah's bed and proceeded to go through several, doing all the parts in different pitches of her voice, while Sarah giggled.

She was just in the middle of "The Three Bears," doing Baby Bear's voice when Sarah sat up, smiling from ear to ear and cried, "Daddy!"

Meredith felt her face burn, her heart start to pound, as he came into the room, dressed in a gray business suit, sparing her a curious glance as he handed something to Sarah.

"Something from Dallas," he told the child. "It's a puppet."

"I love him, Daddy!"

It was a duck puppet, yellow and white, and Sarah wiggled it on her hand while Blake turned to Meredith with a cool smile.

"Where's Amie?" he asked.

She told him, adding that Amie had promised to phone as soon as she knew something. "She couldn't get Elissa, and there wasn't anyone else, so she asked me."

"We had lots of fun, Daddy!" Sarah told him. "Merry and me played dolls and watched TV together!"

"Thank you for taking the time," Blake said, his whole attitude antagonistic. He'd done nothing but think about the irritating woman for days. And there she sat, looking as cool as a cucumber without a hint of warmth in her cold gray eyes, while his body had gone taut and started throbbing at the very sight of her.

Meredith got to her feet, avoiding him. "I didn't mind. Good night, Sarah," she said, running a nervous hand through her loosened dark hair to get it out of her face.

"Good night, Merry. Will you come back to see me again?"

"When I can, darling," she replied absently, without noticing the reaction that endearment had on Blake. "Sleep tight."

"Go to sleep now, young lady," Blake told his daughter.

"But, Daddy, what about the monsters?" Sarah wailed when he started to turn out the light at the door.

He stopped and looked uncomfortable. He wasn't about to start chasing monsters from under the bed and dragging them out of the closet in front of Meredith. Sarah loved the pretend housecleaning and he'd grown used to doing it to amuse her, but a man had to have his secrets. He cleared his throat. "When I walk Meredith to her car, okay?"

That pacified Sarah. She smiled. "Okay, Daddy." She looked at Meredith. "He kills the monsters every night so they won't hurt me. He's very brave and he weighs one million pounds!"

Meredith glanced at Blake and her face went red as she tried to smother laughter. He glared at her, breaking the spell. She rushed out into the hall and kept going.

He caught up with her downstairs and walked her out onto the porch.

"I'm sorry Amie involved you," he said curtly. "Bess would have kept Sarah."

"Bess and Bobby were going out," she replied. "I didn't mind."

"You didn't want to come here, though, even while I was away," he said perceptively. "You don't care for this house very much, do you?"

"Not anymore," she said. "It brings back some

painful memories." She moved away from him, but he followed.

"Where's your car?" he asked, searching for it.

"I walked. It was a beautiful night and it's only a short walk."

He glared down at her from his superior height. In his gray suit and pearl-colored Stetson, he looked enormously tall and imposing. He never seemed to smile, she thought, searching his hard features in the light that shone from the windows onto the big, long porch.

"If you're looking for beauty, you won't find it," he said, his mouth twisting into a mocking smile. "The scar only makes it worse."

She gazed at it, the long white line that marred his lean cheek all the way from his high cheekbone to his jaw. "I remember when you got it," she said quietly. "And how."

His expression became grim. "I don't want to talk about it."

"I know." She sighed gently, her eyes searching over his dark face with more poignancy than she knew. "But you were always handsome to me, scar and all," she mused, turning away as the memories came flooding back. "Good night...Blake!"

He'd whipped her around, his lean hands biting into her arms. She was wearing a sleeveless lemon yellow blouse with her jeans, and it made her skin look darker than it was. Where his fingers held her, the flesh went white from the pressure.

"I..." He eased his hold a little, although he didn't release her. "I didn't mean to do that." He drew in a silent breath. "I don't suppose you'll ever get over the fear I caused you in the past, will you?" he added, watching her eyes widen, her body stiffen.

"It was my first intimacy," she whispered, flushing. "And you made it...you were very rough."

"I remember," he replied. His pride fought him when he tried to tell her the truth, although he wanted to. He wanted to make her understand his roughness.

"As you said, it was a long time ago," she added, pulling against his hold gently.

"Not that long. Five years." He searched her eyes. "Meredith, surely you've dated men. There must have been one or two who could stir you."

"I couldn't trust them," she said bitterly. "I was afraid to take a chance with anyone else."

"Most men aren't as rough as I am," he replied coldly.

Her breath was sighing out like a whisper. He made her nervous, and the feel of his hands was affecting her breathing. "Most men aren't as much a man as you are," she breathed, closing her eyes as forgotten sensations worked down her spine and made her ache.

His pride burned with what she'd said. Did she think him masculine, handsome? Or was that all in the past, part of the love he'd killed?

He drew her closer and held her against him warmly but chastely, her legs apart from his. He didn't want her to feel how aroused he already was.

"I'm not much gentler now than I used to be, Meredith," he said deeply, as his head bent toward her. "But I'll try not to frighten you this time...."

She opened her mouth to protest, but his lips met hers. They probed her soft mouth while his lean, strong hands slid up to frame her face.

She stiffened, but only for a minute. The taste of him made her dizzy with pleasure. She liked what he was doing to her too much to protest. After a minute she relaxed, letting his mouth do what it wanted to hers.

"God, it's sweet," he whispered roughly, biting at her lips with more instinct than expertise. His voice was shaking and he didn't care if she heard it. "Oh, God, it's so sweet!"

His mouth ground into hers and his arms slid completely around her. He pulled her body up against his so that his legs touched hers, and he felt her sudden shocked tautness.

He let her move away, his eyes glittering, his breath rustling out of his throat. "I shouldn't have done that," he said gruffly. "I didn't mean to let you feel how aroused I was."

Having him mention it shocked her more than the feel of his body, but she tried not to let him see her reaction. She stepped back, touching her mouth with light fingers. Yes, it had been sweet, as she'd heard him whisper feverishly. Just as it had been five years ago in the stable, when he'd put his mouth on hers and she'd ached to have him touch her.

"I have to get back to Bess's house," she said unsteadily.

"Just a minute." He took her hand and pulled her farther into the light. He held her gaze so that he could see the fear mingled with desire that lingered in her eyes, the swollen softness of her mouth.

"What are you looking for?" she asked huskily.

"You're still afraid of me," he said, his jaw going taut.

"I'm sorry." She lowered her eyes to his chest, to its quick, hard rise and fall. "I can't help it."

"Neither can I," he replied bitterly. He let her go,

turning away. "I'm not much good at lovemaking, if you want the truth," he said through his teeth.

That was true. He had the patience, but not the knowledge. Nina had taught him a few things, but she'd been indifferent to his touch and her response to him had always been just lukewarm. She hadn't known he was innocent, but she had known he was inexperienced, and at the end of their relationship she'd taunted him with his lack of expertise. It was one of the things he hated remembering. Better to let Meredith think he was brutal than to have her know how green he was.

Watching him, Meredith was surprised by the admission. She'd always considered him experienced. If he wasn't, it would explain so much.

Suddenly, she understood his fierce pride a little better. She went closer to him, reaching out to lightly touch his sleeve. He jerked a little, as if that impersonal contact went through him like fire.

"It's all right, Blake," she said hesitantly.

He looked down at the slender hand that rested lightly on his sleeve. "I'm like a bull in a china shop," he said unexpectedly, looking into her eyes. "With women."

She felt a surge of emotion at that rough admission. He'd never been more approachable than he was right now. Part of her was wary of him, but another part wanted once, just once, to give in without a fight.

She went up on her tiptoes and pulled his head down to hers. He stiffened and she stopped dead.

"No!" he whispered huskily when she started to draw back in embarrassment. "Go ahead. Do what you want to."

She couldn't believe that he really wanted her to kiss him, but he was giving every indication that he did. She didn't know a lot about it, either, since all she'd ever done with men was kissing.

She drew her lips lightly over Blake's hard ones, teasing them gently. Her breath shook at his mouth while she held his head within reach, but she didn't relent. Her fingers slid into the thick, cool hair at the nape of his strong neck and her nails slid against his skin while her mouth toyed softly with his.

"I can't take much of that," he whispered roughly. His hands held her hips now, an intimacy that she should have protested, but she was too weak. "Do it properly."

"Not yet," she whispered. Her teeth closed softly on his lower lip, tugging at it sensuously. She felt him tremble as her tongue traced his upper lip.

"Meredith," he bit off, and his hands hurt her for an instant.

"All right." She knew what he wanted, what he needed. She opened her mouth on his and slid her tongue inside it, and the reaction she got from him was electrifying.

He cried out. His arms swallowed her, bruising her against his hard chest. He was trembling. Meredith felt the soft tremors with exquisite awareness, with pride that she could arouse him that easily after a beauty like Nina.

"Blake," she whispered under his mouth, and closed her eyes as she gave him the weight of her body, the warmth of her mouth.

She felt him move. Her back was suddenly against the wall and he was easing down over her body.

Her eyes flew open and his head lifted fractionally, and all the while his body overwhelmed hers, his hips lying heavy and hard against hers, pressing against her.

She could feel the full strength of his arousal now,

and it should have frightened her, but it didn't. He was slow and gentle, not impatient at all as his hands slid to her hips, holding her.

"This should really frighten the hell out of you, shouldn't it?" he asked huskily, searching her eyes. "You can feel what I want, and I'm not quite in control right now."

"You aren't hurting me," she whispered. "And I started it this time."

"So you did." He moved down, letting his mouth repeat the soft, arousing movements hers had made earlier. "Like that, Meredith?" he whispered at her lips. "Is that how you like it?"

"Yes," she whispered back, excitement making her voice husky. Her hands were against his shirt and she could feel the heat from his body under the fabric.

"I want to open my shirt and let you touch me," he whispered roughly. "But that might be the straw that breaks the camel's back, and there's a long, comfortable sofa just a few feet inside the door."

The thought was more than tempting. She could already feel his skin against hers, his body overwhelming hers. She wanted him, and there wasn't really any reason to say no. Except that her pride couldn't take the knowledge that he wanted only her body and nothing else about her.

"I can't sleep with you," she said miserably. She let her head rest against him, drowning in the feel of his body over hers. "Blake, you have to stop," she groaned. "I'm going crazy…!"

"So am I." He pushed himself away from her, breathing roughly. His darkened green eyes looked down into hers. "You wanted me," he said, as if he were only just realizing it.

She flushed and looked up at his hard face. "I don't understand what you want from me."

"Sarah needs a woman's companionship," he said tersely.

"That isn't why you made love to me," she returned, searching his eyes.

He sighed deeply. "No, it isn't." He walked to the edge of the porch and leaned against one of the white columns, looking out over the wide expanse of flat land. The only trees were right around the house, where they'd been planted. Beyond was open land, dotted with a few willows at the creek and a few straggly bushes, but mostly flat and barren all the way to the horizon.

"Why, Blake?" she asked. She had to know what he was after.

"Do you know what an obsession is, Meredith?" he asked a minute later.

"Yes, I think so."

"Well, that's what I feel for you." He shifted so that he could see her. "Obsessed," he repeated, letting his green eyes slide over her sensually. "I don't know why. You aren't beautiful. You aren't even voluptuous. But you arouse me as no other woman ever has or ever will. I couldn't even feel for Nina what I feel for you." He laughed coldly. "After she left me, there wasn't anyone else. I couldn't. I don't want anyone but you."

She didn't know if she was still breathing. The admission knocked the wind out of her, took the strength from her legs. She looked at him helplessly.

"You haven't...seen me in five years," she said, trying to rationalize.

"I've seen you every night," he ground out. "Every time I closed my eyes. My God, don't you remember what I did to you that day in the stable? I stripped you...."

He closed his eyes, oblivious to her scarlet face and trembling body. "I looked at you and touched you and put my mouth on you." He bit back a curse and opened his eyes again, tormented. "I see you in my bed every damned night of my life," he breathed. "I want you to the point of madness."

She caught the railing and held on tight. She couldn't believe what she was hearing. It wasn't possible for a man to feel that kind of desire, she told herself. Not when he didn't feel anything emotional for the woman. But Blake was different. As Elissa said, he'd never been loved, so he didn't know what it was. But all men felt desire. A man didn't have to love to want.

"Don't worry—" he laughed mockingly "—I'm not going to force you into anything. I just wanted you to know how I felt. If that sensuous little kiss was some sort of game, you'd better know how dangerous it is. I'm not sane when I touch you. I wouldn't hurt you deliberately for the world, but I want you like hell."

Her swollen lips parted. "I wasn't playing," she said with quiet pride. "It was no game. You…" She hesitated. "You seemed so disturbed because you'd been rough. I wanted to show you that you hadn't made me afraid."

He watched her unblinkingly. "You weren't, were you?" he said then, scowling. "Not even when I brought you close and let you feel what you were doing to me."

She shifted. "You shouldn't have," she murmured evasively.

"Why hide it?" he asked. He moved toward her, encouraged by her response and her lack of bitterness. He was taking a hell of a chance by being honest with her, but it might be his only way of reaching her. "You might as well know it all."

She lifted her face as he stood over her. "Know what?"

"Nina was my first woman," he said bluntly. "And the only woman."

She wanted to sit down, but there was no chair. She leaned against the banister, her eyes searching his hard face. He wasn't kidding. He meant it.

"That's right," he said, nodding when he saw the memories replaying in her eyes. "The day we were in the stable together, I was as inexperienced as you were. That's why I was rough. It wasn't deliberate. I didn't know how to make love."

Her lips opened on a slow breath. "No wonder..." she whispered.

"Yes, no wonder." He brushed a strand of loosened hair from her pale cheek. "Why don't you laugh? Nina did."

She could feel the hurt under that mocking statement. What it must have done to his pride! "Nina was a—" She bit back the word.

He laughed coldly. "She certainly was," he agreed. "She taunted me with it toward the end," he added, his eyes bitter and cynical. "I didn't want to risk that kind of ridicule again, so there weren't any more women."

"Oh, Blake," she whispered, closing her eyes on a wave of pain. "Blake, I'm so sorry!"

"I don't want pity. I wanted you to know the truth. If you're ever tempted to give in to me, you're entitled to know what you'd be up against. My God," he said heavily, moving away, "I don't even know the basics. Books and movies don't make up for experience. And Nina wasn't interested in tutoring me."

"I wish I'd known," she said huskily. "I wish I'd known five years ago."

He looked back at her, his thick eyebrows raised. "Why?"

"I wouldn't have fought you," she said simply. "I thought you were terribly experienced." She lowered her eyes. "I'm sorry. I guess I hurt your ego as much as you frightened me."

He studied her in a tense silence. "You don't have a thing to apologize for. I'm the one who's sorry." He waited until she lifted her head, and he caught her eyes and held them. "You haven't wanted anyone, in all this time?"

"I wanted you," she said frankly. "I...couldn't feel that for anyone else. I'd rather have been frightened by you than pleasured by the greatest lover living." She laughed coldly. "So I guess I'm in the same boat that you are." She clutched her purse. "I really do have to go," she said after a long, quiet moment during which he stared at her without saying anything at all.

He escorted her down the porch steps. "All right. I'll walk you to the woods and watch you through them. Sarah Jane will be all right until I get back, and the house is in full view the whole way."

"Sarah is very much like you," she said.

"Too much like me," he replied. His fingers brushed hers as they walked, accidentally or deliberately she didn't know, making her all too aware of him. "She almost got trampled the other day, climbing into the corral to retrieve a handkerchief."

"She told me. I suppose you were livid."

"Mild word," he said. "I blew up. Scared her. I found her hiding in the closet, and I felt like a dog. I went to town the next day and bought her half a toy store to make up for yelling at her." He sighed. "She scared me blind. I kept thinking what could have happened if my reflexes had been just a bit slower."

"But they weren't." She smiled. "You were always quick in an emergency."

He looked down at her and his fingers lazily entangled themselves in hers. "Luckily for you," he murmured darkly, watching her flush. "I haven't had an easy life," he said then. "I had to be tough to survive. They weren't good days before I came here to live with my uncle. I got in a lot of fights because of my illegitimacy."

"I never heard you talk about that," she said.

"I never could." His fingers tightened in hers as they got to the small wooded area and stopped. "I can't talk about a lot of things, Meredith. Maybe that's why I'm so damned alone."

She glanced toward Bess's house. Bess and Bobby must have come home, because their car was in the driveway next to hers. She hesitated, not eager to leave Blake in this oddly talkative mood. "You've got Sarah now," she reminded him gently.

"Sarah is getting to me," he confessed ruefully. "God, I don't know what I'd do if I could sit down in a chair without crushing a stuffed toy, or go to bed without running monsters out of closets." He smiled mockingly. "It cut me to pieces when she started crying after I raged at her about getting in with the horse."

"She doesn't seem that sensitive at first glance, but she is," she replied. "I noticed it that first day, at the children's shop, and again when she played with Danielle. I gather she was neglected a lot before they sent her to you."

"I got the same feeling. She had a nightmare just after she came here," he recalled quietly. "She woke up in the early hours, screaming her head off, and when I asked what was the matter, she said they wouldn't let her out of the closet." His face hardened, and for an instant he looked relentless. "I've still got half a mind to send my lawyers after that housekeeper."

"A woman that cruel will make her own hell," Meredith said. "Mean people don't get away with anything, Blake. It may seem that they do, but in the end their meanness ricochets back at them."

"The way mine did at me?" he asked with a mirthless laugh. "I scarred you and pushed you out of my life, married Nina, and settled down to what I thought would be wedded bliss. And look where it got me."

"You've got everything," she corrected. "Money, power, position, a sweet little girl."

"I've got nothing except Sarah," he said shortly. His green eyes glittered in the faint light. "I thought I needed money and power to make people accept me. But I'm no more socially acceptable now than I was when I was poor and illegitimate. I've just got more money."

"Acceptance doesn't have anything to do with money." She stared down at the big, warm hand clasping hers. "You're not the world's most sociable man. You keep to yourself and you don't smile very much. You intimidate people." She smiled gently, her eyes almost loving despite her reluctance to give herself away. "That's why you don't get a lot of social invitations. This isn't the Dark Ages. People don't hold the circumstances of their birth against each other anymore. It's a much more open society than it was."

"It stinks," he returned coldly. "Women propositioning men, kids neglected and abused and cast off…."

"They don't burn witches anymore, though," she whispered conspiratorially, going up on tiptoe. "And the stocks have been eliminated, too."

His face cracked into a reluctant smile. "Okay. You've got a point."

"Who propositioned you?" she added.

He cocked his head a little to study her. "A woman at the workshop in Dallas I just came back from. I didn't believe she meant it until she put her room key in an ashtray beside my coffee cup."

"What did you do?" she asked, because she had to know.

He smiled faintly. "Took it out and handed it back." He touched her cheek gently, running a lean finger down it. "I told you on the porch. I don't want anyone but you."

She lowered her eyes to his chest. "I can't, Blake."

"I'm not asking you to." He let go of the hand he was holding. "I'm archaic in my notions, in case it's escaped your notice. I don't seduce virgins."

Her body tingled at the thought of making love with Blake. It was exciting and surprising to know how much he wanted her. But her own conscience wasn't going to let her give in, and he knew that, too.

"I guess you'd rather I got my autographing over and left town…" she began.

He tilted her chin up so he could see her face. "Sarah and I are going on a picnic Saturday. You can come."

The suddenness of the invitation made her blink. "Saturday?"

"We'll pick you up at nine. You can wear jeans. I'm going to."

Her eyes lifted to his. "Blake…"

"I like having things out in the open, so there aren't any more misunderstandings," he said simply. "I want you. You want me. But that's as far as it goes, and there won't be any more of what happened on my porch tonight. I'll keep my hands off and we'll give Sarah a good time.

Sarah likes you," he added quietly. "I think you like her, too. She could use a few good memories before you go back to the life you left in San Antonio."

So he was going to freeze her out. He wanted her, but he wasn't going to do anything about it. He wanted her for Sarah, not for himself, despite his hunger for her.

She hesitated. "Is it wise letting her get used to me?" she asked, her voice echoing the disappointment she felt.

His hand on her chin became faintly caressing. "Why not?" he asked.

"It will be another upset for her when I leave," she said.

His thumb moved over her lips, brushing them, caressing them. "How long are you going to stay?"

"Until the first of the month," she said. "I do the autographing a week from Saturday."

His hand fell just in time to keep her from throwing herself against him and begging him to kiss her. "Then you can spend some time with Sarah and me until you leave. I won't force you into any corners and we can help Sarah find her feet."

Her eyes searched his night-shadowed face. "Why do you want me around?"

"God knows," he muttered. "But I do."

She sighed audibly, fighting her need to be near him.

"Don't brood," he said. He didn't smile, but there was something new about the way he was looking at her. "Just take things one day at a time and stop analyzing everything I say."

"Was I doing that? Okay, I'll try." She wished there were more light. She managed a smile. "Good night, Blake."

"Go on. I'll watch you."

She left him standing there and went running down to the house, her heart blazing with new hope.

If there was any chance for her to have Blake, she'd take it willingly, no matter what the risk. She now understood the reasons for his actions. And if she went slowly and didn't ask for the impossible, he might even come to love her one day. She went to sleep on that thought, and her dreams were so vivid that she woke up blushing.

Chapter 6

Meredith was awake, dressed and ready to go by eight on Saturday morning, with an hour to kill before it was time for Blake and Sarah to pick her up.

Bess, an early riser herself these days, made breakfast and smiled wickedly at her friend.

"It must feel strange to have Blake ask you out after all these years."

"It does. But I'm not kidding myself that it's out of any great love for me," she said, neglecting to tell Bess that Blake's main interest in her was sensual. All the same, just remembering the way he'd kissed her Wednesday night made her tingle from head to toe. And he'd shared secrets with her that she knew he'd never tell anyone else. That alone gave her a bit of hope. But she was afraid to trust him too much just yet. She needed time to adjust to the new Blake. She sighed. "I haven't been on a picnic in years. And I'm looking forward to it," she confessed with a smile, "even if he only wants me along because Sarah likes me."

"Sarah's a cute little girl." Bess sighed. "Bobby and I are ready to start a family of our own, but I can't seem to get pregnant. Oh, well, it takes time, I guess. Do you want something to eat?"

"I'm too nervous to eat," Meredith said honestly, her eyes still soft with memories of the night before. "I hope I'm wearing the right thing."

Bess studied her. Jeans, sneakers, a white tank top that showed off her pretty tan and emphasized her full, high breasts, and her dark hair loose around her shoulders. "You look great," she said. "And there's no rain in the forecast, so you should be fine."

"I should have slept longer," Meredith wailed. "I'll be a nervous wreck… Oh!"

The jangling of the telephone startled her, but Bess only smiled.

"If I were a gambling woman," Bess said as she went to answer it, "I'd bet my egg money that Blake's as nervous and impatient as you are." She picked the receiver up, said hello, then glanced amusedly at Meredith, whose heart was doing a marathon race in her chest. "Yes, she's ready, Blake," she said. "You might as well come get her before she wears out my carpet. I'll tell her. See you."

"How could you say that!" Meredith cried. "My best friend, and you sold me out to the enemy!"

"He isn't the enemy, and I think Blake needs all the advantages he can get." Bess's smile faded. "He's such a lonely man, Meredith. He was infatuated with Nina and he let himself be suckered into marriage without realizing she only wanted his money. He's paid for that mistake enough, don't you think?"

"There are some things you don't know," Meredith said.

"I'm sure there are. But if you love him in spite of those things I don't know, then it's foolish to risk your future out of spite and vengeance."

Meredith smiled wearily. "I don't have the strength for vengeance," she replied. "I wanted to get even for a long time after I left here, but when I saw him again…" She shrugged. "It's just like old times. I can't talk straight or walk without trembling when he gets within a foot of me. I never should have come back. He's going to hurt me again if I give him an opening. After what Nina did to him, he's not going to make it easy for any woman to get close. Least of all me."

"Give it a chance," Bess advised. "Nothing comes to us without some kind of risk. I've learned a lot about compromise since Bobby and I almost split up a few years ago. I've learned that pride is a poor bedfellow."

"I'm glad you two are getting along so well."

"So am I. I went a bit bonkers over my sexy brother-in-law for a while, but Elissa came along and solved all my problems," Bess confessed with a grin. "King Roper has a gunpowder temper, if you remember." Meredith grinned, because she did. "I couldn't stand up to him, but Elissa didn't give an inch. Not that they do much fighting these days, but they had a rocky start."

"She's so sweet," Meredith murmured. "I liked her the minute I met her."

"Most people do. And King would die for her."

Those words kept echoing in Meredith's brain as she sat in the car, with Blake behind the wheel and Sarah chattering away in the back seat. She looked at Blake's

taut profile and tried to imagine having him care enough
to die for her. It was a forlorn hope that he'd ever love
her. His reserved nature and Nina's cruelty wouldn't let
him.

He glanced at her and saw that sadness in her eyes.
"What is it?" he asked.

"Nothing." She smiled at Sarah, who was looking
worried. "I'm just barely awake."

Blake lifted an eyebrow as the powerful car ate up
the miles. "That explains why you were up and dressed
at eight when I said we'd be at Bess's at nine."

"I couldn't sleep," she muttered.

"Neither could I," he replied. "Sarah was too excited to
stay in bed this morning," he added, just when Meredith
was breathless at the thought that the memory of the way
he'd kissed her had been the reason he didn't sleep.

"I'm so glad you came, Merry," Sarah said, hugging
her new Mr. Friend stuffed bear in the back seat. "We'll
have lots of fun! Daddy says there's a swing!"

"Several," he returned. "Jack's Corner has added a
new park since you were here," he told Meredith. "It
has swings and a sandbox and one of those things kids
love to climb on. We can sit on a bench and watch her.
Then there are plenty of tables. I thought we'd pick up
something at one of the fast food stores for lunch, since
Amie wasn't around to fix a picnic basket."

"Did she call?"

"Yes. Her sister is recovering very well, but it will be
at least two weeks more before Amie comes back."

"How are you managing?"

"Not very well," he confessed. "I'm no cook, and
there are things Amie could do for Sarah that I'm not
comfortable doing."

"Daddy won't bathe me," Sarah called out. "He says he doesn't know how."

A flush of color worked its way up Blake's cheekbones and Meredith felt the embarrassment with him. It would be hard for a man to do such things for a daughter when he'd rarely been around a woman and never around little girls.

"I could..." Meredith hesitated at his sharp glance and then plowed ahead. "I could bathe her for you tonight. I wouldn't mind."

"Oh, Merry, could you?" Sarah enthused.

"If your father doesn't mind," she continued with a concerned glance in Blake's direction.

"I wouldn't mind," he said, without taking his eyes from the road.

"And you can tell me some more stories, Merry," Sarah said. "I specially like 'The Ugly Ducking.'"

"Duckling," Blake corrected, and he smiled faintly at his child. "I guess that story fits both of us, sprout."

"Neither of you," Meredith interrupted. "You both have character and stubborn wills. That's worth a lot more than beauty."

"Daddy has a scar," Sarah piped up.

Meredith smiled at the child. "A mark of courage," she corrected. "And your father was always handsome enough that it didn't matter."

Blake felt his chest grow two sizes. His gaze darted to Meredith's face and he searched her eyes long and intently. As she was feeling the effect of that glance, he forced his eyes back to the road barely in time to avoid running the car into a ditch.

"Sorry," Meredith murmured with a grimace.

"No need." He turned the car down the street that

led to the city park and pulled it into a vacant parking space.

"It's beautiful," Meredith said, looking at the expanse of wooded land with a children's playground and a gazebo. There was even a fountain. At this time of the day, though, the area was fairly deserted. Dew was still on the grass, and as they walked to the benches overlooking the playground, Meredith laughed as her sneakers quickly became soaked.

"Your feet are getting wet," Sarah said, laughing, too. "But I have my cowgirl boots on!"

"I think I can spare your feet," Blake murmured.

Before she realized what he intended, Blake bent and whipped Meredith off the ground, carrying her close to his chest without any sign of strain.

"Gosh, you're strong, Daddy," Sarah remarked.

"He always was," Meredith said involuntarily, and her eyes looked up into Blake's, full of memories, full of helpless vulnerability.

His arms contracted a fraction, but he didn't look at her. He didn't dare. He could already feel the effect that rapt stare had on his body. If he gazed at Meredith's soft, yielding face, he would start kissing her despite the small audience of one watching them so closely.

He put her down on the sidewalk without a word and moved to the bench to sit down, leaning back and crossing one booted foot over his jeans-clad knee. "Well, sit down," he said impatiently. "Sarah, play while you can. This place probably fills up in an hour or so."

"Yes, Daddy!" Sarah said and she ran for the swings. Meredith sat down beside Blake, still glowing and warm from the feel of his arms and savoring the warm, cologne-scented fragrance of his lean body. "She's already a different child," she commented, watching

Sarah laugh as she pumped her little legs to make the swing go higher.

"She's less wild," Blake agreed. He took off his hat and put it next to him on the bench, pausing to run his hand through his thick black hair. "But she isn't quite secure yet. The nightmares haven't stopped completely. And I've had less time to spend with her lately. Business goes on. A lot of jobs depend on the decisions I make. I can't throw up my hands and stay home every day."

"Sarah likes Amie, doesn't she?" Meredith asked.

"Amie won't be here for several weeks, Meredith," he said impatiently. "That's what I'm worried about. Monday morning I've got a board meeting. What do I do with Sarah, take her along?"

"I see your problem." Meredith sighed, fingering the face of her watch. "Well...I could keep her for you."

He didn't dare let himself react to that offer, even if it was the second time in a day that she'd volunteered to spend time with Sarah. It wouldn't do to get his hopes up too high.

"Could you?" he asked, and turned his head so that his green eyes pinned her gray ones.

"All I have to do is the autographing," she said. "And that's next Saturday. The rest of my time is vacation."

"You'd need to be at the house," he said with apparent unconcern. He pursed his lips, watching Sarah. "And considering how late I get home some nights, it's hardly worth rousing Bobby and Bess to let you in just for a few hours. Is it?"

She colored. "Blake, I don't care if this is the nineteen eighties, I can't move into your house...."

He glanced at her and saw the rose-red blush. "I won't seduce you. I told you that Wednesday, and I meant it."

The blush deepened. She averted her gaze to Sarah

and her heart shook her with its mad beat. "I know you won't go back on your word, Blake," she whispered. "But it's what people would think."

"And you're a famous author," he said, his eyes narrowing. "God forbid that I should tarnish your reputation."

"Don't start on me." She sighed miserably and got up. "This isn't a good idea. I shouldn't have come…!"

He got up, too, and caught her by the waist, holding her in front of him. "I'm sorry," he bit off. "I've never given a damn what people thought, but I guess when you aren't looked down on to begin with, reputations matter."

She looked up at him with soft, compassionate eyes. "I never looked down on you."

His jaw clenched. "Don't you think I know that now?" he asked huskily. He pulled her hand to his chest and smoothed over the neat pink nails, his eyes on her long fingers. "You were always defending me."

"And you hated it," she recalled with a sad smile. "I always seemed to make you mad—"

"I told you," he interrupted. "I wanted you, and I didn't know how to handle it. I knew it was impossible to seduce you, and I'd given my word that I was going to marry Nina." His shoulders lifted and fell. "It wasn't conscious, but afterward when I thought about what I did to you that day, I thought maybe it would be easier for you if I made you hate me." He looked up into her gray eyes with quiet sincerity.

Her face felt hot. She searched his hard expression for a long moment. "I suppose in a way it was," she said finally. "But it undermined my confidence. I couldn't believe any man would want me."

"Which worked to my advantage," he whispered,

smiling faintly. "Because you weren't tempted to experiment with anyone else." The smile faded. "You're still a virgin. And your first man, Meredith, is going to be me."

Her heart stopped and then ran wild. "That's the most chauvinistic—"

He stopped her by simply lowering his head until his lips were almost touching hers. She could taste his coffee-flavored breath and the intimacy of it made her knees feel rubbery. "I am chauvinistic," he whispered. "And possessive. And hard as nails. I can't help those traits. Life hasn't been kind to me. Not until just recently."

His hands were on her shoulders, holding her in place, and his eyes were on her mouth in a way that made her breath rustle in her throat.

"Sa-Sarah Jane…" she stammered.

"Is facing the opposite direction and doesn't have eyes in the back of her head," he murmured. "So just give me your mouth without a struggle, little one, and I'll show you how gentle I can be when I try."

He felt her mouth accept his with the first touch, felt her body give when he drew her against his hard chest. She sighed into his mouth, and his brows drew together tightly over his closed eyes with the sheer pleasure of holding her.

She reached up under his arms to hold him and her body melted without a vestige of fear. Even when she felt the inevitable effect of her closeness on his powerful body, she didn't flinch or try to move away. He was her heart. Despite the pain and the anguish of years ago, he was all she knew or wanted of love.

His hands smoothed her hair as his hard mouth moved slowly on hers. She'd dreamed of this for so many years, dreamed of his mouth taking hers with exquisite tenderness, giving as much as he took. But the dreams paled beside the sweet reality. Her nails scraped against his back, loving the way the muscles rippled under her fingers.

His mouth lifted a fraction of an inch, and his breath was audible. "Who taught you to do that?" he whispered huskily.

"Nobody. I…guess it comes naturally," she whispered back.

His hands slid up her back to her hair and tangled gently in it. "Your mouth is very soft," he said unsteadily. "And it tastes of coffee and mint."

"I had Irish mocha mint coffee," she said.

"Did you?" He searched her eyes slowly. "Your legs are trembling," he remarked.

She laughed nervously. "I'm not surprised," she confessed. "My knees are wobbly."

He smiled, and the smile echoed in his eyes. "Are they?"

"Daddy, watch how high I can go!" a small voice called out.

Blake reluctantly loosened his hold on Meredith. "I'm watching," he called back.

Sarah Jane was swinging high and laughing. "I can almost touch the sky!" she said.

"Funny, so can I," Blake murmured. He glanced at Meredith, and he wasn't smiling.

She looked back, her heart threatening to burst. He took her hand in his, threading his fingers through hers so that he had them pressed in an almost intimate hold.

"To hell with your reputation," he said huskily. "Move in with us for a couple of weeks. Nobody will know except Bess and Bobby, and they're not judgmental."

She wanted to. Her worried eyes searched his. "Your

company is an old and very conservative one. Your board of directors wouldn't like it at all."

"My board of directors doesn't dictate my private life," he replied. "We could sit close on the couch and watch television at night with Sarah. We could have breakfast together in the kitchen. If Sarah had nightmares, she could climb in with you. You could read her stories and I could listen." He smiled crookedly. "I don't remember anybody ever reading me a story, Meredith," he added. "My uncle wasn't the type. I grew up in a world without fairy tales and happy endings. Maybe that's why I'm so bitter. I don't want Sarah to end up like me."

"Don't run yourself down," she said softly. Her eyes searched over his face warmly. "I think you turned out pretty well."

He touched her hair with a big, lean hand. "I never meant to be as cruel to you as I was." He sighed wearily. "And I guess if it hadn't been for Sarah, you wouldn't have come near me again, would you?" he asked.

She lowered her eyes to his chest. "I don't know," she said honestly. "I was still bitter, and a little afraid of you when I came back. But when I saw you with Sarah…" Her eyes lifted. "You might not realize it, but you're different when she's around. She takes some of the rough edges off you."

"She's pretty special. No thanks to Nina," he added curtly. "God knows why she kept the child when she so obviously didn't want her."

"Maybe her husband did."

"If he did, he sure changed his tune when he found out she was mine. He turned his back on her completely. I'm damned if I could have done that to a child," he said coldly. "Whether or not we shared the same blood, there are bonds equally strong."

"Not everyone has a sense of honor," Meredith reminded him. "Your sense of honor was always one of your strongest traits."

"It still is." He sat down on the bench again, tugging her down beside him and drawing her closer while Sarah stopped the swing and ran to the sandbox. "She'll carry half that sand home with us," he murmured ruefully.

"Sand brushes off," Meredith reminded him.

He smiled. "So it does." He leaned back and his hand contracted on her shoulder. "She's crazy about you."

"I like her, too. She's a wonderful little girl."

"I hope you'll still think so after she's treated you to one of her tantrums."

"Most children have those," she reminded him. She leaned back against his arm and looked up at him. Impulsively she reached up and touched the white line of scar tissue on his face, noticing the way he flinched and grabbed her hand. "It's not unsightly," she said softly, and she smiled. "I told Sarah it was a mark of courage, and it is. You got it because of me. It was my fault."

His fingers curled around hers and pressed before he led them back to the scar and let her touch it. "Saving you from a wild bronc," he recalled, smiling because it was a lot like what had happened to Sarah in the corral. "You weren't after a lacy white handkerchief. Instead it was a kitten that had run into the corral. I got to you in the nick of time, but I ran face first into a piece of tin on the way out."

"You used words I'd never heard before or since," she murmured sheepishly. "And I deserved every one of them. But you let me patch you up, anyway. That was sweet," she said unthinkingly, and then lowered her eyes.

"'Sweet.'" His hard lips pursed as he studied her face.

"You'll never know what I felt. The atmosphere was electric that day. I gritted my teeth and forced myself to glare at you. It kept me from doing what I really wanted to do."

"Which was?" she asked, curious, because she remembered too well the cold fury in his face and voice as she'd doctored him.

"I wanted to pull you into my lap and kiss the breath out of you," he said huskily. "You were wearing a cotton blouse with nothing, not a damned thing, under it. I could see the outline of your breasts under the blouse and I wanted to touch them so badly that I shook with longing. It wasn't more than a day later that I did just that, in the stable. You didn't know," he guessed, watching the expressions play across her face.

"No," she admitted breathlessly. "I had no idea. Of course, I was shaking a little myself, and trying so hard to hide my reaction from you that I didn't notice what you might be feeling."

"I lay awake all night, remembering the way you looked and sounded and smelled." He glanced at Sarah, watching her make a pointed castle in the sand and stack twigs around it for doors and windows. "I woke up aching. And then, days later, they read the will, and I went wild. Nina was clinging to me, I was confused about what I felt for you and for her." He shrugged. "I went crazy. That's why I said such cruel things to you. I wanted you so badly. When I saw you later, I couldn't resist one last chance to hold you, to taste you. So I kissed you. It took every last ounce of willpower I had to pull back."

"I really hated you for that," she said, remembering. "I knew you were getting even for the will, for what your uncle tried to do. I never realized that you really wanted me." She smiled self-consciously.

His lips twisted. "Do you think a man can fake desire?" he asked with a level stare.

She flushed and avoided his gaze. "No."

"At least I know now that I'm still capable of feeling it," he said heavily, his eyes going again to Sarah. "It's been a long dry spell. I couldn't bear the thought of having some other woman cut up my pride the way Nina did. And no one knows better than I do that I'm not much good in bed."

"I think that depends on who you're in bed with," she said, staring at his shirt. "When two people care about each other, it's supposed to be magic, even if neither of them has any experience."

"It wasn't magic for us, and we both fit into that category the day the will was read," he murmured softly.

"That's true. But I fought you. I didn't understand what was happening," she confessed.

He studied her down-bent head. "Do you think it might be different now that we've both had five years to mature?"

"I don't know," she said.

His lean hand touched her hair hesitantly and trailed down her cheek to her soft mouth. "I haven't learned a lot," he said, his voice quiet and deep. He drew in a slow breath. "And you knock me off balance pretty bad. I might frighten you if things got out of hand."

He sounded as if the thought tormented him. She lifted her eyes and looked up at him. "Oh, no," she said softly. "You wouldn't hurt me."

His heart stampeded in his chest when she looked

at him that way. "Would you go that far with me?" he whispered.

She couldn't sustain that piercing green-eyed gaze. Her eyes fell to his hard mouth. "Don't ask me, Blake," she pleaded. "I would, but I'd hate both of us. All those years of strict upbringing don't just go away because we want them to. I'm not made for a permissive life. Not even with you."

She made it sound as if he were the exception to the rule, and he felt a sting of pure unadulterated masculine pride at her words. She wanted to. He smiled slowly. That made things a little easier. Of course, the walls were all still up. The smile faded when he realized that those scruples of hers were going to stop him, because his own conscience and sense of honor wouldn't let him seduce her. Not even if she wanted him to.

"I guess I'm not either, if you want the truth." He sighed. "You and I are a dying breed, honey."

She heard the endearment with a sense of awe. It was the first time he'd used one with her, the very first time. She was aware of a new warmth deep inside her as she savored it in her mind.

"Daddy, look at my sand castle!" Sarah Jane called. "Isn't it pretty? But I'm hungry. And I want to go to the bathroom."

Blake smiled involuntarily. "Okay, sprout. Come on." He moved slightly away from Meredith. "She doesn't settle for long. Her mind is like a grasshopper."

"I think it's the age." Meredith smiled. She knelt and held out her arms for Sarah to run into, and she lifted the child, hugging her close. "You smell nice," she said. "What do you have on?"

"It's Daddy's," Sarah said, and Blake's eyebrows shot

up. "It was on his table and I got me some. Isn't it nice? Daddy always smells good."

"Yes, he does." Meredith was fighting a losing battle with the giggles. She looked at Blake's astounded face and burst out laughing.

"So that's where it went," he murmured, sniffing Sarah and wrinkling his nose. "Sprout, that stuff's for me. It's not for little girls."

"I want to be like you, Daddy," Sarah said simply, and there was the sweetest, warmest light in her green yees.

Blake smiled at her fully for the first time, his white teeth flashing against his dark tan. "Well, well. I guess I'll have to teach you how to ride and rope, then."

"Oh, yes!" Sarah agreed. "I can ride a horse now. And I can rope anything. Can't I, Merry?"

Meredith almost agreed, but Blake's eyes were making veiled threats.

"You'd better wait a bit, until your daddy can teach you properly," Meredith said carefully, and Blake nodded in approval.

"I hate to wait," Sarah muttered.

"Don't we all," Blake murmured, but he didn't look at Meredith as he started toward the car. "Let's find someplace that sells food."

They found a small convenience store with rest rooms just a little way down the road, where they bought coffee and soft drinks and the fixings for sandwiches, along with pickles and chips. Blake drove them back to the park, which was beginning to fill up.

"I know a better place than this," he remarked. "Sarah, how would you like to wade in the river?"

"Oh, boy!" she exclaimed.

He smiled at Meredith, who smiled back. "Then let's

go. We're between the Canadian and the North Canadian rivers. Take your pick."

"The North Canadian, then," Meredith said.

He turned the car and shot off in the opposite direction, while Sarah Jane asked a hundred questions about Oklahoma, the rivers, the Indians and why the sky was blue.

Meredith just sat quietly beside Blake as he drove, admiring his lean hands on the wheel, the ease with which he maneuvered through Jack's Corner and out onto the plains. He didn't try to talk while he drove, which was good, because Sarah wouldn't have let him get a word in edgewise, anyway.

Sarah's chatter gave Meredith a breathing space and she used it to worry over Blake's unexpected proposal. He wanted her to move in with him and Sarah, and she was more tempted than he knew. She had to keep reminding herself that she had a lot to lose—and it was more than just a question of her reputation and his. It was a question of her own will and whether she could trust herself to say no to Blake if he decided to turn on the heat.

He wasn't a terribly experienced man, but that wouldn't matter if he started kissing her. She still loved him. If he wanted her, she wasn't sure that all her scruples would keep her out of his bed.

And being the old-fashioned man he was, she didn't know what would happen if she gave in. He'd probably feel obliged to offer to marry her. That would ruin everything. She didn't want a marriage based on obligation. If he grew to care about her, and wanted her for his own sake and not Sarah's...

She forced her mind back to the present. It didn't do to anticipate fate. Regardless of how she felt, it was Blake's feelings that mattered now. He had to want more than just her body before she could feel comfortable about the future.

Chapter 7

Blake drove over the bridge that straddled the Canadian River, but he didn't stop on its banks. He kept driving until finally he turned off on a dirt road and they went still another short distance. He stopped the car under an oak tree and helped Meredith and Sarah Jane out into the shade.

"Where are we?" Meredith asked, disoriented.

He smiled. "Come and see." He took Sarah's hand and led them through the trees to a huge body of water. "Know where you are now?" he asked.

Meredith laughed. "Lake Thunderbird!" she burst out. "But this isn't the way to get to it! And this isn't the North Canadian or the Canadian. It's in between!"

"Don't confuse the issue with a lot of facts," he said with dry humor. "Isn't this a nice place for a picnic?" he went on. "We have shade and peace and quiet."

"Who owns this land?"

He pursed his lips. "Well, actually, it's part of what I inherited from my uncle. It's only fifteen acres, but I like it here." He looked around the wooded area with eyes that appreciated its natural beauty. "When I need to think out something, I come here. I guess that's why I've never built on it. I like it this way."

"Yes, I can see why," Meredith agreed. Birds were singing nearby, and the wind brushed leafy branches together with soft whispers of sound. She closed her eyes and let the breeze lift her hair, and she thought that with Sarah and Blake beside her, she'd never been closer to heaven.

"Sarah, don't go too near the edge," Blake cautioned.

"But you said I could go wading," the child protested, and began to look mutinous.

"So I did," he agreed. "But not here. After we eat, there's a nice place farther down the road where you can wade. Okay?"

For several long seconds, she matched her small will against his. But in the end she gave in. "Okay," she said.

Blake got out the cold cuts and bread, and a heavy cloth to spread on the grass. They ate in contented silence as Sarah offered crumbs to ants and other insects, fascinated with the variety of tiny life.

"Haven't you ever seen a bug before, Sarah?" Meredith asked.

"Not really," the little girl replied. "Mama said they're nasty and she killed them. But the man on TV says that bugs are bene...bene..."

"Beneficial," Blake said. "And I could argue that with the man on TV, especially when they get into the hides of my cattle."

Meredith smiled at him. He smiled back. Then the smiles faded and they were looking at each other openly, with a blistering kind of attraction that made Meredith's body go hot. She'd never experienced that electricity with anyone except Blake. Probably she never would, but she had to get a grip on herself before it was too late.

She forced her eyes down to the cloth. "How about another sandwich?" she offered with forced cheer.

After they finished the makeshift meal, Blake drove them down to the small stream. It ran across the dirt road, and Sarah tugged off her cowgirl boots in a fever to get to the clear, rippling water. Butterflies drifted down on the wet sand, and Blake smiled at the picture the child made walking barefoot through the water.

"I used to do that when I was a boy," Blake said, hands in his pockets as he leaned against the trunk of the car and watched her. "Kids who live in cities miss a hell of a lot."

"Yes, they do. I can remember playing like this, too. We used to get water from streams occasionally in oil drums, when the well went dry." Her eyes had a wistful, faraway look. "We were so poor in those days. I never realized how poor until I went to a birthday party in grammar school and saw how other kids lived." She sighed. "I never told my parents how devastating it was. But I realized then what a difference money makes."

"It doesn't seem to have changed you all that much, Meredith," he said, studying her quietly. "You're a little more confident than you used to be, but you're no snob."

"Thank you." She twisted the small gold-braid ring on her finger nervously. "But I'm not in your class yet. I get by and that's all."

"A Porsche convertible is more than just getting by," he mused.

"I felt reckless the day I bought it. I was thinking about coming back here and facing the past," she confessed. "I bought it to give me confidence."

"We all need confidence boosters from time to time," Blake replied quietly, his eyes on Sarah. "She's slowly coming out of the past. I like seeing her laugh. She didn't in those first few days with me."

"I guess she was afraid to," Meredith said. "She hasn't really had much security in her young life."

"She's got it now. As long as I live, I'll take care of her."

The pride and faint possessiveness in his deep voice touched Meredith. She wondered how it would feel to have him say the same thing about her, and she blushed. Blake might allow himself to become vulnerable with a small child, but she had serious doubts about his ability to really love a woman. Nina had hurt him too badly.

They stayed another few minutes, and then Sarah announced that she needed to find a bathroom again. With an amused smile, Blake loaded them into the car and set out for a gas station.

They drove around looking at the countryside until almost dark. Then they went home and Meredith helped Sarah get a bath. After that, she settled down by the child's bedside to tell her some stories before she fell asleep.

She was halfway through "Sleeping Beauty," when Blake came into the room and sat down, legs crossed, in the chair by the window to listen. He was a little intimidating, but Sarah laughed and encouraged Meredith, and in no time she was lost in the fantasy herself.

She told the child two more stories and Sarah's eyelids grew heavier by the second. By the time Meredith had started on "Snow White," Sarah Jane was sound asleep.

Meredith got up, tucked the covers around the tired little body and bent impulsively to kiss Sarah goodnight.

"That's another thing she's missed," Blake remarked as he joined her by the bed. "Being kissed good-night." He shifted, his hands in his pockets as he looked down at his daughter. "Showing affection is difficult for me." He glanced at Meredith. "My uncle wasn't the kissing sort." He smiled a little. "And I guess you know that."

She laughed. "Yes. I remember. He was a sweet man, but he hated touching or being touched."

"So do I," Blake replied. His eyes slid over Meredith's soft oval face. "Except by you," he added quietly. "I used to love to get cut up when you were here because you always patched me up. I loved the feel of your hands on my skin. I remember how soft and caring they were." He sighed heavily and turned away. "We'd better get out of here before we wake her up."

It was obviously embarrassing to him to admit how much he'd enjoyed her doctoring. That was surprising. She hadn't realized until he'd said it just how many minor accidents he seemed to have had in the old days, when she was around. She smiled to herself. That was one more tiny secret to cherish in the years ahead, when these sweet days were just a memory and Blake was far out of her reach.

"Why are you smiling?" he asked curtly.

She looked across at him as she closed Sarah's door. "I was thinking how ironic it is. I loved it when you needed patching up because it gave me an excuse to get close to you." She colored a little as she averted her eyes.

"Isn't it amazing how green we both were?" he asked. "Considering our ages. We weren't kids."

"No."

The atmosphere was getting tenser by the second. She could almost feel the hard pressure of his mouth on her lips, and the way he was watching her, with that single-minded level stare, made her knees feel weak under her.

"How do you remember all those fairy tales?" Blake asked to relieve the tension that he was feeling.

"I don't know. It's a knack, I guess. Blake, you really do need to get her some storybooks," she said.

"You'll have to pick them out," he replied. "I don't know beans about what kids her age read."

"All right. I'll see if Mrs. Donaldson has any in her shop. I noticed some books in the back, but I didn't take time to look at them."

"I appreciate your help tonight," he said. "Some facets of being a parent are difficult. Especially dealing with frilly underwear and baths." He leaned against the wall, in no hurry to go downstairs, and his green eyes wandered slowly over Meredith's exquisite figure in the revealing button-up white tank top and well-fitting blue jeans. His eyes narrowed on that top because he didn't think there was anything under it and her breasts were hard tipped when they hadn't been a minute ago. "You're very maternal."

"I like children. Shouldn't we go downstairs?" she added nervously, because she felt the impact of his eyes on her breasts.

"Why? Do you suspect that I'm going to drag you into my bedroom and lock the door?"

"Of course not," she said too quickly.

"Pity," he remarked, shouldering away from the wall. "Because that's exactly what I'm going to do."

And he did, quickly, smoothly and with deadly efficiency. Before Meredith had time to say anything, he had her in his room. He paused to lock the door and then lowered her onto the middle of the king-size bed.

She lay there breathless, staring up at him, as he bent over her, one lean hand on either side of her head, his green eyes biting into hers.

"How afraid of me are you, Meredith?" he asked quietly. "If I start making love to you, are you going to kick and scream for help?"

Her lips parted as she looked up at him. She wasn't afraid of him at all. During the day, something had happened to both of them. The time they'd spent together had acted to bring them close. She knew more about him now than she ever had, and the thought uppermost in her mind was how much she loved him. Her eyes fell to his hard mouth, and she wanted it, and him, almost shockingly.

"No, I'm not frightened," she said. "Because I know you won't hurt me or force me to do anything I don't want to. You said so."

He seemed to relax a little. "That's true. I meant it, too." His eyes slid down her body, lingering on the thrust of her breasts against the tank top and the way her jeans clung to her rounded hips and long legs. "You can't imagine the effect you've had on me all day in that getup. Do you know how sexy you are?"

"Me?" she asked with a faint, delighted smile.

"You." He lifted his gaze back to collide with hers. "And you aren't getting out of here yet."

She felt tiny tremors shooting up and down her spine at the delicious threat. "I'm not?" she asked huskily.

He lowered himself down over her so that his chest was almost touching her breasts and his mouth was within an inch of hers. "No," he breathed. "You're not."

Her hands slid up around his neck and her eyes dropped to his mouth. He smelled of cologne and she loved the feel of his shoulders and back under her hands, the hard muscles under the thin shirt. Her breath jerked out of her throat as she felt the warm threat of his body and tasted his coffee-scented breath on her lips.

"Just relax," he whispered as his mouth brushed hers. "I won't hurt you."

Her hands slid into his thick hair and she let her body sink under the warm weight of his chest as it pressed against hers. His mouth was slow and hungry, and she didn't mind when it began to probe inside her own. She'd never kissed anyone except Blake this way, and she loved the sensuality of it. She let his tongue enter her mouth and her hands clung as the new sensations ran like fire along her nerves and made her weak.

She kissed him back, savoring the warm hungry mouth on hers. One of his hands supported her neck, but the other slid over her shoulder and suddenly covered her soft breast.

She took an audible breath and he lifted his head, but he didn't remove his hand.

"You're a woman now," he whispered. "And we've done this together once before. Except that this time, I'm not so green."

"Yes." She touched his fingers, lightly brushing them, while her eyes looked into his glittering ones with building excitement. Her swollen lips parted. "You could...unbutton it," she whispered shakily. "I'm not wearing anything under it."

She colored as she said it, and he realized how much courage it took for her to make him such an offer. Was she trying to prove that she trusted him, or could she feel the same hunger he did?

His fingers slid to the buttons and slowly began to slip them out of the buttonholes. And all the while, he searched her eyes, held them. "Why aren't you wearing anything underneath?" he asked when he'd finished and the edges were still touching.

"Don't you know, Blake?" she whispered with aching hunger. She arched just a fraction of an inch.

The invitation was as blatant as if she'd shouted it. He slowly peeled the edges of the tank top away from her full, firm breasts and let his eyes fall to them. They were as beautiful as they had been five years ago. A little fuller now, firmer. The color of seashells and rose petals, he thought dizzily as his eyes lingered on the hard tips that signaled her desire.

"Have you ever let any other man see you like this?" he whispered, because it was suddenly important.

"Only you," she replied, and her eyes were warm and soft, almost loving as they met his. "How could I let anyone else...?" she asked huskily.

"Meredith, you're exquisite," he bit off. His fingers brushed over one perfect breast lightly, barely touching it, and she cried out.

The sound startled him. He stopped at once, scowling at her in open concern. "Did I hurt you?" he asked softly. "I knew you were delicate there. I didn't mean to be rough with you."

She stared at him curiously, biting her lower lip as she

tried to control the tremors he'd set off. "Blake...it didn't hurt," she said hesitantly.

"You cried out," he said, his eyes steady and honestly worried.

She colored furiously. "Yes."

The scowl stayed as his hand moved again. His green eyes held hers the whole time while he stroked her gently, smoothed the hard tip between his fingers and cupped her in his lean, rough hand. And she whimpered softly and cried out again, her body shivering and lifting up to him.

"Damn Nina!" he whispered roughly.

Meredith was too drugged to understand what he'd said at first. Her whirling thoughts barely registered in her mind. "What?"

"Never mind," he whispered huskily. "Oh, God, Meredith...!" His mouth went down against her breast, and she moaned, arching under him. The sound and her trembling drove him crazy.

He kissed every soft inch of her above her hips, savoring both breasts, nibbling at her creamy skin, dragging the edge of his teeth with exquisite tenderness over her stomach and rib cage. And all the while his hands caressed her, adored her. He made a meal of her, and long before he lifted his head, she was crying and pleading with him for something more than he was giving her.

He dragged air into his lungs, his eyes wild, his chest rising and falling raggedly as he looked down into her abandoned eyes.

Her face fascinated him. She looked as if he was torturing her, but her hands were pulling at his head, her soft voice was begging for his mouth. She moaned, but not in pain. And the most exquisite sensations racked his lean body as he poised over her. "You want me," he whispered huskily.

"Yes."

"Badly," he continued.

"Yes!"

His hands smoothed over her breasts and she shuddered. His breath caught. "I never dreamed a woman could sound like that. I never knew…" He bent to her mouth and kissed it softly. "My God, she was suffering me, and I didn't even have the experience to realize it."

"What?"

He dragged himself into a sitting position, and when she made a halfhearted effort to cover herself he pulled her wrist away. "Don't do that," he said quietly. "You're the most beautiful thing I've ever seen in my life. I won't hurt you."

"I know that. I'm just…embarrassed," she faltered, flushing.

"You shouldn't be," he said firmly. "The first intimacy I ever shared with a woman was with you. And your first one was with me. I know what you look like. I've seen you every night in my dreams."

She relaxed a little, sighing as she sank back on the bed. "It's just new," she tried to explain.

"Yes, I know." He brushed his fingertips over a firm breast and watched her shiver with pleasure. "That's sweet," he breathed. "That's so damned sweet, Meredith."

Her breath sighed out. "Blake…"

"What do you want?" he asked, reading the hesitant curiosity in her eyes. "Tell me. I'll do anything you want."

"Could you…unbutton your shirt and let me look at you?" she whispered.

His blood surged in his veins. He flicked buttons open with a hand that was deftly efficient even as he trembled inside with the hunger she aroused. He moved the fabric aside, and when he saw the sheer delight in her eyes at the thick mat of hair over impressive muscle, arrowing down to his jeans, he stripped the whole damned shirt off and threw it on the floor to give her an unobstructed view.

She held out her arms, and he groaned as he went into them, shuddering when he felt her nipples press against his chest as he crushed her into the mattress.

"Blake," she moaned. Her arms clung and her lips searched blindly for his. She found them and kissed him with all her heart, feeling his mouth tremble as it increased its hungry pressure.

He slid over her. His hands found her hips and urged them up against his, moving them against his rhythmically, letting her experience the full surge of his arousal.

She was whimpering, and he felt his control giving. It would only take another few seconds...

"No!" he bit off. He jerked himself away from her and rolled over, but he couldn't get to his feet. He lay there doubled up, while Meredith managed to get her trembling arms to support her. But she didn't touch him. He was shivering and she wanted to cry because she knew it was hurting him that he'd had to stop.

"I'm sorry," she wept. "It's all my fault."

"No, it isn't," he said through his teeth. He drew in sharp breaths until he could get himself under control. His body relaxed and he lay there for a long moment, fighting the need to roll over and strip her and submerge himself in her soft warm body.

"I wouldn't have stopped you," she breathed.

"I know that, too." He finally dragged himself up and ran his hands through his damp hair. His eyes darted to her half-clad body, softening as they swept over her full breasts. "Button your top," he said gently. "Or I'm going to start screaming my head off."

She managed a shaky smile as she pulled her top together and buttoned it with trembling fingers. "You make me feel beautiful," she whispered.

"My God, you are," he returned. His darkened green eyes held hers. "I can't begin to tell you what those sweet little noises you were making did for my ego. I didn't know women made noise or looked like that when they made love."

She searched his eyes. "I don't understand."

"Meredith," he began heavily, "Nina smiled. All through it, all the time. She smiled."

It took a minute for that to get through to her. When it did, she went scarlet. "Oh!"

"I hurt you, that first time," he continued. "So I didn't get any passionate response. I didn't have any other experience when I married Nina, so I thought women were supposed to smile." A corner of his hard mouth lifted ruefully. "But now I know, don't I?"

Her face felt as if she might fry eggs on it. "I couldn't help it," she confessed self-consciously. "I never dreamed there was such pleasure in being touched by a man."

He caught one of her hands and pressed its soft palm hungrily to his mouth. "The pleasure was mutual," he said, his glittering gaze holding hers. "I almost lost it. You let me hold your hips against mine, and I went crazy."

"I'm sorry," she said softly. "I should have pulled away."

"Are you supposed to be superhuman?" he asked

reasonably. "I couldn't stop, either. Together we start fires. I wanted nothing more in life than to feel you under me and around me, skin on skin, mouth on mouth, absorbing me into you."

She caught her breath and trembled at the words, seeing the quiet pride in his eyes when he realized the effect they had on her.

"I want to make love to you," he whispered roughly. "Here. Now. On my bed."

"I can't." She closed her eyes. "Please don't ask me."

"It isn't lack of desire. What, then? Scruples?"

She nodded miserably. "You know how I was raised, Blake. It's hard to forget the teachings of a lifetime overnight, even when you want someone very, very much."

"Then suppose you marry me, Meredith."

Her eyes opened wide. "What?"

"We get along well together. You like Sarah. You want me. You've got a career, so I know you don't need my money, and you know I don't need yours. We could build a good life together." He searched her shocked face. "I know I'm not the best matrimonial prospect going. I'm short-tempered and impatient, and I can be ruthless. But you know the worst of me already. There won't be any terrible surprises after the vows."

"I don't know…" she argued.

"You want hearts and flowers and bells ringing." He nodded. "Well, that doesn't always happen. Sometimes you have to settle for practicalities. Tell me you don't want to live with me, Meredith," he challenged with a faintly mocking smile.

"That would be a lie," she said, sighing, "so I won't bother. Yes, I want to live with you. And I'm very fond of Sarah Jane. Taking care of her wouldn't be any trial to me. But you're still not going to let your emotions get in the way of a good business deal, are you, Blake?" she returned. "You want me, but that's all you have to offer."

"For a man, lovemaking is one big part of a relationship," he said, choosing his words. "I don't know much about love. I've never had any." He lifted his eyes back to hers. "If it can be taught, you can teach me. I've never been in love, so you've got a good shot at it already."

She sighed at his summing-up of the situation, despite the ache in her heart for something he might never be able to give her. He was locked up emotionally, and nobody had a key.

He leaned down, his face poised just above hers. "Stop thinking, Meredith," he whispered. His mouth nibbled at her lower lip, smoothing over its delicate swell. His hands cupped her breasts, hot even through the fabric of her tank top and sensual as they caressed her. One long leg insinuated itself between both of hers and she felt it begin to move lazily.

"This isn't fair," she whispered shakily.

"I know. Unbutton your top again," he whispered, and proceeded to tell her exactly why he wanted her to and what he intended to do when she unfastened it.

Her body tingled with heat. She wanted him. Her moan was pure surrender, and he knew it. His heart leaped as he felt her fingers working at the buttons. And then she was all silky warmth under him, her breasts soft and yielding under his searching hands, his hungry mouth.

"You aren't…going to stop…this time, are you?" she whimpered as his mouth grew even bolder.

"That depends on you," he said in a strange, thick tone. "I'd never force you."

"I know." Her mind tumbled while she tried to decide what to do. Part of her knew it was a mistake. But it had been so many years, and she'd done little else but dream of him, of lying in his arms and loving him.

His hand slid to the fastening of her jeans and he lifted himself so that he could see her eyes. "If I start this, I'll have to finish it," he said gently. "I'll go all the way. You have to decide."

Her fingers lingered on his. "I don't know," she moaned. "Blake, I'm afraid. It's going to hurt...!"

"Only a little," he whispered solemnly. "I'll be as slow and tender as I can. I'll do anything you want me to do to make it easier for you." He bent to her mouth, touching it lightly with his. "Meredith, don't you want to know all the secrets?" he asked huskily. "Don't you want to see how much pleasure we can give each other? My God, just kissing you makes my blood run like fire. Having you..." He groaned as he kissed her. "Having you...would be unbearably sweet."

"For me, too." Her arms tightened around his neck, and she buried her face in his hair-roughened chest, savoring the smell and feel of him in her arms.

His hands smoothed down her hips and his weight settled over her, gently, so that he wouldn't frighten her. His mouth trembled as it found hers, and he kissed her with exquisite warmth and tenderness.

"This is how much I want you," he whispered as he moved sensuously against her.

She felt his need, and an answering hunger made her tremble. "Blake...what about...precautions?" she choked out. "I don't know how."

His lips lifted just above hers. "I'm going to marry

you," he told her roughly. "But if precautions are important to you, I can use something."

Heat shot through her. She felt her nails digging into his back, heard her own wild cry as she lifted to him. His face hardened and she saw his eyes darken as his mouth came slowly back down to cover hers.

"We should…" she whimpered.

"Yes," he whispered. But his mouth grew demanding, and his last sane thought was that creating babies with Meredith was as natural as wading in country streams and walking in the park. He closed his eyes, shaking with the need to join his aching body to hers and give her the same sweet pleasure he felt when he touched her.

Chapter 8

Meredith trembled, half blind with pleasure as Blake's mouth became more demanding. It was almost enough just to kiss him, to feel the exquisite weight of his body on hers as his hand worked at the fastenings of her clothes.

"The light," she whispered huskily.

He touched her mouth tenderly. "I know," he said deeply, reaching for it. "You might not believe it, little one, but I've got more hang-ups than you have."

The room was in darkness then, except for the faint moonlight seeping in through the white curtains. His hands smoothed down her breasts, savoring their warm fullness. She gasped and he searched for her mouth in the darkness.

"Meredith," he whispered huskily.

"What?" she breathed.

"One of us needs to do something if you don't

want me to make you pregnant. You haven't really answered me."

She felt the heat in her cheeks. He was right, it was something they had to consider. She swallowed. "I'm not on the pill," she confessed.

"Do you want me to take care of it?"

Her fingers touched his face, involuntarily running down the scar, while visions of his son in her arms made her tremble with hunger. "I...I don't mind, either way," she said unsteadily.

"God!" He buried his face in her throat and shuddered. It was so profound to hear her say that. It would be all of heaven to see her grow big with his child, to share the sweetness of raising it.

"Blake?" she whispered, uncertain.

"I don't mind, either," he said roughly. "Come here."

He pulled her closer still and she melted against him with blinding hope as he began to tease her breasts with his hands. He trailed his fingers around the outer edges, feeling the tension in her body, the heat of her skin as he drew his caresses out, making her wait, building the need, until she caught his wrists and tried to make him touch her.

And he did, finally, so that it was like a tiny fulfillment, and she shuddered and arched into his warm, lean hands. He liked her reactions, delighted in her responses. She had to care about him, he thought dizzily as his hands smoothed away her clothing, to let him do these things to her and to feel such pleasure when he did.

He was slow. Deliberately slow. More patient than he'd ever dreamed of being. He loved the soft sounds that came whispering out of her throat, the way her hands were clinging to him. He loved the very texture of her skin, the sound of her quick breathing like a rustle in the darkness as he touched her more intimately.

He should be out of his mind with the need to have her, he thought in the back of his mind. But stronger than passion was the need for her to feel the same exquisite sensations that were rippling through his powerful body and making him tremble with each new touch, each soft kiss. He wanted much, much more than quick fulfillment. He wanted to touch all that was Meredith, to join his body to hers and feel the oneness that he'd read was possible between two people who cared for each other.

His lips smoothed over hers, barely touching, while his hands found her where she was untouched and gently, tenderly probed. She gasped under his mouth. Thank God for books, he thought while he could. He hadn't known anything about virgins until he'd done some reading the other night.

"It's all right," he whispered tenderly. "I'm going to be very gentle, Meredith. I just want to make sure that what we do won't be any more painful than it has to be."

"I don't mind," she told him softly, clinging. "Blake... I'd give you anything...!"

"Yes." His mouth whispered against hers. "I'd give you anything, too, Meredith. I'd do anything to please you, even forgo my own pleasure."

That didn't sound like lust. Neither did the exquisitely slow movements of his hands, the gentle crush of his body. He was hungry, she could feel his need, but he wouldn't take his pleasure at her expense. That consideration, incredible given the length of abstinence for him, made her want to cry. He had to care a little to be so...!

Her mind went crazy as his hand moved and she felt a stab of pleasure so sweet that it lifted her and she cried out.

She clung to him, telling him without words that it was pleasure, not pain, she was feeling. He warmed, remembering his own earlier withdrawal when she moaned or gasped, because he'd never known how a woman responded when giving herself to pleasure.

He opened his mouth on hers and let his tongue gently stab inside her lips, aching at the implied intimacy, delighting in the way her soft, slender body turned in his hands when he did that. She was loving this, he thought dizzily. Loving every second of it, reveling in his mouth, his touch. He could feel her pleasure even as his built and built until he couldn't contain it any longer.

She was trembling now, and tiny whispers of excitement were moaning past her lips as she lay waiting for him, her body twisting sensually with mindless abandon.

He was heady with pride at his own latent abilities. He hadn't dreamed that with his inexperience he could bring her to this frenzy.

He stripped with quick, deft movements and slid onto the coverlet beside her, his hands moving on her body, holding her while he kissed her with whispery tenderness.

"Pl…ease." She managed the one word, and her voice broke on it.

"I want you, too, little one," he breathed against her mouth. "I want you so much."

He balanced his weight on his forearms and slid over her, trembling at the soft warmth of her legs tangling with his. She moved, helping him, and he let his hips ease down.

She felt the first hesitant probing and shuddered, but she didn't tense. She forced her body to relax, not to fight him.

He could feel that, and his mouth smoothed over her lips in silent reassurance.

His hands went to her face, holding it while he kissed her, and he felt her soft cry go into his mouth as he pushed gently against the veil of her womanhood.

And it was easy then. He felt the faint tension go out of her body, felt her sigh feather against his lips.

"I won't ever have to hurt you again," he murmured unsteadily. "I'm sorry it has to be this way for a virgin."

"But it wasn't bad," she whispered back. Her fingers slid into his cool, thick hair. "Oh, Blake..." she whimpered. She kissed him softly. "Blake, it's...incredible!"

"Yes." He touched her eyes, closing them; he touched her nose, cheeks and forehead with lips that were breathlessly tender. And all the while his body moved with equal tenderness, drowning her in the exquisite sensation of oneness. She pulled his mouth to hers as his movements began to lengthen and deepen with shuddering pleasure, her breath filling him, her tiny cries making him feverish with contained passion.

His hands slid under her, savoring the warm, soft skin of her back and hips, holding her to him.

"Meredith—" His voice broke on her name. His eyes closed. He felt the tension growing in his powerful body with each torturously slow movement, felt the control he had beginning to slip. But her control was going, too. She was trembling, clinging, her mouth ardent and hungry. He lifted her up and overwhelmed her with desperate tenderness, and when the spasms came, they were white hot, blinding, but with a gentleness that he couldn't have imagined.

She bit him in her passion, but he was riding waves of completion and he hardly felt her teeth. His hands contracted. He cried her name against her damp throat and the tide washed over him in pulsating shudders.

He heard her crying an eternity later and he managed to lift his head and search her face. "Meredith?" he whispered huskily. "Oh, God, I didn't hurt you, did I?"

"No!" She buried her face against his chest, kissing him there, kissing his throat, his face, everywhere she could reach, with lips that worshipped him. "Blake!" she moaned, her arms contracting around his neck. "Blake…!" She shuddered again and again, and when he realized why, he put his mouth gently against hers and began to move.

The second time was every bit as sweet, but slower, more achingly drawn out. He hadn't dreamed a man could hold out as long as he was managing to. But he adored her with his mouth, his hands, and finally, when she was crying with the tension he'd aroused, he adored her with the slow, worshipping motion of his body in one long, sweet pinnacle of fulfillment.

She couldn't seem to stop crying. She lay in his arms with her wet face pillowed on his chest where the thick hair was damp with sweat. She couldn't let go of him, either, and he seemed to understand that, because he held her even closer and gently brushed her hair away from her face while he kissed her tenderly and soothed her.

"I thought…passion was uncontrollable and…and quick…and men couldn't…men were rough," she told him.

"How could I be rough with you?" His mouth touched hers, brushing softly over her trembling lips. "Or make something that beautiful into raw sex?"

Her breath sighed out, making little chills against his damp skin. "I'm so glad I waited for you," she said simply, shaken by the experience. "I'm so glad I didn't give in to some man I didn't even like out of curiosity or because everybody else was doing it." She nuzzled her face against him. "You are so wonderful."

He drew her mouth up to his and kissed her possessively. "So are you," he whispered. "I didn't know what lovemaking was until tonight. I didn't know that there could be such pleasure in it," he murmured against her mouth.

"I thought men felt the pleasure with anyone," she replied.

"Apparently it's an individual thing," he said quietly. "Because I never felt anything approaching this before." He heard the words without realizing their importance, until it suddenly came to him that he'd hardly felt anything with Nina. But Meredith's soft young body had sent him spinning into oblivion and he'd done things with her and to her that had come naturally. Perhaps it was instinct. But what if it was something stronger?

He'd called it lovemaking, and it had been. Not sex, or the satisfaction of a need. And he couldn't imagine doing that with anyone except Meredith. Not that way. Not with such staggering tenderness. He hadn't even known he was capable of it.

"I wasn't sure I could wait for you," he confessed, nuzzling her face. "Was it enough?"

Her body burned with the memory, and she kissed his throat with breathless tenderness. "Yes. And…was it for you?" she asked, worried.

"Yes." Only the one word, but there was a wealth of unspoken pleasure in it.

She was beginning to feel self-conscious, and he seemed distant all of a sudden, as if he were withdrawing. Had he satisfied his hunger for her and now he was looking for a way out of what could become an embarrassing situation? Did he regret what they'd done? He had old-fashioned ideas about sex, after all. In fact, so did she, but they hadn't helped once he'd started kissing her. Her love for him had betrayed her into his bed.

"Blake, you don't…I mean, you don't think I'm easy…?" she asked suddenly.

"My God!" he exclaimed. He reached over and turned on the light, blinding her with stark illumination and embarrassment.

She fumbled for the cover, scarlet faced, but he stayed her hand.

"No," he said quietly, his eyes as solemn as his face. "Look at me, Meredith. Let me look at you."

Her eyes darted over him and she looked away quickly as the heat grew in her face, but he turned her eyes back gently.

"I'm not a monster," he said softly. "I'm just a man. Flesh and blood, like you. There's nothing to be frightened of."

She managed not to look away this time, and after the first shock, she found him beautiful, in a very masculine sense. He was looking, too, his eyes reconciling sweet memories of her five years ago with the reality of today.

"You've blossomed," he said after a minute, and there was no masculine mockery or teasing in his tone. It was deep and soft as he searched over her swollen breasts, her flat stomach, the curve of her hips, the elegant sweep of her long legs. "You're much more pleasing to my eyes than the Venus, Meredith," he said huskily. "The sight of you knocks the breath right out of me."

Her breath caught at the emotion in his voice. "You make it sound so natural," she said with faint curiosity.

"Isn't it?" he asked. His green eyes searched her soft

gray ones. "We made love. I know your body as well as I know my own. We touched in more than just the conventional way, and you're part of me now. Isn't it natural that I should want to see the lovely body I've known so intimately?"

She colored, but she smiled. "Yes."

"And to answer your other question, Meredith, no, I don't think you're easy." He smoothed back her dark hair and his eyes slid over her face. "We both knew it wasn't going to be a casual encounter. I knew you were a virgin." He brought her hand to his lips and kissed the palm tenderly. "We're going to get married and spend the rest of our lives together. That's the only reason I didn't pull away from you. If sex had been all I wanted, I could have had it long before now, and I wouldn't have seduced you in cold blood for my own pleasure."

She searched his darkened eyes. "It isn't just because of Sarah that you want to marry me, is it? Or just because you wanted me—"

He stopped the words with his mouth. "You talk too much. And worry too much. I want to marry you." He lifted his head. "Don't you want to marry me?"

Her eyes softened. "Oh, yes."

"Then stop brooding." He got up, stretching lazily while she watched him with shy fascination. He dug in his chest of drawers and pulled out a set of navy silk pajamas. He tugged the bottoms up over his hard-muscled legs and snapped them before he carried the pajama top to the bed, lifted Meredith into a sitting position and eased her arms into the sleeves.

"It's economical to share these," he murmured dryly when her eyes asked him why. "I used to sleep raw, but I have to wear something now that Sarah's here. Except that I never wear the tops." He looked down at the soft thrust of her breasts, swollen and dark tipped in the aftermath of passion. He bent slowly and brushed his lips over them, tautening as the tips went hard involuntarily. "I've never felt more like a man than I feel when I touch you," he said roughly, his eyes closing, his brows knitting in the most exquisite pleasure.

She held his dark head against her, loving the feel of his warm mouth. "Are we going to sleep together?" she asked.

"We have to," he murmured, sliding his lips slowly over her breast. "I can't let you go."

She slid her arms around his neck as he lifted his head. "But, Sarah…"

"Sarah will be the first to find out we're going to be married," he murmured. "I'll get the license. We can have a blood test on Monday morning and the service two days later. Will that give you enough time to close out your apartment in San Antonio and change your mailing address?"

"Yes." She was breathless with his impatience, but not irritated. She wanted to live with him, and the sooner the better, before he woke up to what he was doing and changed his mind. She couldn't bear it if he'd only proposed in the heat of the moment.

He read that fear in her eyes. "I'm not going to change my mind. I'm not going to back out at the last minute or decide that I've satisfied my hunger for you and I don't need you anymore. I want you, Meredith," he emphasized. "I want to live with you, and not in some modern way with no ties and no legal status. To me, living with someone involves a thing called honor. It's a lost word in this society, but it still means a hell of a lot to me. I care enough to give you my name."

"I'll try to be a good wife," she said solemnly. "You

won't mind if I just sit and stare at you sometimes, will you?"

He searched her eyes quietly. "Do you love me?"

Her lips trembled and she averted her gaze, focusing on his bare chest.

"All right. I won't force it out of you." He brought her forehead to his lips, his chest swelling with the knowledge that she did love him, even if she wouldn't admit it. He could see it in her eyes, feel it in her body. Apparently love could survive the cruelest blows, because God knows he'd hurt her enough to kill anything less. He closed his eyes and nuzzled his cheek against her soft dark hair. "I'll take care of you all my life," he promised. "Don't be afraid."

She trembled a little, because she was. Afraid that he didn't care enough, that he might regret his decision. He might fall in love again someday with someone else like Nina, and what would she do? She'd have to let him go....

It was happening so fast. Almost too fast. She hesitated. "Blake, maybe we should just get engaged..." she began worriedly.

He lifted his head and searched her eyes. "No."

"But—"

He put a long finger over her lips. "Do you remember what we said to each other when we came in here? About precautions?"

She colored. "Yes."

"Marriage and children are synonymous to me," he said quietly. "I think they are to you, too. I'm illegitimate, Meredith. I won't let my child be called what I was."

She sighed. "Does it really bother you so much?"

"I'd like to know who my father was at least," he replied. "Half my heritage is lost forever, because I have no idea who he was or what his background is. I can't tell Sarah anything about him. She'll ask someday."

"She'll understand, too," she replied. "She's a very special little girl. She's so much like you."

His green eyes searched hers. "We could have another daughter," he said. "Or a son."

She held her breath while he touched her flat stomach under the long open pajama top. Her heart went crazy when he looked down, watching the tips of her bare breasts harden helplessly.

She tried to pull the fabric together, but he caught her hands and held them gently.

"No," he said. "You can't imagine the pleasure it gives me just to see you like that."

Her breath sighed past her parted lips. "It's hard."

"I know." He lifted his eyes back to hers, searching them in a long, static silence. "It was for me, too, believe it or not. But I let you look at me, and I wasn't embarrassed." He smiled faintly. "I couldn't let Nina."

She reached up and touched her lips to his. "I'm glad," she said huskily.

He pulled her against him, nudging the pajama top out of the way so that her breasts brushed slowly against his hair-roughened chest, and she caught her breath with pleasure at the exquisite friction.

"We've got a lot to learn about this," he said softly. "We can learn it together."

"Yes." She touched her mouth to his throat, his collarbone. He took her head and guided her lips to his own nipples, groaning at the pleasure that shot through him when he felt the moist suction of her mouth.

"God, that feels good!" he ground out, forcing her mouth closer.

"Let's take our clothes off and experiment some

more," she suggested brazenly, teasing him for the first time.

It delighted him. "You hussy!" he accused, and tugged her head up. His eyes were playful, and his face had never looked less hard.

"You started it," she pointed out, smiling back.

"But I can't finish it," he said ruefully. He sighed over her breasts before he buttoned them out of sight. "It's too soon," he said, answering the question in her eyes. "I don't want to rush you. You're much too new to this for any more experimenting."

She studied his face quietly. "How do you know?"

"Simple logic." He touched her lips. "And a book I read," he confessed, brushing his mouth over them. "In case I ever got this far with you, I wanted to make sure I knew enough so that I wouldn't make you afraid of me again."

"Oh, Blake." She hugged him hard, nestling her face against him. "Blake, I adore you."

His heart skipped when she said it. He smiled, aglow with satiation and the knowledge that she cared. "Lie down with me. We'll sleep in each others' arms."

She tingled all over as he pulled back the cover and tucked her in, turning out the light before he climbed in beside her. He drew her to him with a long, warm sigh and kissed her.

"Good night, little one," he whispered.

"Good night, Blake."

He closed his eyes, sure that he'd never been happier in his entire life. He pulled her closer and sighed when he felt her arms go around him. For a beginning, it was perfect.

But the next morning, when he awoke and found Meredith lying asleep in his bed, the perfection waned.

His body surged at the sight of her, and he realized belatedly that the hunger he'd thought assuaged last night had only grown with feeding. He wanted her more now than ever, with a fever that actually made him shake as he looked at her sleeping body.

The realization terrified him. He'd never been vulnerable. Even Nina hadn't really knocked him off balance very far, or tested his control over his emotions. But Meredith did. She was the very air he breathed, the sun in his sky. He felt a rush of possessiveness when he looked at her, a desperate need to keep her, to protect her. He got out of bed and stared at her as if he'd gone mad. He'd sworn that he would never let her get to his heart, but last night he'd given her a lien on it. This morning, she owned him lock, stock and barrel.

He swallowed down a wave of nausea. The tender loving of the night faded into cold fear with the dawn. He didn't trust women, and now that distrust had extended itself to Meredith all over again. As long as he could persuade himself that it was only physical, marriage hadn't bothered him. But what he was feeling this morning gave new meaning to the situation. He could care for her. He could go crazy over her after a few more nights like last night. He could be so enamored of her that he'd do anything she wanted just to feel her arms around him. And that realization was what caught him by the throat—that he might not be able to keep his pride, his independence. He was afraid of her because he might love her, and he couldn't trust her enough to give in to her. She might be just like Nina. How could he know before it was too late?

Like a trapped animal, he felt the need to run, to get away, to think it through.

He got up and got dressed, taking one long, hungry

look at Meredith before he forced himself to jerk open the door and go out. Last night everything had been so simple, until he'd touched her for the first time. And now he was mired up to his neck in quicksand. He didn't know what to do. He had the most ridiculous urge to go out and get Meredith an armload of roses. God knows, it must be the first stages of insanity, he thought as he went down the stairs and out the back door.

Chapter 9

Meredith woke up slowly, aware of new surroundings and light coming into her room from the wrong direction. Then she moved, and her body told her that the light wasn't the only difference.

She sat up. She was in Blake's bedroom, in Blake's bed, wearing Blake's pajama top. Her face burned. The night before came back with startling clarity. She'd given in. More than given in. She'd participated wildly in what she and Blake had done together.

Her breath came unsteadily as wave after wave of remembered pleasure tingled in her sore body. She looked around, wondering if Blake was in the bathroom. But she spotted his pajama bottoms laid across the foot of the bed, and his boots were missing. They'd been sitting beside the armchair last night.

She got out of bed slowly, a little disoriented. "Bess!" she exclaimed, then remembered that she'd called Bess just after they'd gotten home last night to tell her that she was spending the night to help Blake with Sarah. Wouldn't Bess be grinning when she got back home this morning, she moaned to herself.

She put back on the clothes she'd taken off—the clothes that Blake had taken off for her, she corrected—and pulled on her socks and sneakers before she combed her hair.

In the mirror she could see the imprint of her head and Blake's on the pillows, and she blushed. Well, it was too late now for regrets. He'd said that they were getting married, so she might as well reconcile herself to her new status in his life. At least they were physically compatible and she loved him desperately. Perhaps someday he might learn to love her back. He was already different, mostly due, she was sure, to Sarah's gentle influence.

She opened the door and went to Sarah's room, but the little girl was nowhere in sight.

"If you're awake, breakfast is ready," Blake called from the foot of the staircase.

She looked down, thrilling to the sight of him, tall and dark headed, dressed in gray slacks and shirt with a lightweight tan sport coat and brown striped tie. He looked very elegant, and just a little somber.

That didn't bode well. She almost missed a step on her way down, nervous and shy with him after the night before. Her face was wildly colored and she couldn't look at him.

She paused two steps above him because his hand shot out and kept her there. His green eyes forced her to look at him, and he searched her face quietly.

"Come here," he said gently. "I've got something for you."

His big, lean hand curved possessively over hers and

his fingers tangled in her cold ones as he led her into the hall and stopped her at the chair, which was covered with waxed paper that held dozens of small pink roses, their fragrance like perfume.

"For me?" she whispered, breathless.

"For you. I went out into the field and cut them early this morning."

She lifted them, burying her nose in their beautiful scent. "Oh, Blake," she moaned with pleasure, and looked up with her heart in her eyes.

He was glad then that he'd followed the crazy impulse in spite of his disturbing thoughts after waking. He bent and brushed his mouth over her forehead, his mood light. "I hoped you might like them," he murmured. "They looked as virginal as you did last night."

Her face felt like fire. "I'm not anymore," she said hesitantly.

He smiled slowly. "I'll carry last night in my heart until I die, Meredith Anne," he told her huskily. "It was everything it should have been. Magic."

She smiled into her roses, feeling all womanly and soft when he said things like that.

"Are you sorry that I took the choice away from you?" he asked unexpectedly, and his eyes were serious. "I carried you into my room without asking if it was what you wanted, and I didn't give you much chance to get away."

"Don't you think I could have gotten away if I'd really wanted to?" she asked honestly.

He smiled back at her. "No."

She traced rose petals. "Well, I could have. You didn't force me."

"In a way I did," he replied worriedly. "I didn't try to

protect you. I don't want to force you into marriage with the threat of pregnancy."

Her eyebrows lifted. "Threat?" she picked up on the word. "Oh, no, it isn't that. A baby is…" Her breath caught as she searched his eyes and felt the hunger for a child. "Blake, a baby would be the sweetest thing in the world."

His heart began to race as he looked at her. "That's what I thought, too," he said. "That's why I didn't try to hold back." He smiled ruefully. "And the fact is, I don't think I could have. Years of abstinence makes it pretty hard for a man to keep his head."

Her eyes widened. "You meant it?" she exclaimed. "It was actually that long?"

He nodded. "Now I'm glad," he confessed. "It made it that much more intense with you." He framed her face with his lean hands and bent to savor her lips with his warm, moist ones. "So intense," he whispered roughly, "that I want it again and again and again. Every time I look at you, my body burns."

His mouth became demanding, and she felt the quick, violent response of his body to the feel of hers.

"So does mine," she whispered back, reaching up with her free hand to cling to his neck. "Blake," she moaned as his hands dropped to her hips and pulled her hard against him.

"God!" he groaned, and his mouth covered hers urgently.

Somewhere in the fever they were sharing, a door opened.

"Daddy? Meredith? Where are you?"

They broke apart with heated faces, trembling bodies and faintly crushed roses. "We're here," Blake said, recovering quickly. "We'll be there in a minute, Sarah. I was just giving Meredith her roses."

"Okay, Daddy. Aren't they nice, Merry?"

"Yes, darling," she murmured absently, but her eyes were on Blake as the child went back through to the kitchen.

"You aren't going home tonight," he said huskily. "I've got you and I'm keeping you, and to hell with gossip. I'll get the license tomorrow and arrange for blood tests with my doctor. I'll phone you from my office in the morning with the time. Meanwhile—" he smiled slowly "—you can go over to Bess's and get a change of clothes."

"What will I tell her?" she groaned.

"That we're getting married and you're taking care of Sarah while Mrs. Jackson's away," he said simply. He pulled her hand to his lips and kissed it warmly. "Sarah and I will even go with you to make things respectable. But first we'll have breakfast. Okay?"

She sighed with pure delight. "Okay. But I'll have to go to my apartment in San Antonio this week," she added.

"I'll take time off to go with you Tuesday. Sarah can come, too." He bent, half lifting her against his lean, hard body. "I'm not letting you out of my sight any more than I have to. You might decide to run for it."

"If you think that, you underestimate yourself," she murmured, and buried her face in his throat. "I don't have the strength to get away."

His hands contracted. "How sore are you?" he asked intimately.

She burrowed closer. "Blake...!"

"Is it bad?"

She grimaced and looked up at him, hesitating.

"Tell me the truth," he said. "It will spare us a lot of

frustration later—if I start making love to you and have to stop."

"It's uncomfortable," she confessed finally, averting her eyes.

But he tilted her chin and forced her to look at him. "No secrets between us," he said. "Not ever. I want the truth, no matter how much it hurts, and you'll always get it from me."

"All right," she said. "I want it that way, too."

His eyes brushed over her soft features with lazy warmth. "You look very pretty without makeup," he remarked. "As pretty as these roses." He glanced at them and frowned. "We've bruised them a bit."

"They'll forgive us," she said. She reached up to kiss him softly. "Will your board of directors understand your taking two days off in one week?" she asked. "For a blood test and a license and then to go with me to Texas?"

"I haven't taken two days off in five years, so they'd better." He let her go. "Let's get breakfast. Then we'll go see Bess and Bobby."

She curled under his arm and, carrying her precious roses, let him guide her to the table.

It was cozy in the kitchen. Blake kept watching her and Meredith could hardly keep from bursting into song with the sheer joy of having him look at her that way. He might not love her, but he was already very, very possessive. And in time, love might come.

"Meredith and I are going to get married, Sarah," Blake said. "She's going to live with us and take care of you and write books."

Sarah's eyes lit up and the expression on the small face was humbling. "Are you, Merry? Are you going to be my mommy?" she asked, as if they were offering her the earth.

"Yes." Meredith smiled. "I'm going to be your mommy and hug and kiss you and tell you stories and—oh!"

Sarah ran to her like a whirlwind, almost knocking the breath out of her as she climbed onto her lap and clung, crying and mumbling things that Meredith couldn't understand.

"What is it, honey?" Blake asked, torn out of his normal calm by the child's totally unexpected reaction. He touched Sarah's dark hair gently. "What is it?" he repeated.

"I can stay now, can't I, Daddy?" Sarah asked him with wet red eyes. "I don't have to go. Merry is going to live with us and I'll be her little girl, too."

"Of course you can stay," Blake said shortly. "There was never any question of that."

"When I first came," she reminded him, "you said I could go to a...a home!"

"Damn my vicious tongue," Blake burst out. He got up, lifting Sarah out of Meredith's arms and into his own. He held her close, his green eyes steady on hers. "You'll never live in any home but mine," he said huskily. "You're my own flesh and blood, my own little girl. I..." He choked on the words. His jaw worked. "I...care for you—very much," he bit off finally.

Even at her age, Sarah seemed to realize what a difficult thing it was for him to say. She lowered her cheek to his shoulder with a sigh and smiled through her tears. "I love you, too, Daddy," she said.

Blake didn't know how he managed not to break down and cry. His arms contracted around her and he turned so that Meredith couldn't see his face. In all his life he'd never been so shaken.

"How about some more coffee?" Meredith asked gently. "I'll get it, okay?" She went to the stove to pour coffee from the percolator into the carafe, and her eyes were wet. She felt stunned by Blake's brief display of vulnerability, his hope for the future. If he could love Sarah, he could love others. She dabbed at her eyes and filled the carafe. Miracles did happen, after all.

When she turned back to the table, Sarah was sitting on Blake's lap. And she stayed there for the rest of breakfast, her small face full of love and wonder. Blake just looked smug.

"What about your work?" Blake asked when they'd finished breakfast and Sarah had excused herself to go and watch her eternal cartoons in the living room.

"I just need a place to set up my computer," she said.

His eyebrows arched. "What have you got?"

"An IBM compatible," she said. "Twin disk drives, over 600K memory, word processing software, a big daisy wheel printer and a modem."

"Come and look over my setup."

She let him take her hand and lead her into the study. "It's just like mine!" she exclaimed when she saw what he had on his desk.

He smiled at her. "A good omen?"

"Wonderful! Now we'll both have a spare," she said with a dancing glance.

"You can work here when I'm not home. And if you want to set up your equipment in the corner, we'll order another desk and some filing cabinets."

"It won't bother you?" she asked hesitantly. "I work odd hours. Sometimes, if I get on a streak, I may work into the small hours of the morning."

"I'm marrying you," he said. "That includes your job,

your eccentricities, your bad habits and your temper. I don't mind what you do. You're entitled to a life that allows you the right to be your own person, to make your own dreams come true in business."

"I thought you were a chauvinist," she said. "That's the wrong attitude. You're supposed to refuse to let me work outside the home and say that no job is going to come before you."

He arched an eyebrow. "Okay, if that's what you want."

She hit his chest playfully. "Never mind. I like you better this way." She reached up and slid her arms around his neck. "Sarah says she won't mind if I hug and kiss her. So can I hug and kiss you, too?" she asked daringly.

His mouth quirked a little. "I guess so."

"You might show more enthusiasm," she said.

He bent his head and whispered, "I can't. You're sore."

She blushed and opened her mouth to protest just as his came down and settled over her lips. He kissed her gently, swinging her lightly in his arms from side to side as he held her mouth under his.

"That was nice," she told him huskily.

"I thought so, too." he let her go abruptly, the hardness back in his face. "I'll line up a charter flight to San Antonio for Tuesday. We can have your furniture sent out."

"It's a furnished apartment." She smiled. "All I have is my clothes, a few manuscripts and my computer stuff."

"Okay. We'll have that sent out."

"Blake, you're sure, aren't you?" she asked seriously.

"As sure as you are," he replied. "Now stop brooding over it. I'll get the license and set up the blood test for you tomorrow. Sarah can go with you to the doctor, because it will only take a minute."

"All right. It sounds like a nice day." She sighed.

"Every day is nice with you, Meredith," he said unexpectedly and with a wry smile.

But just as they started to go down to Bess's, a friend of Blake's arrived out of the blue, and Meredith went by herself, letting Sarah stay with her dad and his friend while she told Bess what was going on.

Bess was overwhelmed when she heard the news. "Congratulations!" She laughed. "It's the best thing that could have happened to both of you. You'll make a good marriage."

"Oh, I hope so." Meredith sighed. "I'll do my best, and at least Blake likes me."

"At least," Bess said, and laughed. "If you need witnesses, Bobby and I will be glad to volunteer. Elissa and King, too."

"You can all come," Meredith promised. "I'll need as much moral support as I can get." She shook her head. "It seems like a beautiful dream. I hope I don't wake up. Well, I'd better get my things and get back up to his place. I hope you don't mind, but he, uh, doesn't want me out of his sight until the ceremony Wednesday."

"Fast mover, isn't he?" Bess grinned and hugged her friend warmly. "I'm so happy for you, Merry. And for Blake and Sarah. You'll make a lovely family."

Meredith thought so, too. She carried her single suitcase out to the Porsche and drove up in front of Blake's house. Sarah Jane met her at the door as she set her case down, and Blake came out of the living room smiling.

"Well, what did she say?" he asked. He answered her

silent glance into the living room. "He's gone. What did Bess say?"

"She said congratulations." Meredith laughed. "And that we'll make a lovely family."

"Indeed we will," Blake murmured gently.

"Merry, can I be a flower girl?" Sarah asked from behind her.

"You certainly can," Meredith promised, kneeling beside the child to hug her. "You can carry an armload of roses."

"But, Merry, they're all crushed."

"Daddy will cut some more," Meredith said, warming when she remembered how the roses had gotten crushed. She glanced at Blake and the look in his eyes made her blush.

The next two days went by in an unreal rush. The blood tests were done, the license obtained, and a minister was lined up to perform the ceremony at the local Baptist church where Meredith's parents had worshipped when she was a child. For reasons that Meredith still didn't understand, Blake had given her a guest room to sleep in until the wedding, and although he'd been friendly enough, he hadn't really attempted to make love to her. She preferred to think it was because she was still uncomfortable from their first time rather than because he had any regrets.

The ceremony was held late Wednesday afternoon, with King and Elissa Roper and Bess and Bobby for witnesses. Meredith said her vows with tears in her eyes, so happy that her heart felt like it would overflow.

She'd bought a white linen suit to be married in, with a tiny pillbox hat covered in lace. It was so sweet when Blake put the ring on her finger and lifted the veil to kiss her. She felt like Sleeping Beauty, as if she'd been asleep for years and years and now was waking to the most wonderful reality.

The reception was held at the Ropers' sprawling white frame house outside Jack's Corner, and Danielle and Sarah Jane played quietly while the adults enjoyed champagne punch and a lavish catered buffet.

"You didn't have to go to this kind of expense, for God's sake," Blake muttered to big King Roper.

King pursed his lips and his dark eyes sparkled. "Yes, I did. Having you get close enough to a woman to marry again deserved something spectacular." He glanced at Meredith, who was talking animatedly to Elissa and Bess a few feet away while Bobby, the exact opposite in coloring to his half-brother, King, was watching the kids play.

"She's a dish," King remarked. "And we all know how she felt about you when she left here." His dark eyes caught Blake's green ones. "It's not a good thing to live alone. A wife and children make all the difference. I know mine do."

"Sarah likes her," Blake replied, sipping punch as his eyes slid over Meredith's exquisite figure like a paintbrush. "She's a born mother."

King smiled. "Thinking of a large family, are you?"

Blake glared at him. "I've only just got married."

"Speaking of which, why aren't you two going on a honeymoon?"

"I'd like that," Blake confessed. "But neither Meredith nor I like the idea of leaving Sarah behind while we have one. She's had enough insecurity for one month. Anyway," he added, "Meredith's got that autographing in town Saturday, and she doesn't want to disappoint the bookstore."

"She always was a sweet woman," King remarked. "I remember her ragged and barefoot as a child, helping her mother carry eggs to sell at Mackelroy's Grocery. She never minded hard work. In that," he added with a glance at his friend, "she's a lot like you."

Blake smiled faintly. "I didn't have a choice. It was work or starve in my case. Now that I'm in the habit, I can't quit."

King eyed him solemnly. "Don't ever let work come before Meredith and Sarah," he cautioned. "Bobby had to find that out the hard way, and he barely realized it in time."

Blake was looking at Meredith with faint hunger in his narrow eyes. "It would take more than a job to overshadow Meredith," he said without thinking. He finished his punch. "And we'd better get going. I've got reservations at the Sun Room for six o'clock. You're sure you and Elissa don't mind having Sarah for the night?"

"Not at all. And she loves the idea of sleeping in Danielle's room," King assured him. "If she needs you, I promise we'll call, even if it's two in the morning. Fair enough?" he added when he saw the worry in Blake's eyes.

"Fair enough," Blake said with a sigh.

A few minutes later, Blake and Meredith said their goodbyes, kissed Sarah good-night and went to the Sun Room for an expensive wedding supper.

"I still can't quite believe it," Meredith confessed with a smile as she looked at her husband across the table. "That we're married," she added.

"I know what you mean," he said quietly. His eyes caressed her face. "I swore when Nina left that I'd never marry again. But it seemed the most natural thing in the world with you."

She smiled. "I hope I don't disappoint you. I can cook and clean, but I'm not terribly domestic, and when I'm writing, sometimes I pour coffee over ice and put mashed potatoes in the icebox and make coffee without putting a filter in it. I'm sort of absentminded."

"As long as you remember me once in a while, I won't complain," he promised. "Eat your dessert before it melts."

She picked up a spoon to start on her baked alaska. "Sarah was so happy." She sighed.

"You'll be good for her." He sipped his coffee and watched Meredith closely. "You'll be good for both of us."

Meredith felt as if she were riding on a cloud for the rest of the evening. The Sun Room had a dance band as well as a wonderful restaurant. They danced until late, and Meredith was concealing a yawn when they got home.

"Thank you for my honeymoon," she said with a mischievous smile when they were standing together in the hall. "It was wonderful."

"Later on I'll give you a proper one," he promised. "We'll go away for several days. To Europe or the Caribbean."

"Let's go to Australia and stay on a cattle station," she suggested. "I wrote about one of those in my last book, and it sounded like a great place to visit."

"Haven't you traveled?" he asked.

"Just to the Bahamas and Mexico," she said. "It was great, but no place is really exciting when you have to see it alone."

"I know what you mean." He pulled her against him and bent to kiss her. "You still taste of ice cream," he murmured, and kissed her again.

"You taste of coffee." She linked her arms around his neck and smiled at him. "I want to ask you something."

"Be my guest."

"Do you have any deeply buried scruples about intimacy after marriage?" she asked somberly. "I mean, I wouldn't want to cause you any trauma."

He smiled in spite of himself. "No," he replied. "I don't think I have any buried scruples about it. Why? Were you thinking of seducing me?"

"I would if I knew how," she assured him. She smiled impishly. "Could you give me a few pointers?"

He reached down and picked her up in his arms. "I think I might be able to help you out," he said. He started for the staircase with his lips brushing hers. "It might take a while," he added under his breath. "You don't mind, do you? You don't have any pressing appointments in the next few hours…?"

"Only one. With you," she whispered, and pressed her open mouth hungrily to his, shivering with delight as his tongue pushed softly inside it and tasted her. She moaned with the aching pleasure.

His lips drew back a little. "I like that," he whispered huskily. "Make a lot of noise. Tonight there's no one to hear you except me."

Her teeth tugged at his lower lip and she obliged him with a slow, sultry moan that caused his mouth to grow rough with desire. She smiled under the heat of the kiss, and when he lifted his head and saw her expression, for just an instant he wondered if, like Nina, she was pretending pleasure that she didn't feel. And then he saw her eyes. And all his doubts fell away as his mouth bit hungrily into hers. He thought that in all his life he'd never seen such a fierce passion in a woman's soft eyes….

This time he left the lights on. He undressed her slowly, drawing it out, making her dizzy with pleasure as he kissed every inch of her as he uncovered her body. When the clothes were off, his mouth smoothed over her adoringly, lingering on her soft, warm breasts. He'd never realized how infallible instinct was until now. Apparently it didn't matter how skilled he was. She cared for him, and that made her delightfully receptive to anything he wanted. His heart swelled with the knowledge.

By the time he'd undressed, she was trembling, her body waiting, her eyes so full of warm adoration that he felt like a lonely traveler finally coming home. This was nothing like the indifference Nina had shown when he'd touched her. He looked at Meredith's lovely face and wanted nothing more in life than her arms around him.

She raised her feverish eyes to his, drowning in their green glitter. His lips parted and she trembled, because he wasn't in any hurry.

His hard mouth brushed at hers while his hands touched her with reverence. His wife. Meredith was his wife, and she wanted him. He groaned softly. "Merry, love me," he whispered as his mouth bit hungrily into hers. "Love me."

She felt her body trembling with delight as she heard the soft words and wondered dizzily if he even realized what he was saying. Poor, lonely man....

Her arms went around him hungrily and she kissed him back, willing to give him anything as tenderness and love welled up within her.

"You're...killing me," she bit off minutes later, when his slow, exquisitely tender caresses were making her shudder with need for him.

"Liar," he told her, smiling gently at her even through

his own trembling need. He moved suddenly, and watched her eyes dilate, felt her body react. "That's it. Help me," he coaxed. "Show me what you want, little one. Let me… love you," he groaned when she lifted her body up into his.

Blinded with the passion they were sharing, she pulled his head down to her mouth and kissed him with all the lonely years and all her smothered love in her lips. She felt his powerful body tremble until it gave way under his hunger for her and he overwhelmed her with exquisite tenderness.

Her cry was echoed in his as unbearable pleasure bound them, lifted them together in a fierce buffeting embrace, and they clung to each other as the wave of fulfillment hit them together.

Meredith could barely breathe when she felt the full weight of Blake's body against her. He was shivering, and her arms contracted around him.

"Darling," she whispered. Her lips touched his cheek, his mouth, his throat, damp with sweat. "Darling, darling…!"

The endearment went through his weary body like an electric current. He returned her tender kisses, smoothing her bare body against his and loving the soft curves caressing him. His hands felt almost too rough to be touching her. He savored the warm silk of her skin, the cologne scent of her, the pleasure of just being close to her.

Somewhere in the back of his mind, he remembered whispering to her to love him. He buried his mouth in her throat, kissing it hungrily as his need broke through his reserve and made him just temporarily vulnerable.

He pulled her into the hair-roughened curve of his chest and thighs, holding her with a new kind of possessiveness. His mouth brushed her forehead and her closed eyes with breathless tenderness. He felt the tension of pleasure slowly relax in her soft body, as it had in his own.

"I've been alone all my life until now," he said quietly, his face solemn. "I never realized how cold it was until you warmed me."

Tears formed in her eyes. "I'll warm you all my life if you'll let me," she assured him huskily.

He searched her soft face and bent to take her mouth under his. "Warm me now," he breathed against her lips, and his hands slid to her hips. As he pulled her close, he heard her voice, heard the soft endearment that broke from her lips, and his heart almost burst with delight that she cared too much to be capable of hiding it.

Later, curled up together with the lights out, Blake lay awake long after Meredith was enveloped in contented sleep. He couldn't quite believe what had happened so quickly in his life. He'd been alone, and now he had a daughter and a loving wife, and the way it was affecting him made him nervous.

Something had happened tonight with Meredith. Something incredible. It hadn't been just the satisfying of a physical desire anymore. It went much deeper than that. There was something reverent about the way they made love, about the tenderness they gave to each other. He was being taken over by Meredith and he had cold feet. Could he really trust her not to walk out on him as Nina had? If he let himself fall in love with her, would she betray him? He looked down at her sleeping face, and even in the darkness he could see its warm glow. The distrust relaxed out of him. He could trust her.

Of course he could, he told himself firmly. After all, he could live with her profession and she'd have Sarah to keep her busy. Her writing wasn't going to interfere in their lives. He'd make sure of it.

Chapter 10

But Meredith's job did interfere with their marriage. Her autographing session was the first indication of it. Blake and Sarah had gone to the bookstore Saturday to watch, and Blake had been fascinated by the number of people who'd come to have her sign their books. Dressed in a very sexy green-and-white ensemble, with a big white hat to match, Meredith looked very much the successful, urbane author. And she was suddenly speaking a language he didn't understand. Her instant rapport with people fascinated and disturbed him. He didn't get along well with people, and he certainly didn't seek them out. If she was really as gregarious as she seemed and started to expect to throw lavish parties and have weekend guests, things were going to get sticky pretty fast.

As it happened, she wasn't a party girl. But she did

have to do a lot of traveling in connection with the release of her latest book.

Blake went through the ceiling when she announced her third out-of-state trip in less than three weeks.

"I won't have it," he said coldly, bracing her in the study.

"*You* won't have it?" Meredith replied with equal hauteur. "You told me when we married that you didn't mind if I worked."

"And I don't, but this isn't working. It's jet-setting," he argued. "My God, you're never here! Amie's spending most of her time baby-sitting Sarah because you're forever getting on some damned airplane!"

"I know," Meredith said miserably. "And I'm sorry. But I made this commitment to promote the book before I married you. You of all people wouldn't want me to go back on my word."

"Wouldn't I?" he demanded, and he looked like the old Blake, all bristling masculinity and outraged pride. "Stay home, Meredith."

"Or what?" she challenged, refusing to be ordered about like a child of Sarah's age. "What did you have in mind, tying me to a tree out in the backyard? Or moving to your club in town? You can't, you know, you don't have a club in town."

"I could use one," he muttered darkly. "Okay, honey. If you want the job that much, go do it. But until you come to grips with the fact that this is a marriage, not a limited social engagement, I'm sleeping in the guest room."

"Go ahead," she said recklessly. "I don't care. I won't be here!"

"Isn't that the gospel truth," he said, glaring at her.

She turned on her heel and went to pack.

From then on, everything went downhill between them. She felt an occasional twinge of guilt as Blake reverted to his old, cold self. He was polite to her, but nothing more. He didn't touch her or talk to her. He acted as if she were a houseguest and treated her accordingly. It was a nightmarish change from the first days of their marriage, when every night had been a new and exciting adventure, when their closeness in bed had fostered an even deeper closeness the rest of the time. She'd been sure that he was halfway in love with her. And then her traveling had started to irritate him. Now he was like a stranger, and Meredith tossed and turned in the big bed every night, all alone. In the back of her mind, the knowledge that she had failed to conceive ate away at her confidence. As the days went on, Blake was becoming colder and colder.

Only with Sarah was he different. That was amusing, and Meredith laughed at the spectacle of Blake being followed relentlessly every step he took by Sarah Jane. She was right behind him all weekend, watching him talk to the men, sitting with him while he did the books, riding with him when he went out over the fields in the pickup truck to see about fences and cattle and feed. Sarah Jane was his shadow, and he smiled tolerantly at her attempts to imitate his long strides and his habit of ramming his hands in his pockets and rocking back on his heels when he talked. Sarah was sublimely happy. Meredith was sublimely miserable.

She tried once to talk to Blake, to make him understand that it wouldn't always be this way. But he walked off even as she began.

"Put it in your memoirs, Mrs. Donavan," he said with a mocking smile. "Your readers might find it interesting."

In other words, he didn't. Meredith choked back tears and went to her computer to work on her next book. It was taking much longer than she'd expected, and the tense emotional climate in the house wasn't helping things along. It was hard to feel romantic enough to write a love scene when her own husband refused to touch her or spend five minutes in a room with her when eating wasn't involved, or watching the news on television.

"You're losing weight," Bess commented one day at lunch when Meredith had escaped to her house to avoid the cold silence at home.

"I'm not surprised." Meredith sighed. "It's an ordeal to eat over there. Blake glares at me or ignores me, depending on his mood. I tried to explain that it wasn't going to be like this every time a book came out, but he refuses to listen."

"Maybe he's afraid to listen," Bess said sagely. "Blake's been alone a long time, and he doesn't really trust women. Maybe he's trying to withdraw before he gets in over his head. In which case—" she grinned "—it could be a good omen. What if he's falling in love with you and trying to fight it? Wouldn't he act just that way?"

"No normal man would," Meredith grumbled.

"Bobby did. So did King, according to Elissa. Men are really strange creatures when their emotions get stirred up." She cocked her blond head and stared at Meredith. "You might put on your sexiest negligee and give him hell."

"There's a thought. But he'd probably toss me out the window if I dared."

"You underestimate yourself."

"All the same, it's his heart I want to reach. I can't really do that in bed," Meredith said with sad eyes. "He's always wanted me. But I want more. I'm greedy. I want him to love me."

"Give it time. He'll come around eventually."

"Meanwhile I'm miserable," Meredith said. "At least he and Sarah are getting along like a house on fire. They're inseparable."

"Camouflage," Bess said. "He's using her to keep you at bay."

"He wouldn't."

"You greenhorn." Bess sighed. "I wish I could make you listen."

"Me, too." Meredith got up. "I've got to go. I have to fly to Boston for a signing in the morning. And I haven't told Blake yet." She grimaced. "He's been in an explosive mood for two weeks. This will sure light the fuse, I'm afraid."

"Do you have to go?"

She nodded. "It's the very last trip, but I did promise, and the bookseller is a friend of mine. I can't let her down."

Bess searched Meredith's face. "Better Blake than her?" she asked quietly. "It seems to me, from an objective standpoint, that you're running as hard from this relationship as he is. Do you really have to make these trips, or are you doing it to spite him, to prove your independence?"

"I can't let him own me," Meredith said stubbornly.

"Good for you. But a man like that isn't going to be owned, either. You're going to have to compromise if you want to keep him."

Meredith felt herself going pale. "What do you mean, if I want to keep him?"

"Just that you could drive him away. He isn't like other men. He's been kicked around too much already. His pride won't take much more abuse. You see these trips as simple tours," she explained. "Blake sees that you prefer your work to him."

Meredith felt sick. "No. He couldn't think…"

"I did with Bobby," Bess said simply. "I was sure that he would walk over my dying body to get to the office. I very nearly left him because of it. I couldn't bear being second best." Her eyes narrowed. "Neither can Blake. So look out."

"I've been blind," Meredith groaned. She wrapped her arms around herself. "I thought it was important not to be led around like a dumb animal, so I was fighting for my independence." She closed her eyes. "I never dreamed he'd think I considered him less important than writing."

"If you want some expert advice, tell him while there's still time," Bess suggested.

Meredith hugged the blond-haired woman. "Thanks," she said huskily. "I love him so much, you know, and it was like a dream come true when he married me. Maybe I was afraid to let myself be happy with him, afraid of being hurt, of losing him again. I guess I just lost my perspective."

"Blake probably lost his for the same reason. Get over there and fight for what you have."

"Ever thought about joining the army?" Meredith murmured on her way out the door. "You'd make a dandy drill sergeant."

"The marines offered, but then I found out they expected me to take showers with the men." Bess grinned. "Bobby would never approve of that!"

Meredith laughed and waved as she got into her car and sped back up to the house. Bless Bess for making things so clear. It was going to be all right now. She'd tell Blake the real reason she'd insisted on the tours, and it would smooth over the tension.

She got out of the car and ran into the house, but there was no sound. Odd. She was sure Sarah had been playing in the living room.

She wandered into the kitchen, but there was no one there except Amie.

"Where is everybody?" Meredith asked, excitement shining in her eyes as she savored speaking to Blake.

Amie looked at her worriedly. "Surely Blake told you, Merry," she said hesitantly.

Meredith blinked. "Told me what?"

"Why, that he was taking Sarah to the Bahamas for a few days," Amie said, dropping the bombshell.

Meredith knew her face was like rice paper, but she managed to smile. "Oh. Yes. Of course. It slipped my mind."

"You're crying!" Amie put down her dishcloth and hugged Meredith. "Poor little thing," she mumbled, patting the weeping woman. "He didn't tell you, did he?"

"No."

"I'm sorry."

Meredith reached into her pocket for a tissue and wiped her red eyes. "I've given him a hard time lately," she said. "It's no more than I deserve." She took a deep breath. "I have to fly to Boston in the morning, but when I come back, that's the end of my traveling. I won't go on tour again. Not ever."

Amie searched her white face. "Don't do that," she said unexpectedly.

"What?"

"Don't do it. If you let him get the upper hand now, if you ever let him start ordering your life, you'll never be your own person again," she said simply. "He's a good man in many ways, but he has a domineering streak a mile wide. If you let him, he'll tell you how to breathe. I know you want peace with him, but don't sacrifice your freedom for it."

Meredith felt torn. Bess had said give in, Amie was saying don't. She didn't know what to do anymore. Who was right? And what should she do?

Her heart shattered, she went upstairs to pack. What had begun as a beautiful marriage had turned sour. It was partly her fault, but Blake was as much to blame. She wondered if he was able to admit fault. Somehow she didn't think so.

Boston was lovely. She did her autographing and stayed an extra day to enjoy the historic places and spend a little time in the local library. But her heart was broken. Blake had gone away without her, without even asking if she wanted to go with him. She didn't know if she even wanted to go home again.

She did go home again, of course—to an empty house. She and Amie ate together and Meredith worked on her newest book because there was nothing else to do. And all the while she wondered what Blake and Sarah were doing. Most of all, she wondered if his eye was wandering to a more domestic kind of woman, one who would be content to stay at home and have his babies.

She stopped writing and sat with her head in her hands, daydreaming about having Blake's child. Even though they hadn't taken precautions she hadn't conceived. In a way that was a shame. A baby might have helped bring them together. On the other hand, if Blake decided to leave her, it would be better for both of them if there were no blood ties.

Leave her. She closed her eyes. *If Blake should leave*

her... She couldn't bear even to think of it. She loved him so, missed him so. Tears ran down her cheeks, blinding her. If only he could love her back....

Blake, meanwhile, was riding around New Providence in a jitney with Sarah at his side, smiling as she enthused over the beautiful flowers and the unbelievable colors of the ocean and the whiteness of the sand. If Meredith had been with them, it would truly have been paradise.

His eyes darkened at the thought. Meredith. He hadn't really given her a chance, he supposed. Her traveling made him mad and he'd pushed her out of his life because she refused to stop. In a way he was glad she had the spirit to stand up to him. But in another, he felt miserable because she was telling him he was nothing compared to her career. It hurt far more than Nina's betrayal. Because he hadn't loved Nina. And he...cared...for Meredith.

He couldn't bear to think about her. He'd come down here with Sarah to hurt her. Probably she was in tears when Amie told her they had gone. His face hardened. She was going to take a long time to forgive him for that slap in the face. He was sorry he'd done it. He'd been hurting and wanted to strike back, but now it all seemed so petty and unnecessary. Being cruel wasn't going to win Meredith back. He sighed. He didn't quite have the hang of marriage yet. But he was going to work at learning how when he got back. He had to. He couldn't bear to lose Meredith. These past few cold weeks had made his life hell, especially at night. He missed her soft body, her quiet breathing next to him. He missed her laughter and the lazy talks they'd had late at night. He missed a lot. He only hoped he hadn't left things too late.

"Sarah," he said, "how would you like to go home tomorrow?"

"I'd like that, Daddy," she said. "I miss Merry something awful!"

"Yes, so do I," he murmured under his breath.

Meredith was sitting at the computer with her reading glasses on when she heard the front door open.

"Merry!" Sarah Jane cried, and flung herself at Meredith to hug her convulsively. "Merry, why didn't you come with us? We had such fun, but it was lonely without you!"

"It was lonely without you, too, baby." Meredith sighed, hugging Sarah close.

She heard Blake's step in the hall, and her heart ran away. Her body quivered. She didn't look up because she didn't dare. He'd hurt her enough. She wasn't giving him any more openings.

"Hello, Meredith," he said quietly.

She lifted cool gray eyes to his. "Hello, Blake. I hope you had a pleasant time."

He shifted. He had a faint sunburn, but he looked almost gaunt. She realized that he'd honed down a little, too, during their cold war, and guilt made her throat constrict.

"It was all right," he said coolly. "How have you been?"

"Oh, I've had a ball," she said nervously, hiding her lack of confidence from him. She smiled at Sarah. "I went to autograph in Boston and researched a new book while I was there."

Blake's expression closed up. He'd imagined her sitting home crying, and she'd been in Boston working on another damned book. He turned on his heel without another word and left her sitting there.

"And I'm going to have a party and everything, Merry, 'cause Daddy said so!" Sarah was chattering excitedly. She looked pretty. Her hair was neatly combed and she had on a soft, lightweight cotton dress with red and beige patterns on it, obviously bought for her in the Bahamas. Blake had even put a bow in her hair.

"A party?" Meredith echoed. She hadn't been listening, because the cold look on Blake's face had hit her hard. She'd put her foot in it again by raving about her trip.

"My birthday, Merry!" Sarah said with forced patience.

"That's right," Meredith said. "It's coming up."

"And we have to have a party," Sarah said. "Dani can come, and you and Daddy, and we can have cake."

"And ice cream," Meredith said, smiling at the child's obvious excitement. "We might even have balloons and a clown. Would you like that?"

"Oh, yes!"

"When are we having the party?" Meredith asked.

"Next Saturday," Sarah said.

"Well, I'll see what I can do." She took off her reading glasses and Sarah picked them up and tried to look through them, making a face when everything was blurry.

Mrs. Jackson fixed the birthday cake with a favorite cartoon character of Sarah's on the top and Meredith arranged for a local clown to come to the party to entertain the children. She invited Dani and some of Dani's friends, anticipating bedlam. Maybe if they ate in the kitchen, it would be less messy.

"Why should they eat in the kitchen?" Blake asked icily when Meredith got up her nerve the day of the party to approach him about it. "They're children, not animals. They can eat in the dining room."

Meredith curtsied and smiled. "Yes, my lord," she said. "Anything you say, sir."

"That isn't funny," he said. He stalked out of the room and Meredith stuck out her tongue at him.

"Reverting to childhood?" Mrs. Jackson asked with a gleam in her eye as she opened the hutch to get out plates and glasses, since the party was less than two hours away.

"I guess so. He infuriates me!" She sighed. "He says we have to have it in here. Doesn't he know that cake and ice cream are terrible on carpet?"

"Not yet," Amie said with her tongue in her cheek. "But he will."

Meredith smiled conspiratorially at her. "Yes, he certainly will."

They had the party in the dining room. There were seven four-year-olds. In the middle of the cake and ice cream, they had a food fight. By the time Meredith and Elissa, who'd volunteered to help out, got them stopped, the room looked like a child's attempt at camouflage. There was ice cream on the carpet, the hutch, the tablecloth, and even tiny splatters on Blake's elegant crystal chandelier. Waterford crystal, too, Meredith mused as she studied the chocolate spots there. The chairs were smeared with vanilla cake and white frosting, and underfoot there was enough cake to feed several hungry mice.

"Isn't this fun, Merry?" Sarah Jane exclaimed with a chocolate ring around her mouth and frosting in her hair.

"Yes, darling," Meredith agreed wholeheartedly. "It's

fun, indeed. I can hardly wait until your daddy gets here."

Just as she said that, Sarah Jane's daddy walked in the door and stopped as if he'd been hit in the knee with a bat. His lower lip fell a fraction of an inch and he stared at the table and children as if he'd never seen either before.

He lifted a finger and turned to Meredith to say something.

"Isn't it just such fun?" Meredith asked brightly. "We had a food fight. And then we had chocolate warfare. I'm afraid your chandelier became a casualty, but, then, you'll have *such* fun hosing it down…."

Blake's face was getting redder by the instant. He glared at Meredith and went straight through to the kitchen.

Seconds later, Meredith could hear his deep, slow voice giving Amie hell on the half-shell, and then the back door slammed hard enough to shake the room.

Elissa's twinkling blue eyes met Meredith's gray ones. "My, my, and he insisted on the dining room? Where do you think he's gone?"

"To get a hose, I expect," Meredith commented, and then broke into laughter.

"I wouldn't laugh too loud," Elissa cautioned as she helped mop Dani's face.

The clown arrived just after the children were tidied, and he kept them occupied in the living room with Elissa while Meredith and Amie began the monumental task of cleaning the dining room.

Meredith was on the floor with a wet sponge and carpet cleaner when Blake came in, followed by two rugged looking men wearing uniforms. Without a word, he tugged Meredith up by the arm, took the sponge from her hand, tossed it to one of the men and guided her into the living room.

He left her there without a word. Belatedly she realized that he'd gone to get some cleaning men to take care of the mess. Oddly, it made her want to cry. His thoughtfulness had surprised her. Or maybe it was his conscience. Either way, she thought, it had been kind of him to do that for Amie and her.

Seconds later, Amie was pulled into the living room. She stared at Meredith and shrugged. Then she smiled and sat down to enjoy the clown with the children.

It was, Sarah Jane said after the guests had gone, the best party in the whole world.

"I made five new friends, Merry," she told Meredith gaily, "And they liked me!"

"Most everyone likes you, darling," Meredith said, kneeling to hug her. Her white-and-pink dress was liberally stained with chocolate and candy, but that's what parties were for, Meredith told herself. "Especially me," she added with a big kiss.

Sarah Jane hugged her tight. "I love you, Merry." She sighed. "I just wish…"

"Wish what, pet?"

"I wish my daddy loved you," she said, and her big green eyes looked sadly at Meredith.

Meredith hadn't realized until then how perceptive Sarah was. Her face lost its glow. She forced a smile. "It's hard to explain about grown-ups, Sarah," she said finally. "Your daddy and I have disagreed about some things, that's all."

"Why not tell her the truth?" Blake demanded coldly from the doorway. "Why not tell her that your writing comes before she does, and before I do, and that you just don't care enough to stay home?"

"That's not true!" Meredith got to her feet, her eyes flashing. "You won't even listen to my side of it, Blake!"

"Why bother?" He laughed mockingly. "Your side isn't worth hearing."

"And yours is?"

Neither of them noticed Sarah Jane's soft gasp, or the sudden paleness of her little face. Neither of them saw the tears gather in her green eyes and start to flow down her cheeks. Neither of them knew the traumatic effect the argument was having on her, bringing back memories of fights between her mother and stepfather and the violence that had highlighted most of her young life.

She sobbed silently and suddenly turned and slipped from the room, hurrying up the staircase.

"Your pride is going to destroy our marriage," Meredith raged at Blake. "You just can't stand the idea of letting me work, or giving me any freedom at all. You want me to stay home and look after Sarah and have babies—"

"Writers don't have babies," he said curtly. "It's too demeaning and limiting."

She felt her face go pale. "I never said that, Blake," she said. "I haven't done anything to prevent a baby." She lowered her eyes to the carpet and hoped the glitter of her tears wouldn't show. "I just can't…can't seem to get pregnant."

His breath sighed out roughly. He hadn't meant to say such a cruel thing. It was cruel, too, judging by the look on her face. She seemed to really want a child, and that warmed him.

He moved forward a little, his hand going out to touch her hair. "I didn't mean that," he said awkwardly.

She looked up. There were tears in her eyes. "Blake," she whispered achingly, and lifted her arms.

He cursed his own vulnerability even as he reached for her, lifting her hard against him, holding her close. "Don't cry, little one," he said against her ear as she sobbed out the frustration and loneliness and fear of the past few weeks against his broad shoulder.

"There's something…something *wrong* with me," she wailed.

"No, there isn't." He nuzzled his cheek against hers. "Unless you count a husband with an overdose of pride. You're right. It was just feeling second best, that's all. You can't stay home all the time."

"I promised I'd go on tour," she said huskily. "I didn't want to. But then, when I kept not getting pregnant, I hated having so much time to sit and worry about it." Her arms tightened around his neck. "I wanted to give you a son…."

His arms contracted. He'd never considered that as a reason for her wandering. He'd never dreamed she wanted a child so much.

"We've been married only a few weeks," he whispered at her ear. "And the past several, I've been sleeping in another room." He smiled faintly in spite of himself. "It takes a man and a woman to make babies. You can't do it by yourself."

She laughed softly, and he felt warm all over at the sound, because she hadn't laughed in a long time.

"If you want to get pregnant, Mrs. Donavan, you'll have to have a little help."

She drew in a breath and looked into his soft green eyes. "Could you do that for me?" she whispered playfully. "I mean, I know it would be a sacrifice and all, but I'd be *sooo* grateful."

He laughed, too. The joy came back into his life again. She was beautiful, he thought, studying her face. And he cared so damned much. His eyes darkened and the smile faded. Cared. No. It was more. Far more than that. He... loved.

"Kiss me," he said, bending to her soft mouth. "It's been so long, honey. So long!"

His mouth covered hers hungrily, and she felt her body melting into him, aching for his touch, for the crush of his mouth on her soft lips. She moaned, and his kiss became suddenly ardent and demanding.

"Merry?" Mrs. Jackson called suddenly from the hall.

Blake and Meredith broke apart with breathless reluctance, but there was a strange note in Amie's usually calm voice.

Meredith moved to the closed door and opened it. "Amie, what is it?" she asked, wondering at the closed door, because it had been open when Sarah was in the room with them—"Where's Sarah!" Meredith asked suddenly.

Blake felt himself pale when he remembered the argument. Sarah Jane had heard.

Amie grimaced. "I don't know where she is. I can't find her," she said. "She isn't in her room. And it's raining outside."

It was thundering, too. And it was almost dark. Meredith and Blake didn't waste time on words. They rushed down the hall and out the back door, forgoing rain gear in their haste to find the child they'd unknowingly sent running out into the stormy night.

Chapter 11

Blake wanted to throw things. He searched the stable, every nook and cranny of it, and every one of the outbuildings, with Meredith quiet and worried beside him. The rain was coming down heavier now, and the last bit of light had left the sky, except for the occasional lightning.

"Where can she be?" Meredith groaned as they stood in the doorway of the barn and looked out into the night.

"I don't know," Blake said heavily. "God, I could kick myself!"

She slid her hand into his big one and held on tight. "I'm every bit as responsible as you are, Blake," she said gently. "I was being stubborn and proud, too." She went close to him, nuzzling her cheek against his broad chest. "I'm sorry for all of it. I never looked at things from your point of view."

"That goes double for me." He bent and kissed her forehead. "I wish we'd remembered that Sarah was in the room. She's had nightmares about arguments her mother and stepfather used to have. Violence upsets her. Any kind of violence. When I yelled at her about getting in the corral with the horse she—" He stopped dead, remembering. He straightened. "No," he said to himself. "No, she couldn't be. That would be too easy, wouldn't it?"

"What would?" Meredith asked as she tried to follow his train of thought.

"Come on!"

He ran toward the house, tugging her along behind him. They were both soaked. Meredith's blouse was plastered to her skin, and her hair hung in wet tangles over her face. Blake didn't look much better. His tan shirt was so wet that she could see right through it to the thick tangle of black hair on his chest.

"Did you find her?" Amie asked worriedly from the sink, where she was washing dishes.

"I'm almost sure I have," Blake said. He dragged Meredith with him and shot up the staircase.

He opened the door to Sarah's room, went straight to the closet and, with a silent prayer, opened it.

And there was Sarah Jane, sobbing silently in the very far corner of the closet floor, under all her pretty things.

"You…hate each other," Sarah sobbed, "just like my mommy and Daddy Brad. I'll have to go away…!" she wailed.

Blake eased into the closet and caught her up in his arms. He held her and hugged her and walked the floor with her while she cried. His shirt was soaked, but Sarah didn't seem to mind. She held on with all her might.

"I love you, baby girl," he whispered in her ear. "You'll never have to go away."

"But you fought!" Sarah said.

"Not the bad kind of fighting," Meredith said, smoothing the child's soft hair as she rested against Blake's wet shoulder. She smiled. "Sarah Jane, how would you like to have a brother or sister?"

Sarah stopped crying and her eyes widened. "A real live baby brother or sister?"

"A real live one," Meredith assured her. She looked up into Blake's soft, quiet eyes. "Because we're going to have one, aren't we, Blake?"

"Just as soon as we can," he agreed huskily, his eyes full of warmth and faint hunger.

"Oh, that would be so nice." Sarah sighed. "I could help you, Merry. We could make clothes for her. I can sew. I can make anything."

"Yes, darling," Meredith said with an indulgent smile.

"And Meredith isn't going anywhere," Blake added. "Neither are you, young lady." He chuckled as he put her down. "I can't do without my biggest helper. Who'll go out with me to feed the horses on weekends and help me talk to the men if you leave?"

Sarah nodded. "Yes, Daddy."

"And who'll help me eat the vanilla ice cream that Mrs. Jackson has in the freezer?" he added in a whisper.

Sarah's eyes brightened. "Vanilla?"

"That's right," he said. "Left over from your birthday party. Would you like some?"

"Blake, it's too late..." Meredith began.

"It is not," he said. "It's her birthday, and she can have more if she wants it."

"Thank you, Daddy." Sarah grinned.

"I guess birthdays do only come once a year," Meredith said, relenting. "I'll go and get it. And some cake."

"Amie will get it," Blake said, eyeing Meredith's clothes. "You and I have to change before we can join the party. We got soaked on your account, young lady," he told Sarah with a faint smile. "We thought you'd run out into the fields."

"Oh, I couldn't have done that, Daddy," Sarah said matter-of-factly. "I would have gotten my lovely party dress wet."

Blake laughed with pure delight. "I should have thought of that."

Mrs. Jackson had followed them upstairs and was sighing with relief. "Sarah, I'm so glad you're all right," she said, and smiled. "I was worried."

"You're nice, Mrs. Jackson," Sarah said.

"So are you, pet. Want to come and help me dish up some ice cream and cake while your mommy and daddy change clothes? And we could even make some cookies if you want to. It's not at all late. If your daddy doesn't mind," she added, glancing at Blake.

"Please, Daddy!" Sarah asked.

"All right," he said, relenting. "Go ahead. Your mommy and I will expect some when we get showered and changed. And they'd better be good," he added.

Sarah laughed. "Me and Mrs. Jackson will make lots," she promised. She took Mrs. Jackson's hand and went with her.

"We are a mess," Meredith said, looking down at her clothes.

"Speak for yourself," he returned. "I look great soaking wet."

She eyed him mischievously, her gaze running possessively over his hard muscles. "I'll drink to that."

He took her hand. "Well, come on. We'll get cleaned up together."

She went with him, expecting that he'd leave her at the door to the master bedroom, but he didn't. He pulled her into the bathroom with him and closed the door, locking it as an afterthought.

Meredith's heart went wild. "What are you doing?" she asked.

"We have to shower, don't we?" he said softly. His hands went to her blouse. "Don't panic," he whispered, bending to touch his mouth gently to hers. "We've seen each other before."

"Yes, but…"

"Hush, sweetheart," he breathed into her open mouth.

She was hungry for him. It had been so long. Too long. She gave a harsh moan, and the blood went to his head when he heard it.

"Do that again," he whispered roughly.

"Do…what?"

"Moan like that," he bit off against her mouth. "It drives me crazy!"

She felt his hands on her breasts when he pushed the blouse out of his way, and she did moan, not because he'd said to, but because the pleasure was so exquisite.

He reached out to turn on the shower and adjust the water, and then, his jaw set, his eyes glittering with desire, he stripped her and then himself and lifted her into the shower.

In between kisses, he soaped her and himself, and it was an adventure in exploration for Meredith, who'd never dreamed of touching and being touched so intimately. The soap made her skin like silk and the feel of his hands against her most secret places was unbearable delight.

He rinsed Meredith off, and himself, then turned off the water and reached for a towel. But he didn't dry them with it. Holding her eyes, he spread the towel on the tiles of the big bathroom floor, and catching her waist, he lifted her against him and kissed her with probing intimacy.

"We're going to make love. Here," he whispered, "on the floor."

She shuddered at the images that flashed through her mind. "Yes," she groaned, pressing hard against him so that her soft breasts flattened against the thick pelt of hair on his muscular chest.

He spread her trembling body on the thick towel and himself over her, his mouth demanding and slow, his body making the sweetest kind of contacts as he moved sensually over her.

She felt his hands on her and she shivered, but he kept on, evoking sensations she hadn't dreamed existed. She opened her eyes and looked at him and cried out, her nails digging into his shoulders as she lifted against his hand.

"I've never wanted you this badly," he whispered as he poised above her. "I don't want to hold back anything this time."

"Neither do I." She lifted her hands to his face. "I love you," she said, parting her lips as they brushed his with open sensuality. "I love you, Blake."

His hands contracted on her hips as he moved down, very slowly, his eyes holding hers so that he could see them while his body began to merge with hers. "I love you, too, honey," he whispered shakenly, jerking a little with each deepening movement. She started to lift up, but his hands held her still. "No," he murmured breathlessly, his eyes still on hers. "No, don't…move. Don't rush it… God!" His eyes closed suddenly and he shuddered.

She felt him, breathed him, tasted him. Her body shook with what he was doing to it, with the exquisite slowness of his movements, the depth… She clenched her teeth and cried out in protest, her hips twisting helplessly.

"Blake…if you don't…hurry!" she wailed in anguish.

"Ride it out," he whispered at her ear. His body flowed against hers like the tide, lazy and deliberate, despite the sudden hot urgency that was burning them both. "It's going to be good," he groaned. "Good…so good… Meredith!" His body clenched. "Merry, now!"

She felt his control slip and she let go of her own, yielding totally, trusting him. And the tension all but tore her to pieces before she felt the heat blinding her, burning her, and she fell into it headfirst with tears streaming down her cheeks.

His hands were in her hair, soothing her, smoothing the wet strands away from her rosy cheeks. He was kissing her, sipping the tears from her eyes, kissing away the faint sorrow, the fatigue, the trembling muscles.

She opened her eyes and his face came into focus. She couldn't breathe properly. Her body felt as if it had fallen from a great height. His eyes held hers, and there was adoration in them now, openly.

"The bed would have been better," he said, brushing her mouth lazily with his. "But this was safer."

"She's making cookies," she told him wearily.

"She's unpredictable." He nuzzled her nose with his. "I love you," he breathed, his eyes mirroring the statement. "I couldn't admit it until today, but, oh, God, I feel it, Meredith," he said huskily, his face taut with emotion that made her heart jump with excitement. "I feel it when

I look at you, when I'm with you. I didn't know what it was to love, but now I do."

"I've always felt that way about you," she whispered, smiling adoringly. "Since I was eighteen. Maybe even longer. You were the moon, and I wanted you so much."

"I wanted you, too. But I didn't understand why I wanted you so badly." He kissed her again. "You complete me," he breathed. "You make me whole."

Her arms linked around his neck, she buried her face in his throat. "I feel like that, too. Was it necessary to torture me to death?" She laughed shyly.

"It was good, though, wasn't it?" he said. "So intense that I thought I might pass out just at the last. I like losing control with you. I fly up into the sun and explode."

"Yes, so do I." She cuddled closer. "The floor is hard."

"The bed is unprotected."

She sighed. "Well, there's always tonight." She drew back a little. "Are you going to sleep with me?"

"No, I thought I'd sack out with one of the horses—oof!"

She withdrew her fist from his stomach. "Sarah Jane wants a brother or sister."

"At the rate we're going, that won't take long. There's nothing wrong with you," he added, emphasizing it. "And meanwhile, Sarah's going to have time to adjust to us and feel secure. Okay?"

"Okay. I'll stop worrying," she promised.

"Good. Now let's go get some ice cream," he said, moving away to get to his feet and pull her up with him. "I'm starving!"

She wanted to make a comment about men and their strange appetites, but she was too hungry to argue. Her eyes adored him. So much had come out of such a stormy, terrible night, she thought as he wrapped a towel around his lean hips and tossed an extra one to her. He loved her. He actually loved her. She smiled, tingling all over with the newness of hearing the words, of having the freedom to say them. It was like a dream come true. Or it would be, she thought, if she could ever give him a child. She had to force herself not to think about it. Anyway, Blake had said there was plenty of time.

Epilogue

Eight months later, little Carson Anthony Blake Donavan was born in Jack's Corner Hospital. Looking down at the small head with its thick crown of black hair, Meredith could have jumped for joy. A son, she thought, and so much like his father.

Sitting by her bed, Blake was quiet and fascinated as his first son gripped his thumb. He smiled down at the tiny child. "He's a miracle," he said softly. "Part of us. The best of us."

She smiled up at him tiredly and her hand touched the finger that was caught in the baby's grasp. "He's going to look like you," she said.

"I hope so, considering that he's a boy," he replied dryly.

She laughed. Her eyes made soft, slow love to his. "I'm so happy, Blake," she whispered. "He's the end of the rainbow. And I was so afraid that I couldn't give you a child."

"I knew you could," he said simply. "We love each other too much not to have a child together." He bent and kissed her soft mouth. "Sarah wanted to come, too. I explained that they wouldn't let her in here, but you're getting out tomorrow and she can see her brother all she wants to. She's coloring a pretty picture for him."

"She's been almost as excited as we have," Meredith said. "She'll love not being an only child. And it will give her some security. She still doesn't quite believe that she's safe and loved."

"It will take time," he said. "But she's coming around nicely."

"Yes." She smoothed her fingers lovingly over the baby's downy soft hair. "Isn't he just perfect, Blake?"

"Just perfect," he said, smiling. "Like his mother."

She searched his eyes. "No regrets?"

He shook his head. "Nobody ever loved me until you and Sarah Jane came along," he said quietly. "I can't quite get over it. I'm like Sarah—happiness takes some adjusting to. You've given me the world, Meredith."

"Only my heart, darling," she said softly. "But maybe it was enough."

He bent to kiss her again. "It was more than enough," he replied. The light in his eyes was so full of love for Meredith and his child that it was almost blinding. He smiled suddenly. "I meant to tell you—I met Elissa and Danielle in town just before I came here. They're bringing over a surprise for you." His eyes twinkled. "The store was a little crowded, full of people. I walked in, and do you know what Danielle said?"

Meredith smiled lazily. "No, what?"

"She pointed to me and said, 'Look, Mama, there's

Sarah Jane's daddy!'" He grinned. "And do you know what, Merry? I think I'd rather be Daddy than president."

Meredith reached up and touched his mouth lovingly. "I'm sure Sarah Jane and little Carson will agree with that." She took his hand in hers and held it. "And so do I."

He looked down at his son, and foresaw long days ahead of playing baseball in the backyard and board games at the kitchen table. Of drying Sarah's tears and helping Meredith patch up Carson's cuts and bruises. Together, he and Meredith would raise their children and make memories to share in the autumn days. He brought Meredith's hand to his mouth and lifted his gaze to her quiet face. There, in her gray eyes, was the beginning and end of his whole world.

* * * * *

COMING NEXT MONTH

Available January 11, 2011

REQUEST YOUR FREE BOOKS!

**2 FREE NOVELS
PLUS 2
FREE GIFTS!**

Passionate, Powerful, Provocative!

YES! Please send me 2 FREE Silhouette Desire® novels and my 2 FREE gifts (gifts are worth about $10). After receiving them, if I don't wish to receive any more books, I can return the shipping statement marked "cancel." If I don't cancel, I will receive 6 brand-new novels every month and be billed just $4.05 per book in the U.S. or $4.74 per book in Canada. That's a saving of at least 15% off the cover price! It's quite a bargain! Shipping and handling is just 50¢ per book.* I understand that accepting the 2 free books and gifts places me under no obligation to buy anything. I can always return a shipment and cancel at any time. Even if I never buy another book, the two free books and gifts are mine to keep forever.

225/326 SDN E5QG

Name	(PLEASE PRINT)	
Address		Apt. #
City	State/Prov.	Zip/Postal Code

Signature (if under 18, a parent or guardian must sign)

Mail to the **Silhouette Reader Service:**

IN U.S.A.: P.O. Box 1867, Buffalo, NY 14240-1867
IN CANADA: P.O. Box 609, Fort Erie, Ontario L2A 5X3

Not valid for current subscribers to Silhouette Desire books.

**Want to try two free books from another line?
Call 1-800-873-8635 or visit www.morefreebooks.com.**

* Terms and prices subject to change without notice. Prices do not include applicable taxes. N.Y. residents add applicable sales tax. Canadian residents will be charged applicable provincial taxes and GST. Offer not valid in Quebec. This offer is limited to one order per household. All orders subject to approval. Credit or debit balances in a customer's account(s) may be offset by any other outstanding balance owed by or to the customer. Please allow 4 to 6 weeks for delivery. Offer available while quantities last.

Your Privacy: Silhouette Books is committed to protecting your privacy. Our Privacy Policy is available online at www.eHarlequin.com or upon request from the Reader Service. From time to time we make our lists of customers available to reputable third parties who may have a product or service of interest to you. If you would prefer we not share your name and address, please check here. ☐

Help us get it right—We strive for accurate, respectful and relevant communications. To clarify or modify your communication preferences, visit us at www.ReaderService.com/consumerschoice.

SDES10R

HARLEQUIN®

A Romance

FOR EVERY MOOD™

Spotlight on

Classic

Quintessential, modern love stories
that are romance at its finest.

See the next page
to enjoy a sneak peek from
the Harlequin Presents® series.

Harlequin Presents® is thrilled
to introduce the first installment of
an epic tale of passion and drama by
**USA TODAY Bestselling Author
Penny Jordan!**

*When buttoned-up Giselle first meets
the devastatingly handsome Saul Parenti,
the heat between them is explosive....*

"LET ME GET THIS STRAIGHT. Are you actually suggesting that I would stoop to that kind of game playing?"

Saul came out from behind his desk and walked toward her. Giselle could smell his hot male scent and it was making her dizzy, igniting a low, dull, pulsing ache that was taking over her whole body.

Giselle defended her suspicions. "You don't want me here."

"No," Saul agreed, "I don't."

And then he did what he had sworn he would not do, cursing himself beneath his breath as he reached for her, pulling her fiercely into his arms and kissing her with all the pent-up fury she had aroused in him from the moment he had first seen her.

Giselle certainly *wanted* to resist him. But the hand she raised to push him away developed a will of its own and was sliding along his bare arm beneath the sleeve of his shirt, and the body that should have been arching away from him was instead melting into him.

Beneath the pressure of his kiss he could feel and taste her gasp of undeniable response to him. He wanted to devour her, take her and drive them both until they were equally satiated—even whilst the anger within him that she should make him feel that way roared and burned its resentment of his need.

She was helpless, Giselle recognized, totally unable to withstand the storm lashing at her, able only to cling to the man who was the cause of it and pray that she would survive.

Somewhere else in the building a door banged. The sound exploded into the sensual tension that had enclosed them, driving them apart. Saul's chest was rising and falling as he fought for control; Giselle's whole body was trembling.

Without a word she turned and ran.

Find out what happens when Saul and Giselle succumb to their irresistible desire in

THE RELUCTANT SURRENDER

Available January 2011 from Harlequin Presents®

HPEXP0111